PENGUIN BOOKS

CHILD OF ALL NATIONS

Pramoedya Ananta Toer was born on the island of Java in 1925. He was imprisoned first by the Dutch from 1947 to 1949 for his role in the Indonesian revolution, then by the Indonesian government as a political prisoner. Many of his works have been written while in prison, including the Buru Quartet (*This Earth of Mankind*, *Child of All Nations*, *Footsteps*, and *House of Glass*) which was conceived in stories the author told to other prisoners during his confinement on Buru Island from 1969 to 1979.

Pramoedya is the author of thirty works of fiction and nonfiction. His novels have been translated into twenty languages. He received the PEN Freedom-to-write Award in 1988 and the Ramon Magsaysay Award in 1995. He is currently under city arrest in Jakarta where his books are banned and selling them a crime punishable by imprisonment.

Max Lane was second secretary in the Australian embassy in Jakarta until recalled in 1981 because of his translation of Pramoedya's Buru Quartet.

CHILD OF ALL NATIONS

Pramoedya Ananta Toer

Translated from the
Indonesian by Max Lane

PENGUIN BOOKS

PENGUIN BOOKS

Published by the Penguin Group

Penguin Books USA Inc., 375 Hudson Street, New York, New York 10014, U.S.A.

Penguin Books Ltd, 27 Wrights Lane, London W8 5TZ, England

Penguin Books Australia Ltd, Ringwood, Victoria, Australia

Penguin Books Canada Ltd, 10 Alcorn Avenue,
Toronto, Ontario, Canada M4V 3B2

Penguin Books (N.Z.) Ltd, 182–190 Wairau Road, Auckland 10, New Zealand

Penguin Books Ltd, Registered Offices: Harmondsworth, Middlesex, England

First published in Australia by Penguin Books Australia Ltd 1984
First published in the United States of America
by William Morrow and Company, Inc. 1993
Reprinted by arrangement with William Morrow and Company, Inc.
Published in Penguin Books (U.S.A.) 1996

5   7   9   10   8   6

Originally published in Indonesian by Hasta Mitra Publishing House, Jakarta, 1980.

THE LIBRARY OF CONGRESS HAS CATALOGUED THE HARDCOVER AS FOLLOWS:
Toer, Pramoedya Ananta, 1925–
[Anak semua bangsa. English]
Child of all nations/Pramoedya Ananta Toer;
translated from the Indonesian by Max Lane.
p.   cm.
Translation of: Anak semua bangsa.
ISBN 0-688-12726-6 (hc.)
ISBN 0 14 02.5633 4 (pbk.)
1. Indonesia—History—1798–1942—Fiction.   I. Title.
PL5089.T8A25   1993
899'.22132—dc20   93–3516

Printed in the United States of America
Set in Bembo

TRANSLATOR'S NOTE

To preserve something of the rich texture of cultures, languages, forms of address, dialects, beliefs, and milieus of the Indies, I have retained numerous Malay, Javanese, and Dutch terms.

These are italicized the first time they appear. If explanations or translations are required, they can be found in the Glossary at the back of this book. The Glossary also contains some English words or acronyms and certain identifications that may not be familiar to the English-speaking reader. The explanations given have been kept to the minimum. A richly rewarding project that awaits scholars of Indonesian history is the preparation of a detailed guide to all the historical and cultural material contained in Pramoedya's tetralogy.

The production of such a complex translation is not easy. The contributions made by Susanna Rodell and Jackie Yowell at Penguin Australia to the editing of this manuscript have been very important.

I am grateful to Professor A. H. Johns of the Australian National University for providing facilities, including an office, while I was working on this translation.

I would like to thank, once again, Anna Nurfia for her tolerance of the time taken up by this project. I must also thank those concerned in Indonesia for their continuing friendship, which has been a cable that has kept the energy of my commitment to Indonesia flowing here in Australia.

INTRODUCTION

"We fought back, Child, as well and as honorably as possible."

These were the words that ended Pramoedya Ananta Toer's novel *This Earth of Mankind,* the first in a quartet of which *Child of All Nations* is the second. *This Earth of Mankind* was indeed a story of people fighting back, of resisting the worst of colonial oppression and greed.

It was also a gripping story of remarkable characters caught in the cultural whirlpool that was the Dutch East Indies of the 1890s. Because Pramoedya's vision extends far beyond parochial politics to reach for more universal human concerns, it is a bitter irony that, in 1965, he was arrested by Suharto's junta, and his entire library, including research and notes assembled over many years, were burned to ashes. He was jailed, without trial, for fourteen years. Denied access to writing materials, he kept his literary vision alive by recounting his stories to other prisoners. Only in 1975 was he permitted the facilities to commit his novels from memory to paper.

A year after his release from Buru Island concentration camp in 1979, *This Earth of Mankind* was published in Jakarta as *Bumi Manusia.* Soon after, its sequel *Anak Semua Bangsa (Child of All*

Nations) was published. Both novels became best-sellers in Indonesia, as reviewers hailed Pramoedya's return to the nation's literary life. However, in May 1981 both books were banned in Indonesia. The government accused the books of surreptitiously spreading "Marxism-Leninism"—surreptitious because, they claimed, the author's great literary dexterity made it impossible to identify actual examples of this "Marxism-Leninism." Later in the year students from the University of Indonesia were arrested and expelled when they invited Pramoedya to speak on campus. One of the publishers of Pramoedya's books, Yusuf Isak, was imprisoned for over three months, without being charged. Pramoedya himself and Hasyim Rahmam, Yusuf's partner in the publishing house Hasta Mitra, were repeatedly interrogated.

In *This Earth of Mankind* Minke is an eighteen-year-old Javanese, the first to be educated in an exclusive Dutch school in Surabaya. Striving for his own personal and intellectual development, he is drawn into the more immediate and dramatic struggle that faces his formidable native mentor, and then mother-in-law, Nyai Ontosoroh. Sold as a girl to a wealthy Dutch businessman by her ambitious father, Nyai had become acquainted with the true character of the colonial system early in life, and fought back at it with vengeance. After her corrupt and insane Dutch master is murdered, she rises to restore and control his business, Boerderij Buitenzorg. Minke, on the other hand, has been spoiled by the system. He has received an elite Dutch education. He is attracted to Dutch ways by the apparent superiority of the West, such as the modern achievements of electricity, machines, photographs, and books.

Minke's struggle, sparked off by his association with Nyai, becomes essentially against himself—against his integration into, and identification with, the colonialists' civilization. Nyai Ontosoroh is self-taught; she has never been to an elite Dutch school, nor any school, except that of life itself. Yet she proves herself again and again to be capable of both defending her principles and self-respect, and imparting to Minke knowledge and understanding that he would never learn at school. Nyai Ontosoroh's dignity is evidence of an alternative and superior civilization developed in spite of rather than because of Dutch colonial authority.

The separate struggles—Minke's against his illusions about Western values, and Nyai's against their brutalizing effects—are complicated and intensified by their coming together. They are brought together by Nyai's Eurasian daughter, Annelies, whom Minke loves and marries. Minke moves into Nyai's mansion to live with Annelies. Annelies's deep and unqualified love for Minke is an attempt to resolve her own complex contradictions. Annelies is not legally Nyai's daughter and, after Annelies's Dutch father dies, she "reverts" to being the property of his far-off Dutch relatives. Nyai and Minke's personal struggles are put aside as they fight (unsuccessfully) to protect Annelies from being taken to the Netherlands.

Minke's eyes are opened by these experiences. He is amazed by the cold, legalistic language of the court. In the colonialists' eyes, Natives are just items on inventories. Minke and Nyai become one force as they rally all their energies and friends to resist the plans of the dead Dutchman's relatives. Minke's outstanding talents as a writer are tested to the full: His passionate challenges to the inhumanity of colonial "justice" are circulated far and wide.

The use of language in this period was an important indicator of a person's social caste. Dutch, of course, was the language of the governing caste; Javanese, the Native language of the Javanese; and Madurese, the Native language of Madura (an island off Java). Malay was the language of interracial, or rather intercaste communication (as many elite Javanese could speak Dutch), as well as the language of many Eurasians. Indeed, in situations where the caste order needed to be emphasized, Natives were forbidden to use Dutch. Not only did colonialism install Dutch as the supreme caste language of Java, it helped reinforce and even exaggerate caste distinctions in the Native languages themselves, especially Javanese. The Javanese language already operated on at least three different levels, each used according to the person to whom one was speaking. This feudal stratification was given extra force as Javanese feudal notables, devoid of real political power in the face of the Dutch cannon and Dutch capital, channelled their oppressive energies into culture, something Dutch cannon and capital were, in turn, frequently ready to buttress. The egalitarian and colloquial Javanese that was used in the palaces and royal houses of

Java actually died out in this period. Only the masses of peasants and other toilers retained such an egalitarian Javanese.

The terms *Native, Mixed-Blood* and *Pure* are capitalized. This is because they do not simply identify the racial origin of the persons involved, but manifest how, even in everyday life, racial caste dominated all of Netherlands Indies society. These categories were eventually given legal status. Thus racism was institutionalized as a caste system by colonialism.

Among the many complex interrelated themes of political, cultural, and social life in the Indies, Pramoedya describes the emergence of a bourgeois from a feudal culture; the demands for rights of indigenous language and culture; the divisions amongst the colonialists over their treatment of the Natives; the intervention of Dutch colonial capitalism into the Javanese countryside; and the humiliation of the Javanese nobility in their dependence on Dutch officialdom. Most importantly, he writes of the development of those energies that would galvanize the Indonesian people into finally standing up and throwing off the yoke of colonial domination.

These themes are brought to life by the richly drawn characters in *This Earth of Mankind,* many of whom reappear in *Child of All Nations:* Nyai, Minke, and Annelies; Ah Tjong, the corrupt Chinese brothel owner who murders Herman Mellema, Nyai's Dutch master; Robert Mellema, his and Nyai's son, who imitates his father's Pure-blood Dutchness and hates Natives; Robert Suurhof, Minke's Dutch rival from school; Magda Peters, the liberal Dutch teacher expelled from the Indies; Jean Marais, the one-legged Frenchman, painter, and veteran of the colonial war in Aceh; Mr. de la Croix, the liberal but interfering Dutch district officer, and his two socially conscious daughters, Miriam and Sarah; Maiko, the Japanese prostitute used by both father and son Mellema; Robert Jan Dapperste (alias Panji Darman), the Native boy adopted by a Dutch preacher; Maarten Nijman, the editor of the powerful Dutch newspaper published in the Indies, the *Soerabaiaasch Nieuws;* Kommer, the exuberant Eurasian editor of a popular Malay-language newspaper; Dr. Martinet, a representative of Dutch science and education at its best; Darsam, the tough fighter and right-hand man of Nyai; Mr. D——. L——., the cowed Dutch accountant; the mysterious Fatso, shadowing Minke everywhere; Minke's authoritarian, aristocratic father and his gentle, Javanese-educated mother; as well as a host of minor characters.

While *This Earth of Mankind* saw the losing battle to defend Annelies brought to a climax, the struggles of Nyai and Minke continue in *Child of All Nations*. The fate of Nyai's "first child," the business, is not resolved. But more fundamental is the fate of Minke. With Annelies seemingly lost, how will he deal with the lessons he learned in the course of that battle? His environment has been completely changed; no longer is it limited to his school, his old boarding house, Nyai's home, and the gallery of Jean Marais, with whom he is a partner in a furniture business. Minke has been drawn into the vortex of colonial society and must now confront all its harsh implications.

In *Child of All Nations,* Minke has become part of the vanguard that would change the face of the East Indies. Like iron on the anvil, he is beaten into shape by the forces of change operating in the early twentieth century. It is not only a time of change for the Indies: China is awakening—a phenomenon Minke has to face personally; Japan is aroused and will soon defeat Russia in war; the Filipino people have created, even if only briefly, the first Asian republic. At home he is confronted by things he had never dreamed of. Most importantly, he becomes involved with representatives of his own people: the peasants. There are certainly new lessons to learn and greater challenges to come in *Child of All Nations*.

—Max Lane

1

Annelies had set sail. Her going was as a young branch wrenched apart from the plant that nourished it. This parting was a turning point in my life. My youth was over, a youth beautifully full of hopes and dreams. It would never return.

The sun was moving slowly, crawling like a snail, inch by inch across the heavens. Slowly, slowly—not caring whether the distance it had traversed would ever be traversed again.

The clouds hung thinly across the sky, unwilling to release even a single spray of drizzle. The atmosphere was gray, as though the world had lost its multitude of colors.

The old people teach us through their legends that there is a mighty god called *Batara Kala*. They say it is he who makes all things move further and further from their starting point, inexorably, towards some unknown final destination. A human blind to the future, I could do no more than hope to know. We never even really understand what we have already lived through.

People say that before humankind stands only distance. And its limit is the horizon. As the distance is crossed, the horizon moves away. There is no romance so strong that it could tame and hold them—the eternal distance and the horizon.

Batara Kala had pushed Annelies across many distances and had pushed me across others. The further apart we were forced, the clearer it became that no one could tell what the future held. The distance opening out before me made me understand she was not just a fragile doll. A woman who can love so deeply is not a doll. Perhaps, also, she was the only woman whose love for me was pure. And the further Batara Kala pulled us apart, the more I came to feel that truly, I loved her.

And love, like every other object and situation, has its shadow. And love's shadow is called pain. There is nothing without its shadow except light itself.

Whether light or shadow, nothing can escape being pushed along by Batara Kala. No one can return to his starting point. Maybe this mighty god is the one whom the Dutch call the Teeth of Time. He makes the sharp blunt, and the blunt sharp; the small are made big and the big made small. All are pushed on towards that horizon, while it recedes eternally beyond our reach, pushed on towards annihilation. And it is that annihilation that in turn brings rebirth.

I don't really know whether this beginning to my notes is fitting or not. At the very least everything must have a beginning. And this is the beginning I have written.

Mama and I hadn't been allowed out of the house for three days nor permitted to receive guests.

A district police head rode up on his horse. I didn't leave my room. It was Mama who met him, and hardly a moment passed before the shouting started in Malay. Mama called me out of my room. The two of them stood facing each other.

She pointed to a piece of paper on the table: "Minke, the police chief here says we were never under arrest. Yet we haven't been able to leave the house for over a week now."

"Yes," the policeman explained, "you now are being officially notified: The two inhabitants of this house are free to come and go."

"The police chief here thinks that now, with this written notice, our period of detention never existed."

These last few days Mama's nerves had been so on edge that

she was ready to fight with anyone at all, especially a servant of the state. I was reluctant to join in the fight. I could see that Mama, her face fiery red, was ready to erupt with rage.

The police chief jumped on his horse and made his escape.

"Why didn't you say something?" Mama rebuked me. "Afraid?" Her voice subsided into a low rumble. "They need us to be afraid, Child, no matter how badly we Natives are treated."

"Ah, everything is all over now anyway, Ma."

"Indeed, all over. We were defeated, but still they have violated a principle. They have detained us illegally. Don't ever think that you can defend something, especially justice, if you don't care about principles, no matter how trifling an issue."

So she began to lecture me about principles—a lesson I had never learned at school, had never read about in books, magazines, or newspapers. My heart was not yet calm enough to receive such new teachings, no matter how beautiful and good. Yet still I listened.

"Look, no matter how rich you are," she began, and I listened half-heartedly, "you must resist anyone who takes what is yours, even if it's only a clump of soil below the window. Not because the soil is so very valuable to you. A principle: Taking someone's possession without permission is theft. It is not right; it must be opposed. And in the last few days, it is our very freedom they have robbed us of."

"Yes, Ma," I answered, hoping that she would end her lecture quickly.

But it wasn't so easy to stop her and, if I hadn't been there, she would probably have delivered it to whoever else was around.

"Those who are not faithful to principles become open to evil, to have evil done to them or to do evil themselves."

Then she seemed to realize that her timing was wrong. "Go out and get some fresh air, child. You've been locked up too long. You look stale."

I went back into my old room, which I had shared so briefly with Annelies. Yes, I needed to go for a stroll, to get some fresh air. I opened the wardrobe to get out a change of clothes. All of a sudden I remembered Robert Suurhof. There was something of his in this wardrobe: a gold and diamond ring.

Mama had thought it was a very expensive gift for a friend to give as a wedding present. The diamond alone was about two carats. Only somebody who was rich, or who really loved you, would give such a present. Mama's guess was probably right—Robert Suurhof might indeed have given it as a sign of his love. Now that Annelies had gone, the time had come to return this thing to him, to his family. Now it seemed no mere coincidence that Mama had spoken of principles.

After I'd dressed I opened the wardrobe and took out Annelies's metal jewelry box. Robert's ring wasn't there. I checked the drawer again. It was lying unwrapped in a corner. I picked it up and looked at it closely.

I had never taken much notice of women's jewelry. Yet I could still enjoy the stone's pure shining blueness, sparkling within itself, the rays multiplied by its polished walls. Why must I admire this destructive object?

I put back the jewelry box, which I had just opened for the first time. Beside the box was a folder. Inside it was a Bank Escompto bank book, a pile of salary receipts from the business, and two letters from Robert Suurhof. They had never been opened! I fought my desire to open and read them. I had no right, I told myself. She had received those letters before she became my wife.

I rose to leave for my walk, then stood hesitantly at the door. There was something I hadn't done. Yes, of course: I usually read the newspapers before I went for a walk. Who knows how long it had been since I'd opened one? I returned to the desk, sat down, groped through the pile of mail. The desire to read was gone.

Why was I feeling so listless? I forced myself to start on a newspaper. No. I couldn't. I separated the letters from the rest of the mail and went through them one by one: from Mother, from my elder brother, from . . . Robert Suurhof for Annelies. Anger burned in my heart, my jealousy was awakened. From Sarah de la Croix, from Magda Peters, from Robert Suurhof for . . . from Miriam de la Croix, from . . . again from Robert Suurhof for Annelies. I began to sort more quickly.

There were eleven letters from Suurhof. Scalding lava erupted into my heart. Lunatic! Damn him!

I took a letter, tore it open, and read:

Miss Annelies Mellema, Goddess of My Dreams . . .

I didn't go on. I rushed outside and ordered Marjuki to prepare a buggy. The ring in my pocket weighed me down. I would go and hurl this thing to the ground before his parents.

"Quickly, Juki!"

The buggy flew off in the direction of Surabaya.

Neither my thoughts nor my vision would focus. All was blurred, without direction. Then, in the distance, I saw an old school friend, one who had never passed his exams. But even concern for my friends had faded away. Only after he had disappeared from sight did I feel ashamed for having treated a school friend so dishonorably. Perhaps he was one who had been sympathetic to us in our troubles.

Near Kranggan I saw Victor Roomers strolling happily along, kicking the roadside pebbles. This Pure European fellow graduate didn't seem to have anything to do that afternoon. He was wearing white shorts, white shirt, white shoes; as usual, he looked quite fresh. After three years of studying with him, I had grown to like him. He was a lover of athletics; he had a sportsmanlike attitude towards the world and never turned a sour face to it. And most important of all, he held no racial prejudices.

"Hello, Vic!" I ordered Marjuki to pull the buggy over to the side of the road. I jumped down and shook hands. Victor invited me into a roadside drinks stall.

He began quickly: "Forgive me, Minke, for not being able to help you in your difficulties. I came once to see you at Wonokromo, but the Field Police broke up any groups that collected around or near your fence. Some of our other friends also tried to visit you, but in vain. No one could help, Minke, especially not someone like me. I asked Papa about it all once. It had never happened before, he said, a Native daring to oppose a decision of the white court. All our friends regretted not being able to ease your suffering. We truly share your sorrow in all this, Minke."

"Thank you, Vic."

"Where are you off to? You look so pale."

"Would you like to come along?"

"Very much, but I can't just now. Where are you going?"

"I've got a bit of business to fix up at Robert Suurhof's house."

"A waste of time. What do you want to go there for?"

"There is something—"

17

"Robert's vanished. Who knows where he's gone," Vic said casually, as if nothing of note had happened.

"Vanished?" Somehow it didn't feel right to use that word about a fellow graduate.

"Yes. So you haven't been reading the newspapers. Robert's name wasn't mentioned. It was Ezekiel's name that was printed."

"You're right, I haven't been reading the papers. You mean the Ezekiel who owns the jewelry shop?"

"Who else? Surely there is only one Ezekiel left in this world, eh?"

The diamond ring jumped in my pocket, piercing my thighs and demanding to be taken to Ezekiel's shop. So Suurhof had stolen it.

"That's the kind of person our friend Robert Suurhof is," Vic said with disappointment. "He had big ambitions. He wanted to master the world in a week. In the end . . . "

"Oh, so now it's *in the end,* Vic. Robert stole from Ezekiel's."

"If I were you, Minke, perhaps I wouldn't be reading newspapers either. You've been through too much lately."

"Forget it, Vic. Tell me about Robert."

The diamond ring started jabbing and stabbing me in the thigh again. Imagine what would happen if a policeman stopped and frisked me; it would mean another trial.

"It's just like any other crime story. It always starts with someone's great ambition to overwhelm the world in a week. Pity the Suurhofs, Mr. and Mrs. Suurhof. Both were already so gaunt, perhaps they're even worse now. Two of their children gave up school altogether just so Robert can graduate from H.B.S. Straight after graduating, he turns into a bandit, and a cheap bandit at that."

"What did he take from Ezekiel's?"

"Not even that! If he'd robbed Ezekiel's shop, at least he'd have had some style. At least he would have had to fight several neighborhood guards or speak with a golden tongue and outwit them. All he did was rob a Chinese grave, shaming his school friends, his school, and his teachers. It's lucky he's disappeared and escaped arrest. Who knows where he is now?"

"I know where he is. But keep on with the story."

"The story's quite simple. Remember how he used to carry on about becoming a lawyer? His parents would never have been able to pay for it, especially as he'd have had to finish another five years of H.B.S. in Holland. His parents could never pay his boat fare, let alone his school fees there. They're both ill; they've used up all their money for medicines. Ah! That Robert! He wanted to be rich, to have a wife of unrivaled beauty, to be number-one man, a lawyer—and all in a week. Straight after graduating he goes and knocks down the watchman at the Chinese cemetery, hitting him from behind and stealing from one of the graves."

So that's the story, I thought. Damned bejeweled ring, that's how you've come to be in my pocket! If somehow the police knew where to find you now. . . . I became a bit nervous. I asked: "How was the crime discovered?"

"You're going pale, Minke. Are you ill?"

I shook my head.

"He sold the booty to Ezekiel. It was discovered by the dead man's family. They checked all the jewelry shops and found one of their things at Ezekiel's; then they reported it."

Vic then told the rest of the story; it was easy to guess. The crime was exposed; the police searched Suurhof's house. Robert had vanished. Nothing was found. No one knew where Robert had gone, not even his parents.

"You say you know where he is, Minke?"

"Well, at least where he's been sending his letters from."

"Letters? To you?" he asked, amazed. His eyes questioned mine. Then, abruptly, he turned the conversation: "There's no point, Minke. There's no point complaining to his parents about those letters. You'll only cause more grief."

I became suspicious. How embarrassing if he knew about Suurhof's letters to my wife! How humiliated I would be as a husband! The ring itched in my pocket. Perhaps this cursed ring was the cause of all our misfortune.

Victor could tell I was trying to hide something. "No, Minke, don't go there. That scoundrel Robert is capable of anything."

I turned the conversation: "What are you doing these days, Vic?"

"Just as you see me now: in and out of the villages. You know what I am? Don't laugh. An agent for the shipping company that takes pilgrims to Mecca. Being a *sinyo* like this, it's hard to get my customers' trust. I intend to get some other kind of work, but . . . ah well. Hey, Minke, do you know how many pilgrims will travel

19

to Mecca from South Africa this year? Five hundred! From an English colony! If I could just get five hundred people here in Surabaya . . . "

He too wanted to avoid talk about Robert's letters. He must have known they were addressed to my wife. So it was no secret. How did people know?

"Say, Minke, would you like to swap jobs with me?"

"Thanks, Vic. But I must get on now."

I left Victor Roomers in the stall. I left with an angry heart—hot, jealous, furious.

The buggy raced off towards Peneleh. From others I met along the way I got the same story and the same advice: Stay away from the Suurhofs. One even said, straight out: "Don't take any notice if you get letters from him. He's crazy."

So all my school friends knew about the letters to Annelies. I was the only one who didn't. How blind I had been.

Willem Vos, who was working in a timber yard, even went so far as to say: "He made it clear that he was out to get you, Minke. Be careful. He hinted to some people at the graduation party that day that he would get you. But people like him would never dare say such things openly."

I deliberately avoided the girls from school. Now that they had graduated they were no longer school friends but maidens awaiting proposals from one official or another—Pure European if possible. I would only disturb their waiting.

Late in the day, another friend pointed out: "Ezekiel has been kept under detention, yet Suurhof's name has never even been mentioned. Why? Because Suurhof has European status. Ezekiel is a Jew from Baghdad, with only Oriental status."

At five-thirty in the afternoon, my buggy entered the Suurhofs' front compound. My eyes went straight for the mango tree, where the family liked to sit and enjoy the afternoon air. Yes, there they were, sitting on the wooden benches around the tree trunk, talking amongst themselves.

I had not been to this house since the incident between Robert and me when I first met Annelies at Wonokromo. When they saw my fine buggy enter the yard they all stood up and stared in amazement. I recognized Mr. and Mrs. Suurhof straight away. Both were thin and wasted from consumption. Of their twelve children, only Robert, the eldest, was missing.

As soon as I alighted, Mrs. Suurhof called out in her Indo accent, "Ai-ai, *Nyo,* it looks like you're a big *tuan* now!"

"Good afternoon, Mr. Suurhof, Mrs. Suurhof, children," I greeted them, thinking at that moment that my friends were right: I shouldn't have come.

The whole family looked thin and sickly. What was the use of showing them this cursed ring? And what was the use in protesting about Robert's letters? Pent-up anger, fury, a hot and jealous heart—all were slowly pushed aside by pity.

The children stood up and moved aside to make a place for me. They sat surrounding me in a horseshoe shape.

"Ah! The newspapers were full indeed of reports about you, Sinyo," Mr. Suurhof began.

"Yes, but things have eased now. It's all over."

"It's a great pity that it ended so unhappily, Nyo," Mrs. Suurhof added.

"What can be done?" and the conversation ended.

But our quiet reflections were interrupted. One of the children attacked with the news: "Brother Robert has gone. He's not here anymore. Didn't he say good-bye to you?" On seeing me shake my head he went on, "He's gone to the Netherlands."

"Who said he's gone to the Netherlands?" Mr. Suurhof quickly took over the conversation. "He went away just before Sinyo got married. You must know, as a child he was never at ease with himself. A young person, an H.B.S. graduate, restless, forgetful, never wanting to stay at home. Sinyo knows what he was like." Old Suurhof threw a hard look towards his children. It seemed he meant to forbid them to talk about their elder brother.

But one of the younger children didn't understand the signals. He came up to me and passed on some proud news: "Yes, *Bang,* in the afternoon Bang Robert would work and in the morning go to H.B.S."

"That's very fine. He was a very advanced pupil. What kind of work did he do?" I asked.

"He never used to say, Bang."

"He might be restless," Mrs. Suurhof took over from her children, "but we never believed there was evil in his heart. Yes, sometimes he was naughty, uncontrolled, Nyo—you know what he's like from school, yes?—but a wicked boy? No."

The smaller child wasn't going to be ignored. He went on

with his report with great enthusiasm: "He sent us some money, Bang! Fifteen guilders!"

"What are you talking about, Wim?" his mother reprimanded.

"Yes, it's true, Bang," another little brother confirmed. "Mama used the money for clothes for us children."

"It's true, Bang, they're being made up now," Wim added.

"Children!" Mr. Suurhof cut in. He wanted to say something else, but his coughing stopped him.

"It's true, Bang, it's true." Some of the other children supported their brothers.

"That wasn't from Robert. You heard wrong. The money is from your father's pension," Mrs. Suurhof scolded.

"Back pay for a wage increase due five months ago, Nyo," Mr. Suurhof explained, then tried to divert the conversation: "So Sinyo works for *Nyai* now?"

"Yes, just helping around the place, sir, that's all."

"How does it pay?"

"Well enough, sir."

"Yes, it's a big company; the salary would be big too."

"Bang, Bang," Wim charged in head first again. "Bang Robert has been adopted by a wealthy merchant. He's living in a three-storied building in Heerengracht."

"Where's Heerengracht?" I asked.

"Ah, fancy listening to children's talk. Don't take any notice, Nyo."

The eldest child—who hadn't been able to continue his schooling—observed the conversation with big suspicious eyes. He listened to each of his parents' words, and to what I said, but paid no heed to his younger brothers and sisters.

"Robert said"—another child came forward—"after he becomes a lawyer, he's going to open an office in Surabaya."

"So he's living in Heerengracht now?" I repeated my question.

"It's not true, Nyo. Even my husband and I don't know where he is now," Mrs. Suurhof contradicted her children.

Husband and wife were trying to avoid each other's eyes, while doing their utmost to silence their children.

The eldest, the one who hadn't even graduated from primary school, didn't relax his attention for a moment.

"Go on, over there, fix some drinks for Nyo Minke."

The eldest moved slowly away from the mango tree, his head bowed.

"Come on! All out the back! Check that all the dishes have been washed. You too!" she ordered the smallest. They all obeyed.

"I don't know where those children learned to fantasize about their brother," said Mr. Suurhof, frowning at his wife.

"Yes, that's children for you, Nyo," Mrs. Suurhof added. "If Sinyo has many children later on, you'll find out. They eat out your heart. Don't pay them any attention now, Nyo."

It was pathetic to see how these two parents tried to defend their family's good name by refusing to admit anything to the world, and by painting for their other children a flawless picture of their eldest son.

And what of the ring in my pocket? What must I do with it? Must it smolder forever in my pocket and my thoughts? These people will be even more tormented if I return it and tell them it came from Robert. Look: Both of them are waiting to see what will come out of my mouth next, like the accused awaiting the judge's verdict.

Seeing I was hesitating, Mr. Suurhof began: "You must know yourself, Nyo, what Robert was like. I myself don't know what he wants, Nyo. He has never given any thought to the troubles he causes his parents."

"Tuan, where is Robert now?"

"No one knows, Nyo."

"I know he set sail for Europe on board an English ship," I said.

Both husband and wife looked at me with hopeless eyes. The approach of one of the younger children, crying, from the direction of the house, saved them. The child complained: "Someone's stamped on my foot, Ma."

"Nah! Nyo, this is how it is. Fighting every day. If God permits, you'll end up thin and dried up! Even when they're grown, there's no guarantee they'll be of any use to you," Mrs. Suurhof advised. She spoke to the child and led him back into the house.

Now, left with only Mr. Suurhof's eyes on me, I at last felt more at ease. Yet still there was not enough resolve in my heart to act on my intentions. The ring began to burn again in my pocket.

The gaunt man before me was still trying to guess the reason for my visit.

"So how is your wife, Sinyo?"

His question gave me an opening: "I am here precisely on my wife's behalf, Tuan."

"Ha? She had no business with us."

Pity returned to erode my resolve. No, you must not be weak! Do what you must, I encouraged myself.

Tuan Suurhof searched my face.

"Yes, Tuan," and I reached down into my trouser pocket. But once again I became unsure and couldn't do it. "My wife, yes, Tuan, my wife . . . "

"We've never had anything to do with Sinyo's wife." Old Suurhof was beginning to feel boxed in.

" . . . is returning something that she received from Tuan's family, the Suurhof family."

"Returning something? We've never lent anything to your wife." He was becoming more and more guarded.

Before I lost my nerve again I reached into my pocket and drew out the handkerchief in which the ring was wrapped. I put it on the table, explaining, "Yes, Tuan, only a small object. On the day we were married, my wife received this gift from Robert. We felt it was too valuable. We wanted to return it."

"We never agreed with Robert about any present."

I opened the handkerchief. The diamond glistened in the bright twilight, lying there like an eyeball gouged from its socket.

Tuan Suurhof was abruptly seized by a coughing fit, turning his face away and bending over. His right cheek quivered uncontrollably. He waved the object away: "Wrap it up again, Nyo. I know for certain that Robert had gone before Sinyo was married. Robert, and even we ourselves, have never owned anything like that."

"It is indeed a very expensive ring, Tuan, perhaps worth more than four hundred guilders, but it did come from Robert."

"No, Sinyo is mistaken. It couldn't have been from him. He had long gone."

"Yes, he was indeed gone, Tuan, but not before our marriage. Even now he is sending letters."

"How is that possible, Nyo? He doesn't even write to us. They must be fake."

"No, Tuan, I know his handwriting well. So what about the ring?"

"No, Nyo, Robert never owned a ring like that. Put it back in your pocket, before anyone sees it," he said nervously.

"Robert himself put this ring on my wife's finger. I thought that if we gave it back to you, you could use it for something."

"No, Nyo, I am happy enough as I am, a clerk in the post office."

"But we don't want it," I persisted.

"Neither do we, Nyo. Indeed we don't have any right to it."

The haggard man's eyes darted everywhere, even behind himself, steadfastly refusing to look at the ring on the table.

"If that is the case, let me take my leave of you." I stood up.

He too stood up. I walked away but he jumped up and blocked my path. He pleaded: "Take the thing back, Nyo. Don't be angry with me. Don't make things even more difficult for us." He held my hand, pleading.

"It's up to you, Tuan; you can throw it away. You can burn it."

"Don't, Nyo. I don't even dare touch it."

I kept walking away. He tugged at me to stop me from going.

"Why are you afraid? It's Robert's. If you don't like it, then keep it and give it back to him when he returns."

"Don't, Nyo, don't cause us more trouble, Nyo. Sinyo knows how many children we have." His tugs grew stronger.

I stopped, unsure. Indeed I had no right to make trouble for him and his family. They had already suffered enough because of Robert. Victor Roomers was right after all. I shouldn't be adding to their troubles. Mama's teachings about principles were being tested. But it wouldn't be right to go on with this.

I allowed myself to be pulled back, and sat again under the mango tree. I listened to his pleas: "Take it back, Nyo," he said, pointing with his chin to the ring, which still lay on the handkerchief.

I wrapped up the ring and put it back into my pocket. For the second time, I took my leave. He seemed relieved. All of a sudden, he asked: "Where to now, Nyo?"

"To hand this ring over to the district police officer, Tuan."

"God, Nyo, is there no other way?"

"No, Tuan," I answered firmly.

"If that's what Sinyo wants." He paused momentarily, then didn't go on. He escorted me back to the buggy. Before climbing aboard, I felt I had to ask his pardon: "I'm sorry, Tuan. There is nothing else I can do."

The buggy took me to the district police chief's office. Along the way I couldn't help but marvel at the presence of the police in this world. In troubles such as these, they appear as a kind of godfather—able to solve almost any problem. The civilized world could not continue without them. People say they began as groups of private individuals in Spain, hired to protect the wealthy and powerful from criminals and from the poor. Later they were taken over by governments. As in other places, the police had not been around long in the Indies, only for the last few decades. Imagine if criminal cases had still been in the hands of the officers of the Dutch East Indies Company. There would be even more trouble before I could get rid of this ring.

The district police officer received me politely, listened to my story, took the ring, and examined it. He seemed to know what he was doing. It was not fake, he said, and was about two carats, but he called someone else in to examine it more closely.

He handed me a receipt to sign which gave details of the ring's diamond-carat value, its gold-carat value, and weight.

"Can you get witnesses that this was a gift from Robert Suurhof?"

He took down the names I gave.

"Do you know where Suurhof is now?"

"I do know, Tuan, from his letters."

"Can we borrow those letters?" he asked politely. "No? Very well. If you have no objections, could you give us his address?"

"His actual address isn't written there, Tuan. But the stamps on the envelope were postmarked Amsterdam Post Office."

"Good. Then let us borrow the envelopes. The more the better."

"Just the envelopes?"

"If you have no objections, Tuan. Otherwise, please just write out a declaration giving the details."

I wrote out the declaration he asked for.

On the way home I felt freed from the disturbances caused by that accursed object, as though freed from some thorn stuck in my throat.

"Only rich people like going to the police, Young Master," Marjuki suddenly said. "Little people like me are afraid. If I weren't your driver, I swear I'd never have entered that yard, Young Master."

"Yes, Juki," I answered. Indeed they had no need of the police. They had little interest in the security of their wealth, selves, and name; in fact, they owned nothing. These thoughts, emerging so suddenly, aroused feelings of sympathy for them— those who had nothing, who had no need of the services of the police. To them a ring, especially a two-carat one, was like a legend from the heavens, not something of this earth. What need did they have of the police?

On arriving home, I went straight to my room. Once inside, I began to relax. The wardrobe no longer housed any accursed object. The police would do their job and search out Robert in the Netherlands. The Suurhofs would have to understand; their son would have to accept the consequences of his actions.

If I had not acted, perhaps those old people and their children would still go on living in a fantasy world forever. It would only hurt them all in the end. And me? I had been able to resolve quite a difficult problem, to balance pity and justice—and still ensure triumph of principle.

And more than that: I had overcome my own weakness of heart, overcome out-of-place sentimentality. I saw all this as a personal victory.

2

It was none other than Mama who said: A name can change a hundred times a day, but the object itself stays the same. The bureaucrats and aristocrats of Java, my people, liked to give themselves wonderful names as adornments to impress everything and everyone around them, including themselves, with the beauty of these names. Shakespeare, that English dramatist, never knew the powerful men of Java who liked to wax lyrical with names, to ensconce their positions and offices in the security of names. A clerk likes to use the name *Sastra,* meaning "of letters," so *Sastradiwirya* will mean a clerk who is good and firm of will. A bureaucrat *priyayi* in charge of irrigation will strengthen his standing with the name *Tirta,* meaning water, so *Tirtanta* will mean an official who administers irrigation.

What's in a name? People called me Minke. Perhaps it was indeed a mispronunciation of the word monkey. But it is a name, and it will still make me respond if I hear it called out.

Is it true that a name cannot change the subject of a thing? Was Shakespeare right? For the time being we'll have to reject that theory. Take, for example, Robert Jan Dapperste, the Native child who was adopted by the preacher Dapperste. His body was thin and weak. He always needed protection and support. Every day he was the object of insults; he was called *de Lafste,* the most cowardly. The more people he came to know, the more he became the object of insults and laughter. Because of a name, just a name, he developed into a shy, introverted person, full of resentment and cunning.

Yet he was loyal to people who helped him and protected him, who didn't insult or torment him. He ran away from his adoptive parents because of that name too. Now he had obtained a determination of the governor-general of the Netherlands Indies. He had a new name: Panji Darman. And he himself had indeed changed. Imagine: Only three weeks after obtaining his new name, he had already become happy, free of the name Dapperste, free of any burden, with his good characteristics unchanged. And he turned out to be a very courageous person.

While still so young, two years younger than I, he was ready to carry out Mama's order to escort Annelies to the Netherlands or wherever else she might be taken.

I will not say much about him. It will be enough if I show you his letters. They are in the order in which they were written.

I write this letter on board a ship heading for Betawi, *on the Java Sea, this calm and windless day. Mama and my good Minke, this is the first time I have sailed on a ship. Even so I have had no chance to dwell on my own feelings.*

Before boarding the ship, my carriage waited at the edge of the road, waiting for the carriage that was bringing Madame Annelies. I saw several other people sitting along the side of the road also waiting to see Annelies pass. It seems that newspaper reports about Madame Annelies being taken away from Mama and Minke and being sent back to the Netherlands had spread by word of mouth, and had reached right down into the villages. There were many people who felt they must come and express their sympathy by standing for hours along the side of the street.

Then there appeared a military carriage escorted by a troop of Marechausee *in other carriages. That particular carriage was closed. In there was Madame Annelies. She must have been there. I ordered Marjuki to follow them after the troop* escort had passed by. I couldn't help but watch the faces of those who were standing along the road. They were all disappointed that they couldn't see inside the carriage. Many of the older women, Natives, were wiping away their precious tears with handkerchiefs or the corners of their clothing.

The closer we came to Tanjung Perak harbor, the bigger were the crowds along the road. In some places people threw stones at the Marechausee. Even some little children showed their sympathy with catapults and small slings. I could not but be moved by all this. They were enveloped in a sense of justice—a sense of justice that had been outraged. It was as if Madame Annelies had become one of them, a member of their own families.

I had never seen so many people come together to express their sympathy and solidarity for another person.

The Marechausee rode on, ignoring the flying stones. But some soldiers were actually hit and bleeding. They rode on as if nothing had happened. How resolved were their hearts in carrying out their evil orders! I worried, worried very much: It mustn't happen that any of these stones hit Madame Annelies's carriage. But no, neither her carriage nor its driver became targets.

The closer we came to Perak, the greater the number of people waiting along the road. And now they weren't just throwing stones, they were shouting out too: "Infidels! Infidels! Thieves!"

About two thousand feet from the harbor, across a road hemmed in on either side by mangrove trees, a string of Madurese buffalo carts were lined up, blocking the way. The carriages of Marechausee stopped, as did Madame Annelies's. My heart pounded anxiously as I watched the incident from a distance. Would there be another fight?

"Oh no! It's terrible, Young Master," said Marjuki, "Miss Annelies is in that carriage."

It was indeed a tense moment, and neither of us could do anything. The Marechausee were all jumping down from their carriages, blowing on their whistles. They charged the Madurese buffalo-cart drivers. The fight was over quickly. The Marechausee were quickly in control of the situation. The now driverless buffalo carts were pushed aside; many tumbled over *into deep channels along the side of the road. Injured cattle and damaged carts filled the channels.*

I'm not really sure whether all this is the proper subject of my letters to you. Marjuki must have told it all to you already. My intention is to let you know just how many people came to express their sympathy in their own way, perhaps in a way that is unknown in Europe. But maybe it too is a European way, if we remember how people expressed their anger against Louis the Sixteenth in France.

Madame Annelies's carriage now went straight on to the harbor without stopping at customs. We arrived not long after. When I went into customs, I suddenly realized: Mama and Minke were not accompanying Annelies. You must have been forbidden from doing so, I thought. And because of that thought, a great, deep anger arose within me: Mama and Minke weren't even allowed to come with her to the ship. And these Dutchmen professed themselves the servants of Christ in the Indies. My feelings were outraged by this. Christ would never have become involved in an abomination such as this. Mama, Minke, let alone Madame Annelies, had never slapped anybody's cheek, but now you were being forced to put forward your right cheek, I thought. Those Dutchmen were not following the Christianity I was taught, yet your own behavior had been Christian enough.

Perhaps it is also because of that great anger that I am able to write such a long letter as this. Forgive me, Minke, if this letter is not well put together, because, of course, I cannot write as you can. I write this because of my responsibility to report to you both everything that you should know.

I waited on the wharf as the skiff took Madame Annelies out to the ship. My turn to be taken hadn't yet arrived. Forgive me for not being able to keep close to Madame Annelies. But I could see from a distance that she was being watched over by a European woman dressed in white, perhaps a nurse.

Even as I boarded the ship, I heard someone discussing the decision of the White court, saying that it was not very wise or just and was too harsh, and that the court had treated Mama's family as if they were criminals. I pretended I knew nothing about it so I could get to hear more. But, a pity, the talk went no further than that.

I saw several Marechausee disembark from the ship. And with that I judged that the incident was over.

Two hours later, the ship blew its steam whistle and departed.

Through the efforts of the shipping agent, I have been given the cabin next to Madame Annelies's. But from the beginning, she has never used it. It appears that she is in a special room under the care of the ship's doctor. I have tried to get close to her: She might feel I am a friend, or at least an acquaintance. But she is never to be seen. I don't know exactly where she is being kept. And I don't yet dare ask about her; being afraid that such inquiries may give away my true purpose. Forgive my stupidity and clumsiness.

But I am still trying to find out which is her room. Don't be disappointed, Mama and Minke, if this is all I am able to tell you now. I will write again soon, and please pray that my efforts might bear fruit, just as we all hope.

My unbounded respects, Panji Darman

Several days later, eight days to be exact, his second letter arrived. This time it was postmarked Medan.

It was only when the ship entered Singapore harbor that I got to see Madame Annelies. She was in a white gown and was escorted by the nurse. She was brought up on deck so she could have a look at Singapore. But it was clear she wasn't really taking any notice of anything at all. I guessed from the first that it was actually the nurse who wanted to get a look at Singapore, not Madame Annelies. It was as if she had lost interest in everything.

I quickly moved closer to her, pretending not to know her. She was not looking at Singapore at all. Her head was bowed down as if to watch the waves playing against the side of the ship. But it was clear she wasn't paying attention to anything really. Her hair was neatly combed, and from where I stood I could smell perfume.

Her face was very pale. The nurse never let go of Madame's waist, a sign that she was in a very weak state.

A few score passengers went ashore to have a look around

Singapore. Before disembarking they all had to stop and take a look at Madame Annelies. Those who intended to get their view of Singapore from the ship's deck felt, just like me, that they must seek a place close to her. Their feeling of pity and compassion showed on their faces, but no one spoke, except here and there somebody might whisper.

Madame Annelies's paleness was most evident in her lips, and she took no notice of anybody's stares.

I tried to get as close as possible without arousing suspicion. I was going to try to let her know that she wasn't alone on her journey to the Netherlands. But it seemed she paid no heed to either sound or voice. I spoke out my name as loudly as possible to an old Chinaman who, in fact, did not at all wish for my company: Jan Dapperste alias Panji Darman.

The old Chinaman was quite surprised at my attentions, but Annelies still didn't seem to care about anything going on around her. She didn't even glance around. She just kept on with her observation of the sea below. It was her nurse who turned around. I couldn't look her in the eye because of a feeling that I was doing something wrong. And the nurse seemed to understand: I had deliberately spoken my name aloud.

She pulled Madame along, leading her off by the hand away from that spot. I didn't dare follow close behind. But then just for a moment, no more than a moment, Madame looked at me; I think she recognized me. But she stayed silent, not showing any special interest.

I followed them from a distance. Annelies was led up and down other stairs with great difficulty and effort until, at last, they went into a cabin that was clearly not a passenger cabin. Perhaps that was her room, perhaps not. There was no name on the door, just a number.

After I discovered this cabin, I began to hang about there. But there was still no sign of Annelies. Perhaps tomorrow or the day after. But her nurse does from time to time come out of the cabin. Perhaps it is the ship's clinic? But I soon rejected that idea, because the clinic clearly isn't there; I know that for sure.

My good Mama and Minke, this is as much as I can report at the moment. Perhaps at our next port of call there will be some further progress which I can report.

Then there was Panji Darman's letter stamped Colombo.

It appears that the nurse did notice me. One day I was summoned by the captain. His letter was addressed to Panji Darman, alias Robert Jan Dapperste. I went to the cabin mentioned in the letter and, indeed, I found the captain there.

"You are going to the Netherlands, yes?" I nodded. "You came on board at Surabaya, yes?" I nodded again. "You will continue your schooling there?"

"No, I am going on business," I answered.

"Business. As young as you?"

"Yes. I think the younger one starts the better."

"Very good. What will you be trading in?"

"Spices, cinnamon from East Java mainly."

"Yes, Europe has a craze for cinnamon at the moment. What is the name of your company? Oh, yes, Speceraria, isn't it?"

The captain just watched me, completely at ease, then asked as if totally disinterested: "You no doubt have heard the name Mellema?"

"Everybody in Surabaya has."

"What about Annelies Mellema?"

"I saw her with her husband once at the H.B.S. graduation ceremony."

"Does she know you?"

"Perhaps. Her husband did introduce me to her once."

"Don't keep using that word husband. *She has no husband yet."*

"I know her husband. We graduated together."

"Forget all that, Tuan. Are you willing to help us—that is, if you do know Miss Mellema? Her condition is very pathetic, very sad. Every day she must be forced to eat even porridge or an egg. She must also be forced to take a drink. She no longer wants to care for herself. She has handed herself over to others to do as they wish with her. She has lost all her will. Her beauty moves the heart of all who see her."

Even though I tried my best to hide my feelings, I still feel my words were too enthusiastic.

"What can I do to help?"

"She doesn't want to speak at all. If she was willing to

talk to someone, her condition might improve. Will you help
us? Though I must remind you again that she is not Mrs. but
Miss."

"Of course I am willing to help, Captain."

"As long as you remember, she is not Mrs.," he repeated.

Mama and Minke,

Now I will try to tell you in as much detail as possible of
my meeting with Madame Annelies. But forgive these inadequate writings of mine. As I said in an earlier letter, I write not
because I am good at writing, but in order to carry out my
responsibilities.

The captain took me to his cabin where I had earlier seen
the nurse take Madame Annelies. He knocked and then entered. I followed behind. Madame Annelies was sitting propped
up in bed. Her eyes were closed. The nurse inside greeted the
captain with a "Good morning," and reported on the patient's
health.

"Has the doctor been in yet?"

"Yes, Captain."

"This is Mr. Dapperste."

"Oh, yes, Mr. Dapperste, can you help us? Keep Miss
Mellema company? She won't speak to us. We will leave you
here with Miss Mellema. Perhaps because she knows you, she
will want to talk. We thank you beforehand, Mr. Dapperste,"
and she left with the captain.

Madame Annelies just sat there propped up in the bed.
Under the bed there was a chamber pot and bottles of water.
Everything was tidy, lacking in nothing. The porthole seemed
to be kept always half closed. The washbasin and cupboard
were both clean. There were no cockroaches to be seen anywhere.

I came up close to Annelies and whispered into her ear:
"Mevrouw, Mevrouw Annelies."

She showed no reaction. I pulled a chair over and, sitting
down, I watched her. She looked so thin and weak. I took hold
of her arm and I felt how loose and thin her flesh was. I tried
to think what to do. I tried to recall everything I had ever heard
about her and about how she was looked after when she was ill
the other time. After observing her for quite some time, I sat on

35

the edge of the bed. I repeated my earlier whisperings. Still no reaction.

I whispered again: "Mevrouw, Mevrouw, Minke!"

She opened her eyes but still had no desire to look at me. Then I remembered what Mama said once, as she herself had been told by Dr. Martinet: Annelies didn't like white people. I held out my arm under her eyes and called her again. She lifted up her eyes and looked at me.

Mama, Minke, how startled I was to see those eyes without any sparkle in them. How different she had been on that day of the graduation party! How different on her wedding day when I was so busily tidying up all the wedding presents in the wedding room! How great was the torment she had suffered that it could cause the light in her eyes to be put out!

I know Annelies well, and Mama and Minke too. How much she has suffered, Mama and Minke. I know you all as people of noble heart. No, Mama, Minke, I have no regrets at shedding tears for people who are so generous, helpful, noble; and all these are things praised highly in Christianity. Why now are you all suffering this torment, which none of you deserve?

I continued my whispering: "Robert Jan Dapperste alias Panji Darman is here. Mevrouw is not alone."

Her eyes blinked quickly. How grateful I was to have my efforts answered! She was going to talk. But no. She didn't blink again, her awareness died away, and I heard a long drawn-out breath blown out from her chest. She held my hand. She was going to speak: Madame Annelies moved her lips. But no sound came from her mouth. She nodded weakly.

I also knew that Dr. Martinet had drugged her the other time. As if I were a doctor, I took a sniff of her breath. There was no smell of medicine. She was obviously not being drugged. But her condition was that of someone under sedation: She was half awake, half asleep.

All right, it doesn't matter if there is no response to my whispers. Who knows, she still might be awake. So I explained to her that I had been sent by Mama and Minke to guard her and befriend her on her journey. On hearing the name Minke, her eyes blinked out a flash of light again. But it too lasted only for a moment, then it died away once more.

I had heard about the advice Dr. Martinet had once given to Minke, so I began to carry out that advice. As if I were Minke himself, I began to tell her beautiful and wonderful stories. I didn't know whether she was listening or not. I whispered close into her ears. Ah, even if she wasn't conscious, at least my whisperings would find their way into her dreams. I came so near to her as I whispered that I felt ashamed because I was so intimately close to the wife of a true friend. I shook myself free of those feelings. Forgive me, Minke.

For about an hour I talked and talked; then I realized that she had fallen asleep, really asleep, propped up against the wall. I laid her down on the bed and covered her with a blanket.

To be honest, my dear Mama and Minke, I have not been successful. She is still shutting herself off from the outside world.

Mama and Minke, I promise I will keep on trying, whatever the results. It is God who decides in the end.

The next letter from Panji Darman was postmarked Port Said and it read as follows.

Since leaving Colombo and right up until entering the Red Sea, the weather has been exceedingly hot during the day. I can hardly stand staying in the cabin. And on top of all that, there were the great waves and ocean swell before the entrance to the Bab-el-Mandeb Straits; it has been almost unbearable. The ship's clinic is always full of people. But despite these conditions, Madame Annelies hasn't been affected at all. It is as if she has become immune to the effects of changes in weather, or has already lost her sensitivity to such things.

She was never taken to the clinic. The nurse says that the doctor always visits her cabin. But I never meet him, even though I care for Annelies and keep her company every single day. Perhaps he visits before I come to the cabin.

Mama, Minke, I am caring for and befriending her in appearance only. The reality is not what I hoped for. I still haven't been able to get her to speak. It is as though there is some dense mist that blankets her mind. I don't know whether that mist is the result of medicines or something that has grown from within her. I don't know. Because I have never met the doctor, I have never been able to get an explanation.

The nurse too has never been willing to give an explanation.

Forgive my stupidity.

In that hot weather and during those high seas, Madame Annelies never left her bed. Her health was worsening. Several times I have seen the food spoon-fed into her mouth by the nurse only to stop there, unchewed. I began to worry that the nurse would become cranky with all this. So I have taken over her task. Let her go up on deck to get some fresh air, or do whatever she likes.

Mama, Minke, forgive me, because I don't know what Madame Annelies's religion actually is, even though I know she was married according to Islam. I need to ask your forgiveness because every time I leave her cabin I need to pray at her bedside. I pray for her safety, health, and happiness, then I say good night and return to my own cabin.

I am not in error to do that, am I? I only know Christian teachings and I only know how to pray in the Christian way. I could never bring myself to surrender her at night to that nurse without leaving her with a little prayer.

Every night before I sleep I pray also for Mama and Minke, that you both stay strong and wise.

I am never able to sleep before eleven o'clock. My thoughts do not seem able to get away from Madame Annelies and her withdrawal from the world. Ya, God, Allah, allow me a day when I can meet Annelies again in good health, smiling and talking happily as I have so often seen her in Wonokromo. So far it is only her muteness that I meet.

Even so, I have not lost hope. God will always give me the strength to try to guard and befriend her.

The letter postmarked Amsterdam was the longest.

As time goes on I become more anxious and saddened. Mama, Minke: Madame Annelies's health is deteriorating rapidly. This started happening after we left the Mediterranean Sea and the Straits of Gibraltar. Somewhere near the Bay of Biscay the ship was attacked by a storm. Great waves rolled over, washing forth all over the ship's deck. All the ship's portholes were closed up tight. For the first time, Madame Annelies groaned.

Only I was there to befriend her. The floor of the cabin swayed beneath my feet and it felt as if it was going to turn over. The engine's voice trembled as if giving up all hope. I didn't stop vomiting.

In this situation I knelt down beside Madame Annelies's bed, gripping it with one hand, and I prayed that the ship would not sink and that Madame would quickly recover once we had made land and that she would be recovered forever and that she be given the strength to endure the period of her guardianship, only one or two years.

Only twice she groaned; then she gave voice no more.

This storm receded about four hours later. It was then that Madame Annelies started to soil her bed. The nurse only rarely attended to her now. Forgive me, Minke, that I had to care for your wife in such a situation. Christ was leading me in this work. May His love lighten her suffering.

And that was the situation as we entered the Channel. I prayed even more, because that was all I could do, pray and pray. If the hearts and minds of men can accomplish no more, is it not to God that we then call out?

I had such high hopes when the ship entered the 't Ij Canal. I whispered to her:

"Mevrouw, we have arrived in the Netherlands, the land of your own ancestors. Awaken now. We will not be tormented by the sea any longer. You can laugh and smile now! Face these new things with courage and in health."

She still didn't speak, just lay there, rolled over on the bed.

"Mevrouw, we've arrived in the Netherlands."

Ya Allah! Mama, Minke, she opened her eyes. Her hand moved; she seemed to be looking for my hand.

"Jan Dapperste is here," I said to her.

"Jan," she called out weakly for the first time.

"Mevrouw, Jan is here."

Without looking at me, she said weakly: "Be a friend to my husband."

"Of course. He is following on the next ship. You must get well quickly, Mevrouw."

She didn't speak again.

Then the captain came into the cabin with the nurse. He

thanked me and requested me to leave Madame Annelies. I hesitated but I had no choice; it was an order.

All the passengers were ordered to assemble so that their identity papers could be examined, as well as, for those who weren't Netherlands Indies subjects, their health cards and passports. Because I had been in the cabin all this time, I didn't know where these officials had boarded. There were also Marechausee among them.

After the inspection I hurriedly found my suitcase and then took up a position where I could keep an eye on the cabin. Two dock workers stood outside. Without my realizing it, the ship had already docked. A policeman then passed me, accompanied by an old woman dressed all in black. They too were headed towards Annelies's cabin.

Perhaps that was Mrs. Amelia Mellema-Hammers?

Then I heard them talking as they walked past me, frowning seriously: "Why has no one from the Mellema family come to meet her?"

"It's enough that I am here with that letter of authority I showed you," answered the old woman, who, it now turned out, was not Madame Annelies's guardian.

"She is seriously ill. You will not be able to take her. She must go straight into a hospital."

"A contagious disease?"

"No!"

"I will take care of it all in the proper manner."

They headed for the cabin where I had spent so much time lately. They ordered the dockers to enter the cabin too. Not long afterwards, Annelies was carried out on a stretcher, accompanied by the nurse, Marechausee, the policeman, and the old woman in her black clothes. I trailed behind them as they disembarked.

It was drizzling rain and the cold made its way into my bones.

Seeing me, the nurse said: "You don't have to follow us."

"I only want to know which hospital she's being taken to. I would like to visit her."

"This lady," she spoke again and pointed to the old woman—"will take her straight to Huizen."

"If that's the case, then let me help her."

"I won't be able to pay you anything," said the old woman.

"I hope for no payment, Mevrouw," I answered.

"I have no money to pay for your train fare," she said.

"I will pay for it myself. You don't need to worry."

"I have no money for food for you either," she said.

"I will buy my own food."

"You can buy your food from me."

"Good."

"Very well. Then let's go."

We left for the train station in a horse carriage. The old woman got down and went to buy the train tickets. Madame Annelies was left in my care. We all climbed aboard the train. We laid Annelies down on a seat with her head on my lap. Luckily, there weren't many passengers that day.

The woman sat across from me. She didn't speak. I forced myself to speak to her. Her name was Annie Ronkel, a widow.

"I already regret taking on this work," she then said. "If I had known it was going to be like this . . . . "

"I don't."

"Who is paying you?"

"God Almighty, Mevrouw."

Madame Annelies didn't move at all, at least not of her own will. Sometimes the swaying of the train would heave her body a little. She no longer even opened her eyes. She wasn't interested in seeing the Netherlands.

The nurse hadn't stayed with us. The train moved off slowly, as if it hated leaving its stable.

"Where are we taking this sick one?" I asked.

"According to the agreement, to my own house," answered the old crow, who still showed no interest in either my name or where I came from.

"Agreement with whom, Mevrouw?"

"With those who have hired me."

"Mrs. Amelia Mellema-Hammers?"

"How did you know that?"

"Let's take her to a hospital," I proposed.

She wouldn't agree. It would mean disobeying her orders and she might lose her job.

It seemed a very long time. My legs had gone to sleep. Madame Annelies showed she was alive only by her breathing. The train stopped at Huizen. We transferred her to a hired horse cart. Only then did I realize that all Annelies had with her was an old suitcase. It was very light, as if it had nothing in it. Were there other things left on board ship? Ah, what meaning did they have, I thought almost in the same second. So I looked upon that lone suitcase as all that came with her from the Indies.

The horse cart left Huizen and made its way straight to a village, B——., a peasant hamlet. The road was rough and rocky and in bad repair.

We carried Annelies upstairs. It was a small room, smelling of new hay. The house itself was a farmer's cottage made from earth and stones with a thatched roof, just like in all the pictures. Its occupants were the old woman herself, her daughter and son-in-law, and their two children, both still very small.

After all this was finished, Mama and Minke, and Annelies lay in an old iron bed, maybe two centuries old, covered in a thick blanket, I fed her some hot milk. She finished half a glass.

After many different approaches, I was finally able to obtain the address of Mrs. Amelia Mellema-Hammers. I returned to Huizen and sent off a telegram telling her of Madame Annelies's severe illness. After that I looked for some accommodation. The innkeeper only wanted me if I paid more than the normal tariff because I wasn't European. Perhaps they equated me with a demon or devil. It was there, in that inn, that I started to think about what I must do next in order to help Madame Annelies. If there was no word from Mellema-Hammers within two days, I would go and see her.

My dear Minke, that event which shook all of Surabaya did not reach the attention of a single person here. There is no concern over Madame Annelies anywhere. Everyone seems busy with their own affairs. So I thought again of Miss Magda Peters, our teacher who was expelled from the Indies. Didn't she once tell us that progress in this age was pioneered by the radicals? I will find Magda Peters and get her help. Sooner or later I will find out her address.

I write this letter at the inn in Huizen. Forgive me, for I

have left Madame Annelies now for almost twenty-four hours.
As soon as I finish this letter, I will be off to the village again.
May God continue to give strength to Mama and Minke.

Another letter stamped Huizen read like this.

I don't know what I must write under these anxious and wor-
rying circumstances, Mama and Minke. But even so I must
write and tell you. I must not make Mama and Minke wait too
long. Dear friends, you must be even more worried and anxious
than myself.

I have already been to Amsterdam and protested to Mrs.
Amelia Mellema-Hammers. Engineer Mellema wasn't to be
found at home that day. That woman only hunched her shoul-
ders and then said: "There is no need for you to involve your-
self. There is already somebody taking care of the matter."

At that moment I came to understand how one human
being could murder another. But Christ still guided me. Noth-
ing happened.

I explained to her that I had been looking after Madame
Annelies ever since she set sail from Java.

"Are you demanding to be paid?" she asked.

"If it was only a matter of being paid, Madame Annelies's
husband and mother would be far more able to look after that
than you," I answered, infuriated. "Are you not her guardian?
At least you could visit her while she is so ill."

She told me to leave. I threatened that I would take the
whole affair to the liberal press. She became even more fierce
and slammed the door shut in my face. I had no formal rights in
any of this; I knew that, so I could do nothing else but go away.

Amelia Mellema-Hammers never did come to Huizen, let
alone that three-house village. She owned a dairy business, but
it wasn't so big as your business in Wonokromo.

I returned to Huizen without being able to get in contact
with Speceraria. I was lucky that the old woman looking after
Annelies still allowed me to come and visit each day. I made up
a flower arrangement and placed it on the bedside table, near
Annelies's head.

Madame Annelies herself is no longer conscious of any-

thing. Only God knows what her condition really is at this moment.

Just a few hours after we received this last letter, a telegram arrived.

MY DEEPEST AND SAD CONDOLENCES ON THE PASSING AWAY
OF MADAME ANNELIES. PANJI DARMAN.

And so the tension of all this time, which had utterly destroyed our nerves, reached the moment of explosion.

And Mama looked calm, though of course I knew that inside she would be feeling the same as me. She had lost her daughter, and was soon to lose her business. I had lost my wife.

After reading the telegram she covered her face with both hands. Her cries were stifled by her palms. She groaned and ran upstairs. My head collapsed upon the table as if a sword had cut through my neck. How cheap was life. We will never while away the time talking as we used to. You will never again listen to my stories. Between us there is only a cluster of beautiful memories, and they were all beautiful.

Her smile, the light from her eyes, her voice, her sometimes childlike words—all were now lost forever, to me, Mama, and to the world. Mother, your daughter-in-law is no longer with us. You will have no grandchildren from her. You will never attend their wedding.

I don't know how long my head lay on the table. Rapid footsteps from behind startled me. Mama was standing there, still overcome: "It's as I predicted, Child, they set out to destroy her and for no other reason than to obtain this company. They have murdered her in the manner available and permitted to them."

"Ma—"

"The same as Ah Tjong, but more vile, more cruel, more barbaric."

"Ma," and I could say no more than that.

"And there is nowhere we can turn."

"Ma."

"A satanic alliance more evil than Satan himself. Everything has come to pass."

"That a human being could be treated that way, Ma."

Mama stroked my hair, as if I were her own small child, and as if I were the only person in the world in mourning at that moment.

"Ya, Child, this is what they have been doing all along, only now it is our turn to experience it." She spoke again but as if it had nothing to do with her own grief. "Three years ago neither of us knew the other existed; we had never met. In just a little while we have become friends. Now this grief we shall bear together forever."

"Ma."

"My two children have gone, and this business too will soon go. I do not want to lose my son-in-law too—you, Child."

Even in my grief I could sense that Mama would now become isolated from everything outside. She would return to being the maiden-girl who was thrown out by her family, sold to the house of Master Mellema.

"Child, if I ask you to remain my son . . . ?"

Ah, what is the use of writing about this dark time in our lives? Let me just say that from the arrival of that telegram Mama felt closer to me. And I to her.

Panji Darman's letter following the telegram said his task was over now, so he would come home to the Indies. Mama answered in a telegram that it was best he rested for a while in the Netherlands. If he wanted to continue his studies, she would pay for it.

Panji Darman answered with another telegram. He was a thousand times grateful, but he was not willing to be a burden on someone who was threatened by disaster. Indeed, it was he who should be helping Mama. Anyway, the Netherlands had given him only bad things to remember it by. He would come home quickly.

His letters kept coming.

The newspapers presented all sorts of reports from all over the world. But I saw only Annelies.

"For nine months I bore her, then I gave birth to her in pain. I brought her up. I educated her to be a good administrator. I married her to you. . . . She should now be growing into her full beauty . . . murdered, dying in the grip of somebody who never knew her, who had never done a single good thing for her, and who only abused her," Mama moaned during those days.

Finally I marshaled the courage to answer her. I repeated Panji Darman's words. "All we can do is pray, Ma, pray."

"No, Child, these are the deeds of human beings. Planned by the brains of humans, and by the warped hearts of humans. It is to people we must speak our words. God has never sided with the defeated."

"Ma."

"It is to people we must speak."

I knew that revenge was raging inside her heart. She needed nobody's pity.

And so it was that I too began to feel the fire of revenge.

3

Life went on without Annelies.

I returned to my old activities: reading the papers and certain magazines, books, and letters; writing notes and articles; and helping Mama in the office as well as with the outside work.

All this reading taught me a great deal about myself, about my place in my environment, in the world at large, and in the unrelenting march of time. Looking at myself this way, I felt I was being carried along by the wind, with no place on earth where I could stand secure.

This is the story, put together in my own way:

Eighteen ninety-nine—the closing year of the nineteenth century.

Japan has become increasingly interesting. These people, who arouse such admiration, are achieving more and more amazing things. I read from my notes: The Netherlands and Japan signed a treaty of friendship about half a century ago. One by one the European nations have come to look upon Japan as an Asian people different from the others, exceptional. And about five years ago I read in an article that Japan had entered the arena, not wanting to be left behind by the white nations in dividing up the world. Japan has been taking its share too. She attacked Manchuria, the territory of China. And the Netherlands, and the Netherlands Indies itself, announced official neutrality in that war. Neutral! Neutral towards an ally that is on the attack. I could see in my imagination: a small child, clever and strong, thieving the possessions of an old giant riddled with disease—an old giant, laid out on a stretcher, powerless.

Elsewhere, a war had broken out between Greece and Turkey: The whole civilized world, they said, was watching the Bosporus Straits. Meanwhile, Japan continued to overrun the possessions of the decrepit giant China. The Spanish-American war broke out in the Philippines at the edge of the Indies. Two Dutch frigates sailed back and forth around the waters of Manado Sangi-Talaud on the one hand, and in the waters between Geelvinkbaai and the Mapia Islands on the other, both, no doubt, ready to defend the neutrality of the Indies. So the civilized world then turned its eyes to the Philippines. And Japan was still overrunning the possessions of the decrepit giant China. Victory after victory. Her power swelled; she became more resolute, more self-confident. Amazing Japan!

Three years ago, one history book said, a treaty had been signed between the Netherlands Indies and Japan. In it the Netherlands Indies had claimed the right to look upon Japanese residents of the Indies as having the status of Orientals. That was three years ago. One year after that agreement the Indies government hurriedly prepared a new law that gave the same legal status to Japanese residents as to Europeans.

Now, at the time of my writing, Japanese residents in the Indies have the same status as Europeans.

How proud must the Japanese be. How proud must Maiko be. And why not? They were the only people in all of Asia that had the same status as the white-skinned peoples! I could only sit, mouth agape, in wonderment. What had transformed these people? As a single grain of sand of the great sand-mountains of Asian peoples, I secretly felt some pride too, even though, yes, even though as a Javenese youth I felt far below them. I was a child of a conquered race. The European teaching that I had received had not equipped me to understand Japan, let alone the greatness of Europe.

What I was feeling then was that Europe had obtained its glory from swallowing up the world, and Japan from overrunning China. How strange it was if every glory was obtained only at the cost of the suffering of others. How confused I was, surrounded by the reality of the world. I was overcome by directionless ideas and feelings. Perhaps I was still too young to expect to reach any clear conclusions. Yet it was precisely conclusions that I needed. Conclusions—the mother of a clear and firm stance in life.

The conferring of equal status on the Japanese in these Dutch-conquered islands startled all who heard of it. Japan had left the Arabs, the Chinese, and the Turks behind—flying by themselves up into the heavens to join the ranks of the Europeans, and not just on paper, but in the treatment they received.

People said that on the plantations and in the workshops, the businessmen and foremen now called them tuan. But Maiko certainly marred Japan's good image. It was even being said that the Japanese had the right to be paid the same wage as Pure Europeans for the same work. I didn't know if it was true. The Japanese, it happens, don't like working for employers who aren't Japanese themselves.

Perhaps, in all of the Indies, I am the one and only Native who keeps notes like these. Who else is interested in other peoples? Notes like these bring no respect, let alone any material benefit.

Mama, like the others, was not interested. It is true that she once said there was no point in hiring Japanese if Natives could do the work. Even so, because she had never paid attention to the matter, she was surprised to find several auction papers urging, "Sack all the Japanese coolies! Their labor is too expensive!" In the midst of all these proposals and demands the papers also got an opportunity to advertise the goods they had for auction. Indeed, several of our own workers told how three Japanese had been sacked from a carriage workshop and a bakery. Both businesses were owned by Europeans.

Then the news was announced: The Country of the Rising Sun, of the Meiji Emperor, was appealing to all its people overseas, advising them: Learn to stand on your own feet! Don't just sell your labor to whoever is willing to hire you. Change your status from a coolie to an entrepreneur, no matter how small. You have no capital? Join together, form capital! Learn together! Be diligent in your work.

I felt that appeal was addressed to me too, like a voice from the heavens, just like in the *wayang,* shadow puppet plays when a god calls out from the heavenly ether above.

The reality, however, was that the colonial newspapers and magazines were savagely and angrily opposed to the new legal reality. They did not want the position of the Japanese equal to that of the Europeans.

And Jean Marais said that those accustomed to enjoying the suffering of the Asian peoples will, of course, never be ready to lose even a small part of the respect that they consider their right, as well as a gift to them from God.

Then there were others who wrote rudely—in auction and advertising papers naturally. Japan, they said, the biggest exporter of prostitutes and cooks in the world, with its new status will be able to ruin the world with its pleasures and its delicious food, bankrupting good families, bringing the disaster of moral collapse, creating chaos in Indies European society. The cities will fill up with red-light areas, with slant-eyed, kimono-wearing misses whose behavior will offend the hearts of civilized European ladies. Will granting equal status to the Japanese mean the acceptance of prostitution? Before it is too late and things have gone too far, would it not be better for this Indies State Decision No. 202 to be reconsidered?

Just imagine, growled my old landlord Telinga, what would become of the world if Europeans had to accept equality with colored peoples, peoples who can in no way be properly considered equals? All sit on the same level? Perhaps it could happen. Stand at the same level? No! All this while our heads have been bowed in obedience to the knives and scissors of Japanese barbers, our stomachs have been caressed by their restaurants, and perhaps even our fertility and potency have been thieved by their prostitutes . . . as if there aren't enough half-breed Indos in the Indies already!

A fellow graduate angrily gave his ideas on the whole matter. He was well known as a regular patron of the *Japanese Gardens.* "If things keep on like this, one day that slant-eyed dwarf, with legs shortened by too much sitting cross-legged, will be found everywhere—sitting in our offices where we ourselves should be sitting. How shameful! Would we have to bow first? Sadly, I feel this will happen. But I will refuse to look at even a Chinese officer! Even if they have hundreds of sacks of money!"

Another friend, the son of a former consul to Japan, had something different again to say. It was, perhaps, a rather imperfect repetition of something his father or mother once said: "Japan? But they have been of great service to us, the Dutch. In the battles and wars to conquer the Indies, didn't a great many die for the *Dutch East Indies Company, the VOC?* When we had to defend Batavia from the attacks of Mataram? . . . Even so, it doesn't seem quite right."

And Maarten Nijman wrote: "Indeed the concern, unease, and disagreement with this decision to give equal status to Japanese has succeeded in casting a shadow over the hearts of all you colonial gentlemen. There are grounds for your fear, but there is also something strange about it. The great Roman Empire never entertained such feelings, not even towards those peoples it had defeated and then colonized. And in this matter, the Netherlands never defeated and colonized the Japanese. Relations between Japan and the Netherlands have always been without blemish since the beginning of the seventeenth century. Yes, there was a fight in 1863–1864, but that was only with one particular lord of the central government of the Dai Nippon Empire. And in the end that gave birth to the Shimoneski Convention of 1864, which improved Dutch-Japanese relations even further. So it is indeed strange that you colonial gentlemen feel so worried and unhappy over this!

"You gentlemen have defeated the peoples of the Indies, so you have the right to expect their respect. You have the right to demand anything whatsoever from them: a right that the law of history, where victory in war determines all, has conferred upon you. But in the case of the Japanese, it makes sense to acknowledge them as equals."

And Telinga again: "It's a pity I don't know anything about the Romans, though it must be true if it's written in the histories. But there is a difference with the Japanese. It's not possible to acknowledge them to be equally tall in all climes. That would be directly violating the laws of nature."

And Jean Marais: "Why can't those who disagree with the decision restrain their need to hurl insults? Amongst ourselves—if all we want to do is hurl insults—it has to be acknowledged that we all don't stand equally tall; with stupid insults we will only strike back at ourselves. It's true, isn't it, that you could get together a number of colonial gentlemen who are dwarfs, either because their growth was stunted or because they were naturally small."

Another voice again: "Japan has been given equal status with Europe. And that is only possible because of our own generosity and sense of charity. Now it is law. And this is the question: If China achieves some little progress like Japan, will China also be given equal status? There's nothing wrong with daring to put such a question. We must dare also to answer it. If it turns out that we must answer yes, what then will become of these Indies? What will our position be then?

"The Japanese and Chinese people are famous for their wandering, a wandering caused by their poverty. The latest news is that the Japanese are flooding into Hawaii, and have already begun arriving in America—both north and south. The Chinese have come into Southeast Asia in wave after wave. Those who know say it started before Christ. In the Indies itself, the number of Chinese is several times greater than the grand total of all the Pure and Mixed-Blood Europeans. Can we forget the Chinese War of 1741–1743 when the Chinese Imperial Fleet swept the Dutch East Indies Company from all its footholds on the north coast of Java? And then the fall of the *Court of Katasura*? It is hoped that our great colonial leaders, whom we all honor and respect, will spare some moments to contemplate these things.

"Look at our colonial investments: How much money and how many lives have we already flushed down the drain to put down every resistance of the Natives—from the moment we set foot here up to this very second? How many thousands of our soldiers have died in Java and Sumatra because of war and malaria? We have waged continuous war in order to retain power. Every barracks-child can tell you! Even now in the very center of the Indies there are enclaves of power that have not bowed down before Her Majesty the Queen. Now there is a yellow-skinned people who have been made our equals: a nation of imitators. With our European technology, they have tried to sow the seeds of pride in their breasts by attacking and conquering Manchuria.

The scholars say Japan wants to strengthen itself with the iron and steel of Manchuria.

"With iron and steel, and the science and learning of Europe, we dare not imagine what will happen to the fruits of all our strivings and efforts in the future. Ask any soldier who has had to go into battle time and time again! Ask the men who have served in the Field Police. Just count up how many have died or been disabled for life for the glory of the Greater Netherlands! Be careful!"

I myself, as a result of all this, was forced to imagine Japan as very very close to the Indies, ready at any moment to replace the power and authority of the Netherlands.

The Malay-Chinese papers, which mostly printed advertisements, remained silent; they gave no opinion. Even the turmoil in China itself was hardly ever reported.

Here are my own conclusions on this matter. There was fear among the colonial classes in the Indies. It was as if they had lost faith in their own strength. And how can such a tall people be so afraid of another race—a race it despises, upon which it is always heaping insults? I did not understand. But I could sense that something was making the Europeans and their Mixed-Blood relatives very anxious.

Mama had not been reading the newspapers over the last several days. She was still busy, and not paying much attention to her makeup and dress. Dark rings shadowed her eyes. She rarely spoke, rarely greeted me. When she wasn't working, I usually found her lost in thought. I didn't bother her with my questions.

If I forced myself to understand what was going on—even with my current limited capabilities—I came to the conclusion that the colonials were frightened of their own imaginings, imaginings of things far away on the distant horizon. For me Japan still represented something abstract. My admiration of her was admiration of an abstraction. In my mind I could not yet feel Japan in its concreteness. It was different with the Chinese, who could be seen and met almost anywhere in the Indies, their bare feet tramping the highways and village lanes, their backs loaded with peddlers' merchandise, their skin clear and clean. And they never complained! No one ever got to know them well because of their different language, their different habits and beliefs. But for me there was always something special about them. Without ever swinging a hoe or machete, without ever turning soil or planting seeds, they were able to eat and live better than most Natives. Nobody wanted to see this special achievement, but only to stare wide-eyed at their foreignness. If the Chinese had this extra ability, surely the Japanese would be even further advanced.

Then an image of Maiko came to me—the one and only Japanese I'd ever seen and whom I met during the court trials. She was just one among so many Japanese prostitutes who had left the land of their birth, determined to accumulate some capital so that they could return and set up a business with their husbands. And how much capital had already been gathered by all these prostitutes throughout the world? How much had been taken back to Japan by people other than prostitutes? How many businesses had been set up in Japan by now? I could not even imagine—except for how busy that nation must be with every kind of business and enterprise.

Even though I was a great admirer of Japan I had never dreamed that this people, who had never been conquered by Europe, could become so highly respected among the international community of advanced nations. Their warships patrolled all the world's waterways. The mouths of their cannons gaped out at both sky and sea. How proud any Asian would be to be so respected, never having to crawl and kowtow to some foreign power.

And then one day, quite unexpectedly, Maarten Nijman started a new controversy: "The Yellow Peril from the North." In contrast to his earlier article, he gave the following warning: "Only one step away from Japan is China. A sense of restlessness has lately been in the air among all the peoples of the European colonies of Southeast Asia, from Cochin China to the Indies. The target of this restlessness has been colonial authority. And there's another restlessness that is not so well known but deeper and more hidden—the restlessness of conquered peoples who have had enough, who are tired of satisfying the wants of those who have made themselves masters—all those who must be called Sir. This is the restlessness of the religious leaders of the people in the conquered areas. It has been there for a very, very long time. But an even more important source of restlessness, which hasn't been recognized as such, is the 'yellow peril from the north.' The reform movement, the renaissance in China, however small and meaningless it may seem, will, as time goes on, grow larger and larger."

I didn't really understand what he meant by restlessness, so I made sure I remembered that word. Restless! restless!

And it was none other than Herbert de la Croix who, through a letter from Miriam, completely dumbfounded me.

> *My good Minke, please don't become bored with us because we're always nagging you with our opinions about your people and your country. Papa says that right up to today, Minke, the nations of the north have come to your country to tread upon you. Yes, even in our times, Minke. You yourself have experienced this. The north has always been sacred to your people, even in their dreams. Isn't a dream of sailing northward considered an omen of approaching death? And haven't your people, since the forgotten ages, buried their corpses pointing to the north? And your ideal home, isn't that one that faces north? According to Papa, this is because it is from the north that the marching feet of conquering peoples have come, ensuring your backwardness, then deserting you, and leaving you only the waste of their civilization, their diseases, and just a little of their learning.*
>
> *I write this with a heavy heart, my dear Minke, not to hurt your feelings, but only to pass on a message: The north contains no magic. But it is true that you must keep your eyes to the north always in vigilance.*

Jean Marais said: "I think, Minke, that your country is too isolated—it can't bear the life-beat of other countries. They can come out here into warm and gentle lands, relax, live like kings. Even a small nation like the Dutch. And your people can do nothing about it. Three hundred years, Minke. Not an insignificant time."

Shameful. And there was more. I felt furious in my impotence.

This tumult of ideas and opinions from so many people made me more and more confused. School was simpler; you just had to listen and have faith in a few teachers. The best marks went to the student who could turn himself into what the teachers wanted.

Maarten Nijman wrote: "The Chinese Young Generation, so

well schooled, are jealous of Japan's achievements, the same Japan that is robbing China of parts of its own territory. They are jealous! And furious and angry because they are aware but powerless."

Just like me.

"Pity the Chinese Young Generation," said Nijman. "They are forty years behind the Japanese, the cousins of whom they're so jealous. Imagine, just to rid themselves of their *thau-cang*—pigtails—and to free the feet of their women from that tormenting, deforming custom, will need at least fifteen more years. Even then there is no guarantee of success. Ah yes, because 'custom' will oppose the Chinese Young Generation with the force of arms. If they do succeed in ridding the byways of the world of pigtails and the tiny deformed feet of their women, they will still not have freed themselves from that habit of coughing up phlegm and spitting it out—a revolting habit that makes one's hair stand on end—a habit that has caused the Chinese to lose the sympathy of the whole world! To get rid of that habit the Young Generation would have to work for another twenty-five years at least. So it will still be about seventy-five years before the world won't feel disgusted when standing near a Chinese."

Still Nijman's opinion: "Japan is now looked upon as equal with Europe, China not yet. What people say is true: There is only one step between China and Japan. But it cannot be measured in miles or kilometers. It is a step in civilization. It can be measured only in terms of the Chinese people's own capacities."

Nijman's writings were interesting. One day I would ask his opinion of my own people. Are my people as pathetic as the de la Croix family says? Perhaps he has some kind of abacus he can use to calculate how many dozens of years it will take the Javanese to reach the same level as the Japanese.

And more Nijman: "That distance in civilization, however many steps it may be, is not important. In the end the strong always swallow the weak, even if the strong are only small in number. Just try to imagine: the Chinese nation is a big nation; what if it were strong as well? The Yellow Peril, sirs, the Yellow Peril. Be careful, very careful. Japan is already a reality; China can likewise become a reality, whether we like it or not. Perhaps we won't ever see it ourselves. But be very careful, because time keeps moving on, whether we like it or not."

Then one day a letter from Nijman landed on my desk—for me. He hoped that I could come to the editorial offices to write up an English-language interview with a Chinese youth.

An interview in English, not Dutch! If there is anyone who cannot see that this is a great advance, I don't know what to say to them. Mama had no objections. Like my own mother, she never forbade me anything. Also like Mother, she supported everything I did, as long as I was prepared to bear the risk and as long as it did not harm anyone else.

So it seemed that it was only Jean Marais who objected. He began the argument a week ago. "Minke, I've wanted to talk to you for some time, but I've always held back," he said, "even though I feel it my duty."

"What is it, Jean?"

"It's like this, Minke. You have become famous and respected because of your writings. No one can deny that. But my opinion is different. Perhaps my opinion originally comes from you. Look, Minke, I feel the respect you have obtained doesn't come from your writing. It is respect for your character. You present and show things differently. It is all uniquely Minke. Your writing is only an emanation, no, not even that, just a reflection of your character. You are a very interesting individual. Fortunately you have mastered Dutch, so you write in Dutch."

From the beginning my suspicions were aroused. Perhaps his opinions were only secondhand too—he didn't read Dutch. And he didn't normally speak for so long at once. I didn't like being lectured to like this. If all he wanted to do was to free himself from his dependence on me, I didn't see why he had to start off with a speech. It was his right to stand on his own feet. It was good if he felt he could stand alone now. I too would join in thanking God.

But the way he delivered his little speech made me feel he was letting out some suppressed emotion, ready to explode.

"Yes, Jean?"

"There is something I feel is a great pity. Something that thousands of other people feel is a great pity too: Why do you only write in Dutch? Who do you only speak to the Dutch and the others who understand their language? You owe nothing to them, just as your mother once told you. What do you expect from them that makes you want to speak only to them?"

My prejudice made me feel his words were jumping out at

me, without any humility: arrogant, piercingly lecturing, even reprimanding me. My anger welled up and overflowed. I sensed he was preparing to entrap me. He wanted me to write in Malay so that he himself could read my writings directly, while destroying my fame and achievement and prestige. I gazed at him with bulging, angry eyes.

"Are you angry, Minke?" he asked in an arrogant tone of voice.

I restrained my fury. Whatever else, he was my friend, not an enemy. He must not become a former friend. Perhaps he simply didn't want to face reality: my character, my individuality, could not be separated from the Dutch language. To separate these things would only make this person named Minke nothing better than roadside rubbish.

"So you want me to write in Malay," I asked, "so that no one will read what I write? In a language that you can understand?"

"You've got it wrong, Minke. I personally am not a factor in this. I'm only speaking like this for your own benefit. Malay is used more than any other language in the Indies, much more than Dutch."

I rejected his proposition. "Why don't you accept reality? Only those with little or no education read Malay."

Jean seemed to be offended, perhaps because he himself couldn't speak Dutch. And indeed I wanted him to be offended, to be hurt. His heart must suffer the hurt that mine was now feeling.

However he then whispered harshly: "You're an educated Native! While Native people are not educated, it is you who must ensure they become educated. You must, must, must speak to them in a language they understand."

"Malay readers are, at the most, only uneducated European Mixed-Bloods who work in the plantations and factories."

"Don't belittle," he said more harshly. "Do you consider Kommer uneducated? He writes in Malay. He translates your writings into Malay. Do you think it was Dutchmen who defended you in your difficulties? How many of those uneducated ones were prepared to go to jail to defend you? And for how long? They defended your marriage because of Kommer's translations, because of Kommer's writings, not because of your Dutch articles."

"You're lying!"

"That's what Kommer said."

"You're a liar!" I roared.

"He understands Natives better than you!" he hissed in accusation. "You don't know your own people."

"You're going way too far now!"

"Through the Malay readers, even the illiterate eventually found out. Their feelings were moved, their sense of justice was offended—"

I left his house, no longer able to control my fury. I went straight to the buggy, jumped aboard, and ordered Marjuki to get going.

"Just had an argument, Young Master?" Marjuki asked.

I didn't answer.

The buggy started off. From behind I could hear the sharp-pitched cries of little Maysoroh Marais: "Uncle! Uncle!"

Damn! Keep going, Juki! Maysoroh be damned as well! It's no loss to me if I no longer know you. Then suddenly the words of Marais from two years ago echoed in my mind: "You are educated! You must be fair and just—beginning with your thoughts."

Have I been just? I turned around. The little girl was still chasing after the buggy, crying out and calling me to come back. Was it right for me to treat her this way, this child who had done me no wrong? Was my treatment of her father proper? Was I right that he only wanted me to write in a language that he knew? What has this girl done to you, Minke?

"Go back!" I ordered Marjuki.

"Go back where, Young Master?"

"To where we've just come from. Stop by that little girl."

By the time we reached May, she was panting desperately. I jumped down. Her face was wet with tears and her hand was still waving futilely in the air. I picked her up and carried her.

"What's the matter, May?"

Between her sobs she said in French: "Don't be angry with Papa. Uncle is Papa's only friend."

That truly cut my heart. I hurriedly whispered in her ear: "No, May, I'm not angry with your papa. Truly, I'm not. Let's go home."

"Uncle shouted so loudly at Papa," she protested.

"I won't shout at your papa again, May," I promised.

"I prepared a drink for you," she spoke again, "and you wanted to leave, just like that. Doesn't Uncle love May any more?"

Wiping away her tears with a handkerchief, I carried her back inside the house on my shoulder. Jean Marais was still sitting, thinking. He didn't lift his eyes to look at me, as if he no longer wanted to know me. Maysoroh ran out to the back and returned with drinks. Then she rushed to her father's side. Her clearly spoken words were interspersed with sobs: "Papa, Uncle is not angry with you anymore."

Jean Marais was silent.

I regretted everything that had happened, as did he. I swallowed the drink May had brought. I caressed her hair, then excused myself.

"No!" protested May. She began to cry again. "You still haven't spoken to Papa." She collided into me, her red eyes moist, protesting in her own way. I too was now shedding tears. I ran to Jean Marais. I embraced him; I kissed him on his thickly whiskered cheeks: "Forgive me, Jean, forgive me." I cried and Jean cried.

All this happened a week ago.

Now, with Nijman's letter in my hand, I went to Jean's place again. Eight-thirty in the morning. May was at school. Jean was painting. My anger would now avenge itself. Not only does Minke not need to write in Malay, but he has taken another step upward: He is going to do an interview in English.

He didn't seem bothered by my arrival. I went up to him and began: "Jean, once more forgive me my unworthy behavior of the other day."

Without turning, and while still sweeping the canvas with his brush, he answered: "I understand your difficulties, Minke. You've suffered a lot of sadness lately. You're still in mourning. I was also in the wrong; I wasn't very clever in choosing the time. Forget it, Minke. And more than that, it's not right for me to interfere in how you dedicate your life. I didn't mean anything bad by what I said."

His pronouncement sounded long and formal—a warning bell.

"Of course, nothing bad would come from you."

Now the moment had arrived for me to avenge his earlier

arrogance. I would show him the letter from Nijman so that he would know: Minke was always advancing. He would be startled. He must be startled. He had to understand just who this person Minke was.

"Jean, Nijman has written to me. He wants to see me at his office, but not to write in Dutch. You don't agree, do you, with me writing in Dutch?" He put down his brush and stared at me in great surprise.

"It's not that I don't agree," he answered, but didn't continue.

"Nijman has asked me to write. Do you know in what, Jean? English!"

As if he understood that this was my revenge, his hand nervously sought his brush; he knocked it and it fell to the floor. He didn't retrieve it. He brushed his hands on his trouser legs and then held one out to me. He said coldly: "Congratulations, Minke. You are indeed progressing."

Now feel what it's like! I shouted silently, thrilled, in my heart. Filled with my victory, I examined his paintings.

Following Dr. Martinet's sales talk at my wedding, Jean had received many orders for portraits that didn't come through me. He'd already finished more than ten paintings. The one of Dr. Martinet was the only one I recognized. Quite accurate, with the dusky sky as background. His eyes gazed at me without blinking. The point of his nose shone in its sharpness. I could recognize in the painting both Dr. Martinet and his kindness.

"Those pictures are all finished, Minke. They just need to be collected." Suddenly he turned the conversation. "You're still an admirer of Japan, Minke, aren't you?"

"That's right, Jean."

He didn't go on, but began to identify each of the portraits for me: this administrator, that official or police officer . . . as if showing off his triumphs, showing that he could succeed without me, and even succeed better.

"You're doing very well too, Jean," I praised him.

"No, Minke. None of this is the proper work of an artist. Just the work of a day-laborer, a coolie."

"But these pictures are all of important people—all of them."

"That's got nothing to do with the art of painting. It's only to make a living, not for making life fulfilling. There is nothing of any importance that I want to say that I can put in those portraits. Except perhaps for the one of Dr. Martinet."

"I understand your words, Jean, but not what you mean." I glanced at him out of the corner of my eye, and my impression was that he wasn't jealous of my success—he really was dissatisfied with his work.

"Do you remember Maiko, the Japanese prostitute?"

"Of course, Jean. That small, fragile woman?"

"Servicing people for no other reason than to make a living. I'm no different from Maiko. It makes me ashamed."

"The comparison is extreme," I said.

"Just think: I get paid for pleasing other people who have no spiritual or emotional relationship with me. In art, that's called prostitution. You're lucky to be able to pour out what you feel in your writings. I can't."

He limped across to the window on his crutches. With his back to me, he said: "So you're still an admirer of Japan?"

"Why, Jean?"

"If all the Japanese didn't want to write in their own language . . . "

Straight away I knew he was launching a counterattack. I returned to my earlier vigilance.

But he changed direction: "Do you remember what I once said about Jepara carving? I got more satisfaction out of working Jepara-type motifs into my furniture. At least it meant I was doing something to ensure that one of the beautiful creations of your people would be permanently preserved for others to see. I often hear from Kommer that the Javanese have many beautiful writings. I think that if I knew about Java, I'd be more happy translating them and bringing them to the French people than working like Maiko with all this."

Now I was at an even greater loss to understand. Yet I had the feeling that with this puzzle too he was still on the attack.

"You're confused, Jean."

"Yes, I'm confused."

We both went silent. I began to think over his words. Then all of a sudden the hidden meaning came to me, emerging as the meaning of one sentence linked up with another: an admirer of Japan . . . if all Japanese didn't want to speak in their own language . . . preserve forever some of the beautiful creations of

Java . . . translate and bring them to the French people rather than work like Maiko. . . . yes. He was still on the attack. And I could sense that the purpose behind his attack was the same as before: to get me to change from writing in Dutch to writing in Malay or Javanese. It was clear he didn't think much of my getting the English interview at all.

I steered his attention in another direction: "How's the picture of my wife going, Jean?"

"Annelies is so beautiful and alluring. She doesn't need any adornments. Her last experiences gave a special substance to her character. Only the brush stroke of a painter who truly knew her, Minke, can realize her potential as a subject for a portrait."

I didn't understand about art. So: "Naturally, Jean."

"Moreover, I don't need to lie to you or Nyai." It seemed he was reading my thoughts. He stressed the word *lie* as if inviting me to recall our argument of a week ago.

"It's not right to lie to a friend," he said.

So he was still pushing me to write in Malay or Javanese. "If you're in a hurry, Jean, I'll meet May later," I said, ending that unpleasant conversation.

"You're always so kind, Minke."

And I left him there with his thoughts.

I arrived too early at Nijman's office. There was a Chinese youth sitting in the waiting room. His pigtail, his thau-cang, looked too long for his thin body. Its light brown color also didn't seem right for his clear ivory-yellow skin. It was as though you could see the whole system of blood vessels through his transparent skin. But that too-long pigtail trailing right down to the waist! Strange! Long and not very thick. Not in balance with the round, fat, healthy red face. Just his face though; his body was gaunt. I looked at the thau-cang's hairs again: coarse and very thick.

I don't know why the pigtailed youth nodded to me, smiling so that his narrow eyes almost disappeared. His teeth became visible: few and far between and very sharp. His clothes of Shan-tung silk were ivory-yellow, clean but old. His reddish face reminded me of a guava fruit.

After nodding and smiling, he just sat silently and didn't try to start a conversation.

I made a guess: This is the Chinese youth Nijman wants

63

interviewed. I was disappointed at the idea that this might be him—just a youth dressed in Shantung pajamas, without any shoes, with pointed and few-and-far-between teeth—just a *sinkeh*. There's no way some sinkeh boy would have any business with a Dutch newspaper! And if this was the one, why didn't he appear to be educated? Coming into a European's office wearing pajamas, even if they were from Shantung silk. He looked more like a peddler from the villages. He wasn't even wearing sandals, but was barefoot.

A Pure-Blood sinyo requested that I go upstairs to the editorial office. Nijman was writing at his desk. He put his quill back into the ink bottle, stood up, and shook hands with me. His words were merry, friendly, yet very polite and gentle.

"I trust that you have now got over your troubles, Tuan. That is why I took the decision to write to you."

"Thank you, Tuan Nijman."

"We all greatly admire the resolve and patience of you and Nyai. How is your wife's health, Tuan?"

"Fine, Tuan, fine," I lied.

"I'm glad to hear it. Do you remember your last article? You compared something with a sparrow in a storm? It's my own opinion the comparison is not quite right. In my view, and it's not just my own, it is you, Tuan, that is the storm, and that which you considered was a storm was really the sparrow."

"This time you are truly exaggerating," I answered, and I remembered Mother's warning always to be wary of flatterers.

"No"—he took out his pocket watch and looked at it for a moment—"I doubt if one in a thousand people could get through what you have got through safely. The reality is that you yourself progress further and further because of these difficulties. That is why I decided to write to you: Begin with English! Defeated in one field of battle, but victorious in another. What's the difference? Isn't that so, Tuan Minke? If you succeed, your voice will be able to reach the international audience without going via the translations of others, yes?"

"You exaggerate."

"Not at all," he said firmly. "Since the Japanese have been given equal status, all sorts of strange things have been happening in Southeast Asia."

"I've studied all your articles but, excuse me, I haven't read about anything strange happening."

He laughed and invited me to sit on the settee: "Not everything is reported in the papers, Tuan. Look, you've read my writings about the Chinese young people who are restless and jealous of Japan?" His eyes pierced mine with the question.

"Yes, and I read a lot more after I received your letter."

"Excellent. It looks like these young Chinese have a real passion to catch up with Japan. Once you have begun to write in English, you'll be able to establish direct contact with publishers in Singapore and Hong Kong. That will bring you closer to the British empire, to the international audience. Your writings about these strange goings-on will be very interesting to the international community, Tuan. Who knows, you might be a big success in this too."

"Ah, you are exaggerating very much, Tuan."

"Not at all. We'll try. To start with, you will note down an interview between myself and a young Chinaman about your age."

I had not been wrong. It was indeed the young sinkeh with the guava-ball face who was going to be interviewed.

"And besides that," Nijman went on, "you will be able to see close up just how these strange goings-on are taking form. It will be very interesting. These young Chinese are nothing but clowns making unfunny and dangerous jokes. Not at all funny, even saddening. And everyone knows you are far more educated than all of them. The Dutch education system is rated among the best in the world. Just look upon this experiment as an enjoyable game."

The Pure sinyo who was outside a while ago opened the door. Guava Face stood in the doorway, bowing his head deeply. When he stood up straight again he seemed even skinnier than before.

"Please come in," Nijman said in English, without moving from his chair. I followed his example.

The Chinaman's bare feet made their way nimbly and quickly across the room and brought him up to us. He stopped in front of Nijman's desk, where he bowed once again and expressed his greetings in an English with which I wasn't familiar.

I got in first by holding out my hand. Then I sensed my own nervousness: I mustn't fail this test. I will suffer great embarrassment if I am unable to catch what he says.

Nijman still sat in his chair. His English was clear.

"Please sit down, sir," he said. "Mr. Minke, this is Mr. Khouw Ah Soe. Mr. Khouw Ah Soe, you must have come across Mr. Minke's name in the newspapers."

Guava Face bowed even while seated. He bowed so often I began to wonder whether it really was Chinese custom, real Chinese custom, in its pure form.

"Ya-ya-ya, Mr. Minke . . . "

I sharpened my listening to accustom myself to his accent.

"The waves of events involving yourself and your family—we followed them closely. We all have sympathy for you and your family. May you remain strong. And what is the news of your wife now?"

"Very good, thank you, Mr. Khouw."

His narrow eyes penetrated mine. I observed them for a second. Standing there with nothing on his feet, wearing only pajamas, he didn't seem to suffer any sense of inferiority at all. He moved and spoke as if he weren't arraigned before a European, but among his own best friends. This approach might not be very pleasant for Nijman, who would be used to being fawned upon by Natives. And that's what made Khouw's behavior so interesting to me. He didn't try to pretend to be anything more than he really was. His face reddened as he talked. His few pointed teeth appeared and disappeared from behind his lips.

"I'd like to talk to you one day if you have the time," he said to me. "In any case, sir, we are very grateful to you that, no matter what the means and route was, you played a role in the destruction of the corrupt Old Generation that Ah Tjong symbolized."

Word by word I followed what he was saying. But, damn it, I didn't know what he meant. All I could do was grimace. It seemed he had already become used to speaking English in his own way. I tuned my ear so as to hear better.

"Your contribution was really greater than ours. May I know where you live? Are you still with that business?" he asked.

"Still, Mr. Khouw." I was amazed that he knew all that.

"May I, perhaps, visit there one day?"

"Of course. And just wait there for me if I haven't arrived home yet."

Nijman intervened: "Let's begin our interview, gentlemen."

I readied myself with pencil and paper. The Pure sinyo appeared at the door again, but Nijman waved him away.

"Now, Mr. Khouw," Nijman began, "would you like to tell us where you come from and what education you have?"

"Of course. I am from Tientsin, the son of a merchant."

"What kind of merchant, Mr. Khouw?"

"Everything that can be sold, sir. I'm a graduate of the English-language secondary school at Shanghai."

"But it's not close to Shanghai—Tientsin—is it?"

"Not at all close."

"Are you a graduate from a Protestant or Catholic mission school?"

I wrote and wrote. Not sentences—just words.

"What kind of school it was and who owned it aren't important. In the beginning I wanted to continue my schooling in Japan. But knowing that there were very few places put aside for foreign students, I didn't try, especially as I knew that several of my fellow countrymen there returned before finishing their studies."

He was silent for a moment. It seemed he was giving me time to take down what he was saying.

"Was their action a protest or the result of discrimination against them?" asked Nijman.

"Neither. They had taken an oath to become good workers for the Chinese Young Generation movement."

"So then you joined them?"

"Exactly. There is no point in becoming a clever expert, as clever as a May tree—"

"What is a May tree?"

"Just the name of a tree that turns the mountains yellow whenever it flowers."

"And it is really tall, this tree?"

"No, not really . . . anyway, any education would be wasted if one had to take orders from the corrupt and ignorant Older Generation that holds power, or if you had to become ignorant and corrupt yourself in order to be able to maintain that power. All a waste, sir. Even the cleverest of experts who became part of an ignorant power would become ignorant also."

"So you object to the nature of the power of the Chinese empire at the moment?" asked Nijman.

"Exactly!"

"But that is rebellion against the emperor."

"Is there any other way?"

"Japan still has an emperor."

"We are not Japan. Japan is experiencing her awakening. China is in the process of collapse. We want to speed up that collapse so as to rise again, free of oppression."

"But the Chinese Older Generation is famed for its wisdom, the great heritage it has left China, books and cultural artifacts, a high civilization. . . . "

"True, but that was the Older Generation when it was the Young Generation. This is the modern age. Any nation and people that cannot absorb the power of Europe, and then arise and utilize it, will be swallowed up by Europe. We have to make our China equal with Europe without becoming Europe, as Japan is doing."

"Do you really believe in what you are saying?"

"That belief is, indeed, precisely the power that mobilizes us. We have never been conquered by another race, and we are not willing to undergo that experience. On the other hand, we have no dreams of conquering other races. That is our belief. Our people have a saying: 'In the sky there is heaven, on earth there is Hanchou,' and we young people have added: 'In the heart is faith.' "

"You speak like a member of the English parliament," Nijman flattered him. "You desire and are struggling for a new form of authority." There was insult in Nijman's voice. "You want China to become a republic?"

"Yes."

"You want to rival the United States and France?" Nijman smiled arrogantly.

"Is there any other road that new nations can take in this modern age?"

"While most of the countries of Europe are not yet republics!"

"That's nothing to do with us."

"Yet you yourself still wear the thau-cang."

Khouw Ah Soe smiled politely, bowing. Nijman seemed unable to restrain his amusement and laughed also. I, on the other hand, was offended. Nijman's words went too far. It was Khouw Ah Soe's right to wear a pigtail.

"Do you know the meaning of the pigtail?" Khouw Ah Soe suddenly asked in reply.

"No. It must be very important." There was a smile on Nijman's face. "Tell us about it."

"It's an unusual story, the story of the pigtail. There was once a time when Europe so admired our civilization that the French took to wearing pigtails. Then, sir, the Dutch took on the practice also. So too did the Americans wear thau-cangs."

Nijman went pale. He murmured agreement.

"But that was when Europe had not known us long. Of course it is not like that now. Even so, it is still quite amazing: Europeans wearing pigtails! Even the Americans, during their revolution! During France's period of triumph and glory, they not only copied the pigtail but also the habit of eating frogs, which the rest of humanity looked upon as degrading. And what was, in truth, the thau-cang, sir? Nothing more than a symbol of slavery and obedience, originating during the period when China was ruled by the people from the north. Sir, the pigtail in China was a symbol of humiliation. In Europe it was the other way around; it was a symbol of triumph, at one time, during one era. In China people used to eat frogs because of their poverty; in Europe it was a part of its grandeur. So topsy-turvy is history. The mighty race that forced us to wear pigtails is now being subjugated by the Japanese, who seek iron and steel and coal to make themselves strong. That is if I'm not mistaken."

"A very interesting interview"—Nijman gave his assessment—"almost a lecture."

"Forgive me, Mr. Editor, it was not my intention to give a lecture. This is a very important moment for me. It is the first time, perhaps, that a member of the Chinese Young Generation has been interviewed like this."

"This Young Generation—it has no publications of its own?"

"In this modern era, there is no movement that does not have its own publications, sir. And vice versa, sir, isn't it so? Every publication must represent some specific interest or power group, even your own publication. I'm not wrong, am I?"

"And when will you cut off your humiliating pigtail?"

"There will be a time for that, sir."

"What was your purpose in coming to the Indies?"

"To see the world."

"Oh. Ya. You are the son of a merchant who sells anything that can be sold, yes?"

Khouw Ah Soe nodded in affirmation.

"You came by yourself. But you are a member of the Young Generation. How is it possible you have no friends with you, and have just come here to see the world?"

"Perhaps we have a different idea of what the word *friend* means. Our members are just workers, carrying out history. That is what I am as well. We are only ants who want to erect a new castle of history."

"Mr. Khouw Ah Soe, it seems to me that you are not just a high-school graduate. It appears that you have studied at university. The way you bow is not Chinese but Japanese. It seems you are trying to hide the fact that you have lived in Japan—for at least two or three years. You are, at the very least, a very intelligent university student."

"Truly a compliment to be valued highly, sir."

"And you haven't come to the Indies by yourself."

"I wish that were true; I would not be so lonely."

"It is not the Chinese way to wander around by oneself."

"Oh yes? It appears you have a great knowledge of the Chinese. Well, if you are right, let me ask you: May not a Chinese with some European education be somewhat different from his own group and people?"

"Mr. Khouw Ah Soe, what is your opinion of an elephant that leaves its herd? Isn't he a very dangerous elephant? Can't you be compared to such an elephant? You are a member of the Chinese Young Generation, a member that has left its group. It is certain you are not here just to wander around and look at the sights."

"Wonderful. Then you must be right."

"Why is that?"

"Because according to our ancestors, the host must always be honored."

"You have a very clever tongue. May I now put to you the last question? Did you enter the Indies legally or did you sneak in?"

"A very good question, one that history will also put to the peoples of Europe: Oh, you peoples of Europe—and not just individuals—did you enter the Indies legally or did you sneak in? It is you yourself who must answer that question, not me. Good afternoon."

Khouw Ah Soe rose from his chair. Smiling, he shook hands with me, then with Nijman, bowed, and left the office.

For several moments Nijman sat numbed, his gaze riveted on the door now closed behind his guest. Then, realizing his condition, he turned to me, saying, "Yes, Mr. Minke, write up the interview in English. It looks like he is hiding quite a lot. He says he's from north China, but he has a southerner's name. Says he has never been to Japan but is unable to rid himself of Japanese customs like that bowing of his. . . . " He didn't go on with his grumblings.

I began to write it up. Less than an hour later I left the office. I still had time to pick up May. I dropped into a shop: I had to buy something for the little girl. I found a doll that looked very much like Annelies.

May's school hadn't finished for the day. I had to wait a few minutes. As soon as school was over, May caught sight of my buggy, ran to us, climbed aboard, and called out to some of her friends to join her. So we had no choice but to transport this gang of little chatterboxes to their homes. May's house was the last one.

As she was about to climb down from the buggy, I opened up the box and handed her the doll. She jumped up and down in excitement. She kissed me over and over again. She kissed the plump, pretty doll too.

"Climb down, May. I have to go straight on."

"No, I don't want to climb down!" she rebelled.

"Ah, you're being naughty. I've still got a lot of work to do."

"Everyone's got a lot of work to do. Me too. Come on, come in."

"No, May."

She went silent. Her eyes moistened, then she cried in French: "Here's your doll. I'm giving it back. Uncle doesn't like Papa anymore."

"You're getting more and more spoiled, May," I said, but the words kneaded my heart. How great was this child's love for her

71

father; she didn't want to see her father lose a friend. "All right then, I'll take you inside."

I climbed down ahead of her, carrying her schoolbag. She carried the doll herself. She ran inside. "Papa!" she shouted. "May was given a doll by Uncle Minke. Isn't Uncle Minke kind, Papa?"

I came in and saw the child cuddle up to her father. I heard Jean Marais answer, "Very kind, May."

I avoided looking at the paintings. My heart was troubled by the girl's behavior, which had thrown my feelings into confusion. In a flurry she brought in some drinks. After putting the glasses on the table she gave me a long look, then those big eyes of hers gazed at her father.

"Why doesn't Papa talk to Uncle Minke?" she demanded.

"That painting is finished now, Minke."

The child observed her father, then me.

"Are there other things that you want to paint, Jean?"

"Yes, there are many more."

"Why isn't Uncle laughing, or smiling and grinning as you usually do?" May demanded.

So I laughed and laughed until I felt my jaw would drop off. Seeing all this, Jean Marais also laughed boisterously. May was the only one who didn't laugh. All of a sudden she embraced her father, and wouldn't let go.

Jean Marais and I went silent on seeing the child's strange behavior.

"What is it, May?" She let go of her papa and ran into her room. We heard her howling; it seemed she would never stop.

I ran into her room. She was hiding her face under her pillow and her arms were hugging the edges of the mattress of the small wooden divan.

"May, May, what's the matter?"

I took the pillow from her face and caressed her head. Slowly the crying faded. I sat her up; she didn't resist.

"Don't cry, May. Don't make Papa and Uncle Minke sad." She didn't want to look at me. Jean Marais came in, limping, and sat on the divan.

"The two of us don't understand, May. What is it?" I asked. Still she wouldn't look at either of us.

"Do you love your papa?" I asked.

She nodded.

"Do you love Uncle Minke?"

She nodded again.

"We both love you very, very much. Don't cry!"

But she started howling again. Between her sobs she protested: "You're lying to me. You've become enemies."

Later in the evening, having convinced May that the two of us hadn't become enemies, I was able to go home.

Soerabaiaasch Nieuws van den Dag hadn't yet published my interview with Khouw.

The next afternoon the much-awaited report finally appeared. It wasn't a headline, but it was placed in a prominent corner with an attention-getting title: "A Meeting with a Member of the Chinese Young Generation." I was tremendously pleased that my first work in English was good enough to be used by Nijman. I would enjoy it after dinner.

After dinner I sat with Mama in the front room. Seeing her so busy with all kinds of calculations, I quickly said: "It's late, Ma. Give them here; let me do them."

"No, this is very personal. That wolf wants fifteen percent. I'm only prepared to let him have five."

I knew the wolf was Mijnheer Dalmeyer, an accountant. There was no need for me to interfere. Why bargain over percentages? But my curiosity was aroused and I asked about it.

"Just read your newspaper."

Now and then I caught a glimpse of the figures on the sheets of paper. Figures and totals with six digits. I made a quick guess: the value of the whole business. She didn't take much longer to finish her work; then she told me: "Tomorrow I'm going to withdraw Annelies's money from the bank, Minke. I want to know how you feel: Do you feel I'm violating your rights by doing that?"

"Mama! What are you saying? I don't have any such rights!"

"No, Minke. No matter what, you are my own son, the same age as Robert. And you know that this business is going to be taken over by somebody that the law says has a greater right to it. I want to start another business. I need Annelies's money. Her savings from the last six years aren't all that much. She saved all of it—less than three thousand. I can invest that money in your name."

"No, Mama, thank you very much. But no."

I began to read. But what was this? From the very first line, there was no similarity to the interview that had taken place. It read like this:

At eleven o'clock last Monday morning there appeared at the editorial office of this paper a member of the Chinese Young Generation. This person wanted to sell us information about his movement. He gave his name as Khouw Ah Soe, his place of birth as Tientsin, and said he was a graduate of an English-language High School in Shanghai, and was aged about twenty years. His entry into the Indies was no doubt illegal! And we would not be wrong in assuming that he arrived as a member of a large group with orders from their organization's headquarters in Japan.

As we all know, there have been many disturbances in the Indies since the arrival of members of this Young Generation. They openly seek the rapid abolition of the pigtail. The violation of this time-honored custom of China must be resisted.

From the very moment they arrived, they have been opposed by the Chinese sinkeh and Mixed-Blood subjects of the Indies. These former love and respect their ancestors, and feel that to lose one's pigtail is to lose one's Chineseness. They condemn the idea and any effort to abolish the pigtail.

Khouw Ah Soe came to Surabaya about two months ago. He doesn't speak Malay, but speaks good English, Mandarin, and Hokkien, and there are reports he has mastered two other southern dialects as well. Within a week of his arrival in Surabaya it appears he was able to influence several people. Together with these he organized a public meeting in the Kong Koan building. There he explained his lie, that the thau-cang was a symbol of humiliation that had its origins during a period of Mongol domination. And that it was a sign of the Chinese people's slavery under the northerners. The pigtail is no symbol of honor for the Chinese, he said.

The Kong Koan building burst into an uproar. The fury of the crowd couldn't be restrained. The whole debate was conducted in Hokkien. They all demanded: Cut his pigtail so he will be cursed by his ancestors!

According to our reporter, Khouw Ah Soe alone remained

calm. He was not unnerved by the threats. He shifted his pigtail from his back across to his chest. Smiling he spoke: "Don't worry! I myself have already begun."

He lifted up his hair, and the pigtail was false. His hair was cut short; he was almost bald.

The crowd charged the speaker and the meeting's organizers. Fighting broke out and there were many cries and shouts. Various martial arts left many people sprawled on the floor, some with broken bones. Khouw Ah Soe himself, with his false thau-cang, was taken to the hospital where he was to undergo treatment for fifteen days.

He has escaped from the hospital and it looks like he has run out of both energy and money. The Chinese community of Surabaya has rejected him. He has not received any support, especially not funds. His attempt to sell us information is a sign of his failure. He is in very, very difficult straits.

What I had transcribed was nowhere to be found; there wasn't even the slightest similarity. One thing was clear however: Khouw Ah Soe would be in great difficulty as a result of this article.

"Why are you gasping like that?" asked Mama.

I told her what had happened. She also read the report.

"How could they lie in an article like this? Something that should be respected because it's going to be read by thousands of people?" I exclaimed.

Mama looked at me with pity in her eyes.

"Don't be sentimental. You've been educated to respect and even deify Europe, to trust in it unreservedly. Then, every time you discover reality—that there are Europeans without honor—you become sentimental. Europe is no more honorable than you, Child! Europe is only superior in the fields of science, learning and self-restraint. No more than that. Look at me, an example that is near to you—me, a villager, but I can hire Europeans and their skills. You can too. If they can be hired by anyone who can pay them, why can't the devil hire them too?"

Why can't the devil hire them? I lifted my eyes to look at her. Nyai was standing before me. She looked so tall, like a giant, like a mountain of coral. What kind of person was she? The whole world admired Europe because of its glorious history, because of its extraordinary achievements, its literary works, because of Europeans' abilities, their forever-new creations, and their newest creation of all: the modern age. My thoughts flew quickly to that anonymous tract that Magda Peters had given me. Among other things, it had said: The Natives of the Indies, and especially the Javanese, who have been defeated again and again in battle for hundreds of years now, have not only been forced to acknowledge the superiority of Europe, but have also been forced to feel inferior. And the Europeans, wherever they saw Natives not contracting the disease of inferiority, viewed them as a fortress of resistance that must be subjugated.

The tract went on to say: Is the European colonial view appropriate? It is not only unjust, it is not right. But colonial Europe doesn't stop there. After the Natives have fallen into this humiliation and are no longer able to defend themselves, they are ridiculed with the most humiliating abuse. Europeans make fun of the Native rulers of Java who use superstition to control their own people, and who are thereby spared the expense of hiring police forces to defend their interests. The Powerful Goddess of the South Java Seas is a glorious creation of Java whose purpose is to help preserve the authority of the native kings of Java. But Europe too maintains superstitions—the superstition of the magnificence of science and learning. This superstition prevents the conquered peoples from seeing the true face of Europe, the true nature of the Europe that uses that science and learning. The European colonial rulers and the Native rulers are equally corrupt.

"So why are you still so easily surprised?" asked Nyai, as if she had just finished reading that anonymous tract which, in fact, she had never seen. "Not only newspapers, Child, but also the courts, and the law itself, can be and are used by criminals to carry out their purposes. Minke, Child, don't be so easily swayed by names. Wasn't it you yourself who told me that our ancestors used great and splendid names in order to impress the world with their magnificence—an empty magnificence? Europe's show of magnificence isn't based on names; Europeans strut around with their science and learning. But the cheat remains a cheat, the liar remains a liar, even with his science and his learning."

Her voice was pregnant with anger. I could understand why: Her already destroyed family was soon to lose all its property. It was about to be confiscated by the person the law said was the only heir, Engineer Maurits Mellema. I mustn't rub salt into her wounds.

"If they can, and indeed do, do such things to us, why shouldn't they treat the Chinese boy in the same way?" she said.

"That anyone would lie in a newspaper report, Ma—"

"In everything they can get their hands on, Child. The predicament of that Chinese boy is the same as ours. He can't defend himself either. There was a time when mankind was oppressed by kings, Child; now he is oppressed by Europe."

"It looks like Khouw Ah Soe is in real trouble," I said, turning the conversation, "not only with his own people, who don't want to see the end of the pigtail, but also with the police, because of the accusation that he entered the Indies illegally."

"So now you know *your* newspaper, Child."

"It is not *my* newspaper, Ma."

"I'm glad to hear that. But you must have the courage to bear the risks, Child."

"What risks, Ma?"

"What risks? At the very least, that Chinese boy will suspect you of being involved in this shameless lie."

"Maybe he will come here."

"If he suspects you of being a liar and accomplice in all this, he won't come here."

"I hope he won't think that, Ma."

"If he doesn't, and he comes here, he is to receive our protection. He can stay in Darsam's house." She sat down again. "He mustn't stay in this building. He mustn't be seen. Give him a good welcome, Child. No doubt his customs and manners will be different. But you will still be able to learn from him, from other ideas that aren't European."

Learn from ideas that aren't European! What could my mother-in-law be thinking?

"Why are you gaping like that? Did I say something wrong? Something not in accord with what your teachers have taught you? You're looking at me as if you've just met me for the first time!"

"Yes, Ma, each day you amaze me more and more."

"So what have you learned from your mama?"

"You're truly my teacher, Ma, a teacher who isn't European.

I will try to make your teachings not just something I possess, but something I practice as well."

"That's not what I meant."

"Mama!"

"Child, you are all I have left in the world now. I am alone in the world now. Why should I go on working like this? I could easily see out my days without doing any more work. But this business must not die of neglect. It is my own child, my first child. It must remain my beloved child, even if it does fall into the hands of others. It may not be hurt or damaged like the others. It may not be treated just like some dairy cow."

Her thoughts were on the predicament of her business, but she still thought of the interests of others.

"It is my first child. Soon none of it will be left. Just you, Child, my son-in-law, indeed my son. You are more to me than my own children. Sometimes my empty heart is tormented, wondering why Robert didn't turn out like you." She paused a moment. Then: "I often say to myself: An imperfect seedling will die before it bears fruit. Indeed it hurts, Child, to have to accept that reality. And it is more painful still when my conscience accuses me of being unable to educate my own children. That is why I talk so much, lecture you so much."

She picked up the *Soerabaiaasch Nieuws* again and fanned herself with it. Only after a lengthy silence did her words come out, slowly and with conviction: "That Chinese boy knows how to learn from Europe, knows how to reject its sickness. He is no doubt a wise young man. He can be trusted much more than this newspaper," and she threw the paper onto the table.

4

The atmosphere in that big house at Wonokromo became more oppressive every day. I didn't even want to write. The office work was equally uninteresting. Working near Mama, I felt like a dwarf at the back of a giant, a pebble at the foot of a mountain. I was insignificant, my individuality drowned in the immensity of her thinking.

If I allowed things to go on like this, I would surely end up overpowered by her and in her shadow. I had already made up my mind to leave this place—Wonokromo, Surabaya—forever. But whenever my eyes fell upon this extraordinary woman, who, like me, had lost so much, I could not bring myself to carry out my decision. How lonely she would be without me. There would be no one to talk to, no one she could confront with her toughness of mind. She would be like a rock of coral in the middle of the ocean.

I must go; I must become an individual in my own right, my growth not stunted because of someone else's sun-obstructing shadow.

Then one day in her office I told her of my intentions: "When Panji Darman returns, Ma, I will be leaving."

I had not reckoned on how much I would regret saying that. She looked so sad and pained. She groped for something in one of her desk drawers to try to hide her face.

"I have no right to hold you back, Child. But you must know that your place here cannot be filled by anyone else, not even Panji Darman."

She could not make herself accept my leaving.

Suddenly she asked, as if she had just finished making a judgment on the way she had treated me all this time: "What is it you really want?"

"I just want to get away from Surabaya, Ma, to Betawi perhaps. I think I will do some more study, some real study, so that one day maybe I can become like Dr. Martinet."

"If you leave now, Child, with your heart still wounded and in turmoil as it is . . . no, don't. You will never be able to study. You'll end up just wandering around like a drifter. You won't find what you're looking for. You'll be even more depressed. Stay here until you feel better. You'll be better able to decide what to do." Then she was silent.

There was an agreement between the two of us not to think back on what had happened to Annelies, or at least not to talk about her. Even Dr. Martinet, who started to visit us again after the charges against him were dropped, never mentioned the subject of my late wife. It was even more the case with Darsam.

During a week-long trial, Darsam, who was charged with resisting the police and the Marechausee, managed to escape conviction. Now he went on with his daily work as if a person called Annelies, who had been so much a part of his life, had never existed.

Once every three days Darsam would come to me for lessons. He could not only read and write a little, but began to read the Malay-language newspapers, and he was learning arithmetic. Sometimes he would even force himself to study how to handle the office work.

On certain days he would go to Kalisosok jail to visit those who were imprisoned as a result of that earlier rioting when Annelies was taken away. Mama always examined the parcels that were going to them, and told Darsam to pass on her greetings. Once she even wanted to go herself, but Darsam forbade her.

About eighteen people had been caught in the fighting against the police. The sentences ranged from two to five years of hard labor, in chains. Their great sympathy and support for us was something we could never fully repay; all we could offer was our equally great gratitude and the monthly assistance Mama provided for their families. Yes, it was true: The river stones, pebbles, and rocks could also make their feelings known. Never belittle or scorn a single person, or even two, because every individual contains unlimited possibilities.

That morning too I sensed a loneliness in Mama's heart. To alter the mood, I summed up the courage to begin: "Ma, there was Annelies's hope, Ma, that Mama would give me a little sister, Ma. Shouldn't we respect that hope?"

"Come here!" she said. She stood up and moved away from the desk. "Here is the key to the drawer. Open it and examine the letters inside."

I didn't understand what she was getting at. I opened the drawer. Inside there were only letters. Some were tied together with thread.

"Yes, read from that bundle."

I pulled one out. The envelope hadn't been opened. From somebody with a European name, a cashier in a bank.

"Read it," she said.

"The envelope hasn't been opened, Ma."

"Open it, and read it. No need to read it out to me, just read it for yourself."

It proved to be a letter proposing marriage to Mama.

"You can read them all; they're all the same. I've only read three of them. Count how many there are, Minke."

I counted them one by one. Among the names I came across were: Doctor Frans Martinet, Controller H. Sneedijck, Lieutenant ter Zee Jakob de Haene . . . and also Kommer! My heart fluttered; maybe even Jean Marais's name would be among them. Letter by letter I counted, but his name wasn't there. Before I could total them up, Mama's voice came to me: "Enough, Child, put them back. What do you think?"

"Mama is still young."

"When I see those letters, yes, I do feel young. How old is your mother?"

"A little over forty I think," I answered.

"Then I would be her youngest sister."

"Mama, I'm glad Mama intends one day to carry out that hope."

"Yes, Minke, but my intentions are based on hard calculations. Life like this is so lonely. But who knows how long a human being will live? So it is you, who are with me now, whom I value most of all. It is you who I hope has learned from these last experiences. Don't worship Europe in its totality. There is good as well as evil everywhere. There are angels and devils everywhere. There are devils with the faces of angels, and angels with the faces of devils everywhere. And there is one thing that stays the same, Child, that is eternal: The colonialist is always a devil.

"You live in a colonial world, you can't get away from that. But it doesn't matter, as long as you understand: He is a devil until the end of the world. He is Satan."

I heard the bitterness in her words. I recognized that she was confronting an enemy who could be neither opposed nor threatened, a devil immune to insults, blows, tears, or pain.

"If you understand and know the satanic nature of colonialism, then any action you take against it will be justified, except collaboration with it." She blew out a great breath.

"Mama."

"Yes?"

"What do you mean by colonial?"

"It's something that must be not only explained but also experienced. You will never understand by reading alone. I've already tried to find it in the dictionaries, Child, three dictionaries. All in vain."

"It should be able to be explained, Ma."

"I can't. It is you who should be able to explain it."

"What if we define it as 'that which has the character of conquest.' "

Mama laughed. I was glad to see her laugh but my heart was not really happy, for she was laughing at me. She went on, ignoring my suggestion. "Everybody in authority praises that which is colonial. That which is not colonial is considered not to have the right to life, including Mama here. Millions upon millions of people suffer silently, like the river stones. You, Child, must at least be able to shout. Do you know why I love you above all others? Because you write. Your voice will not be silenced and swallowed up by the wind; it will be eternal, reaching far, far into the future. As to defining what is colonial, isn't it just the conditions insisted upon by a victorious nation over the defeated nation so that the latter may give the victor sustenance—conditions that are made possible by the sharpness and might of weapons?"

How confusing were this morning's experiences. Everything was indistinct and without a central focus. Every issue and problem was traveling about, crossing back and forth over previous paths, without direction.

"Your hopes for me are too great, Mama."

"No. You have only one deficiency. You don't really know what the word *colonial* means. You must learn to understand. Your new Chinese acquaintance—what's his name again?"

"Khouw Ah Soe, Mama."

"A very difficult name. From what I can tell from your story about him, he has come to understand that which you don't yet understand."

"But China has never been conquered, Ma."

"Every nation that is backward is conquered and colonized by every nation that has progressed."

That morning's conversation, cluttered with crisscrossing traffic heading in no particular direction, was followed by a mutual silence.

Then one evening Khouw Ah Soe arrived. It was obvious he was in trouble. He was still wearing the same Shantung silk pajamas, but they were dirty and torn.

We sat in the small garden next to my room, on the concrete bench. Mama observed his round face intently (it was no longer reddish, but already going brown), as well as his thin reddish pigtail, his narrow eyes. I heard her mumble in Dutch: "So young, leaving country and family, to come so far—what for?"

Khouw Ah Soe bent to catch her words, then said he was sorry, he didn't understand. I put it into English.

"Thank you very much for such kind words. Thank you."

Unasked, I became the interpreter.

"My child here is confused, Mr. Khouw, after reading the report published about you. It was the opposite of what he wrote."

"Only to be expected."

"Not that. I worried that you would be angry with my son."

"No. That's the way it had to be. Their own actions will educate the people to hate them and oppose them—that has also been the case with the Western enclaves in China."

"My Child had already sent a letter of protest . . . tell him yourself, Child."

Khouw Ah Soe laughed happily on hearing my story, as if he wasn't at that moment being harried by his own troubles. Then he added: "That is how they are—those who hold power in the conquered nations. It is sickening to witness the behavior of those whites who live in countries they consider to be their colonies. To hope for anything else from them is a big mistake."

"Yes," added Mama, "my guess is proved correct, Child. But don't translate that for him. This person is very clever. You can learn much from him."

Khouw Ah Soe looked at me, waiting for the translation.

"Mama says," I said, "that you are now in trouble because of the *Soerabaiaasch Nieuws*. Mama guesses you would find it difficult to find anywhere to stay."

Khouw Ah Soe offered neither a denial nor an affirmation. He dropped his gaze to the floor. At once we understood that things were as we imagined. Someone strong like him would not get into some minor, trifling trouble. His problem would be that he had run out of friends.

"Let me arrange a place for him in Darsam's house," Mama said. Then she excused herself.

Khouw Ah Soe continued his talk. I listened carefully to his every word. "How happy I am to have met your mother-in-law—a very advanced woman." He tapped on the table as a way of channeling his nervousness.

"You will stay here, in Darsam's place. He is a fighter."

"The Darsam who was arrested by the Marechausee? He's free?"

Perhaps Darsam too had been mentioned in the newspapers of foreign lands to the north.

"No doubt he is a fighter," he suddenly affirmed. It seemed he didn't know what else to say. He was nervous.

Not long after arriving in Surabaya he received news: A comrade who had been sent to Fiji had been murdered. Another who had been sent to South America was found murdered not far from the saltpeter mines of Chile.

Finally I summoned the courage to ask: "What is it that you actually do?"

"Call out, no more than that. Call out to my fellow countrymen who have wandered overseas that the times have changed, that China is no longer the center of the world, that China has made great contributions to human civilization, but that it is not the only civilized nation in the world, as so many Chinese believe."

So they were like my own people, I thought, the Javanese, who looked upon themselves as the most polite, most civilized, and most noble of all people. A smile appeared on my face.

"My fellow countrymen must come to realize it is not that the white people are superior; they are the ones who control the world, it is their countries that are the center of the world. Without that awareness they will never be shaken free from their wrong views and false dreams. Arise"—suddenly his voice became louder—"because the eastern peoples too can triumph in this new age. Look at Japan"—and his voice became softer—"but my fellow countrymen look upon the Japanese as a people of no consequence, a young people, a small nation, and always only pupils and imitators of China."

On another occasion he condemned the backwardness of his fellow countrymen, especially those working overseas. They were not like the overseas Japanese, who always returned with some new learning, who humbly set out to learn all they could from the countries where they sought their livelihood, and who took home what they learned as a contribution to the development of their own nation and people.

"I'm sorry, Minke, perhaps I'm too sentimental in the way I talk about Japan, and too enthusiastic when I talk about my own work."

"What's wrong with sentimentality and enthusiasm, if they're expressed at the right time and place? You will be safe here."

He had run out of words, realizing that there was someone going out of his way to help him. He looked embarrassed and was silent.

Nyai invited him to eat, alone because we had already eaten. Afterwards I took him across to Darsam's house. The Madurese man greeted him by running about showing him where everything was: where the toilet was, which was the best way out of the complex if there was danger. I translated.

He thanked us over and over again with an elegant bow, not the Japanese bending that he used with Nijman. He thanked Darsam too for his help in overthrowing Ah Tjong's empire. But I didn't translate that.

Sitting in Darsam's front room, it seemed Khouw Ah Soe was able to wrest back his character, his confidence. Darsam didn't sit with us. Khouw Ah Soe spoke a great deal, for about two hours.

On my return to the main building I found Mama had not gone to bed. She wanted to hear what Khouw Ah Soe had said, and I told her.

"To come to another country without knowing the language," she commented, "just because he wants to help his people advance! Meeting danger after danger. Child, that's what a young person should be like. The Europeans came here as gangs of robbers and pirates. You must note the difference!"

Three days and nights he stayed with us.

From his other stories, I was able to gather that Nijman's guesses were not wrong. Almost everything Nijman had said was right.

He had left China with thirty or so others who headed east, west, southwest or south. He himself, a university student from Waseda, and four others, set off for the Indies. He entered through Bagansiapi-api in Sumatra by fishing boat from Singapore. Two of his friends headed for Pontianak in Netherlands Borneo. One stayed in Bagansiapi-api. He and one of his friends went to Betawi. His friend was left to work there. He himself made his way to Surabaya, an area known to be difficult to handle. Surabaya was the center for the Chinese gang, *Tong,* which, through its use of terror, controlled the lives of all the Chinese subjects of the Indies. The Tong gangs throughout the Indies were controlled from Surabaya.

"Yes, the Japanese have even sent people overseas to learn to play and to make pianos—to Europe and to the United States." He went on to tell how his people who went overseas weren't like that. They broke their backs all over the world for no other purpose than to accumulate wealth. Then they came home hoping only to be admired, and to rebuild the graves of their ancestors. And only to fall into the power of bandits, who squeezed money from them every month and every year. For all time, forever, they would be the milk cows of those bandits as well as of the Tong bandits. If the bandits weren't satisfied, their families at home would become the playthings of torment and torture.

In the end they once again left home, spreading out through the whole world, sucking up more of the world's wealth in order to please their bandit-ancestors. Not in order to build something grand, nor to convince the bandits that what China really needs is: Knowledge and learning; awareness of the need for change; and for a new man with a new spirit, ready to work for his people and his country.

So the children of the overseas Chinese must be prepared to receive a modern education. A great, a very great amount of money must be gathered. The tribute paid to the ancestral and Tong bandits must be stopped. Modern schools must be founded, both for now and for the future. If not, the country of his ancestors would be swallowed up by Japan, just as Africa has been swallowed whole by the English.

Even though his words sounded like an advertisement, they were interesting and impressive.

"Every country in Asia that begins to rise and awaken is not just awakening itself, but is helping to awaken every other nation that has been left behind, including China."

"But science and learning are not the one and only key," I said.

"You are right," he answered. "They are only the conditions. Equipped with modern science and learning, a wild beast will only become wilder and more bestial, and a vicious human will only become more vicious and cruel. But don't forget, with science and learning even the most wild and bestial of all animals can be made to submit. You know what I mean: Europe."

The hair on the back of my neck stood up on hearing his last words. Mama would be quick to express her agreement with this young unsandaled sinkeh.

"So don't hold out any hopes that a modern education will ever be given to the conquered countries, such as this country of yours. Only the conquered people themselves know what their country and people need. The colonizing nation will only suck up the honey of your land and the labor of your people. In the end it is the educated among the conquered people who need to recognize their responsibilities." Suddenly he stopped, changing the subject: "You no doubt know what happened in the Philippines."

His words came at me like an accusation. The Philippines was for me no more than a place on a map, a geographical location. The Philippines is not far from my own country but I knew almost nothing about it.

"A pity, but no," I answered.

He laughed and his narrow eyes disappeared completely from his face. His sparse pointed teeth emerged to represent his absent eyes.

"They studied well from the Spanish, from Europe, even before the Japanese. Even before the Chinese. It is a pity they were a colonized people, unlike Japan. The Filipinos could not develop because they were colonized. The Japanese have developed— developed too well. The Filipinos were good pupils of the Spanish. And the Spanish were bad teachers, rotten and corrupting. But the Filipinos didn't just accept their teachings uncritically. The Filipinos are also great teachers for the other conquered peoples of Asia. They were the founders of the first Asian republic. And it collapsed. A great historical experiment."

I watched his lips closely, and their movements, which seemed somehow not quite rapid enough. His pointed teeth rose and sank behind those lips.

"So you don't know anything about the Philippines?"

"Unfortunately, no. I only know there was a war between the Spanish and the Americans there."

He laughed.

"What's the matter?"

"The Spaniards and the Americans—their war—it was all an act. There was no conflict between them; it was all to do with letting the Spaniards sell the Filipino people to the United States without having to lose face before the eyes of the world."

"How do you know all this?"

"How? Wasn't all this reported in the newspapers?"

"I've never come across any such reports."

He nodded. "Don't university students here have their own

newspapers? Oh, I'm sorry, there are no universities in the Indies yet, are there?"

"So students have their own papers?"

"Of course, newspapers that are devoted to ideals, not yet sidetracked by personal and vested interests."

I couldn't say a thing. The way he linked one thing neatly with another made it seem they were indeed all entwined. His explanations rose before me as a great construction. I couldn't see through his argument. Yes, some great construction where every part contributed to strengthening every other part. All the peculiar things about him disappeared at that moment: his round and now brown face, his reddish pigtail . . . suddenly I was discovering something else about him that emanated from his presence. And that something was life itself. You could hear the groans, the cries and complaints, and the pounding of his heart; the glow and lightning brightness of his thoughts. I had never even thought about any of the issues he brought up. Now I could move on to imagine and wonder about many new things.

I told Mama all about it. She meditated for a moment. Her eyes glassed over in emotion, and finally tears made the journey across her cheeks.

"He has shown us how Europe and America are no more than evil adventurers, Child. If they had no cannons, would anyone honor them?"

Before the guava-faced youth left our house, I felt I had to ask one more question: Was Nijman's report true, that he had been beaten up in the Kong Koan building? He confirmed it.

"Dangerous work," I commented.

"There may be worse yet to come."

"You are not afraid?"

"The Philippines cannot be forgotten, can they? Even if they were deceived by Spain and America? It is inevitable that other conquered peoples will follow in their footsteps. Yes, even in the Indies. If not now, then later, when people know how to handle their teachers."

He left one dark night, refusing the use of a vehicle. He walked off to who knows where. He said he might return at any time to seek protection. Only Nyai and I knew of the help we had given him. He had needed friends and help.

I think I can say it was from Khouw Ah Soe that Mama and I heard for the first time about the awakening of a whole people, rising up, advancing and respected, building a modern culture and civilization.

I still remember those words of his, so beautiful, as if they came from some legend:

"In the past peoples could live at peace in the middle of deserts and forests. Now they cannot. Science and modern learning will pursue everyone everywhere. Human beings, both as individuals and social beings, can no longer feel secure. Mankind is forever being pursued because modern science and learning constantly provide the inspiration and desire to control Nature and man together. There is no power that can bring to a halt this passion to control, except greater science and learning, in the hands of more virtuous people."

The Surabaya newspapers reported that the police were busy with the hunt for illegal immigrants from China.

A Malay-Chinese newspaper published a report that quoted from a Chinese newspaper:

> It is true that Khouw Ah Soe entered the Indies illegally. It is now also known that he entered the Indies with several others. There were reports that one of these was a girl, a graduate from the Catholic High School in Shanghai. They have all been using false names since they left the Chinese mainland. In Hong Kong, Khouw Ah Soe was known as Tjok Kiem Eng and was wanted by the Hong Kong police. He was the troublemaker responsible for the cutting off of pigtails along the pleasure waterways of Hong Kong. From Hong Kong, he ran to Hainan.

The paper also published some background. It was estimated that during the previous year 240 Chinese had entered the Indies illegally, and they were mainly concentrated in Bagansiapi-api and Pontianak. None of them spoke any Native language.

Not long after that there appeared another report:

> Differing from most of the immigrants who came to the Indies, this small group of illegal immigrants did not become involved

*in the smuggling trade. Their intention was to create trouble in
the Netherlands Indies by inciting the young people to defy
their ancestors and their own parents.*

*They are anarchists, nihilists, good-for-nothing agita-
tors. . . .*

And I myself?

After the appearance of Nijman's article about Khouw Ah
Soe, I did not visit the editorial office again. Several times he
wrote me letters in an attempt to win me back, saying forget it,
forget it; if you come and see me, I will explain the whole matter
to you. I did not go. Instead it was he who came to see me. Nyai
did not come out to meet him.

He seemed much younger than usual. His clothes, even his
shoes, were all brown. He took a parcel out of his briefcase and
handed it to me.

"You will find this book very interesting," he said.

It was about America, a continent that was totally unknown
to educated Natives, except for the names of a few people and
places, some geography, and a little information about its produce. He didn't say anything more about the book.

"I understand. You are very disappointed, perhaps even angry because of the interview affair. There was nothing else we
could do. Look, this is your country, Mr. Minke. If you read this
book, you will come to understand why America is thirsty for
more inhabitants. It has vast areas of land, it is rich and empty.
Different from Java, Mr. Minke. Fifteen years ago this country of
yours had maybe only fourteen million people; now it is closer to
thirty million. The land is shrinking because of the number of
people. Some action must be taken against these illegal immigrants. It is in the interests of the Javanese themselves. If not, in
just a few decades, this island could become just another little
China. I'm sure that is not what you want."

Another cause for anxiety! I'd never thought of it like that.
On some other occasion I would discuss it with Khouw Ah Soe.

"Look, Mr. Minke, although the Dutch are the rulers, you
can see for yourself that there is no great stream of Dutch families
coming out here. It has never been the intention of the Dutch to
pour out here to set up a colony. Wasn't it right to publish this
article, if it can help stop the flow of all these Chinese coming out

to our country? The Netherlands Indies has spent great amounts of money for this purpose, working in your own interests, Mr. Minke!"

So far I had not found any ground upon which to stand and analyze this problem. All I could do was listen.

"The recognition of Japan as an equal has produced a number of problems," he went on. "The Chinese of Singapore have already become restless. We don't need that sort of thing in the Indies, especially not in Java. Be frank, Mr. Minke, do you agree with the ideas of Khouw Ah Soe?"

"In some things he is right."

"Very true. But the truth does not necessarily bring any advantage." He quickly set up defenses. "I think you would prefer to support your country than a truth that would hurt it."

Another point that wasn't without grounds! I had never thought about any of this. I just had to listen.

He left after he was convinced that he had influenced me. I had to promise to bring some new articles to the paper.

Mama laughed when she heard the story. "You've forgotten already, Child; everything colonial is from the devil. There has never been any colonialist that has cared anything about our people. They are afraid of China itself. They're jealous."

I forced myself to think how all these things came together: the progress Japan was making, the restlessness among the Chinese Young Generation, the rebellion of the Filipino natives against Spain and then the United States, the jealousy of the colonial Netherlands Indies towards China, the colonial hatred of Japan. And why wasn't the Filipino rebellion reported in all the newspapers?

And to the north, Siam was crying out because its silk, so popular in the Indies, was being pushed out of the market by Japan's cheaper and shinier silk. In the land of my own livelihood, Japanese handicrafts were surreptitiously entering the market. The Javanese makers of blouses, combs, and brushes were losing their share of the market, because the Japanese goods were cheaper and shinier. But the Javanese were silent. They did not cry out. They did not understand why their livelihood was drying up.

And the women of Southeast Asia could not live without

combs, brushes, and tweezers to catch head lice—all made in Japan.

With my inner eye I scattered my vision over my own surroundings. There was no movement at all. All Java was fast asleep, dreaming. And I was confused, angry, aware but impotent.

5

Something completely unexpected happened: a letter arrived from Robert Mellema.

I was working in the office at the time. Mama called me from her desk and pushed the day's mail across for me to read. From Robert, from Panji Darman, from Miriam de la Croix.

There was no address on the envelope. On the stamp was a picture of the sea and coconut palms. The printing on the stamp said Hawaii. The postmark was illegible.

My faraway Mama, it started.

I didn't know why that phrase filled my heart with emotion and my eyes with tears. The cry of a regretful child.

"What's the matter, Child?" asked Mama.

"This letter is not for me, Ma. It is written for Mama and Mama alone."

"Read it," she encouraged me.

"I'll read it slowly, yes, Ma?" and I began to read aloud:

I know, Ma, that you will probably never forgive me. That's up to you. Even so, Ma, your son Rob, so far away now, begs

your forgiveness, both in this world and the next. Ma, my
Mama. Sun, moon, and stars have all been witnesses to my sins
against you.

And what meaning does my life have now? As low as
your work might ever be, you will always be far more honor-
able than this child of yours, who has fought against you and
caused you much sorrow.

I have heard the village people say: The greatest forgive-
ness is that which a child asks of his mother; the greatest of all
sins is that of a child against his mother. I am the most sinful
of children, Ma. Your son Robert needs your most profound
forgiveness.

I glanced from the corners of my eyes at Mama. The look on
her face hadn't changed. She kept on with her work, calmly, as if
she weren't listening.

I know my Mama so well, so I know you won't want to read
these writings of mine. No matter. That is a risk I must take.
What is important is that at least there has arisen the intent to
ask forgiveness of the person who gave birth to me, who has
shed blood for me, who has groaned with pain for my life's
sake, and that intent has now been put into words. So if you do
not answer this letter or even if you don't read it, if I remain
alive, I will know you have forgiven me, even though you may
never say it. If I die in the near future, that will be a sign that
you did not forgive me.

Once, on a ship, someone said to me: You can ask for-
giveness of God at any time at all, if you sin against Him. Sins
against your fellow man are different again; it is much more
difficult to get him to forgive you. God is all-compassionate;
mankind is uncompassionate.

I am not telling you where I am. What would be the
point? It would only cause problems. I am on a ship. And I
don't need to give its name, nationality, or the flag it is flying
under.

After what happened in Ah Tjong's house, I ran. By
chance a horse cart was passing by. I jumped aboard and headed
for Tanjung Perak. I was able to get aboard a junk heading for
Manila. I did whatever work I was given, even that of cleaning

the toilets—everyone's toilet, not just the one I used myself.

*Complete humiliation—that is the condition that befell me
as soon as I was away from you, my Mama. I could do nothing
to resist what befell me. I had to stay alive. And what kind of
life is it, Ma, crawling around people's toilets like this?*

*I was only a few days in Manila. Attacks by bandits
threw the whole harbor into confusion. Many sailors disappeared without a trace. From Manila I traveled on board a
small ship to Hong Kong. In that small, crowded city I got a
job as a gardener in the house of an English officer. Soon after,
he found out that I had caught a certain disease and he threw
me out.*

*Yes, Ma, I am ill. The easiest thing for me to do was to
visit a sinshe, a Chinese medicine man. He said I had caught
a "dirty disease" and that it was getting worse. I handed myself
over to him. He treated me with potions and acupuncture until
I looked fresh and healthy again. In the meantime I had become
a vagabond, owning nothing at all. All I had was the clothes on
my body. This is all a punishment from Mama, so I must
accept it.*

*Because I could no longer pay the sinshe, I had to find
another job on a ship. I was amazed that I was still allowed to
live. I sailed all over the world, going from ship to ship. No one
recognized or knew me, because I always used different names.
People didn't care whether I was human, animal, or devil.*

*But then the symptoms returned. I did everything I could
to avoid destruction. As soon as I was in Hong Kong again I
looked up the man who had treated me before. Treat me until
I am cured, I begged. But he told me something new: The
disease can only be controlled; there is no real cure. I knew I
would be tied to him forever. It's not that I didn't try the
doctors. None of them were able to help me, not even to ease the
suffering a bit. My heart shriveled up—all I could see hovering
before me was death. Mama, it was you, Mama, that I then
remembered. Nothing can help me except your forgiveness.*

*My illness meant I had to stay close to my sinshe in Hong
Kong. I had to have more money. He said I would have to visit
him at last once a month. My livelihood was not so generous to
bring me to Hong Kong every month. And to work in Hong
Kong itself was not easy for me, because I didn't want to be*

*known to anybody as the child of anybody, the citizen of any
country. I had no address and did not want to have an address.*

Mama, I know my disease is a death sentence for me.

*I talked to another medicine man and his words frightened
me: There is no cure, he said; there is no one strong enough to
survive for more than two years. How frightening, Ma, two
years for someone as young as me. Mama, my Mama . . .*

Nyai Ontosoroh stood up and left. Before leaving the room, she
turned to me and said:

"There are some other letters. For you."

I didn't go on reading Rob's letter. I picked up the other
letters from Mama's desk. From Betawi, from the Stovia Medical
School: I had been accepted as a student beginning the next academic year; details were to follow.

Was it Robert's letter or the one from Stovia that made Mama
so unhappy that she had to leave the room? I didn't know.

There was a letter from Robert to Annelies. Suddenly I realized that he knew nothing of what had happened to the family.
The letter carried the same stamp as the first one. There was no
date nor mention of place.

*Ann, Annelies, my little sister. I have now traveled around the
world as I once dreamed of doing. More than twice, Ann. I
have set my feet down in all the great ports of the world. And
I have met with too many people. Not one has ever invited me
to visit their house. They all look upon me as being not of the
same species, from a people too far away and too strange,
perhaps like a race of animals.*

*I had wanted to be a sailor. Now I am a sailor. But I am
not happy. Even in the most meaningless of jobs, I am still
considered incapable. My thoughts are always going back and
forth between Mama and you. You know the reasons. Until
now you have refused to talk to me. Yes, Ann, I understand,
understand only too well. And I know too why people never
invite me to their houses. Your brother is indeed not worthy of
being spoken to by you. He is only an animal, lower still than
the horses you ride.*

*The incident in the reed-marshes continues to haunt me.
Forgive me, Ann, forgive me. . . .*

At that moment I had to stop reading a moment and reflect again on Annelies's story. So it was true, what she'd told me, that she had been raped by her brother. I read on.

> *I pray always that you may be happy, Ann. Perhaps indeed Minke is the right man for you, despite Suurhof's making fun of him. I think Robert Suurhof will turn out to be no better than me.*
>
> > *I have seen all kinds of people now, Ann: Indians, Chinese, Europeans, Japanese, Arabs, Hawaiians, Malays, Africans . . . and Ann, there is none among their women, young or old, as beautiful as you, as glorious as you. You are a pearl among women. Your husband will be such a happy man. . . .*

I shoved the letter quickly into my pocket. No, I must not think about Annelies anymore.

When Mama came back in, she did not ask anything. She sat down and continued her work. I went on reading Robert's letter to her.

> *My contract with life is for two years, Ma. Who knows whether the sinshe's prediction will turn out to be right. When I left him, I swore that once I boarded a ship, I would never set foot on land again. I will stay on board until I receive your forgiveness.*

The letter ended.

"Where should I put the letter, Ma?"

"Burn it. What's the use of saving such a letter?" she said without lifting her eyes, without diverting her attention from the papers before her.

So I put it in my pocket as well. There was indeed an extraordinary amount of mail that day. There was a letter from Panji Darman addressed to me:

> *Minke, my good friend,*
> > *There is something I must tell you; I think you should know it. But first, forgive me, as I don't know whether this is the right time to tell you or not.*

I was walking one day in the Java Docks at Amsterdam harbor. I saw a young, strong worker, and he clearly wasn't a Pure-Blood Dutchman. He was pushing a cart. Do you know who he was? Robert Suurhof! He stopped, startled at seeing me. He pulled down his hat to hide his eyes. He was ashamed of his work. Then he went back to pushing the cartload of goods. I called out to him. He kept on going.

I followed him and called out again: "Rob! Rob Suurhof! Don't tell me you've forgotten me already?"

He stopped, turned, greeted me: "You? When did you arrive? It's a pity I'm working just now. Come to my place later. After seven in the evening, all right?"

He gave me an address. And I never found that address, let alone the person. I went again to the wharves. I asked several people whether they knew a harbor worker, a young Indisch. I knew Suurhof was registered as a Dutch citizen, but his citizenship could be of no use for identification here. They didn't know what I meant by Indisch or Indies Native. A laborer, a youth, and dark, I said. They mentioned several names but none of them was Robert Suurhof. There is no one by the name of Robert Suurhof known here, they said. There was one worker from the Indies, someone said, dark, not called Suurhof, but he was arrested about three days ago by the police. He was working in the Java Docks at the time.

I went to the Harbor District Police Station. It was true; Suurhof had been arrested and was being returned to the Indies. They said he was suspected of assault and robbery in Surabaya.

He may already be back in Surabaya by the time you receive this letter, Minke.

I have also met Miss Magda Peters. I will tell you about it another time. I will write to Mama about things to do with her new company, Speceraria.

My greetings and respect to her and to you too.

The letter from Miriam de la Croix was from the Netherlands. There was also a letter from Herbert de la Croix with it. Here is what it said:

My dear Mr. Minke,

With this letter, both Miriam and I, even if somewhat

99

belatedly, take our leave of you. We have left the Indies and are now in the Netherlands. We are truly saddened by all that has befallen you and your family. We ourselves are very much to blame for what happened to you all, though our intentions were good and honorable. . . .

I stopped reading and thought over each incident again. There were no grounds for Herbert de la Croix and his daughter to feel they shared any blame. Why, they had gone as far as sending us a famous jurist, even though he had failed. And why was their letter so excessively polite? They had defended me when I was dismissed from school, they had helped me to obtain a place in the Civil Service Academy at Stovia. They had kept up correspondence with me all this time. Mr. de la Croix himself had even put his position on the line over my case. They had no reason to feel guilty.

Mr. Minke, the governor-general very quickly issued my discharge papers; we then left for Europe. The three of us are together as one again. Whatever has happened, my dear Mr. Minke, whatever I have experienced, it is nothing and indeed means nothing compared to what you have suffered, or what was suffered by your beloved teachers, Multatuli and Roorda van Eysinga.

All these events have come and gone so quickly. There has been almost no opportunity to follow them properly or reflect upon them.

Before we finish this letter we need to let you know that the request for a place for you at Stovia has been approved. You may start there next academic year. If you don't wish to do so because you are still upset by the events of recent times, you only need to write to the school and cancel your enrollment.

Greetings and respects from Sarah, Miriam, and myself. May you triumph in life. Adieu.

There was a letter from Mother but I pocketed it too. I would read it later.

Miriam's letter was different again:

Minke, I don't feel right writing to you about serious issues while you're still in mourning. But at a meeting of housewives in my neighborhood, someone read out one of Raden Adjeng Kartini's letters to Miss Zeehandelaar. People were dumbfounded to hear her reports of life among the Javanese. Relations between men and women seemed so strange and tense. In the discussion that followed, I concluded: Javanese women were living in darkness. Kartini's version did differ from what I knew of the life of Javanese village women, though, of course, I never witnessed it myself. Our servants used to tell how the women would sing while planting or harvesting, and how their men would carry off the harvested paddy. And how the little children would play under the full moon singing praises to the rice goddess. . . . Perhaps Kartini knew nothing of all this.

But I didn't say anything that would change the women's response to Kartini's letters. The gloom of the letters might make it easier for them to sympathize with the plight of Javanese women, and with Kartini herself.

Actually I had planned to bring up your case for discussion at the meeting. Father also agreed, as did Sarah too. Yours was the only such case during the whole of the nineteenth century. They would be interested. The story of the love between an educated Native and a Mixed-Blood girl, which proved to involve many issues that could just as easily have taken place in Europe itself.

I was determined to call out their Christian and European consciences. I was convinced I would succeed. I must admit: It wasn't the time or place to divert people's attention from Kartini and her problems.

The ladies were completely amazed to hear of a Native Javanese woman writing in their language. They had always thought of Native woman as still living in the Stone Age.

And you, my friend, how are you? Someone like you— young, strong, educated—will surely be able to face all things with great resolve. We all have faith in you. And we all believe we will meet with you again one day in circumstances much, much happier than those of today. We believe this, Minke. In the end, all was created by God for us to share. And there is no happiness without testing.

And for Kartini too, I pray that she will pass all her tests, because beyond those tests lies the garden of happiness.

You're not bored with my letter yet, are you? And can you

sense how the length of this letter is a symptom of how I miss the Indies, how I miss Java? You can, can't you? You surely must be able to sense it.

If I may make a suggestion, Minke, you should correspond with that extraordinary girl Kartini. It would not be difficult to find out her address, because she is the daughter of the Bupati of Jepara. I am also going to try to write to her.

Our new life in the Netherlands, just as in Java, has its ups and downs, as is the case with people's lives everywhere. Do you know, Minke, the Germans and English and French are racing to make all kinds of machines that will help make life more comfortable for people? There are people racing to make a machine that will replace the horse carriage, not so huge as a train, and it will be able to travel on ordinary roads.

It seems that the fever to discover new things, new tools, will not allow people to be satisfied with how things are. People are entranced and possessed by everything that is new; new etiquette, new behavior. Women are beginning to lose their shyness and are riding bicycles in the evenings. New, new, new, new! People forget that life basically stays the same, the same as yesterday. New, new, new—anything that is not new is looked upon as a remnant of the Middle Ages. People have become so childish, like little schoolchildren, thinking that with these new things life will be better than yesterday. This is the modern age! Anything that is not new is looked upon as being out of date, suitable only for peasants and villagers. People have been so easily lulled they ignore the fact that behind all these shouts, these urgings, this madness for what is new, there stands a supernatural power whose appetite for victims is never satisfied. This magical power is the columns of protozoa, of figures, which are called capital.

In the Indies, Minke, it is different than in Europe. In the Indies people stand helpless before the might of authority. In Europe people collapse before these rows of constantly multiplying protozoa called capital. Under the banner of furthering science and service to humanity, there are people racing to discover how to make a machine that, together with its passengers, will be able to traverse the heavens, physically overcoming all distance. There is a report from another country that there are others who have caught a fever to make a vessel that can take people to the floor of the oceans. There are even predictions that it will not be long before mankind not only has control over new sources of power but will have mastered vibrations to reach a certain destination.

You were right, Minke, the nature and countenance of mankind stays the same, no better than what it was before. The sermons in the churches continually remind us of that. Man remains a being that does not really know what it wants. The busier people become with their searching and their discoveries, the clearer it becomes that they are in fact being pursued by the anxiousness of their own hearts.

You still blame Europe. Naturally I could not bring myself to fault you for this after your recent experiences. If you lived in Europe for one or two years, though, perhaps your views might change. The percentage of those who are evil is probably the same as among your own people. Only the conditions of life are different. When I listen to Papa's stories from the Babad Tanah Jawi, it is not rare for me to shiver in horror at the viciousness, barbarism, and cruelty: all a luxury, Minke, and all only to achieve control of that small island called Java. I am of the same opinion as Papa: There was indeed a time and an era when Europe was no different from what is described in the Babad. Only I hope you don't forget one thing, Minke. At the time the Babad was being compiled, your people were still worshipping individual all-powerful rulers, while the European nations were gradually forming world empires. The world for your people is Java. Take a look at the names of the kings of Java, even those who still live today. Inscribed in them is always a sense of them constituting the whole universe.

What I am getting at, Minke, is that the Javanese view of things, from the very first time foreigners set foot in your country, had already been left far behind in Europe. It is not true that Java and the Indies were taken over by Europe purely because of Europe's greed. The problem in the first place was the warped attitude of the people of Java and the Indies towards the world. I, of course, worry that all this stems from Papa's opinions, because he is more accomplished in reading classical Javanese literature, but I agree with what he says.

If, for example, the Javanese and the Indies peoples had been more advanced than Europe and had sailed to Europe and *conquered it, do you think Europe would have been a happy place? I really believe, Minke, no one could doubt that any occupation of Europe by the Javanese would have been far more brutal than what you are experiencing now. The European nations have studied the character and capabilities of the Indies Natives, while on the other hand the Natives hardly know anything about Europe. Come to the Netherlands, Minke; you will be astounded to see the collection of material we have about the thinking of your ancestors, beginning with what was chiseled onto stone up until what was inscribed onto palm leaves. And none of it, not one thing, was saved by its heirs, your people, but by Europeans, Minke, Europeans.*

I don't know whether these notes of mine are representative of European thinking or not. Even so, allow me to consider them a European girl's ideas about the Indies Natives. So, Minke, let us work together to do whatever is good for Java, the Indies, Europe, and the world. We will fight European, Javanese, Indies, and the world's evil together. Let us provide Europe, Java, the Indies, and the world with a healthier understanding as was struggled for by the great humanists, and particularly Multatuli, who suffered so much in life.

I am now throwing myself into social and political activities. Sarah has gone on to Teachers' College. In other letters we will discuss new issues. Like Papa, I call out to you: Be triumphant in your life! From Miriam far away near the North Pole . . .

How adroit was this girl. I didn't really know what her situation was like, but I was sure life in the Netherlands would not be as easy as it was here. The three of them would have to struggle to keep their heads above water. Yet she still possessed her adroitness as well as her faith in the gloriousness of the future. She accepts all of life's difficulties and tries to overcome them. Maybe, in that way, all troubles become a sport to exercise brain and muscles. Difficulties make her stronger, not weaker. Her resilience aroused me from my depression. She was truly clever to be able to sweep the cloud from my mind. Very well, I will accept that you represent Europe, Mir, represent Europe's view of the reality of the Indies today. You represent the good side of Europe,

Mir. Perhaps—and this is closer to the truth—you represent your own idealization of Europe. I will answer your letter, Mir.

I don't know how long I had been sitting thinking. Mama spoke: "What are you thinking about now, Child?"

"Ma?"

"I've been watching you lately. You've lost your liveliness. I know things have been difficult lately. Even so, I don't think you need become a daydreamer. I've got an idea, Child: Have you ever thought about getting married again?"

A shameful question. I knew what she intended, of course: She was trying to stop me leaving Surabaya and Wonokromo. I was her son-in-law, but the question still struck my ears as going too far, not right or proper, as if I were someone who'd never set foot in a European school. And before I could reassert my dignity, she spoke again: "I can't look at those eyes of yours—so depressed. You must try much harder, much, much harder to forget the past."

This humoring of each other was beginning to seem like a game of handball.

"Does it still look like I haven't begun to forget, Ma?"

"You don't read seriously any more, you don't write, you're not your old spirited self. Sometimes you pick up a newspaper, but then only read a little bit here and there. Your thoughts are all over the place, Child."

"Mama doesn't seem as fresh as before," I said, hoping to end the ball game.

"Of course. Not without reason. I was born earlier. But I have decided what to do."

"When Panji Darman returns—"

"No need to await Panji Darman's return. I have a suggestion, Child. Will you accompany me on a trip out of town? Perhaps our mood will change as a result."

"Of course, Ma, I'd like that very much. In the meantime perhaps Panji Darman will return."

"And then will you go to Betawi?"

"I think so, Ma."

"You're the wrong kind of person to be a doctor. You know Dr. Martinet. What was he able to do when we were in trouble? You were able to do much more than he to defend us, even though we were defeated in the end. I value the work you do much more than the work of a doctor."

"Let it be, Ma. At least I can study and have a livelihood at the same time."

"You don't really believe your own words. Panji Darman will not be returning quickly. According to his latest telegram he has had to postpone his departure again."

"Yes, Ma, maybe it would be good if we took a holiday. Mama has never taken time off from work. But who will look after things while we're away?"

"Darsam."

"Darsam? What can he do?"

"Don't be insulting. He has a lot of experience now, except in the office. I want to try him, so he begins to know what a headache it is to have to manage everything."

"Do you dare do it?"

"He must begin sooner or later. Someone as loyal as he is must be encouraged, be given an opportunity. He has a sharp sense of who is a good foreman and who isn't."

"But office work?"

"He must be given a chance to do that too. The correspondence can afford to stop for a few days."

"You really dare do it?"

For the first time a big smile appeared on Mama's face. Her teeth gleamed. She had decided a long time ago to take a holiday. Now she wanted to carry out that decision. Do it without hesitation or doubt.

"Forget those letters. Forget them all," she said. "What's life for anyway? Not for taking on a whole lot of unnecessary worries."

6

I went to Jean Marais's place to see how far he had gotten with his painting of Annelies. He had refused to copy from a photograph. "With Annelies," he said one time, "I am going to paint her exactly as you and I knew her—not just as we saw her, but as we really knew her, when she was at her peak." And so he painted from memory alone. A month had passed and the picture was still not ready. He was working on it when I arrived.

Out of a gloomy Rembrandt-like background there emerged the face of my angel, like the moon coming out from behind clouds. Yes, it was only that overcast that had threatened her life—so young, pure, beautiful, without equal. I saw once again that hair of hers which I had so many times caressed, the smoothness of her clear skin, the almost imperceptible furrows on her forehead. She was my wife, my Annelies, always so spoiled with my embraces.

"When it's finished," said Jean, "you mustn't put the picture up for everybody to see, Minke."

"I've got to just store it away?"

"Put it in the most beautiful cover you can find. You don't need to look at it again. You could go mad."

Jean Marais wasn't talking nonsense. Every time I looked at that unfinished picture my heart started to gallop and my thoughts began to wander.

"Put it in a cover of beautiful grape-red velvet, Minke. I will make one for you."

"Will it be ready, do you think, when I leave Surabaya?"

"So it's true you're going to Betawi?"

"I have the right to grow and develop too, don't I?"

"You are right, Minke; while you are too close to Nyai you will not develop." He smiled broadly, but I didn't know what he was smiling at. "You haven't the same charisma. You need to be in another place, another region, breathing other air, with other opportunities, other possibilities."

He wouldn't let go when I excused myself. "Don't rush off. There is something else."

"How is May doing at school?"

"She seems a bit behind."

"Perhaps she's too busy at home, Jean."

"Perhaps. What's the point of being clever if you're not happy at home? Learning to work is also important—learning to build a life. School is no more than something to finish things off, isn't it?"

"When I have a child, perhaps I will think the same way."

"There's no need to copy me. My outlook is based upon this deformity of mine. Without her near me I feel so alone. What do you think of this picture, Minke?"

"You're brilliant, Jean."

"I have never painted so well. It should be hanging on the walls of the Louvre. You must see Paris, Minke: The palaces, gardens, statues, the most beautiful works of art in the history of mankind—the most beautiful and most grand, the biggest churches. There is nothing that rivals them . . . I'm sorry, I shouldn't boast about the achievements of my own ancestors."

"Keep going, Jean. France is indeed greatly admired, by my teachers at school too. I am only their student and haven't ever been to France."

"A guest will be arriving soon." Jean Marais turned the line

108

of conversation. "Kommer. Maybe another ten minutes. You should see him."

"So he comes here often?"

"We have a little business together. He's asked me to design a trap to catch a black panther," he said, continuing with his painting.

There was a sound of footsteps, and Kommer walked in carrying a leather briefcase. He shook hands with me. When he offered his hand to Jean, he didn't take it, just nodded.

"You're angry with me?" asked Kommer.

"It's not a good idea to shake hands with a painter at work, Kommer." He smiled.

Kommer laughed: "You believe in that superstition?"

"It's not that. The paint has poison in it. Let me wash my hands first."

"And how are you, Mr. Minke?" asked Kommer. "You haven't written anything for a long time."

Jean hobbled back and straight away butted in: "Mr. Kommer, Minke was once very angry with me for doing no more than suggesting he write in Malay. You try to talk to him."

Now I was being incited to explode again, after my disappointment with Nijman. I attacked: "What can you say in Malay? An impoverished language like that? Riddled with borrowed words from every country in the world? And even to say 'I am not an animal,' you need all these borrowed words."

"Very true." Kommer smiled broadly. From out of his bag he took several newspapers and put them on the table. "Look, Mr. Minke. This is the *Pelapor Betawi*. This is the *Bintang Surabaya* from Surabaya. Of course you must know it, or at least have heard its name. This is the *Taman Sari*. This new newspaper, the *Penghantar*, is from faraway Ambon. In Javanese? You can see for yourself, here—*Retno Doemilah, Djawi Kondo*. This one is in Malay, from East Sumatra, *Percikan Barat*. Nah, here is a pile of auction and advertisement papers. All published in Surabaya. You know them all. Study them page by page. All of them owned by Dutchmen, Eurasians, and one of them, *Percikan Barat*, by a Chinaman."

I couldn't see where his chattering was leading.

"Yes, Minke, it is not Natives who feel it is important to

109

report the news in Malay or Javanese. Fantastic, isn't it, Mr. Minke. Not Natives. And it isn't Natives either who feel it is important to encourage Malay and Javanese to develop and grow as languages. An impoverished language? Certainly. Everything is born into this world with no more than a body and a spirit. You are no exception to that rule."

My heart no longer felt incited to explode. The reality of it all was making me gasp.

"I myself have just started with the *Primbon Soerabaya*. Just forget my own involvement in it for a moment. Take a look for yourself at all these newspapers that are introducing the Natives to a wider world, to the world of humanity. Looked at in that way, can't you agree that their contribution to the advancement of Natives is indeed outstanding? Even though the Natives don't recognize that contribution or feel they're being helped? Especially when none is able to afford a subscription so that they have to join together to be able to read them?"

It seemed Kommer's speech was going to go on and on, even though it was helping me to understand the situation of the Malay press.

"Nah! Minke, it's not me that's talking now. It's Mr. Kommer." Once again Jean began to interfere. "If you still want to be angry, be angry with him."

But I wasn't angry, just bored. Kommer's way of presenting things was different and didn't anger me: He was actually inviting me to understand the issues. Then the Eurasian Mixed-Blood journalist arranged all the papers in such a way that they just called out to be read. My hands grasped out at one page, another page, and another page. I examined their appearance and typography, the columns, bent and untidily joined together, the wavelike lines, the uneven print.

"The typography!" I protested.

"Yes. Still not very good. The Dutch papers aren't perfect yet either. The point is the things that can be passed on to the Malay reader—issues that touch significantly the interests of the readers themselves. Not just things affecting Europeans."

I understood all that he was saying. But my heart still wouldn't accept it.

"You could begin to learn to write in Malay, Minke," Jean Marais began again.

"Yes, you can see for yourself"—now Kommer got his bit in—"Malay is understood and read in every town, big and small, throughout the Indies. Dutch is not."

I was still examining the Malay-language newspapers. There were too many advertisements and the serialized stories took too prominent a place on the front page. They all carried serials, most of them foreign.

"It won't be long, Mr. Minke. Once you begin writing in Malay, you'll soon discover the key to it. That you have mastered Dutch so well is, of course, deserving of great admiration. But to write in Malay, your own people's language, is a sign of your love for your country and people."

All of a sudden he stopped. He was probably preparing a whole new set of demands. So it was not only Mother, but also Jean Marais, also Kommer, who were making demands of me. And now Kommer—a person whose origins I knew nothing about at all—had appeared before me like a prosecutor with a shortage of victims. And I was not angered. But if I accepted these demands now, there could be no doubt that tomorrow or the day after other new demands would follow.

"Are you making demands of me, Mr. Kommer?"

"Yes, I think, indeed, that is the case."

"And do I not have the right to reject them?"

"Of course, Mr. Minke. He who emerges at the top of his society will always face demands from that society—it is his society that has allowed him to rise. You must know the Dutch proverb, 'The tall tree catches much wind.' If you don't want to catch so much wind, don't grow so tall."

"Where is there a tall tree that can turn away the wind?" Jean Marais backed Kommer up.

"The important thing, Mr. Minke, is loyalty to one's own country and people."

This Eurasian Mixed-Blood was getting more and more out of hand in his rudeness. Mother had argued the same point without pressuring or pushing. Kommer was not just asking, hoping, demanding. He was pushing me into a corner. And still he didn't seem satisfied. He added: "Who gives a damn if Europeans want to read Malay or not? Just think about it: Who will urge Natives to speak out if their own writers, such as yourself, won't do it?"

"Why do you write in Malay, Kommer?" It was my turn to

111

interrogate. "You are not a Native. You're more European than Native."

He laughed. He didn't answer quickly. The whole of my attention was focused on him. The skin of his face, burned by the sun, shone with sweat. He groped in his pocket for a handkerchief, but he didn't wipe his face. He rubbed his lips and the tips of his teeth. With a smile that was both a little upset and a little amused, he said, "Look, Mr. Minke, lineage is not important. Loyalty to this country and people, sir. This is my country and my people, not Europe. Only my name is Dutch. It is not impossible for a non-Native to love this country and people. Look around you. Natives are so still, so quiet, so alone—they never speak with anyone outside themselves. Day and night their lives revolve around just one pivot, in the same space, in the same circle. Busy with their own dreams. Just the same thing over and over again. I'm sorry."

His words were becoming more twisted and winding. And I was more and more caught up by them: "An unbearable life, Mr. Minke. Anyone who is aware of this condition must surely try to speak to them. To speak face to face with such a huge number of people is, of course, impossible. That is why I write, one person speaking to many."

Whether he knew it or not, he was lighting my way, my life as a writer. I saw him anew, as a teacher without a name, a great man without origins. I respected him, even loved him, as if he were a part of my own body and brain. He had no hesitation in stating ideas he felt were true. He was a little prophet.

"Minke," Jean Marais interrupted again, "I can't express myself well. Mr. Kommer speaks for me also. I too have hopes for you—my heart still can't bring itself to demand—you must speak to your own people. You are needed by your own people much more than you are needed by any other people anywhere. Europe and Holland will not miss your absence." He was silent a moment as he looked at me, waiting for my anger to sweep down upon his head. "See, you aren't angry with Mr. Kommer, are you?" He was silent again, awaiting my reaction.

I didn't react at all. Kommer's words were as a great surging wave, moving, alive, shifting me away from earlier opinions.

"If I were a writer, I would write in my own language.

Because I am a painter, my language is color, a language between people, not between peoples."

"So there is no need to study other peoples' languages, especially those of Europe?" I asked.

"Nobody has said that. Without studying the languages of other peoples, especially European languages, we wouldn't understand foreign peoples. And, equally, if you don't study your own language you can never understand your own people." Kommer answered quickly, as if he had readied such a reply.

My question seemed childish, like foam frothed on the surging wave that was Kommer.

"And without knowing other peoples," he continued without letting me regain my composure, "we will never come to know our own society properly either."

I felt like Romulus and Remus, the twins who founded Rome, being suckled by a wolf.

"Why aren't you saying anything, Minke?" Jean Marais returned with his own small wave. "We are talking to your conscience, not just playing at moving our lips. Have you still an excuse for not writing in your own tongue?"

The great wave came again: "People of whatever race who do not write in their own language are usually seeking their own self-satisfaction. They do not care about the needs of the people who give them life. Most of them do not know their own people."

Do not know their own people! The accusation went too far; it was like a blow from a blunt adze. And it hurt even more that it came from people who weren't Natives: from an Indo and a Frenchman. In their eyes I didn't know my own people. Me!

"You still haven't spoken," Jean pressed.

"He needs time to think things over, Mr. Marais. Remember *Multatuli*, Mr. Minke. 'If the Dutch won't read or print my writings,' he said, 'I will translate them into Native languages—Malay, Javanese, and Sudanese.' He was your own teacher, and indeed he did go on to write in Malay."

"You think I don't know my own people."

"The truth is often painful. But that is it, more or less. From your articles, it seems that you know more about Dutchmen and Indos."

"That's not true. I speak excellent Javanese."

"That doesn't mean you know the Javanese people. Have you ever known the villages and hamlets of Java, where most of our people live? You've only passed through them. Do you know what the farmers of Java eat, your own country's farmers? Most Javanese are farmers. The Javanese peasant farmers are your people."

"And what do you mean by 'know'?" I grabbed at whatever straw I could to save myself from the surging wave around me.

Perhaps because he saw that my blood pressure was rising, Kommer headed off in another direction: "I have another appointment. Mr. Marais, where is the design for that panther trap?"

Marais pulled out the desk drawer and extracted a sheet of paper. "This is the best possible, Mr. Kommer. You will get that black one, if the animal does indeed exist."

"Mr. Minke, this is a trap to catch a panther. Please drop in to my home from time to time. I keep a number of different animals: Tigers, crocodiles, snakes, monkeys, all kinds of birds . . . I like to watch their antics."

"We will finish our discussion?"

"Another time, all right? Perhaps this isn't the right time. Yes, Mr. Marais?"

"You catch these animals yourself?"

Kommer nodded.

"The panther is to be an addition to the collection?" I asked, relieved to be free of the wave's pounding.

"No, the German consul has ordered one for the Berlin zoo. The wild black panther is the most dangerous of them all. It lives on the ground, amongst the brush, the tall grass, and the trees. They can only be caught while asleep or if they are still cubs."

"Where will you trap it?"

"In the forests around Sidoarjo. The panther is famous because of its black fur, which is bluish like hardened steel. With this design, I will get the carpenters of Sidoarjo to make a trap. Mr. Marais, aren't these wheels too small?"

"No, the thing is that the trap mustn't be too far off the ground. The measurements of these wheels are such that they will still be able to cope with uneven ground and channels or low embankments."

"Right!" Kommer agreed. "Minke, I would be honored if

you would join me in trapping this animal. You will have an opportunity to mix with your own people. Believe me, sir, I know these people better than you do. You will realize that there is too much that you don't know about them." His words were confident and challenging, almost insolent.

Perhaps he was right, but his words weren't friendly. They offended, yet I was unable to refute them. I would test the truth of his boast. I would ask him whether he read Javanese writing or not. If he answered yes, I would ask which books he had read. If he answered no, I would have him cornered. But I hesitated, and he spoke first: "Once you have come to know your people, sir, you will discover a source of material for your writings that will never dry up, an eternal source of material. Didn't Kartini, in one of her letters to her friend, once say that to write is to work for eternity. If the source is eternal, maybe then the writing will be eternal also."

"You know a great deal about Kartini."

"What can one do, sir—someone as important as she is, her letters are being read everywhere."

"When do you leave for Sidoarjo?"

"You are accepting my invitation?"

"When do you leave?"

"Tomorrow."

"Good. Tomorrow we too are going to Sidoarjo."

Kommer frowned on hearing the word *we*. Then his eyes twinkled: "A coincidence," he said.

"If possible I will join you, Mr. Kommer. If possible. And you, Jean?"

"I must finish this painting. Who knows, perhaps one day it will end up in the Louvre. What do you think I should call it, Minke?"

" 'The Flower that Closed the Century,' Jean."

Jean Marais went silent. Then his eyes shone with life: "That gives me a new idea. The background, and the sparkle in her eyes must be adjusted. Also her lips, Minke; they must be able to talk about the century that has passed, and speak about the hope of the future."

I didn't understand what he was talking about. "You're the painter. It's up to you."

"A painting has a language of its own, too, Minke."

115

"Indeed your wife was too beautiful, Mr. Minke, like the beauty we dream about," Kommer said spiritedly.

"That is its form, Mr. Kommer," interjected Jean. "Appreciation of a painting must not stop with the form. It must include the story contained in the brush strokes, the mood, the character, and the life created through the integration of the colors."

Kommer gazed, head forward in incomprehension, like me, before this copy of Annelies. Jean Marais's eyes came alight as we listened to him. Though his Malay was limited, he was able to explain with the help of his eyes and the movements of his hands.

The longer he went on, the more I came to understand: The art of painting is a branch of learning all of its own, whose language cannot be understood by everyone. Better just to be quiet and listen. For the umpteenth time now, I thought: To graduate from H.B.S. only made you realize your own ignorance. You must learn to be humble, Minke! Your schooling doesn't amount to much after all.

Before setting off for the station, Darsam reminded me: "Be careful, Young Master, guard Nyai well. This time I am not escorting her. Her safety is your responsibility now."

"I will look after her, Darsam."

Marjuki wanted to get the carriage moving. Mama stopped him and called Darsam. From on top of the carriage, she reminded him, "You're in charge now, Darsam; be careful."

Darsam smiled proudly, his mustache spreading: "All under control, Nyai!"

"You're always saying 'all under control, all under control.' You haven't even got your mustache under control."

It was true too. That great mustache of his wasn't symmetrical: One corner was drooping. Darsam's hand immediately went to his mouth, brushing back the mustache.

"Now tell me, all is under control."

"Yes, Nyai, I forgot to tidy it up this morning, everything was done in such a hurry."

" 'Yes—yes—yes' is all you ever come out with when spoken to. Must I be the one who has to check things every day? If even your mustache isn't looked after properly . . . look, what am I always telling you?"

"Yes, Nyai. If you feel good, then . . ."

"So you haven't forgotten. Perhaps because you weren't in such a big hurry. Marjuki, get going!"

The carriage left the front grounds. As we moved onto the main road, my mood changed. You don't know your own people! You don't know your own country! I felt shame and knew that it was deserved. I would redeem myself from these accusations which I could not deny. How much weight do you reckon that man with the scruffy black pants over there is carrying on his back? I don't know. He was carting a tall basket of peanuts. To whom will he sell it? I don't know. Where? I don't know. What is it worth? I don't know. Will it bring in enough money to provide food for, say, a week? I don't know. Don't know! Don't know! Is he strong and healthy enough to carry such a load? I don't know that either. Has he been forced to cart it? My ignorance showed its depths. What was the harvest from each hundred square yards? Crazy! These questions tormented my mind. Yes, and they all stemmed from observing just one man carting peanuts—you arrogant-hearted ignoramus! If your ignorance is so great that you can't answer any of these questions about this man, then all you must see is his body and his movements. It would be so embarrassing if you tried to write about him, you arrogant writer!

Kommer was waiting at the station. I knew he had proposed to Mama. And would never get a reply. She hadn't even bothered to read his letter. He already had a wife and children. I had heard that his wife was also a Mixed-Blood. How he had got up the courage to propose was something I could hardly understand. Wasn't he younger than Mama?

He ran about making sure he bought first-class tickets, as if he were richer than Mama. He stood with his back to me at the ticket window. I shifted my gaze from it—that back, which accused me of not knowing my own people and country! The platform was quiet, as usual. Several people sat on benches. Mama went into the first-class waiting room. I walked slowly along the platform. From one of the benches a woman could be heard reminding her husband that he should hide his white *haji* cap, which signified he had been to Mecca; it would attract attention. There was a railway regulation: Europeans, Chinese, and haji were forbidden to travel third class. They had to travel first or second class. The man put his cap into a basket of souvenirs. His wife went off to buy their tickets. Her husband watched from his seat.

Was this the way to come to know your people? I laughed in my heart. I reckoned there must be more to it than this.

Once Kommer obtained the tickets, we quickly boarded our carriage. I sat next to Mama; Kommer sought a place opposite us.

"It's been more than twenty years since I've seen the villages," Mama began. "Perhaps nothing has changed in all this time."

"Nothing has changed, Nyai; it is just the same," Kommer responded, and then asked: "People say Nyai comes from Sidoarjo. Is it true, Nyai?"

And so Nyai and Kommer became engrossed in conversation. You could tell the journalist was trying hard to find things to talk about, wanting to chat forever while the creaking train rocked on. He was trying to impress Mama with his education, with his interest in commerce, reading, and agriculture, hunting, folklore, and especially colonial politics.

I woke up because I heard my name mentioned, I didn't know in connection with what.

"I have suggested to Mr. Minke that he write in Malay or Javanese. It seems he still has his doubts," said Kommer.

"His own mother longs for him to write in Javanese," Mama explained.

"Nah, Mr. Minke." Kommer attacked as soon as he saw my eyes were open. "Your own mother! None other than your own mother!"

His voice seemed to condemn my sleepiness. I wasn't even given a chance to yawn.

"Perhaps he's right, Child," Mama joined in. "When I read the works of Francis or Wiggers—senior and junior—and also those of Mr. Kommer himself and Johannies, I feel Malay has a deliciousness of its own. You should try, I think."

"There's no point in ending up being *forced* to write in Malay; why not start of one's own accord?" Kommer was getting carried away again.

"Why *forced,* Mr. Kommer?" asked Mama.

"Forced, Nyai. Sooner or later, Native people will be greatly disillusioned by the Dutch colonial press, and they will be forced to write in their own language. The Dutch papers never discuss matters of concern to Natives, as though the only people in the

Indies were Europeans. I reckon every honest writer will, in the end, be disappointed by them.''

I watched them and watched them. They didn't talk about me anymore. I think I fell asleep—giving Kommer a chance to show off his cock's plumage. He wouldn't ask about the fate of his proposal, I thought. And when I awoke again, he was asleep, propped up against the wall in the corner. Mama was looking out at the view. I'm embarrassed to admit it, but this was really the first time I ever took a proper look at my mother-in-law in her own right, not in relation to Annelies. Her grace and beauty now revealed themselves in their full naturalness. Nobody could say she looked old. Her cheeks were still full; there were no crow's feet at the corners of her eyes. She always dressed up as a businesswoman should. Her hair was always shining and the creases in her *kain* were never untidy. From the side she looked exactly like Annelies, only not quite as white, and her nose wasn't as pointed. Her eyebrows were dense, which gave her eyes a sinister look.

Kommer was sleeping with his mouth open. One gold tooth sparkled at the corner of his lips. My heart beat anxiously: I hoped this courageous newspaperman would not let saliva drip from behind his gold teeth. If Mama saw that, he might never get a reply to his proposal.

The train was very slow and stopped every other minute. First class and second class shared one carriage. All the passengers wore shoes or slipper-sandals. The second-class compartment carried passengers wearing slippers or sandals, no shoes. The third-class carriages were all barefoot. Peddlers going either to or from the markets walked up and down the carriage, accompanied by every kind of market smell, as well as flies. In first class there were only the three of us. In second class there were maybe ten Chinese and a haji who hadn't taken off his white haji cap.

There was so much dust and soot, it was certain that passengers from all classes would leave the train with dirty clothes. In a number of places, when the train traveled slowly, I would see a gang of laborers repairing the railway tracks and a Eurasian seated on a horse, with a sword, keeping watch over them. The gangs were mobilized by the Native Civil Service and village heads, and the village heads also mobilized the farmers who worked on government-owned lands. Nobody was paid for this forced labor.

They never received food, or money for transport. They even had to provide their own water for tea.

Had I been born a landless farmer, perhaps I too would have been among those being supervised by the Mixed-Blood on his horse. And perhaps his knowledge wasn't any better than that of a village child who looked after the buffalos. Perhaps too I would have been spat upon by one of the overseer's assistants, a village official in his black shirt, his batik kain, with his *destar* on his head and his *keris* at his back. But I was not a tenant farmer working government land. The comparison made me feel fortunate, and also made me feel that I had the responsibility to be compassionate towards them. Responsible because these feelings of mine arose not from the heart, but from the mind. You are right, Kommer; as soon as I start paying them attention, all kinds of ideas and thoughts, and not just material for later, arise before me. It is likely that among that work gang there are people with skills that neither the overseer nor his assistants have. Perhaps there are *gamelan* makers or experts in making wayang shadow puppets, perhaps experts in Javanese literature. At the very least, they are all master farmers. Their miserable fate is caused only by the fact that they have no land of their own.

I knew for certain that besides being liable for forced labor, they would also be conscripted to take part in night patrols and guarding the village, and in emergency collective labor if something had to be done in the public interest. They would have to pay tribute to their chiefs. Their chickens and eggs could be confiscated whenever some chief they had never seen came visiting their village.

I had known all this since I was small. But only now, traveling along in the train, did they abruptly become real inhabitants of my thoughts. From Multatuli's novel *Saidja and Adinda,* I knew about the suffering of these peasants, but that knowledge had never lived in my mind as it did now. People also said that the peasants had to pay eggs and chickens and coconuts and fruit and herbs, which the village head would take with him each time he sought audience with the Native district chief. Sometimes the chiefs would voice the need, and the village officials would collect special tribute from the peasants to buy a cow or goat on his behalf. It all came from the peasantry, who owned nothing except their hoes and their labor.

The anonymous tract Magda Peters had given me spoke about them as the cork upon which the kingdom of the Netherlands floats. And what kind of cork-float? The pamphlet said it was a cork that will be forced to sink one day when its buoyancy has been soaked up. The whole of the kingdom's and the colony's life floated upon that cork. Any and every foot could step upon its head and shoulders, just as Governor-General *Daendels* had literally done long ago; they, the peasants, would accept every burden without protest. They would not complain, it went on to say, because for centuries they had known only one kind of fate: the fate of a peasant.

As soon as we entered the area around Sidoarjo, sugar cane enveloped the train, nothing but sugar cane, rippling in waves like a green sea upon purple-green sands. All of it would be cut and carried off to the sugar mills. This, it seemed, was the land where Nyai Ontosoroh was born. Everything centered on sugar. Even so, not everything tasted sweet. Mama's own experiences had already proved that. Perhaps I shall be able to discover other things.

Our destination was the family of Sastro Kassier, Mama's elder brother. I did not know much about him. From what I knew I wrote up these notes:

The plague had attacked the village of Tulangan. Every day people fell down, sprawled out dead, including Dr. Van Niel, who was brought in from Surabaya. The Tulangan clinic, just a ten-by-thirteen-foot room, could do nothing. After burying their neighbors each morning, people would roll over and join their friends in death.

Sastrotomo, Sanikem's father, died; his children too, except for Paiman, Sanikem's elder brother. (Nyai Ontosoroh was originally called Sanikem.) Paiman ran away from the house to escape the epidemic that was sweeping away all around him. He knew his father and the brothers and sisters who had died had not been buried yet. He ran: Ran.

He didn't realize it then, but the plague bacteria had already begun to multiply within him.

He wandered aimlessly. In the evening he collapsed in the darkness far outside the sugar-factory complex. He knew he must keep walking but his strength was gone. He rolled his body under a tamarind tree. He remembered that the tree stood at an inter-section. The narrow road to the right led to the graveyard. He did not want to end up there. He must live. He did not want to die just yet.

His body was burning with fever. Pain tormented his extrem-ities. The night was dense with darkness; there was no wind. Those eyes, ah, why are those eyes always pulled towards the graveyard? How many of his acquaintances had been planted there like mandarin seedlings? and mangos and guavas?—seedlings that would never grow or sprout, vanishing, sucked up by the earth. Twenty people? Twenty-five? He could not count. His head was aflame.

In the darkness and stillness of the night, from time to time he could see tongues of fire leaping up from the graveyard, as if blown up into the sky to pierce the darkness of the windless night. They reached their peak, then fell back in a long curve, so long—as if they were flying away to vanish into nowhere. He saw other fiery flames pointing back down towards the villages, including Tulangan.

He was afraid. And his body could not carry his longing to be away from this frightening place. There was only one thing that proved he was still alive: the never-subsiding shout in his heart—live, live, I must live, live, live!

The morning dew woke him. In some obscure way, he felt that the dew had eased his fever. As the sun began to rise, he found himself approached by an old man. He heard the old man's voice, full of compassion, whisper: "So young as this! It's not the right time for you to die yet, Child. You probably have never been out of our village before now."

The man had a white beard and mustache. Paiman wanted very much to ask for help, but even his tongue would not work for him.

He dimly saw the old grandfather take down his woven rattan shoulder bag. From inside it he took a bottle. He poured some-thing into Paiman's mouth, then went away. About four hours later, he returned and poured liquid from the bottle into Paiman's mouth once more. Like some god who had descended from heaven, the old man looked healthy and fresh amid the squalor of the epidemic. There was no fear in his face.

The bottle was empty. He put it back in his bag.

Paiman was saved because of that liquid. He didn't know what the old man had made him drink; it tasted like kerosene. Several more times the old man returned to minister to him.

That was Paiman, who was now called Sastro Kassier, and he was more successful than Sastrotomo, his father, the father of Sanikem alias Nyai Ontosoroh.

Sastrotomo never succeeded in becoming paymaster as he had hoped. He was never thought worthy of consideration. Because he knew that the new manager would not adhere to the agreement made between Sastrotomo and Herman Mellema, Mellema had gone to Tulangan to ask that Sastrotomo's son be taken on as an apprentice clerk. He was to be trained so that later he could become paymaster. Mellema did not tell Mama about this act of conscience.

The new manager of the sugar factory had come to Wonokromo a few times. Herman Mellema used such opportunities to pass on "aid" to his "brother-in-law." It was through such visits that Mama eventually found out: Her elder brother had quickly advanced from being a clerk to an apprentice cashier and then had become full paymaster.

Silently, Mama felt proud to have a brother who had achieved such a high position—the only Native paymaster in a sugar factory in all of Java.

On the day of his promotion, the factory put on a small celebration. Paiman, who had changed his name to Sastrowongso—meaning descendant or with the blood of a scribe—when he married, announced another name change: Sastro Kassier with two s's. His new name was published in the newspapers as a determination of the governor-general.

He had eight children.

Several times Paiman alias Sastrowongso alias Sastro Kassier came to Wonokromo. Mama always received him happily. But as time went on, his visits became less and less frequent. His own position was becoming stronger. After Herman Mellema's death, he was never seen again at Wonokromo.

He did come with his whole family when Annelies and I were married. That time too, Mama received him very affably. His youngest child, a girl, was two or three years younger than Annelies. Twice I saw her from a distance. I guessed that was how Sanikem had looked when she was a girl. Her body, as well as her face, eyes, lips, and nose, were all exactly the same.

From the moment we boarded the train I suspected: Perhaps Mama isn't going to Sidoarjo for a holiday but to ask for Sastro Kassier's permission for his youngest daughter, Surati, and me to marry. No, Ma, it would be impossible for Minke to marry and to live with a woman who was still pure Javanese. Impossible, Ma. I don't mean to insult my mother or any woman who is still fully Javanese in her thoughts and customs. But I must make my own choice. You too, Ma, would never be able to take a husband who was fully a Native. European ideas, whether a little or a lot, have changed the way we look at things, have provided us with new requirements that must be met. And the matter of husband and wife wasn't just one of man and woman. You know that too, Ma. If the purpose of this visit is indeed to propose on my behalf—however beautiful and honorable are your intentions—you must forgive me: I cannot marry her. I just couldn't do it!

These suspicions and presentiments made me anxious, vigilant. On the other hand Mama seemed quite merry, like a young girl. Like a butterfly emerging from its cocoon, she lost that gloomy fearsomeness that had dominated her all this time. She was becoming more cheerful; she laughed, smiled, and chattered. She was no longer engrossed in her business, which was soon to be stolen away by Maurits Mellema.

There was no one from Sastro Kassier's family to meet us at the station. Mama had not told them of our visit. Kommer hailed a carriage and offered to escort us to Tulangan. Mama laughed and refused. "Tulangan is still a long way from here, Mr. Kommer."

"I know Tulangan, Nyai."

"Yes?"

"It is no more than five or six miles," he said.

"You can come and visit if you like. But not now, please."
And our carriage trotted off towards Tulangan.

Sugar cane, sugar cane, sugar cane for almost the whole length of our journey. The unshirted farmers stopped along the road to take a look at who was riding in the carriage. Small, stark-naked children, wet-nosed, filthy, were playing along the edge of the road, looking after livestock. I would have been among them had I been born into a farmer's family.

"This is what my country is like, Child. Only cane. It is true what you said; everything revolves around sugar, whether evil or dreams. There are more than ten sugar mills in my country, Nyo. When the factory starts to mill, there's a big festival, nothing but festivals and parties. Everyone stakes their wealth and their reputations as fighters. Everywhere people lie sprawled in the streets, drunk. And on the gambling mats, children, wives, young brothers and sisters, all change hands as the wages of bets. You need to have a look at one sometime. It's a pity the milling season isn't about to start."

The driver tried to turn around to catch the words he couldn't understand. He asked, "Yes, *Ndoro*?"

"No, Man, I wasn't speaking to you."

I was amazed that Mama followed Dutch practice and called the driver Man. The word did indeed mean man or person, yet I sensed that it still contained a derogatory element: It was used only when talking to lower-class men. The problem was that there was no neutral way to speak to such people in Javanese and Malay. Perhaps this is an aspect of the poverty of my mother tongue, a poverty that forces people to become accustomed to constantly degrading others. Why does my mind go crazy like this? Why won't it stop looking for work?

"Tomorrow or the day after, Child, you can take a look at the villages. Didn't you say yesterday that Kommer had accused you of not knowing your own people? Actually I feel he was accusing me too. He is not totally mistaken. Perhaps he was a bit extreme, but I understand what he meant. He loves all that is Native so much, except their deficiencies and ignorance. He loves all that was ever possessed, created, or known by his mother's ancestors. On the train, he spoke with tremendous enthusiasm about the ancient Hindu temples. He said that he once invited Jean Marais to go on a trip with him to see some. Jean laughed. He didn't understand the significance of these temples. Kommer tried to explain. Jean only laughed more. Kommer became cranky, and took his revenge by belittling the monuments of France that the rest of the world so glorifies."

Not an interesting subject. Suddenly Mama asked, "Have you ever seen one of these temples? Neither have I. They were built to last forever; there must be something about them that their builders wanted to immortalize."

The conversation was becoming even less interesting.

"Have you ever read anything about Paris? about France?"

"Nothing specifically, no, Ma."

"I don't know why, but sometimes that country interests me very much. I can't imagine what it is like, but I'm still interested."

Perhaps it was Jean Marais that Mama was really interested in. But I didn't say anything.

"And Kommer?"

"What about Kommer?"

"What do you think of him?" I asked, fishing.

"He has a lot of enthusiasm. That's all. In a few years, five or ten perhaps, you will far outshine him."

"Ma, I don't mean that."

"Shh! You'd be pleased if I accepted his proposal?"

"What is it that Ma wants?" Mama's face went red like that of a blushing virgin. How happy she was at that moment.

It seemed that Sastro Kassier was very well known in Sidoarjo. The carriage driver knew exactly where his house was. It was a stone house, a respectable house. It was located on the Tulangan sugar-mill complex. Sastro Kassier was the only Native to have a house inside the complex.

The front door was closed, but the windows were open. Beyond the curtains we could see a reception area that wasn't at all small, and furniture one usually finds in the houses of Europeans. The differences were few: No books were in evidence, whereas in a European house they usually took pride of place among the furniture.

"Yu! Yu Djumilah!" Nyai called out several times. She was calling for her sister-in-law, the wife of Sastro Kassier. I had never seen her, though she had come to my wedding, but I knew her husband.

A woman, looking much older than Mama, opened the door. She stood there not understanding what was happening.

"Yu Milah, have you forgotten me? Sanikem?"

"Aiai! Sis Ikem, is this Sis Ikem? Come in. Come in. Still so young too?" She ran back and forth welcoming us, and invited us to sit on the settee of which they were so proud.

"Yes, this is how we live. Please don't compare it to your house, Sis Ikem."

The carriage driver took down all our things and carried them inside the house. Djumilah herself prepared a room. She came back into the parlor and began again: "Yes, just a simple room, please don't be disappointed." She always spoke in Javanese, the only language she knew. "You must be very tired. Let me get you something to drink," and she disappeared to the back.

Not long after that a pockmarked girl came out, bending and bowing as she brought out a tray of drinks. She went down on her knees as she approached us.

From the back came Djumilah's voice: "Have a drink, Sis. There just happens to be water boiling."

The pockmarked girl put the drinks out on the table, shifting them to their proper places.

Nyai got up from her chair and had a look around. Above one of the doors were two pictures of Her Majesty Wilhelmina, a sign that two graduates from the Factory School lived here. No doubt two of Sastro Kassier's children, even though it was unusual for children—boys or girls—from small towns like Tulangan to go to school.

After having a good look around, Nyai went to the other room. I could hear Djumilah's voice, loud and harsh, but friendly: "Yes, Sis, this shirt was woven in Gedangan. There are no weavers in Tulangan. There is no cotton grown here. Very nice?" Laughter. "If you'd like, I'll order one for you later. . . . Yes, yes, I'm amazed too, Sis, why the factories here don't want to make shirts like this. They'd be much better, too, of course."

They came out together. Then Djumilah took Mama's suitcase and my suitcase into a room. I looked at Mama for a second. I heard her hiss: "Stupid woman!"

The basket of presents for the family had been carted into the kitchen by the carriage driver.

As soon as Djumilah reemerged from the room, she said: "Ah, you've stayed young, Sis Ikem. Sir, please feel free to change your clothes and rest up."

"I want to see out the back first." Nyai stood up again and Djumilah took her to the back part of the house.

I was left alone there with my heart in turmoil—I was thought to be Mama's new man! Perhaps worse than that: the kept man of a nyai. Why didn't Mama put things right straight away when only one room was prepared? Why did she merely hiss "stupid woman"? I laughed, seeing the funny side of it. At least it would be good material for a story.

They came in again and sat down, still chattering away and laughing about I don't know what. I was silent, meditating on what I heard. Usually the male guest is received by the man of the house in the front parlor and the female guests by his wife in the back parlor or kitchen. The host wasn't there, so I was now included among the female guests. Another funny side to this awful situation.

The pockmarked girl came in again, bowing and bending as before. Now she put out some of the sponge cake we had brought from Wonokromo. At that moment Mama put the following question to Djumilah: "Elder Sister, where is Surati? I didn't see her out the back there just now."

"Surati? Come here," she shouted shrilly. "Even your auntie doesn't recognize you anymore!"

The pockmarked girl, curling her lip, bowed down: "It is I, Surati," she whispered. "Yes, Aunt, I am now pocked like this."

I too was startled. This was Surati, that pretty girl I had seen twice before. Marked with big broad pocks, some deep and blackish.

"Alah Niece." Nyai stood up and pulled the girl up too. "How could this happen to you?"

"It is my fate, Aunt."

"It was her father's doing, Sis Ikem's own brother, a man with no backbone. He wanted to follow in Sastrotomo's footsteps, and sell his own daughter to the *Tuan Besar Kuasa* factory manager!" Djumilah burst out.

"What? Paiman?" Nyai was suddenly in a fury. "Paiman could do that to his daughter? Didn't he know what I had to suffer? Sit here, Niece!"

Surati sat down, bowing her head as custom required a young girl to do before her elders, especially before a man she had never met before.

Djumilah began to screech out curses on her husband, like a stream of river water that had found a free path in the steepest part of a gully. Every now and then her words would be punctuated by a shrill shout from Nyai: "A child as pretty as she, as sweet as she, look how she is now!"

Silently I followed the three women's conversation. Their questions and answers provided the structure of a story. Mama was overcome by the fire of her emotions. Back here in the environment from which she originally came, she seemed for a moment no more educated than Djumilah, thrown about by waves of extreme emotion while Surati told her the story as if it were the story of someone else's life; as though she had never felt sorrow or regret at the loss of her beauty.

They kept on talking. Mama groaned, accused, attacked; she laughed and smiled no more. The experiences of this once-beautiful blossom of Tulangan, the story of how she came to be pockmarked like this, unattractive to anyone, even to Mama and me, formed the basis of a great short story. It truly moved me and I wanted to write it. I promised myself that I would immortalize her suffering, even if the story was similar to Mama's own.

They talked and talked for more than an hour. They forgot I was there with them. Then the factory whistle reminded us all that it was already five o'clock. The cane workers in the fields now knew the working day was over.

"Ah, Tuan hasn't been able to rest yet?" Djumilah said in a tone that asked forgiveness. "Sis Ikem, please show Sir into the room."

"I see there is another room. He can use that one," said Nyai.

"Why must you be separated?" protested Djumilah.

"Don't be stupid! This is Annelies's husband!"

"Oh, ah, oh, Annelies's husband! Ya-ya, and how is Annelies—people say she was taken to Holland?"

"She's fine, Elder Sister," Nyai lied.

"No news yet?"

"No."

"Well, I had better prepare another room."

Then I realized: Her own sister looked upon Nyai as a woman of low morals. But at least that unspoken matter was now resolved. I got a room of my own, perhaps Surati's.

As I settled into that room, with its tidy bed and clean linen, I began to muse upon how disappointed Nyai must be. She would not try to marry me to Surati now. Her failure was an omen: I would soon be able to escape from Surabaya and Wonokromo.

Twilight arrived. The lights came on and I suddenly realized: electricity! For several minutes I stood gazing in admiration at the globe that gave off light but burned no oil, no gas, no wick. I thought of Edison and I bowed my head in his honor. I had now actually enjoyed two of his discoveries, the phonograph and the electric light bulb. And I was actually seeing an electric light bulb itself, not just a picture in a newspaper or magazine.

After I bathed, instead of taking the usual afternoon stroll, I began to note down the story of Surati's life. But I wasn't able to do it in peace. All of a sudden I heard Mama, running amok with words—and a man's low voice occasionally responding. Sastro Kassier had arrived home and was feeling Mama's wrath.

There was silence at the dinner table that evening and an atmosphere of enmity. I withdrew from the table before the battle began again.

It was Djumilah's voice that first broke the silence. "You were always a man without a backbone. Like a wayang shadow puppet that's lost its stick. It's lucky there's not a war on. How would you behave if you had to go to war?"

"Nothing but the descendant of a slave!" Mama reentered the fray.

"You keep out of this, Sanikem. You've done all right as a nyai," Paiman alias Sastrowongso alias Kassier answered.

"No! You're the one who benefited from my sale as a nyai. You were made a clerk!"

"But you're doing all right too!"

"I'm doing all right now because I've worked and fought hard, not because I was made into a nyai! Idiot!"

I closed the door, and my ears too, and went on writing my notes.

7

These are the notes I made about what happened to Surati, rearranged and rounded out with further material:

The citizens of Tulangan were busy preparing for a farewell party for the tuan manager, tuan besar kuasa. His contract had expired. As soon as his replacement arrived, he would set off for Surabaya among much festivity. He wanted to leave the people with something nice to remember. To the employees whom he was leaving, he kept saying: "May my replacement be better than I. Please help him!"

All the employees, workers, and other ordinary citizens held the same hope. The manager of the sugar mill was a powerful man in Tulangan, more powerful than the *bupati, assistant resident,* or even the resident. He was a little king. People said his wage was bigger than that of the governor-general. Though people didn't bow down and abase themselves before him, as they had to before a bupati or other Native official, his word was law. The old people of the village could still tell the story of the first tuan besar kuasa, the one Herman Mellema replaced, and how he ordered the execution of seven farmers who rebelled and refused to surrender their land. Five others had died of fright after carrying out orders to remove stones from the temples to be used as the foundation of giant constructions for the factory.

The laugh of a manager is something that puts people at ease; his threat is something else: The plantation supervisors, foremen, office employees, even the coolies, will obey him without question. At the crook of his finger, people will come; with just a grunt, people can be knocked to the ground.

The manager of the sugar mill, the tuan besar kuasa: a man with a tongue of fire.

So it was the time for preparations for the arrival of the new manager. The hand-over ceremony was attended by the controller and the bupati of Sidoarjo. Two hours after the ceremony, the new and the old managers came out from the office and went among the festive throng. The gong sounded, and the party began. At the same time, carriages were readied to escort the old manager as he left Tulangan.

The party itself was kept going with hired dancers, with palm wine, and with dice and brawling.

The new tuan manager was called Frits Homerus Vlekkenbaaij. He accompanied his predecessor as far as Sidoarjo railway station. As soon as he returned he strode into the partying crowd. Through an interpreter he rebuked: "What kind of infidel's party is this? Such noise—barbaric! Everyone leave! Go! Quickly!"

Everyone realized at once that gloomy clouds hovered before them.

Mijnheer Frits Homerus Vlekkenbaaij was short, even compared to Natives. His body was like a ball, with a bloated stomach—the stomach of someone who always sat and did no physical work. His eyes were deep, and peered out from under his eyelids, a greenish yellow, but clear, like marbles. He was the first European to appear there in public wearing short-sleeved shirts and short trousers, so that his dense, long, blond body hair was visible. He was bald; his cheeks were round and loose. His heavily lidded eyes gave the impression that he never slept at the right time. He kept to himself, avoiding speech except to spray abuse at people.

Not only the coolies and the villagers, but especially the office employees and foremen were frightened of his power. It was the

Mixed-Blood employees who whispered to the villagers and coo-lies: The new Tuan was *Plikemboh*—"Ugly Penis." The name stuck. The women would look away or giggle, covering their mouths, whenever they heard that name.

From the time of the party a tense atmosphere oppressed all of Tulangan—villagers, employees, and laborers. Plikemboh seemed capable of doing anything to anyone—Native, Pure, or Mixed-Blood. The workers and office employees reacted in their normal way: They would accept any treatment as long as they weren't dismissed.

Plikemboh understood that people were afraid of him. He was pleased. Now he was really someone. He was feared; he was master. He didn't have to work. Fear was his trusted foreman. He was rarely seen at his desk. His only order during the whole first month was: Tighten the supervision over the manufacture of spir-its and hard drink.

Plikemboh was a drinker and a drunkard. Yet he never drank what he had manufactured himself. So one or two sample bottles of drink from his own factory were brought to him, and he would sniff them to assess their alcohol content.

In the second month he started to wander around outside the complex. He would visit the cane plantations and the factory's electric plant. He liked to stand watching the plant's steam gen-erator, proud that it was the very first in the Surabaya area. He would walk around carrying an air rifle with which he hunted birds. He didn't ride horses—unusual for a sugar-mill manager.

In the late afternoons he could be seen sitting in front of his house, perhaps half drunk, with the air rifle on his table. He would take aim and shoot at any Native child who passed by on the street. Soon all the children were afraid of him. They would run away as soon as he appeared in the distance, carrying his rifle. So began the practice that mothers would use his name to frighten disobedient children.

Whenever he spent time outdoors, his face went very red, like that of a hen about to lay an egg. His head hardly ever turned, as if it were just a piece of twisted firewood.

Everyone knew he was a bad shot. He never took home a single bird. Whenever he went hunting a black leather bag hung from his shoulder. People guessed the bag had never held a bird, only a bottle of brandy.

After realizing that the birds would always elude his black leather bag, Plikemboh became bored with his rifle. Now he discovered a new kind of hunting: entering the homes of the Natives who lived near the factory complex, opening the doors to their rooms, their cupboards, even their cooking pots and rice steamers. His reasoning was that Natives could not be trusted; they were all thieves or half thieves, smugglers of contraband, manufacturers of illegal whisky. He never found what he was looking for. Then he began to worry the women. People began to lock their doors and wouldn't open them even if he pounded on the door.

Both men and women felt disgust whenever near Tuan Plikemboh. Not just because of his appearance; more so because of his character. Wherever he was present, people felt the air to be polluted. His body hair, his bloatedness, his transparent eyes, his glistening baldness . . .

One day Djumilah cried out, startled. Plikemboh had entered the house, perhaps through a window. Djumilah ran to the back part of the house, into the kitchen. All the boys were at school. The girls were in the kitchen. Plikemboh came into the kitchen too. The girls, in a daze, scattered in every direction, running faster even than their mother.

Djumilah ran out into the back yard. She shivered; she was unable to speak. She saw Surati pulling up water from the well, ready to do the family washing. Her mother signaled her to run. The girl didn't understand. Plikemboh had rushed out and reached the well. Now he stood before Surati, who was shaking with fear, unable to stand up any longer.

In the distance she could hear Djumilah calling for help. People came running. Seeing Tuan Besar Kuasa up to one of his tricks again, they all disappeared, guarding their own fates.

Fear and revulsion made Surati shiver and collapse into a squat. Seeing this, Plikemboh didn't know what to do. He slunk away behind the other houses and disappeared from view.

Only then did the neighbors return to Surati. They picked her up and carried her to the bench in the kitchen and changed her wet, stinking *kain*. Her face was white and she still couldn't speak.

The tuan manager, carrying his shoulder bag, descended again to the main road and returned to his office. From his books he found out that house number fifteen was occupied by the Sastro

Kassier family. He summoned the paymaster. Before coming to the Indies he had prepared himself by learning a little Malay from a retired controller. The conversation took place in Malay:

"You are Sastro Kassier?"

"Yes, Tuan Besar Kuasa."

"You are the paymaster here?"

"Yes, Tuan Besar."

"You have worked here a long time?"

"More than fourteen years, Tuan Besar Kuasa."

"How many wives to you have?"

"Only one, Tuan Besar Kuasa."

"Liar. No Javanese like you has only one wife."

"On my life, Tuan Besar Kuasa, only one."

"How many children?"

"Eight, Tuan Besar."

"Good. Do you have a virgin daughter?"

Sastro Kassier sat up, startled. The father in him warned him to be careful. The beginning of some catastrophe hovered before his soul's eye. But there was no way to avoid answering. All his children were listed in the company books. He would lose his position straight away if he was discovered to be lying. He admitted he did have one. Plikemboh asked about her age, her schooling, everything about Surati except her name.

"Good. You can go now."

Sastro Kassier returned to his work. He was anxious. He thought of sending his daughter away to Wonokromo. Impossible. From the Eurasian-owned Malay-language press, he knew that Sanikem herself was in trouble. His youngest niece, Annelies, was under the threat of being taken off to the Netherlands under guardianship. He knew too what a big affair that had become. He had wanted to go to Wonokromo to ask about it and at least to show his sympathy. He had hesitated, and ended up not leaving. Now it was impossible to take Surati there.

In the afternoon, after work, he was summoned again by Tuan Manager. He was received in Plikemboh's house. He was served cakes and alcohol. He couldn't refuse any of the things offered to him, afraid of exciting Plikemboh's wrath. All that he drank and ate there he felt was poisoning him, destroying his whole world.

Not a single person knows what they said to each other. Neither Sastro Kassier nor Plikemboh has ever spoken about it to anyone else.

It was evening when he returned home. His wife greeted him roughly—the first time he had ever been treated that way by her: "Look out, you, if you try anything crazy with that Plikemboh!" she threatened.

He realized that the whole of Tulangan knew what was happening. That night he didn't eat, but went straight to his room. He couldn't sleep. His eyes blinked open and shut like those of an old doll.

No paymaster was ever popular. It was the same with Sastro Kassier. The laborers suspected, correctly, that he and the foremen conspired to take a ten percent cut from their wages. None of the coolies could read or write. They could only frown, distrust, hate, make threats behind the backs of those concerned. Sastro Kassier indeed needed the extra money—for gambling and to pay for his mistresses, an honored custom among Native employees.

But one's position—that was everything to a Native who was neither farmer nor tradesman. His wealth might be destroyed, his family shattered, his name dishonored, but his position must be saved. It was not just his livelihood; with it also went honor and self-respect. People would fight, pray, fast, libel, lie, force their bones to the limit, bring disaster down on others, all for Position. People were prepared to give up anything for Position, because, with it, all might be redeemed. The closer Position took a person to the Europeans, the more he was respected, even if all he owned was his one *blangkon* hat. Europeans were the symbol of unlimited power, and power brings money. They had defeated the kings, the sultans, and the princes of Java, the holymen and the warriors. They subjugated men and nature without the slightest quiver of fear.

The next morning Paiman alias Sastro Kassier was called before Plikemboh again. Once again their conversation remained a secret to themselves. That night Sastro Kassier did not come home. He walked and walked through the villages to the north of Tulangan, like a burglar without a job. He thought and he didn't think. He prayed and then forgot what he prayed for. He did not make the rounds of his mistresses. He did not pick up the cards. He had resolved to cleanse himself of all such pollution. He neither drank nor ate. He walked and walked. He did not sleep, just walked.

He went back to his office after bathing in the river and meditated on top of a rock. He would work through the day without visiting home. As soon as he unlocked the door to his office, a messenger arrived: "An order from Tuan Besar Kuasa: As soon as Ndoro Paymaster arrives he must report immediately."

His meditation and ascetic exercises of the night before had not been blessed. Already Plikemboh was calling for him. His heart was still in turmoil. Now people would find out what the two of them talked about. A young coolie was scrubbing the office floor with carbolic acid.

"Eh, Sastro Kassier have you come up with an idea yet?"

"Not yet, Tuan Besar Kuasa," he answered.

"Why not?" He mispronounced his Malay.

"I haven't dared discuss it with my wife, Tuan Besar."

"Don't you know yet who Vlekkenbaaij is?"

"I know, Tuan Besar, I know very well."

"How come then you haven't spoken with your wife yet?" he said in even worse Malay.

"Afraid, Tuan Besar."

"And not afraid of me?"

Sastro Kassier was afraid of them both. He didn't answer.

"So then bring this wife of yours to see me. Why are you still here? Bring her to me! Get going!"

"She's gone, Tuan Besar, gone to rest at her mother-in-law's."

Vlekkenbaaij's eyes popped out. His forefinger wagged up and down as it pointed threateningly: "Watch out if you're lying. You'll regret it later. Get to work!"

Sastro Kassier went to his work. His anxiety did not prevent him from preparing his accounts. Tomorrow, Saturday, was pay-day. After finishing this, he recklessly reported sick and went home early.

His wife was not at all surprised to see her husband not sleeping at home. That indeed was the way of a man with position. She would never ask where he'd been. It was not the custom of a wife to challenge a husband who had position. Indeed even without her ever challenging him, she could be kicked out without a formal divorce. In some matters, the wife of a man with position might dare ask something, but never concerning her husband's "leisure." She was silent, silent in every way, feeling indeed inadequate in her inability to serve her husband as he desired.

Now Djumilah prepared something to eat, even though the day was still young. But Sastro Kassier did not eat. He pulled his wife over and ordered her to sit on the chair beside him.

"Don't think you can trick me." She erected battlements around her daughter.

"He wants to see you."

"No." Djumilah knew she would be powerless once faced with Plikemboh himself.

"It's true; he wants to see you."

"I cannot. Rather than my child be sold . . . shameful! Times have changed. That kind of thing shouldn't happen anymore."

Sastro Kassier knew his wife's answer was a challenge to divorce her. "Then you should go away."

"No. I will defend my daughter."

"Surati!" called Sastro Kassier. The girl came out and squatted, bowing before her father. "You know what's happened. What do you say?"

"Pay no attention to your father!" Djumilah incited her daughter. "You mustn't be like Sanikem, your aunt. May God forgive her."

"Sanikem is now richer than the Queen of Solo," Sastro Kassier contradicted. "Surati could be rich like that too. Well, Rati?"

"The mouth of Satan! Don't answer, Child, don't!"

"Yes, she doesn't have to answer. But both of you have a duty to understand how things are."

"Don't listen."

"Tuan Besar Kuasa," Sastro Kassier went on, not heeding the protests of his wife, "has ordered that I hand you, Surati, over to him. He wants to take you as his mistress. That's enough. That's all you need to know from your father. It's up to you whether you want to reject him or accept. If you don't want to answer, that's all right too."

Surati left.

"Satan!" cursed Djumilah. "Do you think I gave birth to her so she could become someone's concubine? You were always a man without backbone!"

"Don't make me angry. I'm still meditating, trying to find an answer to this." Now it was Sastro Kassier who shouted.

"Meditation! No need to meditate to know the answer: *No!* and the whole thing is over."

"It's not as simple as that."

"Are you afraid of becoming a farmer? A trader at the market? Ashamed? If I were the man, that would be my answer: no!"

"What does a woman know? Your world is no more than the tamarind seed. A wrong step and all of this could fall apart."

The whole day Sastro Kassier did not eat or drink. He left the house and walked and walked as he had the day before, across the dikes around the infertile paddy land which the village people still owned. The most fertile lands, all of them, had been taken over, rented by the mill every cane season, the contract renewed every eighteen months. Peasant farmers who rebelled courted disaster; the factory also controlled the civil service right down to the village officials.

The time of the full moon had passed. The night was shimmering with the half-light of its yellowish glow. The wind blew strongly. Sastro Kassier took no notice of the wind, of the moon, of himself. A sugar-mill official was one of the elect, one of the beloved of God. If that were not so, then could not any Native become a paymaster? Now he longed for an answer, one that didn't come from a human mouth, but from the realm of the supernatural, through some nonhuman being as an intermediary. Perhaps tonight some supernatural being was roaming the dark like him on this half-lit night. Perhaps this being might whisper the answer to him. And, indeed, if at that moment a goat had stood up on his two hind legs, or squatted, or rolled over, or sat legs tucked under as if at prayer, and spoke, and said: Sastro Kassier, carry out the orders of Tuan Plikemboh, he would carry them out no matter what the consequences. As long as Sastro Kassier himself could not be held responsible for his own deeds, did not have to use his own brain. So long as the sign did not come from a human mouth, such as his own.

And if that goat said No! he would never do what Plikemboh wanted, no matter what the cost.

For people like Sastro Kassier, Europeans were only one level below supernatural beings. And Europeans could be found about the place almost any time you wanted one. But he would never dare contradict a European. Like the others, he preferred to hope for a supernatural being. They had to be obeyed as well, but they were much more difficult to find when you needed their advice.

Sastro Kassier had complete faith that he would not collapse or faint for lack of food or drink. Fasting too was a much-honored practice. But he came across nothing supernatural. As if nothing had happened, he turned up for work as usual the next morning. His duties at the office must be carried out as efficiently as possible.

He took out the key to his office. He started: The door wasn't locked! He searched his mind: Had he forgotten to lock the door when leaving yesterday? He didn't go into his office. His eyes examined the steel-latticed walls. It was impossible for anyone to get their hands through and undo the lock from inside. He could see the whole office inside. Everything was lying peacefully in its place. Who had opened the door?

He didn't feel he'd been negligent. He had locked the door when he went home yesterday. He could still remember the click as he had turned the key in the lock and said to the attendant that he was going because he had a headache. Wasn't it the attendant himself who had reminded him: Don't forget the key, Ndoro?

Sastro Kassier was absolutely certain he hadn't forgotten. Locking up was one of his many responsibilities; he could not possibly have forgotten. He turned around and found yesterday's attendant on duty today as well—he was sitting on a bench in the corner. Sastro Kassier asked uncertainly: "Who opened this door?"

"There hasn't been anyone, Ndoro."

"Look, the door's already open. The key's still in my hand."

The attendant went pale, and didn't say anything.

"Go and get the night attendant." He was sure now: Someone had entered his office without permission. Only two people had a key: himself and Tuan Besar Kuasa. It was possible Plikemboh had come in and forgotten to lock up again. But if it were someone else using a copied key, and with evil intentions?

Half an hour later the night attendant arrived.

"You were on guard last night?"

"Yes, Ndoro."

"Who entered my office?"

"Tuan Besar Kuasa, Ndoro."

"You saw him yourself?"

"Yes, Ndoro."

"Watch out if you're lying! What did he do inside?"

"I don't know, Ndoro. I came outside to keep watch on the other doors and windows."

Sastro Kassier felt a bit calmer; yet his suspicions could not be put at rest. He went uncertainly into the office. From his desk drawer he took out his accounting books, anxious. He knew with great certainty: People might do anything for the sake of Position.

He opened his cash box. Yesterday he had sorted the money into piles for today's wages. All he had to do now was set it out on the table. He jumped back in shock. The cash box was empty, its lock undone, a gaping emptiness. He took another step back, his eyes wide open. He bumped into the next table.

"Attendant!" he shouted.

"Yes, Ndoro," replied the attendant from behind the latticed wall.

"Look!" he shouted again. "You are a witness! The cash box is empty. Someone has been in here and opened the cash box. You are a witness! The night attendant said Tuan Besar Kuasa came here last night. You're a witness! a witness!"

"Ndoro!" The attendant was shaking.

"You're the one who guards my office. Go and report to Tuan Besar Kuasa." The attendant, terrified, went off to find Plikemboh. "Today there will be no wages, no pay!" Sastro Kassier cried hysterically.

People gathered around outside the latticed wall gasping at the sight of the open, empty cash box.

"No wages! The cash box has been emptied! Emptied! There will be no wages today, no pay for anyone!" Sastro Kassier shouted more and more hysterically as the crowd watched.

The office work stopped altogether. All came to have a look: European—both Pure and Mixed-Blood—and Natives. Not a single person dared enter the paymaster's office. Only two people had that right: paymaster and manager.

Sastro Kassier was still screaming hysterically when Frits Homerus Vlekkenbaaij arrived and growled: "Shut your snout!" Immediately Sastro Kassier was silent.

Plikemboh entered through the crowd, which was parted by the aura of his power. Sastro huddled in a corner, his eyes unable to move from the gaping cash box.

"What's all this about, you, monkey Sastro Kassier?"

The paymaster, no longer able to feel the sharpness of such an insult, reported nervously: "Someone has broken into the office, broken into the cash box."

"You're the only one here."

"Night attendant! Here!" shouted Sastro.

The night attendant pushed his face up against the iron lattice. "Yes, Ndoro."

"Tell us: Who was here last night?"

The attendant stared at Plikemboh for quite some time, and the manager stared back at him with those marblelike eyes.

"No one, Ndoro. No one was here."

"But what did you just tell me? You said Tuan Besar Kuasa was here last night. Now you're going back on what you said. The day attendant heard you. Day attendant!"

Now the day attendant pushed his face up against the partition. His eyes followed the look of the night attendant, to Plikemboh, to the paymaster, then to the floor.

"You witnessed what the night attendant said to me."

"Yes, Master, Ndoro."

"Tell us what he said: that Tuan Besar Kuasa came in last night."

"The night attendant said that no one entered here."

"Liar! Both of them are liars!"

"You are the lair!" Plikemboh pointed to Sastro Kassier. "What time did you go home yesterday? Eleven! Who inspected your things before you left? Attendant! Did you examine his things when he left, day attendant?"

"No, Tuan Besar."

"Who can witness that you didn't take the factory's money? Who's your witness?"

"Who can witness that I *did* take the money?" Sastro Kassier protested weakly.

"Answer first: Who can witness that you *didn't* take it?"

"There is no witness," answered Sastro.

"So it was you who took it. Report this to the Marechausee!"

"Not yet, Tuan Besar Kuasa. Not yet! We must investigate who has been here first. Only Tuan Besar and I have keys. There are no signs that either the door or the cash-box lock have been forced. They must have been opened by the right key."

"You dare accuse me? The manager?"

"Who knows?" Sastro Kassier began to fight back. "If it wasn't Tuan, it could only have been me. There is no one else who could have opened this cash box except us two."

"Very well, let me just call in the Marechausee. We'll see you admit it all under their riding whips." He started to move away, stopped, and called out, "Karl, Karl!" When the person he had called arrived he gave the order in Dutch: "Draw up a letter of accusation to give to the authorities, for the Marechausee too. Do it now. I'll take it to them myself." And then speaking in Malay: "Everyone back to work! You too, monkey!"

The crowd dispersed. The paymaster was left facing Plikemboh. The closest people to them were the day and night attendants. Both were pale. They were facing away from the paymaster's office but their ears were alert, straining to hear.

"In short," said Plikemboh, "who took the factory's money is not the important thing now. What is important is that all wages due to the foremen and coolies must be paid today. Must be!"

"If there is no money, it's impossible."

"That's your affair, paymaster. Your name is Kassier, isn't it, eh? The factory put its trust in you. It is your responsibility. How much was lost altogether?"

Without opening his books, the paymaster replied: "Forty-five thousand guilders and five cents."

"Quite a lot. No one has ever had that much money. How much are the coolies' wages this week?"

"Nine thousand and forty-four guilders."

"Good. Pay up that nine thousand and forty-four guilders. Don't fall down on your job."

"I don't have even one guilder."

"Where did you go from here yesterday?"

"Home."

"And didn't go out again? People saw you leaving your house. Who did you go to see? Why are you silent? You must have been going somewhere."

Now Sastro Kassier understood: He had fallen into a trap prepared especially for him. He also understood that in a case like this where two people are accused, one a Pure-Blood manager, perhaps also a shareholder, and the other a Native, the Native is in the wrong place and the Pure is in the right. Since he had been paymaster, the money in his care had never been short one cent. That was before; it was different now. Where were you last night? Who is your witness? The night attendant would stand fast with his lies. It was enough to keep saying that no one had come in, for there was no reason for anyone to visit the office at night. And a manager who was perhaps even a shareholder would never rob money from his own factory.

"Come on, tell me. Where did you go? You still won't confess? Whom did you meet? Why are you silent? Fine—you don't want to answer. In short, you still have to pay today's wages and salaries. No delay—that is a factory regulation, part of our agreement with the government. Do you hear? The government!"

Before leaving, he still needed to turn around and add: "Do you want to try to fool the government? The government troops? The Marechausee? The police? You can try if you like." Then he left.

Everyone stared across at the paymaster's office, now like an iron cage. Each thanked God not to be the one singled out for this disaster.

The paymaster stood gazing at the yawning cash box. He did not know what to do. He was no longer concerned with the disappearance of the money, but with his responsibility to ensure that the wages and salaries were paid. He sensed his fingers going cold because he wasn't counting out the money. In a moment, the foremen would start arriving to collect their pay. A gang of coolies would be waiting upon each of them. He knew the danger that threatened if the money wasn't paid over as it should be. He also knew with certainty that the agreement between the factory and the government did exist.

Slowly he closed the cash box and locked it. Without looking at anyone, he left his office, locked the door, and headed for Plikemboh's office, walking with his head bowed.

"Ha, you've come, eh? What do you have to say?"

He wanted to gouge out those marblelike eyes from that European face.

"Tuan Besar Kuasa Manager, I don't have the money to pay the wages. It is up to Tuan Besar Kuasa to decide what is best."

"Sit!" ordered Plikemboh.

For the first time in his fourteen years at the factory he sat on the chair opposite the manager.

"What do you want now?"

"The coolies and foremen must be paid today. There is no time to borrow money from the bank. Tuan must lend me the money."

"Lend you money?" Plikemboh hissed. "That's an insolent request indeed. Nine thousand and forty-four guilders—the same price as four new stone houses with land and furniture. You're crazy!"

"Only Tuan Besar Kuasa can help me."

"You shall be dismissed, punished, everything you own will be taken from you. You'll be a pauper, a vagabond, a beggar. And it will happen today, if you can't pay those wages."

"Whatever may happen, then let it happen. But Tuan too will be in trouble if the wages can't be paid. The factory will be closed for breaking the agreement with the government. What can one do?"

Frits Homerus Vlekkenbaaij laughed to hide his surprise. Then: "You're clever, heh; you've a lot of cunning in you. You want to drag me into it?" Now his tone was more friendly. "Yes, I must help you to pay out those wages. Here, sign this agreement first. Put your signature and your thumbprint on it. You'd better do it."

It became clearer still to Sastro Kassier. Of course it was Plikemboh who had arranged all this. Plikemboh had already prepared the letter of agreement: It demanded the handing over of Sastro's grown-up daughter within three days of signing the letter. On handing her over, his debt to Plikemboh and all the remaining missing money would be taken care of by the manager himself.

Sastro Kassier forced himself to believe that this was indeed the genuine fruit of his meditation and fasting over the last two nights. He had not yet eaten or taken any drink. But today, anyway, the foremen and coolies would receive their money. He knew he could not avoid his responsibilities as paymaster. With a prayer that God lay a curse upon it, he signed the agreement, then added his thumbprint.

He received the money. Plikemboh watched it all, smiling.

The days now passed tensely for Surati. She knew the story of Auntie Sanikem well. She was unwilling to go freely to become someone's concubine, isolated from the world, looked upon by everyone as something strange, a public spectacle.

Her mother kept pressuring her not to agree to anything her father suggested. She was afraid of her father, but sad for her mother. From childhood she had been taught to fear and obey her parents, with words, with beatings, with pinchings. Fear of her parents was a part of her personality. But she was still more afraid of the Europeans and their weapons.

Her happiness in life vanished. Her mother's rebellion against her father turned everything upside down. She could not stand to see her father so abused by her mother; neither could she stand to see her mother belittled and ignored by her father. If the gods and goddesses in the heavens fought each other as viciously as her parents now fought, the earth would tremble and be forced to find a place to anchor itself.

"Don't make your mother and your sisters carry a burden of shame. Become a concubine? Be a nyai? May God protect us, may it never happen. It's not proper, not right. No one can say it's right."

Surati understood. She must carry out her mother's wishes and not shame her sisters. The whole neighborhood agreed with her mother. She understood too, better than they, that it was her father who held power over her, more power than anyone else. If her father wanted her to do it, there was no power that could stop him. Not the police, not the troops, and certainly not just the village head. And she would not dare oppose him.

She lost all desires during those tense days. Must she just surrender herself to whatever was to happen? And so save her parents' marriage? Bring them together again in an atmosphere of perpetual enmity? Or must she rebel, so that when her mother sided with her, a divorce would follow? What would be the fate then of her little sisters? She couldn't decide. She herself had come face to face with Plikemboh. She would never willingly be taken by him! She shivered.

That evening, after the factory whistle had finished its repetitive screaming, she was lying in despair on her bed. In the front parlor, her mother was venting all her fury on Sastro Kassier: "Miserable descendant of the seller of children! As long as you're all right yourself! A man with no backbone! A worm could still crawl on and try!" Her voice was harsh and furious but her muscles were powerless.

"Surati!" called her father.

Surati came out of her room and stood with head bowed and hands clasped before her as was proper. At that moment, she knew: Her voice had volume but no power.

"So, Rati," Sastro Kassier opened his speech, "three more days and I will take you to him, to Tuan Besar Kuasa Manager. In all things it is Allah that hands out fate and good fortune. It is He who decides all things in accord with His wishes."

Surati understood that she must now answer, and it would be an answer from a frightened and obedient child. She knew too that such obedience and fear meant her own destruction. All of a sudden she remembered the smallpox epidemic that was spreading wildly in the south. In a little while everyone would be lashed by the disease. Tulangan too. What was the difference between the destruction looming before her now and the viciousness of smallpox? As a good daughter, she would not disappoint her father.

"I just obey, Father."

"You will do what I say, my Child? What do you mean by obey?"

"In whatever way it is Father's wish."

"Yes, Child, it is only you that can save your father, that can stop your father from being dismissed, from being put in jail."

"Let him be dismissed. Let him be accused, Rati, so that he knows what it means to be a man."

"No, Mother. We would all be ashamed as a result."

"Ah, you, Rati, Surati, to accept being concubine of an infidel, a cursed devil."

"We all eat from him," Sastro reminded everyone.

"Let it be, Mother; my sisters are still many. What does it mean to lose just one egg? I will go there myself. No need to be escorted like Sanikem."

"Thanks be to God, Rati, praise be to God. You are a child who truly understand the difficulties of her parents. A child so devoted to her parents will be honored in both this world and the next."

"Mouth of a liar!" Djumilah screamed. "Not honor. He doesn't know the difference between honor and humiliation."

"But," Surati went on, "allow me to go out tonight to meditate. Don't look for me. When the time has come, I will go myself to the house of Tuan Besar Kuasa Manager."

"What kind of meditation, Child? Late at night like this?" Djumilah could not hold back her tears. All her anger melted away in pity for her daughter. "With so much illness about now?"

"Yes, Mother. If its parents can no longer do anything for an egg, then the egg must roll away itself to find its own way in life."

Djumilah could no longer hold back her emotion. She embraced her daughter.

"Where are you going? All this is your own father's—"

"Let it be, Mother. Now let me leave."

"Where are you going? I will come with you."

"Let it be, Ma. What need is there? This daughter of yours is an egg that must be sacrificed. Stay and live in happiness with Father."

And so it was. With a small bag containing clothes, matches, kerosene, and dried foods, the girl left to make her way into the thick blackness of the night. Her feet took her southward. After traveling quite a long way, she sat down in a daze beside the road. What must she do? All she knew was that she must leave that house. The roof that had always sheltered her from rain and heat now housed a nest of quarrels, had lost its power to shelter and protect its peacefulness, and all because of her. But where must she go now? She knew her mother and sisters would try to follow her. She stood up and walked a bit farther. Quickly, faster and faster. She slipped behind a hedge, disappearing from the view of anyone following her.

She pressed on, her strides quicker. She did not want blame to arise in her heart.

She must resolve the problem herself, because it was she herself who would undergo it all. None of this would be happening if there were no Plikemboh. Plikemboh—Surati shivered. She was supposed to accept that disgusting person. For a moment the vision of Plikemboh disappeared, and was replaced by one of her mother, her father, her little sisters, her Aunt Sanikem. Then for a moment she saw Annelies's marriage again—Annelies sitting beside her husband, looking so happy. Surati knew such happiness as that was not now for her, nor would it ever be. A tear dropped. She too wished for such happiness. But it seemed her fate was to be different. And she was afraid of her parents.

"Why is Father like Grandfather Sastrotomo?" she whispered angrily to herself. "How could he do it to his own daughter, just to keep himself safe? What was the use of having me? Why can't I be like other girls?"

Like lightning, memories flashed by of other friends who had suffered this same fate. All beautiful girls, stolen from their houses, through all kinds of means, by Europeans. Now it was her turn, because now she had reached the age for theft. Like them, she could do nothing. She knew she would have surrendered like the others, had Plikemboh not been so hideous.

The air was cold and the wind whistled and whistled. Her legs walked as if they had a will of their own. To the south, to one particular spot: a village that was at that moment being destroyed by smallpox.

"No one will protect me," she whispered to the night as it covered her in darkness. "If my own parents can't do anything, what is to be done, as long as they never come to curse me."

Without her realizing it, a plan had formed, the plan of a winged ant that wanted to fly into the flames of a fire.

During those tense days, she had tried to gather together the courage to decide. And she could not decide. A maiden dwells in silent loneliness, alone in life. Her only friend is the hope of happiness. Without the hope of happiness, she has lost everything. There is no one with whom she can talk. If she makes what seems like a decision, it is in reality only a surrender to what is going to happen. At the moment Sastro Kassier had decided, such a surrender became an unshakable resolve. One thing that had made its way into her mind at the time was the smallpox epidemic. What must happen now? The coming together of herself and the smallpox epidemic. She would do it.

From behind her came the howls of a pack of wolves that had recently roamed about seeking victims. The curfew had allowed the wolf packs to become kings of the night. Several times already, villagers' stock had been attacked and destroyed. She was not afraid; the oppression in her spirit had overcome fear. She walked on. Only if she heard the lonely cry of a bird did she stop and look. Perhaps the bird was calling after the moon or crying out its longing for a lover who would never arrive.

She had covered almost ten miles. Sweat soaked her body. The moon was starting to peek out from behind the horizon of silhouetted trees. She stopped under one tree, checking whether she could see anything in the distance. She did not want to be seen by anybody or meet anybody. She checked behind her and to her left and right. There was nothing suspicious. But she remained alert at the places shrouded in thicker darkness. Still and quiet, as if she were the only person on this earth. And the cries of the night birds made the night seem even stiller.

Many times during the last two weeks the army had ordered a curfew. People obeyed. Only the army and police were allowed out, but she did not see even a single soldier.

She traveled on for about another five miles. In the distance she could see a blinking glow in the night sky, like a lamp that had almost run out of oil: campfires among clusters of bamboo. That was the village where she was headed. The campfires were army posts. The soldiers weren't visible. She kept on walking. She knew the army had issued orders that no one was to approach closer than a mile. The people in the village weren't allowed out. Those outside weren't allowed in. Those in the village were pitilessly given up to die, without compassion—sacrifice to Lord Smallpox.

If I die there with them, then I will be dead, her heart whispered to the night wind. It would not be long, and all would be over. Surati was going to kill herself. She had accepted what was to happen. And she felt as though she could still decide, not like Aunt Sanikem. She herself must bring an end to herself.

And if I do not die, it must truly be my destiny to become the woman of that hateful and hideous man. What is to be done, Father, Mother . . .

The closer she came to the village, the farther she moved away from the roads, plunging into the paddy and through the broken-down, neglected fields. The scratches on her feet and body from the leaves about her went unfelt. She did not even lift up her kain.

She was startled when she disturbed some ducks sleeping peacefully under a bush. The animals scattered, screeching with frightened protests. The ducks had no one looking after them, she thought; perhaps their owners had been killed by the smallpox.

Now she plunged through fields wrecked by wild pigs and

150

deer. Her clothes were covered with grass blossoms. Her hair had fallen loose and was now tangled. She didn't care. Her hairpin had fallen who knows where.

The moon shone brighter and brighter. The tongues of fire in the distance seemed to grow larger. Some Dutch soldiers could now be seen running back and forth. The wind began to blow strongly. She knew the village perimeter was patrolled continuously. The nearer she came, the lower she crouched. Finally she began to crawl, like a forest pig.

The fires that lit the soldiers' camp receded into the distance as she moved away. She kept crawling, making no sound, like a cat. Her hands and feet were covered in blood, cut by the thorns and sharp brush along the way. She sought a rift in the bamboo that fenced off the village. In vain. It was not easy: The clusters of bamboo weren't smooth bamboo, but thickets of the thorny variety.

She had forgotten her own problems, her own troubles. Her whole being was concentrated on the effort to enter that village, to break through the bamboo fence. Every hole, every gateway, was guarded by soldiers and tongues of fire. Without any sharp instrument, with only her bare hands—the hands of a young girl who had never done any real physical work—she was unable to break through. She had to climb over. So she began her attempts to climb over the bamboo—the first such experience in her whole life.

In the distance she could hear soldiers greeting each other in Dutch:

"Who goes there!"

"A friend!"

In silence, she listened alertly. The voices went away.

I must climb down, she whispered to a stalk of bamboo. But still she didn't climb down. A lone, gaunt cow dawdled silently along. She could vaguely hear the hungry lowing of other cattle. She cast her eyes across the village on the other side of the bamboo fence. Here and there stood huts with grass roofs, like giant animals trying to hide themselves. The moon shone brighter, reluctantly throwing its light upon all that lived on the earth. She no longer wanted to look up at the moon, whereas in the past she had so often gazed at it while singing with her friends. This time she had to force herself to look; perhaps it would be the last time.

She climbed down into the village carefully, freeing herself
from the view of the soldiers and from the jabs of the bamboo's
thorns. The ground below the cluster of bamboo was blanketed in
fallen leaves. They rustled under the tread of her feet. She stood
silently, listening for sounds. Between the whistling shrieks of the
harsh wind as it charged into the bamboo clusters, she heard again
the lowing of starving cattle. Perhaps they were still tethered in
their corrals. No human sound could be heard. Now she was a
member of this village. Like the others, she had surrendered un-
conditionally to the smallpox. She walked on, looking for the
cattle that were lowing so weakly. The moon lit her way to a
house with a corral at the back. She lit a match and looked for the
cross-bar. There was no human inside, just a pregnant cow. She
undid the rope that tied the cow. The animal walked slowly,
heading towards a spot from where the grass sent out its delicious
aroma. She gazed at the animal, which had no intention of saying
thank you, then walked on again. Under a jamblang bush, she saw
a she-goat and its kids, sprawled out dead from hunger and thirst.
The she-goat was still tethered. It seemed it had just given birth,
unwitnessed by anyone.

The moon was shrouded in cloud. Once again Surati forced
herself to look up, as if she wished to memorize its face forever
before the smallpox entered her body and escorted her to the
universe of souls.

Those that live, let them live, she whispered; the dead, lie still
in your muteness; don't disturb me.

Then, confidently, without hesitation, she stepped into a hut.
She heard a weak voice coming from inside.

"Is there someone there?"

There was no answer. She opened another door. Darkness
gaped out at her from the doorway. Yes, she had heard a voice, a
very weak one. She lit a match, and saw a bloated, wheezing baby
lying beside its dead mother. A gaunt baby, fleshless, covered in
filth. Both lay on a tattered bamboo mat. The match burned out.
She lit another and then the kerosene lamp that hung from a nail
on a wall.

The soldiers would never dare come here, she thought.

Behind the door, she found another corpse—a man, bare-
chested, sprawled on the ground, dead. His right hand reached
out. Perhaps he was trying to reach his baby, his loved one.

The man looked very young, less than twenty years old. Surati herself was younger.

The still living baby she took and cuddled. It had the smell of rotten fish about it and its body was hot. She took a bottle of drinking water from her bag and gave some to the baby, but the child was no longer able to swallow. The end for it too was near.

Far away she could hear the trumpets of the soldiers. She didn't know what they signaled. She didn't care. She held the dry, shriveled child, dirty and rotten-smelling, as though holding one of her little sisters at home. She hugged the small weightless body to her breast. She kissed it as if saying good-bye, good-bye forever, then to be together again, also forever.

Under the rays of light from the kerosene lamp, the baby finally reached death's door. Surati began to sing a lullaby so that this very young soul would be able to sleep in eternity caressed by the love of another human being—a human being it had never known. She cleaned the baby's face with the corner of her *kebaya*.

The child convulsed for a moment, quickly expelling its final breaths. Surati did not know the child's name. She had never seen a human being on its deathbed. She was not afraid in this encirclement of death. She felt so close, such a friend to them all; soon she too would be part of it all. Death? What lies beyond death? At least, for sure, she would not be meeting Plikemboh. Why are people afraid of death? And why am I not afraid? When the smallpox has entered my body, and death arrives . . . no, she was not afraid. The curse of one's parents was more terrible than death. Enter, you smallpox, come into me.

She put the baby down beside its mother. She pulled its father over with great difficulty. The corpse was already stiff. At least, now, the baby was sleeping together with its mama and papa. For a moment she looked at the two parents at peace in death, together again forever. She felt happy that she had done this, as if she had done some deed of unrivaled goodness, that had never been done by anyone else ever, except by Surati.

She found nothing in the hut except some torn cloths piled up on an overturned bench. With these she covered them as with a blanket. She put out the lamp, went outside, and closed the door.

She had heard rumors that the soldiers were going to spray the village with kerosene and set it on fire. Not now; that was still five days away. The village heads in the district had protested against the plans: It wasn't right to burn people alive. It was not certain that everyone would be killed by the smallpox. But the government doctor, Lieutenant Doctor H. H. Mortsinger, had calculated that everyone would die within two more days. Even if some hadn't died, they might spread the epidemic, so they should be wiped out as well. The village heads' protests resulted in the decision to postpone the burning for a few days, to give everyone a chance to die naturally. The burning was still to go ahead.

To die by fire, there was nothing wrong with that either, thought Surati.

She found more corpses outside the house. Some parts of the bodies had been bitten by animals. They had all begun to ooze blood, corrupting the air with their smell. She became aware of the stench of carcasses coming at her from all directions. The dense rottenness was like the rising scent of incense sticks, bearing her to a faraway universe, a place she had never realized existed until now.

Surati lived thus for three days and two nights in that village. She began to feel the hair on her body creep whenever the wind blew. I have caught the disease, she told herself. Very early in the morning she found a well and bathed. She took out the best clothes in her bag. She began to adorn herself. She put on all the jewelry and other adornments that she owned. She knew the fever was starting to attack. In the darkness of the night, she climbed once more over the bamboo. She moved quickly, as if she knew by instinct exactly how far she must travel. It was as if she were racing against the fever that was dancing within her. A few more days and I will be dead. And I will take you with me, Plikemboh! Everybody then will be free from your torments: children, women, and your workers! Perhaps the world will be a little more beautiful without you.

The fever in her seemed to weaken, subjugated by her will, unable to suck up her strength and her determination. I must get safely to your house, Plikemboh, looking fresh, young, and pretty.

A girl who was not from a peasant family would never have been taught to walk quickly; indeed she would have been forbidden to do so. But Surati's legs took stride after stride, penetrating the darkness and the night mist, half-running over the paddy-field dikes, now overgrown with weeds. Now she held her sarong by its corners so it would not be soiled by the weeds' blossoms.

She had covered five miles. Yet there was still no sweat on

her. She walked another few miles and a few more again. Then she stopped under some trees and descended into a big ditch. She washed herself again. At the peak of the moon's mist-covered brightness, she put on her makeup once more. For a long time she sat under the tree, not thinking of anything. During those last few days, she had stopped thinking, surrendering herself to the flow of events as they happened, as though she were part of nature itself, like the wind, like the water, like the earth. She began to see people out walking on that dark morning. She too stood up, walking slowly so as not to ruin her makeup and her adornments, just like a woman of the aristocracy. Slowly enough even to control her sway.

As the sun rose, Tulangan became vaguely visible behind the mist. She saw several carriages carrying goods and heading for the markets of Sidoarjo.

On entering Tulangan she stopped and whispered to herself. Here I am, coming to you, Tuan Besar Kuasa Manager. Greet me, Surati!

The factory office was open when she arrived. The roads around the factory were busy with coolies pushing loaded carts. She didn't know what they carried, nor did she have any desire to know. Her legs took her straight to Plikemboh's house.

She announced herself formally. In her imagination she could see Aunt Sanikem, a score or more years ago, standing before this same house, there to become the concubine of Tuan Mellema. The door was open, but no one answered her. She sat on the steps with her back to the house. Her dried food was finished. She felt hungry. The fever was still obedient to her plan.

She heard slippered footsteps behind her. She stood facing the door, bowed, and once again announced herself.

Plikemboh emerged still wearing his pajamas. He stood gazing at her, and at once recognized who she was.

"Sastro Kassier's daughter?" he asked joyfully, and sped down the stairs to fetch her.

"It is I, your servant, the daughter of Sastro Kassier, Tuan Besar Kuasa."

She ascended the steps, escorted by Plikemboh, and surrendered herself to be taken into his room—the place that forever would be the boundary that marked the end of her life as a virgin and the beginning of her condition as a kept mistress.

Take me! Take all you can get from me, she thought, and may you soon be destroyed.

As soon as she entered the room, the smallpox ran amok within her. Her strength was broken. From the moment she lay prostrate on Plikemboh's bed, she was unable to rise again. And very quickly Plikemboh too became infected. During those last few days, they both lay sprawled out on the bed, awaiting death.

Tulangan was pronounced an epidemic area. All work stopped. The traffic was stilled. Those who managed to sneak through the government's encirclement ran for their lives, forgetting position and income. The sugar-cane fields were left unattended. The steam-generated electric plant was mute. The factory whistle went dumb. Tulangan was in darkness. The chimneys lost their grandness, craning forward, looking down on Tulangan as if wanting to know what was happening, nodding sadly, but no eyes cared to look up at them.

The village across the fields, which Surati had left behind, was burned out by the soldiers, destroyed together with all its trees that the villagers had looked after for many years. Tulangan itself was not set on fire. Doctors were brought in from all over Java to end the epidemic. A big sugar mill must not be destroyed just because of smallpox. Capital must be kept alive to grow, and people can be left to die.

Lieutenant Doctor Mortsinger was also called to Tulangan with all the medical troops from the antiepidemic service in Bandung. Inoculation was carried out in Tulangan and all the surrounding areas. But the encirclement of Tulangan was kept unmercifully tight. People could neither leave nor enter. People were even forbidden from leaving their houses. Food was brought in and shared out. Every day people buried the victims.

The first to die was Tuan Besar Kuasa Manager, Frits Homerus Vlekkenbaaij, alias Plikemboh.

Surati was still prostrate on the bed when the heavy corpse was taken from beside her to be burned. Only then did people find out that the maiden had already begun her life as a nyai. And hadn't died.

Even while facing the threat of death by smallpox, all the people of Tulangan, regardless of race, Native, Pure, or Mixed-Blood, stopped to thank God for the death of Tuan Besar Kuasa Manager. To them his corpse was a talisman that would protect

Tulangan from disaster. But no one ever found out who it was that had really killed him.

The young mistress was carried home by her mother, whose insults and abuse of Sastro Kassier never silenced.

Sastro Kassier himself did not stay silent. The death of his boss gave him the chance to make his accusations. Witnessed by local officials, a search was made of his late employer's things. There, in a cupboard, they found the missing money, still intact. Sastro Kassier remained triumphant as the honest paymaster, but his honor as a husband and father was gone, and would never return.

So, too, was Surati's beauty gone forever.

And the sugar mill of Tulangan remained grand in its command over all of Tulangan: humans, animals, and growing things.

8

For three days we had been rest-
ing in Tulangan. The new manager who had replaced Plikemboh
sent a letter to Mama, inviting her to come and have a look around
the factory. Mama turned down the invitation. He then came to
Sastro Kassier's house to invite her in person. He was very young,
about thirty years old. Mama refused the invitation again.

I don't know why the master of that sugar mill felt he had to
invite Mama. Mama herself had never mentioned having any special business with him.

Kommer also sent us a letter: He would not be able to visit us.
He couldn't leave the carpenters while they were making his trap.
It was proving to be quite difficult to make.

Every day Mama and I went for a walk through the paddy
fields, plantations, and villages. She was really changed; the dark,
eerie aura about her had vanished. She was truly enjoying her
holidays. She didn't look at all like a widow, nor like someone out
walking with her son-in-law, himself a widower. She looked like
a young maiden, not yet married.

Her walk was confident and free like that of a European

woman. She always wore the kebaya that for a century had been the fashion for Indos, nyais, and now for Chinese women to wear. Very few Native women wore them, at most a few from the elite classes, and perhaps their children. Most wore a simple cloth wrap or even went totally bare-breasted.

Nyai Ontosoroh's beautiful and delicately embroidered kebaya became the focus of everybody's attention. Such a kebaya was still rare in the villages, and its whiteness and the brightness of its embroidery shone out in the middle of all this greenness, drawing all eyes to it.

On the fourth day she wouldn't go for a walk and sent me out by myself.

So on that day, in European clothes (people called them Christian clothes), carrying a bag containing pen and paper, a bottle of water, and a little dried food, I set off alone in a southerly direction. My plan was to visit the village that the government had burned down, the one that Surati had visited.

In the middle of the ocean of sugar cane I saw something odd: the tiled roof of a house. Whose? Somebody's home, or a place for workers to take shade? The trees behind it showed that cane did not grow around it. Probably somebody's house-garden.

It wasn't out of mere curiosity that I set off in the direction of the house, but because I wanted to accustom myself to taking an interest in everything that was related to the lives of the Natives, my people.

The path, hemmed in on either side by the cane, was still and quiet. Not a single person passed me. But from the direction of the tiled house came the sound of muffled shouts, roughly spoken words.

The sun radiated shafts of heat. Sweat soaked my back. The air was fresh and invigorating. My body felt unconstrained by the etiquette required when escorting Mama. I walked along, enjoying it all to the full, savoring how healthy I was. I felt fortunate to be alone in the middle of this greenness. I had never in all my life gone for a hike alone and so far. Perhaps I had already traveled more than three miles.

This was the same road that Surati had once traveled, not in the midday heat like this, but in night's pitch darkness, before the moon had risen.

The cane to my right and left would ripen in a few months'

time. It would become sugar, helping to make Java the second biggest producer of sugar in the world. The sugar would be dispersed over the earth to many countries and give enjoyment and health to millions of people. And the name Tulangan? No one would ever hear of it.

There were those shouts again.

The path I was following branched out. A lane led to the suspicious-looking house.

A farmer with a hoe at his waist passed me. He raised his bamboo hat, bowed without looking at me—only because I was wearing European clothes, Christian clothes. He was heading towards the main road. Perhaps he was a cane cutter.

"What's all the shouting about?" I asked in Javanese.

"The usual, Ndoro. Old Truno is not like everyone else."

"Who is this Truno?"

"The one who lives there, Ndoro."

"In that house?"

"Yes, Ndoro."

"Why are they shouting at him like that?"

"He won't move out of his house."

"Why must he move?"

My barrage of questions scared the peasant. He shrank back, bowed, raised his bamboo hat again, excused himself. Perhaps he had been among those shouting just now.

The shouts came again. Now it was clear what they were saying, in crude Javanese: "When are you getting out of there?"

Other shouts followed from several mouths at once, but I was unable to pick up what they were saying. Then there were further angry exchanges and cries for Truno to get out. What was happening in the middle of this ocean of cane?

Because I had been accused of not knowing my own people, yes, and because of curiosity, my legs took me closer to the location of the quarrel. Perhaps I could learn to understand their problems. Without my realizing, my feet were now carrying me more quickly. I no longer took any notice of the foliage above me as the branches and twigs squeaked against each other whenever the wind blew.

In this very lane the tile-roofed house stood. It was made out of thick bamboo. In front of the house stood a mustached man with a thick beard, bare-chested, wearing black trousers down to just below his knee. In his hand was a machete with that just-honed shine about it. His eyes were wild. He was now standing alone. On seeing me, his eyes popped out in challenge.

"*Pak!*" I shouted, in friendly Javanese. "Who was making all the noise just now?"

He still stared at me wild-eyed as if I were his enemy. I stopped in front of the bamboo gate.

"What?" he hissed in low Javanese. "You too?" I was offended. I could feel the blood rise into my face. A Javanese had never spoken so roughly towards me, let alone used the familiar form for *you*. No doubt he was that kind of insolent Javanese, hadn't been properly educated, I thought. Then quick as lightning came the voice of Jean Marais, accusing me: You are not fair, Minke; what right would you now have to abuse him? What have you done for him? Just because you are the grandson and the son of a bupati? You say you understand the great call of the French Revolution? What's the use of having graduated from H.B.S.?

A smile of awareness crept onto my lips. I must remain friendly.

"Don't be angry with me, Pak. I'm not your enemy."

"Every single day . . ." The man frowned, yet my friendliness did relax him a little.

"What is it, Pak?"

". . . like a pack of barking dogs!" It poured out in sharp tones.

"Who, Pak," I asked affably, "is like a pack of barking dogs?"

He observed me with suspicion. It was unusual for a Javanese peasant farmer to be suspicious of his superiors. Peasants had no right to be suspicious. It was clear that this one peasant had "escaped the prongs of the rake," had turned his back on the proper way of behaving. Like an elephant that had left its herd, as Nijman had said about Khouw Ah Soe, a Javanese peasant who refused to fit himself to the old mold was also dangerous. Machete in hand, loud voice, not listening to orders: All this was evidence.

"Don't get me wrong, Pak, I've only just arrived."

He wouldn't give up his suspicions. His smallish eyes stood out as if they were not interested in ever blinking again. Indeed they seemed ready to hurl themselves out of their sockets at any minute. I must try to win his trust. Must! Must! There's no way of getting close to somebody without first making contact with his heart.

Daring myself to go on, I took a step forward, passing through the gate, not without having to suppress my fear.

"What's really going on here?" I asked affably.

"Is Ndoro a *priyayi* from the mill?" he suddenly asked in high Javanese, a question that also struck me as insolent.

"No. I have just arrived from Surabaya. I am not an official from the mill. I'm still at school, Pak. I write for newspapers, that's my work."

With savage eyes—not normal either for a Javanese peasant—he looked me over from the top of my head to the tips of my shoes.

"This machete is not just good for cutting down banana trees," he growled threateningly in low Javanese. "One more time, and someone will cop it."

"What is it? What is it?" I asked, in the politest of ways.

"I don't care who he is, Javanese, Madurese, Dutch soldier, one more howl from them . . ."

His anger passed its climax with these growls and threats.

"Is Ndoro one of them or not?" He turned abruptly, interrogating me. More insolence.

"Who do you mean by *them*?"

Once more he challenged my eyes, and looked at my bag. *"They,"* he said savagely, "are those factory dogs who just left. This is my own land. What business is it of theirs what I do with it." He wiped sweat from his back.

Unease squatted in my heart; he had gone back to speaking in low Javanese. He had forgotten what class he belonged to. So why should I treat him so well? But you have resolved to become more familiar with your own people! You must understand their troubles. He is one of those fellow countrymen of yours about whom you know nothing, one of your own people, a people you say you want to write about, once you have begun to understand them.

"Of course this is your own land," I encouraged him, and myself too.

"Five *bahu*, inherited from my parents."

"You're right," I said, "I saw it noted down in the Land Office."

"Yes, it's registered in the Land Office." He spoke to himself. The tension began to recede. Slowly he was returning to being a humble Javanese peasant.

"Can I visit you, Pak?" I said in an even more friendly way. His grip on the machete began to relax. I took another step forward. "If you aren't angry with me, I'd like to know what this is all about. Who knows, perhaps I can help?" I took another step.

He didn't answer, but turned around and headed for the house. I followed. He threw his machete down inside the house. He fetched a straw broom and swept clean the bamboo bench at the entrance.

"Please, Ndoro, this is the best I can offer."

So I sat on the bamboo bench, adorned with a bamboo mat. He stood with hands clasped before me. He was beginning to trust me, I hoped. "All right, tell me why you are so angry," I asked.

"Yes, Ndoro, I have already been very patient. My inheritance was five bahu—three paddy fields, two dry fields—and this house garden. Three bahu are being used by the mill. I didn't happily rent them out but was brutally forced to do so by the mill priyayi, the village head, all kinds of officials, and God knows how many others! The land was contracted for eighteen months. Eighteen months! But now it has been two years! You have to wait until the cane stumps have all been dug out. Except if you want to put your thumbprint to another contract for the next harvest season. What's the contract money worth anyway? You can count it up as much as you like, they never pay in full anyway. Those dogs, Ndoro . . . now even my dry fields—they want those too. The trees will be torn down to make way for the cane!"

"How much do you get for one bahu?" I asked, as I took my writing implements from my bag, knowing that all of Java's peasants respected a pen. I was ready to take notes.

"Twenty-two, Ndoro," he answered fluently. Amazing.

"Twenty-two *perak* for every bahu, for use for over eighteen months!" I exclaimed.

"Yes, Ndoro."

"How much did you receive?"

"Fifteen perak."

"Where did the other seven go?"

"How would I know, Ndoro? Put your thumbprint down, they said. No more than fifteen perak a bahu. Eighteen months,

163

they said. In reality, two years, until the cane stump and roots were dug out."

"They dig out the roots themselves?"

"Of course, Ndoro. They don't want to see the stumps grow and ripen again, become new cane fields again. They don't want the farmers around here to get any leftover cane without paying, without working."

I wrote and wrote; and it seemed that he was beginning to respect me. But I didn't know what he really thought of me.

"Now you must listen; let me read out to you everything that you have just told me. Eh, what's *Bapak's* name?"

"Trunodongso, Ndoro."

I stopped a moment on hearing that name. My grandfather had once warned me against peasants who use the name Truno. Such people, he said, are usually quick-tempered, especially when young. And sometimes they are even quicker-tempered in their old age. People choose that name hoping they will be able to maintain the spirit of their youth, to keep their strength and health right to the end. And, said my grandfather, such people usually study the martial arts before they marry. I didn't know whether he was right or not.

"So Trunodongso is your name. Good, let me read this to you."

I read out in Javanese what I had written and he nodded at the end of each sentence.

"This will be printed in the newspapers. All the clever and important people up there will read it. Perhaps Tuan Besar Governor-General, bupatis, residents, controllers, all of them. They will investigate all this. They will then know that there is a farmer named Trunodongso who is being forced from his land and his paddy, and is recovering only fifteen perak for each bahu that is rented by the sugar mill."

"Wah, Ndoro." He freed his hand from its polite clasp, ready to protest. "It's not like that," he began.

"You're taking back what you've told me?"

"No, Ndoro, it's all true. But I am not the only one who has received only fifteen perak. That's all any of the farmers around here have received, Ndoro."

"Everyone?"

"Everyone, except the village officials."

"How much did they get?"

"No one knows, Ndoro. But we do know that none of them are complaining. Never!"

"But people have the right not to rent their land if that's what they want."

"Yes. That is my situation, Ndoro, I don't want to rent out my land but every day I'm threatened, taunted, insulted. Now they threaten that the lane to my house will be closed off. If you want to get to your house and land, they say, you'll have to fly. They have already closed the channels bringing water to my paddy fields. I couldn't farm the paddy, so I had to rent it out."

This kind of thing was something I had never come across before. I wrote everything down. Trunodongso went on and on. All that he had been unable to say for so long was now poured out to me. I was no longer noting down just words, but the fate of who knows how many thousands, how many tens of thousands of peasant farmers like him. Perhaps this was the fate of all the sugar region's farmers. And he was not facing just Europeans, but Natives too: village officials, civil officials, the factory officials, including Sastro Kassier no doubt. My note-taking became even more enthusiastic. And Trunodongso became even more open with me.

A girl appeared, carrying a bamboo basket, walking towards a well beside that bamboo house. She pulled up the water using a bamboo scoop and started washing some clothes in an earthenware dish.

"Is that your daughter?" I asked.

He nodded.

"How many children do you have altogether?"

"Five, Ndoro. Two boys—they're out hoeing in the field now. The others are girls."

"Five. May I come in and have a look around Bapak's house?" I asked politely.

"Please come in, but it's very dirty."

I went inside the house. There were no windows. There was no cow or buffalo inside, but a tethering post standing in the corner indicated that a large animal had lived with the family at some other time or other.

"Where's the cow, Pak?"

"What's the use of a cow if you have no paddy, Ndoro? I've sold it."

There was no furniture except for a big bamboo bench and a kerosene lamp hanging from a bamboo pole. In the corner lay a hoe with lumps of fresh dirt clinging to it.

I thanked God that this quick-tempered farmer had been restored to the original Trunodongso, friendly, generous with his smiles, polite, and humble, no longer hiding evil feelings.

"Where's your wife, Pak?"

"Just left for the market, Ndoro."

I called to the little girl doing the washing. She ran to her father. Her eyes were tired, as though she had never had her proper fill of dreams—or perhaps because she had ringworm.

"What are you cooking today."

"Depends what Ma brings home, Ndoro, from the market," she answered, looking into her father's eyes.

"Look, I want to eat here tonight, yes; would you like to cook for me?"

Once more she quizzed her father with her sleepy eyes. Her father answered with a little bow of the head. Her voice was very, very polite: "Of course, Ndoro, I would be very happy to cook for Ndoro, but it's sure to taste terrible. A village child, remember, that's what I am."

"So we'll eat together tonight. How many altogether? Seven?"

"Then I must get some firewood," Trunodongso excused himself. "But Ndoro won't be ashamed to eat here?"

How happy was my heart to feel this family was beginning to lose its suspicion of me. I added quickly: "Is the market far from here?"

"No, Ndoro, it's quite close," answered Piah, the little girl. I knew in fact that the market was near Tulangan.

"Here is some money. Go and buy something. It's up to you what you cook," and I handed Piah two coins.

Once more the child looked up at her father. Trunodongso glanced around, pretending not to see. I put my bag down on the bench and went outside the house.

I felt a happiness blooming in my breast. I drew the free air deep into my lungs and threw out my two arms like a *garuda* about

166

to fly into the sky. What Kommer had said indeed seemed true: If you're willing to pay a little attention, a whole new continent arises, with mountains and rivers, islands and waterways. I will stay upon this new continent for a while longer. Columbus was not the only person to discover a new continent. So too have I.

I strolled around outside the house. At the back, clothes were drying—clean rags, really. And he was a farmer with five bahu of his own land, including three bahu of first-class paddy fields! If he'd been able to refuse surrendering his dry fields, why hadn't he been able to refuse handing over his paddy? His remaining dry fields were the last bastion of his livelihood. He had to defend it to the end. If he didn't, his whole family could be turned into vagabonds.

The air streaming through the thickets of trees was truly refreshing. The freshness of the air was present, but also the staleness of life—a continent with great mountain peaks, deep chasms.

A drain carrying the dirty water from the well wound aimlessly about; ducks were scratching in the mud looking for worms. Under a bush, three chicks fought over who was the eldest. A pregnant cat—yellow-colored—slept in the sun on a pile of old leaves. A row of banana trees, not one of which had an upright trunk, leaned sleepily to one side. In the distance, Trunodongso was cutting down a tree with his machete. He chopped it up and piled the wood together in the middle of the thicket.

As I moved farther away from the house, I could see more closely the nature of the tidily farmed corn and sweet-potato fields. The border between the back-yard garden and the fields proper was marked by a row of coffee trees, thick with fruit, and protected by the umbrella of closely planted coconut palms. It seemed that this family could live off their own fields—except for clothes and sugar.

Trunodongso had disappeared into the house carrying a hand of bananas. No smoke came from the kitchen yet. At the edge of the field, where it met the mill's cane, I found two of Trunodongso's sons hoeing the ground. They stopped working as soon as they saw me and laid down their hoes. They showed me great respect, yet were also obviously surprised and afraid. More than that: suspicious.

"Are you Pak Truno's sons?"

"Yes, Ndoro." They took off their bamboo hats and threw

them on the ground. They were aged sixteen and fourteen. There were no pictures of Queen Wilhelmina back in their house—neither had finished primary school.

"This is the border with the factory's cane?"

"Yes, Ndoro."

"Aren't they suspicious of you two if any cane goes missing?"

The two of them consulted with their eyes. I saw suspicion in those consultations, and fear.

"No, I'm not from the factory," I said. Still they didn't seem to believe, and were afraid. "I'm staying at your house at the moment. Later on we'll eat together." They glanced back and forth at each other again; then without answering dropped their gaze to their feet.

"You've never been accused of stealing cane?" I asked again.

They shot a look at me from the corners of their eyes, then their eyes consulted once more.

"Don't really know, Ndoro," the eldest answered.

They were still suspicious and afraid; that's how all farmers felt towards nonfarmers. The anonymous pamphlet that my ex-iled teacher Magda Peters gave me had said: The peasant farmers of Java were afraid of all outsiders, because their experiences over the centuries had shown them that outsiders—individuals or groups—would thieve everything they owned. These two young boys, with hoe in hand, sickle at their feet, were afraid of me for no other reason than because I was not one of them. Because my clothes were not the kind they wore.

What that pamphlet said was exactly right. A European had written it. He knew about the Javanese peasants. And I was just now discovering this continent. I was now witnessing that bottom point in their lives: being under the sway of fear and suspicion.

If one day they should cross the limits of their fear and suspicion—so that brochure said—this group of people living un-der God's sun, who aren't used to thinking rationally, will rise up in an explosion of blind fury; they will run amok. They could explode individually or in a group. And their targets would be anyone who was not one of them, who wasn't a peasant farmer. Such indeed was the condition of these pitiable beings who had never known the learning of the world: In no time at all their fury would be suppressed by the army, and they would be broken forever. For three hundred years! So that anyone from whatever group who can humor and capture their hearts they will follow—in religion, to the battlefield, or to annihilation.

I remembered the pamphlet's words well, and so as not to arouse any more fear in these boys' hearts, I moved away. I walked back towards the house, thinking to myself along the way: Perhaps if I had not come and shown my sympathy to Trunodongso, he might have wielded his machete, cutting down whomever he could. The pamphlet had also said: They would run amok not really in self-defense, nor to attack or to take revenge, but only because they no longer knew what else to do once their last opportunity of life had been stolen.

That pamphlet's author, Anonymous, I had to admit, was very knowledgeable. It was clear that the peasants themselves did not understand their own condition. But in that other corner of the world, in the Netherlands, people did know; they knew exactly what the situation was. They even understood the psychology of the peasantry as a class. And all this was in a pamphlet written by a Dutchman living in the Netherlands. It was true what Jean Marais had said: You study the languages of Europe to understand Europe. Through Europe you can learn to understand your own people. To study the languages of Europe does not mean you cannot speak to your own people, and that you should speak only to Europeans.

I went on towards the bamboo house. It was not only from Europe that so much could be learned! This modern age had provided many breasts to suckle me—from among the Natives themselves, from Japan, China, America, India, Arabia, from all the peoples on the face of this earth. They were the mother wolves that gave me life to become a builder of Rome! Is it true you will build a Rome? Yes, I answered myself. How? I don't know. In humility, I realized I am a child of all nations, of all ages, past and present. Place and time of birth, parents, all are coincidence: such things are not sacred.

Back in the house I went on with my writing. But the first sentence was not what I had been thinking as I walked back: "And evil too came from all nations, from all ages."

I wrote and wrote until all that I wished to write was finished. I flopped my body down upon the bamboo sleeping bench and fell asleep, forgetting all that had been happening around me.

Who knows how long I slept. Indeed I hadn't had enough

sleep the night before. I had been overcome by my passion to finish the notes about Surati. Shouting startled me and my eyes flew open, but I still lay there on the divan-bench.

"I only got five coins for the chicken. Not enough to buy any clothes for you, just some pants for your father."

Realizing that the voice was that of an adult woman, I quickly got up. No doubt it was Trunodongso's wife, home from the market. Her smallest daughters followed behind. On seeing me Truno's wife stopped in front of the house, bowed down again and again, then walked off around the side of the house to the back.

It appeared that Piah had begun cooking in the kitchen. I could smell the aroma of frying chicken. All of a sudden my stomach was calling out for food.

Now I could hear Piah speaking in low Javanese to her mama: "When will I get some clothes, Ma?"

I couldn't hear the answer. I took out the gold pocket watch my mother had given me for a wedding present. It was four o'clock, and my stomach was making wild demands.

Trunodongso came outside to the bench and invited me in to eat. He apologized for not daring to awaken me earlier. Inside there was a woven bamboo mat with the food laid out on it. There was only one plate. The curry was in an earthenware bowl and the rice in a bamboo basket. Ground chili and dried fish lay crushed in the earthen bowl. The stone pestle stood in the bowl on top of the chilied fish.

"Please, Ndoro."

"Let us eat together, Pak, with all the children and Ma Trunodongso."

"It's all right like this, Ndoro; there's only one plate."

"Then we can all eat from banana leaves."

An argument started. Finally Trunodongso gave in. Everybody was mobilized to eat together off banana leaves. More food was brought out from the kitchen. I did not regret doing this, even though I knew it was torture for them to eat with me. They were so afraid of taking any of the chicken, especially the fried chicken. It turned out to be as hard as wood. So then I knew: This family had never cooked chicken before, not even the ones they owned themselves.

Seeing that they were hesitating to start, I finished my meal quickly and went for a stroll outside to get some fresh air.

After dinner the following conversation took place.

"If Bapak worked that land yourself, would you be much better off?"

For the first time Trunodongso laughed. "When my parents were still alive, heaps of paddy surrounded this house. There were many chickens and ducks. A few years before they died, the factory started pressuring them to give over the land. My father refused. Then the village chief came, then his second-in-command. My father still refused. Then the paddy-field water canals were blocked farther up, on factory land. There was no more water. My father—"

"Weren't the canals built by the farmers themselves? Not the factory?"

"Sure, Ndoro. I myself helped build them. A week it took, I remember it well. At the end of clearing my section of land there was a great pile of fallen leaves. There were many snakes—no less than seven."

"No one was bitten?"

"Ah, just little lizards really, Ndoro."

"How much were you paid?"

"Paid? No one paid us."

He liked to watch me write down his answers. And I was certainly not going to disappoint him. I would pour it all out in the newspapers. I could already guess that there would be a great commotion. Perhaps this man before me now would become the main figure in some great story about the farmers of the sugar-cane regions. He was becoming more and more interesting. The more marks I made on the paper, the more he trusted me, and the easier it became to enter his mind.

I recalled again my grandfather's warning about people with the name Truno. Such people, my grandfather told me, would fight the government or become rebel bandits. Uh! the names of Javanese! As a writer of newspaper advertisements, it was my view that if grandfather's words were true, the names that the Javanese took were no different than advertisements, whose messages were by no means truthful.

Very carefully I asked him: Did he like to fight?

171

"No," he said, "but indeed I did study martial arts when I was young." So he was a fighter; my grandfather's words were right. "Have you been involved in fights?" I asked.

His eyes narrowed, as if defending themselves from an attack. Realizing that the question had aroused his suspicion again, I quickly added that my grandfather had made me study martial arts too. I studied for three years before graduating. But, I said, I had never been in a real fight.

He listened to my story with eyes full of life—the narrowness disappeared. He was indeed a fighter. No wonder the factory people didn't dare any reckless attempt to throw him out.

I quickly turned the conversation away from fighting. He must not become suspicious again. Issue after issue emerged. I wrote and wrote. This person was interesting: Unlike other peasant farmers, he dared state his opinion, even though his approach was roundabout and he never went directly to the issue. And the more questions I asked him, the happier he was giving his answers. I thought he might have been a laborer in a town once. But I didn't ask.

"Might I stay here tonight?" I asked.

He was surprised at my request. I wanted to stay overnight so I could study a little about how he lived. As expected, out came excuse after excuse. But I was unyielding. With great reluctance he finally gave his agreement. His youngest child was sent off with a letter to Mama in Tulangan.

So it was that I stayed the night.

That night the fireplace was lit, as was the custom if you kept livestock. Smoke filled the windowless space. My lungs were hot and tight. As the evening wore on, the silence was broken by the croaking of the tree frogs. I was given a place on the edge of the big sleeping bench. The other children, boys and girls, slept on my left. Their breathing seemed to speak to each other; they took turns in coughing. The fire finally went out. Then the mosquitoes attacked from above, the bedbugs from below. Ya Allah, how peaceful they all were in their sleep, and I could not even keep my eyes closed in my torment.

For how many hundreds, thousands of years, generation after generation, have they slept like this? Human beings with great resilience, great strength. Every other moment, my hand moved to get rid of a mosquito or bedbug. My eyes still wouldn't close.

Slowly my irritation increased. I sat up in the dark. But the mosquitoes and bedbugs took no notice of my irritation; they were just as bloodthirsty as ever, as if they were the only beings who had to live. How high was the price I had to pay so that no one might ever accuse me again of not knowing my own people! Perhaps if I had not given them shopping money, I would not have eaten at all that night. What did they really eat each day? I still didn't know.

I had just rested my head back on the sheaf of dried paddy stalks when I heard singing outside the hut. Who would be singing on this insect-ridden night? The voice seemed to hesitate. Before even one verse was finished, I heard the scrape of a door being opened quietly. I listened carefully. I could make out the shuffle of a long sarong on the floor. Obviously Ma Trunodongso. Then another scrape of an opening door. So husband and wife were up and going outside.

They wouldn't be going out to relieve themselves. It was the midnight village song that called them. This was interesting material for my story.

Before I knew it, I was groping my way through the darkness to the door. I must add to my knowledge about them. Not long after, there was another sound of a door scraping open, but this time it was my hand that did the opening. I was now outside the house, with the mosquitoes but without the bedbugs. A black starless sky. My eyes tried to locate any human movement. Nothing but blackness. Where had the husband and wife gone? I tried to remember from what direction the singing had come. My arms and legs groped in that direction. I reckoned I had reached the jackfruit trees. The singing had long since died away.

"Impossible." I heard a warning spoken emphatically.

There were several people under the jackfruit tree—at least three. The voice dropped to a soft whisper. Of course I was drawn in that direction.

"The priyayi staying with you is a factory spy for sure!" I heard. "And you haven't the courage to kill him."

"No, in the name of Allah, he is not a spy."

"He's Sastro Kassier's family!"

"Even so, he is not like the factory people; he's not arrogant like them. From Surabaya, writes for a newspaper, he says. He's

173

going to write for the papers about how we've been cheated all this time."

"Rubbish. As if you didn't know what they're like. Kill him and get it over with."

"No blood shall be spilled in my house," came the voice of Trunodongso's wife. "Factory spies aren't like that."

"Very well, I will tell all this to the *Kyai*. Perhaps tomorrow I'll be back again."

I rushed back to the house while they were still talking. My hands and feet began to grope around again. Now it felt as if the house was far away, another mile or so. They must not find me outside.

Suddenly my feet slipped into a drain. I must be on the wrong path. The foul-smelling drain mud became my second layer of clothes. I must be near the well. I had indeed come the wrong way. The humiliation of it! For the first time in my life I had to bathe at night. And for the first time in my life I had to wash my own clothes, in the darkness and the cold.

With my teeth rattling, I finally reached my sleeping-bench. I had no dry clothes. I lay down but now pulled the bedbug-ridden mat over me as a blanket.

Even so I did not feel any more tormented than before. Rather I felt thankful to God: Trunodongso and his wife's trust in me was a far greater blessing, overcoming the cold and torment.

In the morning, wearing only my underclothes, I washed my pants and shirt again and dried them. Then I wrote and wrote. It was clear they were involved in some kind of conspiracy. My guess was that they were banding together to fight against the factory. Perhaps I was mistaken. I must stay here perhaps another day.

Once again I strolled out the back to get to know my new field of action better.

That night I heard the singing again. I awoke and waited for the husband and wife to leave. The sky wasn't as dark as the night before. The stars lit up the earth. The two figures before me made their way quickly to the jackfruit thicket. This time I didn't dare go so close. From behind the bushes I could make out the silhouettes of several people. They didn't stay long, but left for who knows where.

I returned to the house. For a long time I tried to light the kerosene lamp. When I succeeded, I discovered that Trunodong-so's two sons had also gone. So too had their machete and sickle, which usually leaned against the wall. Only their hoes were left, lying side by side near one of the roof supports.

That morning only the smaller children were at home. Little Piah quickly brought water into the kitchen, aided by her younger sisters. I befriended her while she cooked, and she became restless as a result. I fetched a hoe from its place and went out the back. In bare feet, chafed by the cold, dirty ground, I began to hoe where the boys had finished yesterday. After only five minutes I had to stop. I was panting. I was ashamed of myself. Those boys were far younger than I, and they could hoe the ground for four hours without stopping.

There were no witnesses to my condition. How embarrassed and ashamed I would be if someone saw me out of breath like this. I began to hoe the ground again, but this time more slowly. Then little Piah arrived.

"Ndoro, don't work like that, you'll get dirty, you'll fall ill. There's coffee ready back at the house. Let me carry the hoe."

I was lucky the offer of a drink arrived, otherwise I would have been obliged to continue that voluntary but murderous work.

"Don't keep on hoeing, Ndoro," forbade Piah politely. "If you blister your hand, you won't be able to write."

I didn't even have a blister yet, but already I was unable to write; my hands shook uncontrollably. Still I had now, at least once in my life, hoed the ground. Clearly I would never be a farmer like them.

That afternoon I took my leave. I considered that I had enough notes. But the main thing was that I could not live any longer in these conditions. I now understood that these people were far stronger than I. They had the strength of iron; they were tempered by suffering. It was strange. Why should such a class of people, made so strong by their suffering, just keep on suffering?

Trunodongso stood bowing with hands folded before him and said how he regretted not being able to show me the kind of hospitality that was proper. His eyes were red from lack of sleep.

"If Bapak is ever in Wonokromo, come to our house. Make sure you visit us," I told him.

The whole family escorted me. I groped in my pocket. There was still one rupiah and fifteen cents, and I gave it to little Piah.

"Don't forget to visit us at Wonokromo. Look for the house of Nyai Ontosoroh. Remember it, Pak: *Nyai On-to-so-roh.*"

His wife's and sons' eyes were also red.

Now only Trunodongso was left to escort me. He carried my bag respectfully, as if he were my servant. In the middle of the cane I stopped and said to him: "Pak Truno, by Allah, I am not a spy." He glanced at me for a moment, then bowed his head. He must have guessed that I had heard the conversation on that dark night.

"I respect Pak Truno and all those suffering the same fate. Through my writings I will try to lighten your burden. More than that is beyond me. Let's hope my help may produce some results. Troubles such as these can't always be overcome with machete and anger. It's all right, go home, get some sleep, you're exhausted. Here, let me carry my bags."

He handed them over. I walked along without looking back. Yet somehow I could tell he was still standing there. All of a sudden he shouted out and ran up to me: "Forgive me, Ndoro; may I ask what is Ndoro's name?"

9

On our tenth day in Tulangan, Kommer arrived with a cut of venison. His face was tanned and he looked happy.

Mama went out to meet him. I still had to add a few lines more about Trunodongso. I paid no heed to the chattering of the newspaperman, but the sound of his voice was loud, joyful, full of hope.

After finishing my writing, I went out to meet him.

"How's your panther, Mr. Kommer?"

"Haven't caught it yet. I'm going to have to go home first. They'll pull up the traps themselves," he answered. "What can one do? The paper is also important."

I spoke again. "You look very well,"

"Nyai also looks very well," he answered, "but you seem a little pale yourself."

"He has spent too much time inside, Mr. Kommer," said Nyai.

"What a pity," said Kommer. "If all you do is write, Mr. Minke, life will be short. You must engage in some outdoor activities as well. It's a shame you didn't want to come hunting with me. Perhaps you have never seen how a deer runs along, jumping and constantly turning to look back to glimpse its hunter. Its beautiful many-branched antlers can't save its skin and its life. How beautiful they are, those antlers, especially if the deer is running with its head thrust towards the sky. A futile beauty: Those antlers prevent it from hiding in the brush and running through the jungle. Because of the antlers, Mr. Minke, only because of its antlers, that animal is cursed with the fate of having to live always in the open, on the plains, and is therefore open also to the hunter's bullets. Just because of its beautiful antlers!"

"Perhaps you are engaging in some satire."

"If you want to take it that way, you may. Look, the beauty of your life is your writing. So you seclude yourself in your room, and that indeed is a suicidal kind of activity."

I laughed disparagingly.

"I'm totally serious, Mr. Minke. At the moment you are still very, very young. You are healthy; you've never been ill. If you keep on staying indoors like this, you will lose much of life's richness."

"Well, as far as that goes—"

"Five years indoors like this, stuck in your room, will use up the health and strength of ten years. What a pity if all of a sudden you feel dried up and worn out."

I told him how I'd finished two articles, one of them being the best thing I'd ever written.

"I'm glad to hear that, Mr. Minke; may I read that one?"

"You can read it in printed form later. But you are welcome to read the other one if you like."

I handed him the manuscript of "Nyai Surati" and watched his face. Mama went out the back.

"You can comment on it now too, but don't mention any of the names I've used," I warned him.

The manuscript was quite long. Kommer had not finished it by the time Mama came back with food. He was submerged in the story. Letting out a great breath, he placed it down on the table carefully, as if it would break, stared at me with shining eyes, and commented: "It's becoming clearer from your writing."

I was afraid he might mention Surati's name; but he mentioned no name.

"What do you think?" I asked coolly.

"Your unique characteristics are becoming more and more evident. It's true what people say, that you're going further and further in the direction of humanism, expanding its scope. If people like us say 'expanding its scope' then you must look for the aspect that isn't mentioned." He didn't explain what that unmentioned aspect was. "Your writings cry out to people's sense of humanity, rejecting barbarism, cheating, libel, and weakness. You dream of human beings who are strong and whose humanity is strong also. Indeed, sir, only when all people are strong like that will we have true fraternity. You are truly a child of the French Revolution. As long as you retain these personal characteristics of yours . . ."

Mama listened with great seriousness, not involving herself. I saw Kommer sweep his gaze across to Mama, inviting her opinion. His request wasn't answered, but, as though he'd received some encouragement, the journalist continued: "Have you studied many of the French writers?"

"No, sir."

"That's why your outlook on life is so heavy, so serious, just like Multatuli. You have no sense of humor. If you started reading the French writers, you might be able to change."

"So the piece isn't any good?"

"Good, very good indeed. There's no grounds for doubting how good it is. I'm talking about this outlook of yours. No humor, no sense of fun, heavy like a one-ton weight. You take life and mankind too seriously; you are tense, as though you'd never experienced any pleasure, never played."

"Is it wrong to be serious?"

"No, not at all. But you don't mix with enough different kinds of people, from different classes. This constant tension and seriousness could kill you. Have you never had any interest in the lighter side of life?"

"Yes, Minke, you're always gloomy and serious, Child," Mama intervened.

"Yes, Nyai, gloomy. That's exactly the right word," Kommer flashed.

"I haven't seen any happy side to life yet," I defended myself. Now the newspaper man listened with his full attention.

"The situation is still not very happy for many people, Mr.

Kommer, and that story is about maltreatment, oppression. Where is the light side of it? If I agreed with that kind of treatment of other people, perhaps I could see something funny in the grimaces of others' suffering," I went on. "But I'm not among those who oppress others, Mr. Kommer."

"True, it's all true. You've brought it all to life within you as it has brought you to life. You have become one with your material. That is a matter of intellect and emotion. You are right on every point, isn't that so, Nyai?"

"Ah, I don't understand this sort of thing." Mama was washing her hands of the whole thing.

"Life is a matter of balance, Mr. Minke. A person who concerns himself only with the light side of things is a madman, but someone who is interested only in suffering is sick."

"So you count me among the sick?"

"If you keep on this way—yes. You will lose your resilience, your adroitness will be suffocated by all the suffering you concern yourself with. It would be best if you learned to change, if I may make a suggestion."

Kommer seemed so sure of his words, as if there were no other possibility.

"He only needs a change of atmosphere, Mr. Kommer," Mama interrupted. "I think you exaggerate a bit."

The journalist was silenced by her reprimand. He turned to face Mama, and listened intently.

"If he sees suffering about him, then it's only proper and natural that it colors his writing. He sees all those who suffer as his friends, and all injustice as his enemy. People don't have to see merriment and suffering as being in some kind of balance. Isn't reality itself more real than anybody's opinion about reality?"

A debate then ensued. All in Dutch. Mama proved to know a lot about life. As a child, a latecomer to life, I listened more than I took part. Abruptly the debate stopped. Kommer's question came at me like the point of a cutlass: "You write quite well. I think everyone would agree with me. This last article of yours is your best piece so far. If you continue like this, you won't be able to write stories. You will be making speeches, and you will stop being a writer. Do you want to be a writer or a speechmaker?"

That question hurt me greatly, partly because I couldn't understand his argument properly.

"Why does he have to choose between these two things?" Mama protested. "He has the right to grow and develop. He has the right not to choose between those two things. He is still young; at the very least he still has twenty years in which to develop. Have you been more successful in your career than Minke?"

"Don't get me wrong, Nyai." Kommer began to soften his line. "Minke is the hope of his people. What other Native is there like him? If Minke doesn't accept this challenge, it will be difficult later for him to possess the resilience, the toughness he'll need. He'll be quickly discouraged and won't finish the work he began. Look, Nyai, even in this piece I have just read, already he has begun, although in a disguised manner, to speak out on behalf of his people—"

"Now *you're* making a speech," Mama said.

"What do the Natives hope for from me? Nothing. But much is expected of Minke, with all his talents—too much. I have already urged him to acquaint himself with his people and their lives, a source of material that will never dry up. With this latest piece, he has started on that road. Isn't that so, Minke?"

"Yes," I ansered.

"Nyai, if Mr. Minke here is unable to see the happier side of life, how is he going to be able to show his people what happier future they might build? Suffering is a narrow window through which to look on life, Nyai. And there are many ways to overcome it. Without some joy, some merriment, even in the defeat of suffering, people will only go round and round in circles inside that suffering."

Mama was silent. She seemed to be groping, not knowing what to say.

"Twenty years, Nyai. We have both experienced it ourselves—twenty years is not all that long. Twenty years can pass by and see a person no cleverer than he was before. There are many who become more and more unable to learn from their experiences. These are indeed harsh words, these words I direct at Mr. Minke, and also to myself. But they are better than the flattery so generously handed out by Maarten Nijman. Minke here has been flattered too often. But the seeds that will grow within him, Nyai, where will he get them if not from those of his friends who are honest with him?"

"In twenty years, Tuan, he will have had much greater success, I am sure, than you, Mr. Kommer."

I turned the other way, embarrassed to hear my mother-in-law defend me and boast about me like that. She would rather see me victorious than see the truth.

"That is exactly what I hope will happen. Let me explain. Recently there has been a lot of talk in elite circles about those letters of Kartini, which have been read again for the umpteenth time before the conference of the League Against Moral Corruption in the Netherlands. She talks about the coming of the modern era in Europe, which she only knows second-hand. But in these Indies there is only the darkness of night. The modern era? Ha! Not a single spot of light is yet to be found. The Natives live in pitch darkness. In their ignorance, they make themselves the laughing stock of everyone for their stupidity. One of the lines of her letters—as I understand it from what others have reported—reads: How happy people would be if they could sleep for who knows how long and then wake up to find that the modern era had already arrived. Nyai, many people have interpreted this sentence as a sign that she has given up, lost all hope. And in my opinion, she has indeed given up."

"Now it's you, Mr. Kommer, who have become the speech-maker."

"Indeed I am a giver of speeches. I speak a lot, Nyai, in many places."

"But you too write like Minke."

"True, Nyai."

"Nah, well then, what is wrong with doing both things?"

"It would be a dangerous thing if Mr. Minke made speeches in his writings instead of confining them to his conversations. Mr. Minke doesn't seem to be as clever in nor as inclined to talking as me. And a speech-dominated story is the very worst kind of writing."

"What's all this got to do with Kartini?"

"What's it got to do with Kartini, Nyai? Kartini has given up hope. She no longer knows what to do for her people. So she feels tired, because she always sees suffering and suffering alone. She longs to sleep, and then to wake up and enjoy the bright modern era. The modern era is not being built in people's sleep, by their dreams. Mr. Minke, I, and many others—and indeed your own people themselves—do not hope that it will be like that."

"You deliver a clever speech," Nyai praised him.

"I will do anything, Nyai, if it will be of use. And whatever else might be said about this Kartini, she is the only Native girl to speak out like this, in her letters and articles."

"Child," Nyai said finally, "you have to decide what is best for yourself."

"Mr. Kommer," I began, "I don't really understand what you're getting at. What exactly is it you object to in my writings?"

"The piece is very good; I said so just now. But there are signs that you are turning your story into a speech. And that tendency will become more prominent in your writings if you are not warned. In these Indies there has been what we might call criticism. Criticism can be rejected, but it has to be listened to first, reflected upon. If it isn't necessary to reject it, then it can be taken as a suggestion. No one need be angry just because they have been criticized."

That was the first time that I had come across what Kommer called criticism.

Lunch brought a halt to the conversation. Afterwards listlessness conquered us all. Kommer's enthusiasm for speech-making dwindled away. He sat sleepily in his chair, but didn't want to go home either; he enjoyed displaying his knowledge, and the opportunity to sit near Mama. As the day wore on our heads became heavier from the heat and humidity.

In a voice that had lost its spirit and enthusiasm, Kommer began again: "A good author, Mr. Minke, should be able to provide his readers with some joy, not a false joy, but some faith that life is beautiful. While suffering is man-made, and not some natural disaster, then it can surely be resisted by men. Give hope to your readers, to your fellow countrymen. Haven't I already advised you to learn to write in Malay or Javanese? Give your people the best that you are capable of."

"I will not forget, Mr. Kommer."

"Between my two suggestions there are reciprocal connections."

"I still need time to understand all of what you've said."

"Of course, and you are still young, with plenty of time for that."

"That's why I have brought him here, Mr. Kommer," said Mama, "so he can get some fresh air. A new atmosphere, a new environment, new ideas, a new vigor. It's clear he has found much new material."

"Exactly, Nyai, new material. But the way he approaches the material is exactly as before. Pessimistic. Suffering and gloom are his horizon. But the horizon itself is the base of the sky, where the sun sinks and then rises again, the place where boats and ships disappear from sight, and also the place where they emerge into view as they approach the shore."

"Mama, what Mr. Kommer says is beginning to make sense to me. But I need to think about it calmly."

"Yes, Mr. Minke, you are an admirer of the French Revolution; you want to see human dignity given its proper place. If you look at people from one point of view, that of suffering alone, you will lose the many other aspects of humanity. Reflection upon suffering alone will only give rise to revenge, revenge and nothing else."

"We're on holidays," Mama suggested. "Why don't we talk about something else, something happier?"

"Nothing happy has happened to me just lately, Nyai. I didn't catch the panther I wanted. Tomorrow I've got to go back to Surabaya. When are you going home, Nyai?"

"I think it will be after you go back."

The conversation stagnated. Kommer began to lose his sharpness. He had already yawned three times. I myself had just yawned for the second time. Perhaps also it was because he was such a sleeper that he hadn't caught that panther, and hadn't caught Mama's heart either. He could fall asleep in front of Mama on the train, precisely at the time he was hoping she would say yes to his proposal. Maybe he could even fall asleep in the middle of giving a speech.

"If you're already sleepy," Mama prodded him, "you—"

"It's better I go home straight away, Nyai, Mr. Minke."

We went with him out to his horse. Then he rode slowly out of Tulangan.

"He was just showing off what he thinks he knows," Mama growled, "like a little child showing off her doll."

"Perhaps there is some truth in his words, Ma."

"Of course. But it was the way he put them across, Child, his

184

excessive enthusiasm, his pride . . . that wasn't his heart's voice. He wanted to put his knowledge on display. Perhaps he doesn't really believe what he says."

"He is a good man, Ma," I said.

"Yes, he is a good man. That help he gave us was without any self-interest; at least I hope that's the case. But that speech of his just now, there was self-interest there."

"What self-interest, Ma?" I asked like a whining child.

"Are you bored with staying here?"

"Perhaps Panji Darman has arrived back in Surabaya."

"So you do really intend to leave me?"

"Whatever else happens, Ma, I hope that you will give me a little sister-in-law."

"Hush," and Nyai quickly walked back into the house.

Sastro Kassier's house was usually busy with the sounds of children. It was three o'clock in the afternoon and this time no sounds could be heard. Sitting in the front parlor by myself, gazing at the two portraits of Her Majesty, Queen Wilhelmina, I thought about what Kommer had said. He always ordered and insisted, suppressing me and robbing me of my freedom. I knew his intentions were good—not everything he wished from me was wrong. Perhaps indeed he was right about everything. But why did he have to push his ideas so aggressively? Why was he more interested in bragging about his own greatness and in flooding those around him with his enthusiasm? So he can control them? *Must* and *Don't* are his banners, no matter what the particular idea—as if there were no other point of view. Earlier, when I had only known him a little, and superficially at that, I had been attracted to him. I saw him as a man of decision, and without rival. But the more I got to know him, the more my feelings changed. They were no longer sympathetic, indeed the opposite. Even Mama didn't want to continue the debate with him.

How different he was from Sarah and Miriam de la Croix. Even Magda Peters had not gone around *ordering, insisting*. Jean Marais, who was such a gentle and shy man, was not like that, except for the one time he pressed me about using Malay. And that was probably a result of Kommer's influence.

My father and elder brother were exactly the same as Kommer, full of *musts* and *don'ts*. I smiled: Perhaps that was how they were, those backward people who had never been touched by the spirit of the French Revolution? Men who had become comfort-able with ordering around their wives and children and their neighbors and their relatives who had no power? My smile developed into a laugh. I was pleased with this idea of mine—an idea that was by no means certain to be right.

Yes, perhaps Kommer was right this time. Very likely so. But with so many *musts* and *don'ts* he should entertain no hopes of getting close to Mama's heart.

Why was Jean Marais so easily influenced by him, trying to coerce me to learn Malay? Such a polite and shy person. I tried to recollect what he had said that had hurt me so much. All I recalled was that old reminder of his: Be just and fair, starting with your thoughts. I have always tried to think and act justly, my heart assured me. Have a go now at weighing things up again, as if Marais were testing your true inner thoughts. You still spend more time weighing up the good and bad of other people. What about yourself? Have you really considered all this fairly?

Is it true that you write for Dutch readers when you don't have the slightest debt to them? Just as your beloved Mother says?

I am about to start to learn Malay, I answered. That cannot be achieved in just a day.

Are you absolutely sure that you have never forced and pressured people into doing things, nor gone around forbidding them to do things just because you liked it, as some kind of luxury or enjoyment? Like Kommer?

No, never. Really, never.

If it is true you are an admirer of the French Revolution, why were you so offended when a farmer like Trunodongso spoke in low Javanese to you?

I was ashamed in my heart and unable to answer. And I admitted it: The spirit and ideals of the French Revolution still had not cleared away my old attitudes as I lived my day-to-day life. It was still just something I'd read about, no more than an ornament to my thoughts.

Good, you have admitted that. Now, if a Native starts to talk to you in high Javanese will you advise him to switch to low Javanese? Ha, you can't answer. You are still not able to give up the comforts and pleasures that are yours as an inheritance from your ancestors—rulers over your own Native fellow countrymen.

You're a cheat! The ideals of Liberty, Equality, and Fraternity of the French Revolution?—you have betrayed them for the benefits of that inheritance. It is only the ideal of Liberty that lives within you, and then it is only freedom for yourself, no more. Don't you feel ashamed that you dare call yourself an admirer of the French Revolution?

I shriveled up in shame. Yes, I had to admit it: I was still unable to give up the benefits of my heritage. When someone spoke to me in low Javanese, I felt my rights had been stolen away. On the other hand, if people spoke to me in high Javanese, I felt I was among those chosen few, placed on some higher plane, a god in a human's body, and these pleasures from my heritage caressed me.

You are not being honest as an educated person should be, Minke.

Those peasants addressed me that way of their own free will.

They do not do it of their own free will. They behave that way because of their experiences over the ages, as the slaves of both great and little kings. They would be flattened flush to the ground if they themselves did not flatten their bodies napkinlike before their kings—indeed they had been forced to prostrate themselves that way. If that is how they act towards you, a fellow Native, they will behave the same way before other peoples too. Then why should you be offended when Natives abase themselves before the Europeans? You have not learned and practiced justice; it is not yet part of your character.

One can't throw away all those benefits and pleasures in just one go, I rebutted.

You are learning to know more about your people. You now have a little knowledge about them: How you yourself actually help to enslave your own people through the Javanese language. And then you pretend you want to defend Trunodongso through your writings in the newspapers.

I will defend him.

Do you really want to defend him?

Yes. Truly, I do, by Allah.

Mama says: God is always on the side of those who win.

And so people must struggle to be victors, and thus God will bless their efforts. When Mama speaks like that, she is speaking in the name of her own experiences. She did not accept defeat. But in the final confrontation with Europe she was defeated; God has not yet blessed her struggles.

So now you want to defend them from oppression, using Dutch, your language? Ha, you can't answer. Then they are right: You must begin to write in Malay, Minke; Malay does not hold within it any oppressive character. It is in accord with the aims of the French Revolution.

"Are you daydreaming, Tuan?"

I was startled. Djumilah moved my manuscript away to make room for banana-coconut custard and some thick black coffee. I answered with a laugh and nodded my thanks. I put the manuscript away.

"Perhaps you're thinking of someone, heh?" she jibed me. "Is there someone you've met here in Tulangan?"

"I've met so many people, many indeed," I answered.

"Thanks be to God," and she went out to the back again. I watched Djumilah as she left, a lioness without strength, except to roar. Truly different from the wife of Trunodongso—without needing to roar she goes side by side with her husband, as a friend in life, and as an ally as well. Different too from Mother, who knows only devotion and doing good. Different again from educated Kartini, who longs for the arrival of the modern age. Different also from Mama, an independent human being—the essence of the ideal of Liberty from the French Revolution—who sees the modern era as containing no blessings beyond the advances in tools and technique.

From among all those women it is Mama who most closely resembles the ideal of the French Revolution.

And you yourself? You too are a free human being, like Nyai, but you are not trying to live up to the ideals of Equality and Fraternity. Wasn't the revolution over more than a hundred years ago? What do you say now? More than one hundred years have passed!

Yes, there is very little of these ideals within me. Jean Marais works towards his ideal of filling his life with his paintings, not just obtaining his livelihood from them. Why do I want to write? Just to be famous? Just to feel satisfied with myself? You are being unjust again, Minke. Does your search for your own satisfaction give you the right to fame? Unjust! Others work until they sweat blood, to the edge of death—and there is no fame for them. They may not even be sure of eating two meals a day.

And you are no different from others. You are no taller, no more to be honored than Trunodongso. That is, if you truly understand what the French Revolution was all about. What do you think now, Minke?

And I remembered Khouw Ah Soe. He was fulfilling his life.

And the Filipino Natives who had tried to oust the Spanish, they too had given substance to their lives. And they had fought back against the Americans as well.

Writing is obviously not just a means towards self-satisfaction. Writing must be a way of giving substance to your life, as Jean said. And I was happy: My story about Trunodongso would do that. I would publish it. No need to take notice of Kommer's opinions.

10

Stepping down onto the platform at Surabaya station, I asked Mama's permission to go straight to Nijman's office. In my bag were two manuscripts. One I thought was very good, the other perfect. Both contained eternal values, both were dedicated to eternity. I was most proud of the second article: A defense of all those suffering the same fate as Trunodongso. The world must be told how Java's farmers are being thrown off their rice lands—the most fertile lands with the best irrigation—by the sugar factories, and with the aid of the Native civil servants in colonial employ and of the village officials. If Multatuli had been here in Surabaya, I would have come to him and said: Teacher, today I begin to follow where you have trod before.

Today I am important.

All who have fallen from on high, I began my story about Trunodongso, *have been saved and then restored by the farmers: Kings, ministers, soldiers. And all the treading feet of men: They too have been borne on the backs of the farmers. . . .*

There had never been any fiction written about farmers. Mine was the first. People said I did not understand my own people. Just let them wait! Soon they would know.

At Nijman's offices the Pure-Blood boy invited me to go straight upstairs. Nijman stood and held out his hand: "It's been so long since you have been here. The readers have been waiting for another article from you."

I took out the article about Trunodongso. Proudly I handed it over to him. "Mr. Nijman, here are the results of my silence all this while."

He took it politely and asked if I would allow him to read it now. I nodded. He would be amazed by the advances I had made.

"Poetic!" He nodded very politely and went on reading.

He had never used that word before. Just one word, and I felt it was a measure of the article's worth.

I observed his face. He hadn't finished one page; the smile had disappeared. On the second page, his forehead wrinkled. Before he went on to the third page he raised his eyes and looked at me.

It could be no other way, Mr. Nijman; this is the first time you would have read such a story as this!

He went on again. His face was turning red. On the fifth page, he put the manuscript down. He took up his pipe and began to suck on it. He blew the smoke out slowly into the air. Then: "Do you remember the person who sat on the same chair as you now sit?"

"Of course: Khouw Ah Soe."

"Yes."

He didn't go on. He seemed to be groping for the right words. Why bring up Khouw Ah Soe? I became wary.

"Yes, Mr. Minke. All of a sudden I'm reminded of him. It seems you became friends with him after that meeting."

"I never met him again after that."

"True? As I read this, I get the feeling that you must have talked with him again."

His words came at me like accusations. What was the connection between Trunodongso and Khouw Ah Soe? My pride in the story was overshadowed by a new fear.

"The spirit of this story—your spirit, your enthusiasm—has influenced the story too much."

"Influenced it? How?" I asked anxiously.

He didn't answer, but asked instead: "What were you think-ing of when you wrote this?"

"What was I thinking of? The person about whom I was writing."

"A true character or just someone out of your imagination?"

"A real person."

"So you would dare to claim that all this here is more than just imagination? That it is factual?"

"Of course it is."

"You would dare guarantee that?"

"Yes, I would," I answered, once again the hero, my pride returned.

He said nothing more. He read the story again, starting from the beginning. I was still nervous about being connected that way to Khouw Ah Soe. That wouldn't happen, would it?

Nijman stopped reading and fell into thought.

Yes, he would be impressed by this—my best writing, perfect—a protest about the injustices suffered by who knows how many thousands of Trunodongsos. I would reveal to the world the conspiracy of blood-sucking vampires who were cheat-ing those illiterate farmers of their rents. Who could tell how many decades this deception had been going on?

Before reaching the end of the second page, Nijman raised his eyes again, looked at me very sharply, and asked: "You are the son-in-law of the late Mr. Mellema, yes? And what would your father-in-law think if he were still alive and saw what you have written here?"

My expectation that he would be impressed disappeared abruptly. On his face were signs of restrained fury.

"What's the connection with the late Mr. Mellema?"

"You yourself know, don't you, that he was the administra-tor of a sugar factory? You yourself have written: 'And who knows for how many decades this deception has been going on?' If it has only been twenty-five years, it means you have accused the late Mr. Mellema of carrying out such deceptions for at least four years."

My eyes almost popped out. Such a thing had never crossed my mind. Nijman's lips were still moving; his voice continued. "You have accused your father-in-law of being involved in a con-spiracy to defraud people of their rents. And you must know the implications of such a deception: Nyai Ontosoroh's company, Boederij Buitenzorg, was set up with money obtained from such conspiracies. Yes? Or wasn't that what you meant? Why are you silent? Do you still wish to say that all you have written is true? Not just fantasy?"

I was speechless. My mind worked faster and faster, but whatever I thought of, it was Mama's face that I saw.

"Good; what you have written here is not just fantasy," Nijman went on. His voice was soft but its lashes still hurt. "Could you prove these embezzlements if the appropriate officials demanded evidence from you?" He stared at me as though he would never blink again. "Or indeed is it your intention to publish a libel?"

"No! But these peasants—they have no place to air their grievances."

"Nowhere to take their grievances? There are police everywhere. That's what police are for. They can ask for protection from the police."

"The police are closer to the factory officials than the peasants, Mr. Nijman. You must know that yourself."

"So now you're accusing the police of being in on the conspiracy too?" He awaited my answer. "Are you out to multiply your accusations? Look, Mr. Minke, if another person were here with us now, and he later made accusations against you, as a witness I would naturally have to recount everything that had been said. You are lucky there is no other witness here. And you're luckier still that I am not a police official. If I were, and if I made a case of this, you would be involved in a case of libel, and you yourself, I think, would find many difficulties in obtaining both evidence and witnesses."

Now I began to realize how dangerous it was to be a writer. But why had there been silence about this issue for so long? And why now that I was writing about peasants did Nijman no longer like my writings?

"Don't worry," he finally humored me. "In my opinion, this story is totally untrue, it's just libel. This character of yours, if he does in fact exist, is a liar. You have been taken in by his lies. He's nothing but a liar."

My honor was offended. His words implied: You too are lying through that character of yours, Minke!

"But you know, sir, Minke is not a liar."

"Of course you are not a liar. But a wrong original conception can give birth to many errors," he answered. "There are no peasant farmers who have become poor as a result of renting their land to the sugar mills. They receive a fair rent. They are happy to work as plantation laborers on their own land that they have rented out."

He was silent and I was silent. The atmosphere of enmity pressed down upon my heart.

"Do you know what the wage of a sugar-mill worker is?" Seeing that I could not answer, he went on, "At least one *talen* a day. By working for a factory just one week, he receives the equivalent of the rent he receives himself for one bahu of his land."

At that moment, I was envious of Kommer's skill in debate. Someone like him would easily be able to parry the attacks of this other experienced newspaper man. I was not able to do so yet. At that moment I could do nothing. I had to admit that there was still much that I had not yet learned from Trunodongso.

"You are still silent. I'm not going to do anything, sir. We are friends, yes? Your only lack is that you have not yet mastered all the material about sugar. You need to study the sugar mill's Annual Report. The Tulangan one, in particular. Or for all of Sidoarjo, or even all of Java. Or you can study the Memorial Edition of *History of the Sugar Mills*. If you are indeed interested in these things, I will be very happy to help you."

I could not hold back Nijman's words with talk about justice and truth. He looked at the issue from a completely different angle. It was clear he sided with the factories, that he did not want to know who this Trunodongso was.

"And a good wage for a sugar-cane laborer, Mr. Minke: How much is that? Three talens. Someone working as a coolie, after just five days' work, if he is a good worker, can earn the equivalent of twice the rent he receives for one bahu of land. Who says people prefer to work their own land rather than become sugar-mill coolies? What's the price of a day's labor hoeing? A few cents, no more than that."

His words kept on sliding out, unstoppable, unparried. All kinds of emotions wrestled within my breast. All kinds of information about sugar came forth from his mouth: The cost of the foreman's labor, of the employees, the cost of the hulling machinery, the cost of the sack material and of having them sewn up, the expertise of the sugar-mill engineers, whose education was not available in every town or country.

My pride in this, my best manuscript, the most perfect of all, dissolved in disarray. My faith in myself melted. I saw myself as the most stupid of people, thoughtless, not knowing how to weigh things up, ignorant. But still I felt I was on the side of truth.

"You are a good writer, but not a good journalist. In this you have lost the beauty of writing. You are making a speech"— exactly what Kommer had said.

He didn't read the fifth page.

"It's a pity we have such different opinions," I said. My hand was ready to take the manuscript from his desk.

"We don't have different opinions, Mr. Minke. Don't be mistaken. When you are writing about reality, you must make sure that you provide enough documentation. There are specific ways of doing that."

"I am sure my writings do not contain errors."

"People can believe in many things that are not right. History is indeed the story of liberation from wrong beliefs, of struggle against stupidity, against ignorance."

He looked the other way, as if to give me the chance to regain possession of myself.

"It's best that you keep clear of things that might end up getting you in trouble. One or two untrue explanations in the hands of an educated person could develop into some kind of general disturbance. It will be Natives who suffer in the end. Do you still remember Khouw Ah Soe? An educated young man with wrong thoughts stemming from a wrong explanation of things. He left his own country and came to make trouble here in the Indies. It was lucky the Chinese of Surabaya weren't able to be stirred up by him. So in the end he had to suffer the consequences of his own errors. You've heard what happened?"

"What do you mean?"

"He was killed."

"Khouw Ah Soe?"

"That's who I'm talking about."

"Where, Mr. Nijman?"

"You seem very keen to know. I can tell from that, and from your writings, that you did indeed become friends with him." He put his pipe down on the table; it had gone out. "If you ended up as Khouw Ah Soe did, I too would feel a loss, as would many others, Mr. Minke."

"If you yourself experienced what Khouw Ah Soe experienced, Mr. Nijman, I would be just as keen to know what happened, even though you and I have never really been close friends."

No doubt he knew what my answer meant: I no longer looked upon him as a teacher. I saw him now as a competitor who wanted to box me into a corner. I took my manuscript, put it in my briefcase. And, just as Khouw Ah Soe had done that day, I left his office without excusing myself.

I hired a carriage and headed straight for Jean Marais's house. Along the journey I thought over and over again about those threat-filled words of Nijman's. Perhaps he could do harm to me—and my story about Trunodongso could be used as evidence. He was happy, even joyful, about Khouw Ah Soe's death. He might be equally as pleased by my own.

Quickly I took out the manuscript. Ah, my most beautiful of all works, perfect! I held it in both hands. I tore it once, twice, three times. The paper was now tiny shreds, becoming even smaller, scattered along the road.

Trunodongso, forgive me. I am not yet able!

I found Maysoroh bringing water into the kitchen. She was so happy to see me. Jean was engrossed in watching his workmen. I took him into his own workroom.

"You look upset, Minke," he greeted me.

"You're not wrong, Jean."

"What trouble are you in now?"

"No, it's this . . . for the first time ever, I have torn up my own writing. I scattered it over the road." I told him everything that had happened. And I ended with: "I will never have anything to do with *Soerabaiaasch Nieuws* again. Nor with Nijman. This is the second time he's done wrong by me."

I waited to hear Jean's opinion. He sat silently in his chair. He didn't even look at me, as if my anger, my worries, my fury were of no interest to him. All he did was call May and tell her to be quicker getting dinner ready.

"Don't you have any opinion on this, Jean?" I pressed him. "You're siding with him because he's European?"

He blinked, startled, and turned to stare at me. He spoke slowly: "That is just prejudice," he said in French, then went on in Malay: "I have often tried to explain to you what prejudice is. What you just said is a kind of prejudice, color prejudice, cultural prejudice. You are educated, aren't you?"

"Nijman is no less educated than me. He is more prejudiced. He is siding with the factories rather than with justice and what is right."

"Just a minute, Minke. You haven't seen how things are. Perhaps you're right, but are unable yet to prove that you are right. I am absolutely sure you are right about the factories. Your only weakness is that you don't have any proof. As far as the law goes, you are in the wrong. Charges could indeed be brought against you. You would be found guilty. You could not produce evidence. On the other hand, the court would definitely be able to prove you were making unsubstantiated allegations."

"I could get the testimony of Trunodongso and others like him."

"He has put his thumbprint to every receipt he has received. And the amounts he would have received would be exactly as written on the receipt, not a cent less."

"But that's where the deception lies!" my fury exploded again.

"And that is what you must prove. You must take on a new task besides that of writer; you must become a detective. If you succeed in obtaining evidence that embezzlement and deception are occurring, your writing will be of much greater value. No one will be able to reject it. That indeed is the method used by the great social writers of Europe. Behind each of their works, there is full documentation. They are not afraid of any court. It is rather the courts that are sometimes afraid of them."

I had to listen. This kind of thing had never been taught by Magda Peters.

"They too are like you, writing to achieve a victory for humanity and justice; but your position before the law is much weaker. I hope you will be stronger. You are not in the wrong, you are in the right. It is just that your position is not yet strong enough. Minke, you must never think that I am not on your side. I know you. And it is not just the Indies, but the whole world, that needs writers like you, writers who take positions on what they write about."

"You know all this; why don't you write it yourself?"

"If I could write, why would I become a painter?"

"Thank you, Jean. I understand. You are my friend."

"Don't be discouraged, Minke. There was no need to tear up that story. We could have studied it together. I am always happy to help you."

"I'm furious, worried, bitter, Jean."

"I understand. But your writings pose no danger while they remain unpublished. That's the trouble with looking on Nijman as a god. The time had to come when you would be disappointed. He does not make the rules. He is just one man among millions upon this earth, and every one of those millions has the right to his own opinion. Why then are you angry? Why does the fact that Nijman has a different opinion offend you, upset you? He too has the right to his own opinion."

"He was so rude, Jean. He has never been like that before."

"You must see Kommer. He predicted this, that you would be disappointed."

"Yes, I remember."

"He was let down earlier than you."

"Thank you, Jean. I understand."

Maysoroh came out looking for me. Seeing we were engaged in serious conversation, she didn't join us but sat at a distance looking at me with questioning eyes.

"Kommer was here yesterday," Jean said. "He was upset that his trap didn't work. He was more upset still that you seemed disappointed with his opinions."

"Yes."

"Where's Uncle Minke's drink, May?" May left and returned carrying a tray with drinks—hot, steaming tea. Then she moved away again.

"Perhaps he is a bit rough, a bit rude even. But that doesn't mean he is necessarily wrong, Minke. He was disappointed too that you still wanted to write for the *Soerabaiaasch Nieuws*."

"May, let's go to Wonokromo," I said to her.

"I've got a friend coming over this afternoon, Uncle."

After drinking what May had brought in, I excused myself. Jean Marais felt he had to limp out with me to the carriage. "Where's your buggy?"

"I'm using a hired one, Jean."

"Don't be discouraged; don't let this break you. It would be a loss to me too."

The carriage took me back towards Wonokromo. About a hundred yards from Jean's house, I saw Kommer. Perhaps he was going to Jean's place. He didn't see me, and I didn't really want to be seen by him.

Darsam greeted me with his arm in a sling and his hand bandaged.

"Cursed bad luck, Young Master," he complained.

"Fall off a carriage?"

He shook his head and stroked his mustache with his left hand.

"Just bad luck, Young Master, stupid luck!"

"Fall from a horse? But you don't ride."

"It's all taken care of now, Young Master. It's all in the hands of the police."

"Police? What's happened?"

"Fatso, Young Master, he came back. I'll tell you later tonight, so Nyai can hear at the same time."

On entering the house, I found Mama sitting reading the *Soerabaiaasch Nieuws*. She stopped reading and motioned me to sit down. Then: "Your friend, Child . . . read this." She pushed the paper across to me.

In a big headline the news was reported: THE DEATH OF A RABBLE-ROUSER. I read the report. The person named as a rabble-rouser was Khouw Ah Soe.

This report followed:

> One morning a wig was found nailed to the wooden pylons of the Merah Bridge. The wig had a long pigtail and was covered in blood. It had obviously been nailed there deliberately; the nail was not at all rusted. The police who examined it ordered a Chinaman to translate the writing inside. It read: "If this wig is found forcibly freed from my head, it means they have got me. They = the Tong Terror Society."
>
> Three hours later, a fisherman had to climb down out of his sampan, fifteen meters from the bridge. His net had snagged on something. He hurriedly climbed aboard again and headed

for shore, shouting: "A body! A body! Dead! In the water!"

Once again the police arrived on the scene. All the fishermen nearby were ordered to haul in the net. The victim was a young Chinaman with short hair and but a few sharp teeth. His feet were bound together and tied to a bundle of rocks. On his body they found thirty wounds from sharp instruments.

In a short time the police discovered who the man was: He had gone by the name of Khouw Ah Soe, a rabble-rouser on the run from Shanghai, chased out of Hong Kong, who finally met his end in the Mas River, Surabaya.

No one has come to claim the body.

"Don't try to do anything about the body, Child. He has finished his work. Dying in someone else's country, without friend or family."

"I heard from Nijman, Ma. He seemed happy about Khouw's death."

Nyai Ontosoroh paid no heed to my words. She gazed into the far distance.

"He knew the danger, Ma," I said to humor her.

"It seems anybody who has an opinion must be expelled or annihilated here in the Indies," she said, half to herself.

Mama then bowed her head, and so did I. We paid our respects to a young foreigner a few years older than I, a lone wanderer, here in the Indies to call out to his people to rise and awaken. The danger of Japan had already touched upon China, and Japan would swallow up their country if they remained stagnant in this modern era. Any nation would be proud to have a son such as him.

Khouw Ah Soe appeared in my mind's eye as a giant. I felt very, very small: A youth hanging onto a nyai, whose own country had been swallowed up by the Dutch for three hundred years.

Mama was the first to raise her head. It seemed she was still half thinking to herself: "Any mother would be happy to have such a son as he, even though her heart would be in turmoil."

"He was an orphan, Ma."

"Happy then will his parents be to have him back with them."

The two of us sat silently, recalling all we could of that young Chinese man.

"There was once another orphan like him, like your friend. Even today he is loved by the people in the village, perhaps in all

200

the villages of Java, Child, even though hundreds of years have passed. He too was killed in the end like your friend. Except that he died on the battlefield. He too was brave, intelligent, clever. You know his name: Surapati—Untung Surapati." She pronounced his name syllable by syllable, as if savoring its sound and its memory.

My thoughts moved to Untung Surapati. Mama admired him and loved him. And I felt ashamed, because all this time I had never thought of him as more than a character in a story.

"There is not a single Javanese who does not know of Untung Surapati. Every one of them loves him."

The atmosphere of mourning was abruptly ended by the arrival of a hired carriage. Kommer jumped down and then helped Jean Marais out. The two of them came up to the house.

"Excuse us, Nyai, we've come after hearing of Mr. Minke's recent unhappy experience."

"You mean the report in the paper?"

"Newspaper report?" Kommer asked. "No, his bitter experience with Maarten Nijman."

I quickly told Mama what had happened.

"It wasn't the manuscript I read?" Kommer asked.

"No."

"That one you considered was your best article ever?"

"I think," Mama intervened, "it must have been his best. There was something he wanted to achieve with it."

"I think so too," Kommer agreed. "But Jean Marais's comments are right; Mr. Minke's legal position is weak. But Trunodongso's position is weaker still. He will never be able to prove the truth of his statements, even though he is telling the truth. But I want to give you some more information about Nijman's paper. You should have been told this long ago. Nyai, Mr. Minke, it is only natural that Nijman takes the side of sugar, because he himself lives from sugar. His paper is owned by sugar interests, funded by the sugar companies to protect the interests of the sugar lobby."

Mama and I removed Khouw Ah Soe and Untung Surapati and Darsam from our thoughts. We also put aside Jean Marais, who was always dreamily admiring Mama.

I was impressed by Kommer's explanation. When he was still a teenager, having just graduated from the Dutch language primary school, he went to work for the weekly paper *De Evanaar*.

It was a small and insignificant paper. Its printery was owned by a sugar mill. Then he found out that the paper itself was also owned by Lord Sugar.

"I knew Mr. Mellema already twenty-five years ago," he went on. "He arrived one day with a text he wanted printed in the paper. It attacked the attitude of the *patih* of Sidoarjo, who was putting obstacles in the way of the sugar mill's attempts to expand the area of land it controlled. It rejected the patih's opinion that sugar was impoverishing the region of Sidoarjo; it claimed that sugar was making the region prosperous. The patih was later moved to Bondowoso. Two years later a subdistrict head, a *camat,* argued with Mr. Mellema. The camat himself owned fifty hectares of first-class paddy fields, but he was still greedy to obtain more. A competition arose between the factory and the camat, each trying to expand their land holdings. Mr. Mellema came to the paper again, and ordered me to spy on the camat. Officially I was to go there as a reporter."

"You did it?" Nyai Ontosoroh asked.

"I was just a low-level employee then, Nyai. I did what I was told."

"What else were you ordered to do?"

"Just to report back on his habits and so on. I reported everything to Mr. Mellema."

"That's all?"

"That's all. I returned to Surabaya and continued with my work at the paper. Then I received news: The camat had been replaced. It's not clear where the old camat was moved to. All his land went to an executor and from there across to the sugar mill."

"Did the camat die?" Nyai asked, upset.

"No one knows, Nyai."

"You're not being honest with me," Mama pressed.

"After the camat disappeared, I felt I had been part of something evil too. I was disappointed in my paper. I left it and went to work for the *Surabaya Star.* The paper I left behind grew, coming out twice a week. Once it became a daily it changed its name to *Soerabaiaasch Nieuws.* But it was the same paper it is today: a creature of the sugar lobby. It must defend the interests of sugar. Anything can happen, so long as sugar remains safe! Your writings delivered you into a trap, Mr. Minke. A sugar trap!"

"Just a minute, Mr. Kommer," Mama intervened, "I once

heard of a body that was found in the paddy fields. Gored by a buffalo, the rumors said. The Camat of Sidoarjo . . . ?"

"I don't know about that, Nyai; the papers never reported it."

Mama was silent. Perhaps she was asking herself what other things there were that she didn't know about Herman Mellema. Her face showed the signs of an unsettled heart.

"It wasn't my intention to remind you of the late Mr. Mellema," said Kommer, asking forgiveness.

"I understand, Mr. Kommer; excuse me," she answered, arose, then withdrew.

We all watched Mama as she went out.

"Was she angry, do you think, Mr. Minke?" asked Kommer.

"There have been too many shocks just lately, Mr. Kommer," I answered. "So many deaths, so many injustices, and now you bring up another matter. Too shocking—to find out that Herman Mellema did such things. I am shocked myself. It's understandable."

"That wasn't my intention, Mr. Minke, truly."

"You have only told us what you know. We should be thankful for your frankness."

"It disappoints me too, Minke, it saddens me; not that there is such a good explanation for Nijman's actions, but that it should bring so much hurt and bitterness with it," Jean Marais added.

"There is nothing to regret, Jean. We would have been even more disappointed if nobody had told us. Eh, Mr. Kommer? We are truly grateful you have been prepared to tell us all this. It must have taken a lot of courage. And it was all brought about by my writings. Indeed that story of mine, the one I considered the best of all, I tore up and scattered along the road even before you had a chance to read it. But this other one, Mr. Kommer"—I opened my bag and took out the story "Nyai Surati"—"would you accept this manuscript as a souvenir of this dark day?"

"Why, Minke?" asked Jean Marais. "Do you mean for it to be put into Malay and published by Mr. Kommer?"

"No, Jean. It's for Mr. Kommer himself. Who knows, perhaps one day Mr. Kommer will have time to go through it and change it, rewrite it, as a remembrance of our friendship, and of this day too."

Kommer was unsure, but accepted it.

"You often go to Sidoarjo," I added. "You can do some more research, and won't be in a hurry, as I was. You did say you thought the story had merit, even if written like a speech?"

"Why don't you perfect it yourself?"

"Beginning this day, Mr. Kommer, I close one book. I accept your suggestion. I will learn to see the brighter side of life. The way I am now, all my strength is being sucked away."

"Close one book, Minke? What do you mean? You mean you're not going to write again?"

"Yes, Jean. I must stop writing, at least for a while."

"You're tired, Minke," said Marais gently, "your soul, not your body. You need a new environment, a new atmosphere."

"Yes. I must go."

"Go where, Minke? You'll leave Nyai alone, by herself?"

I couldn't answer. What Jean had said made me realize just how tired and dispirited I was.

"Good, you must get some rest," Kommer proposed. "You have the right to a rest. We only came to let you know about Maarten Nijman and his paper, a sugar paper. You musn't be discouraged. Come, Mr. Marais; we'll go now. Pass on our goodbyes to Nyai."

They left. I escorted them to the front steps and watched as their carriage left our property. Farther and farther away they moved, finally disappearing from sight.

However unrefined Kommer might be, he's proved to be a good and reliable friend. And Jean Marais too. What would happen to me if I had no friends? They have felt all that I have felt over the last months. I will write a letter to Mother and tell her of the beauty of friendship—something she always advised me about but which I never thought about seriously until now.

Back inside the house, I remembered Mama. The news Kommer brought had shaken her greatly. She had lost something which she had always been able to hold on to. I should be with her now.

Slowly I made my way up the stairs. I didn't knock. The door wasn't locked; indeed it was open a little. Coming from inside the room were sounds of crying, almost inaudible. That a heart as hard as hers could shed tears! How much she had suffered already. Still, Kommer's information about *De Evenaar* and *Soerabaiaasch Nieuws* and their connection with Herman Mellema had deeply shocked her.

11

But the book wasn't completely closed. Unpleasant matters still pursued us.

That night I sat beside Nyai in the front parlor. Her eyes were still swollen, though she seemed more lively. The look in her eyes showed that she was still meditating on things; then her eyes would change and you could see she was becoming anxious again.

"Yes, Minke, Child, you should look for a new environment. How I too would like to leave here, leave for some distant place and rid myself of all this. Kommer is right. We will petrify like rocks if we keep getting knocked around like this."

"Where does Mama want to go, so far away?"

"I'm bored with Wonokromo. Perhaps I'm bored too with this kind of life. Wherever we go, it is always bandits that we find."

"To Europe? Or Siam maybe?"

"Perhaps one day I will leave the Indies. This country becomes more and more foreign to me with every day."

"Europe or Siam would be even more foreign, Ma."

She didn't answer. All I could hear was a sigh of complaint.

And that was the first time I had ever heard her complain. She was much disturbed by Kommer's news; I knew what was troubling her. Nijman had snidely hinted to me that Herman Mellema was also involved in the conspiracy to cheat people of their rents. While I had not passed on Nijman's remarks to anyone, especially not to Nyai, a woman so clever could easily work out her late master's involvement in the crimes.

"If I had known before that his capital was obtained by deception, blackmail . . . murder . . ." Mama said.

"We only know now, Ma."

"It's lucky you wrote about Trunodongso. If you hadn't, I'd still feel . . . feel clean. Even after his death that damned man still deceived me. Devil! Barbarian!" She began to burn with fury, exploding into insults and curses. "Acting like a man of honor—in reality just a deceiver of powerless peasants!"

In my mind's eye I saw the young administrator of the mill at Tulangan who had twice invited Mama to his house. He would be no different from Plikemboh and Mellema, my father-in-law.

All of a sudden Mama lost control and began to cry.

"Let me take you upstairs, Ma."

"Let it be, Minke, let my heart speak now. Listen to me. Listen. If you will not, then who will listen to me?"

Her wave of weeping reached a peak, words held back by sobbing, the crying of a strong-hearted woman, courageous, experienced, educated, and intelligent—the weeping of someone who realizes she has built her life on top of mud.

All I could do was bow my head. This woman who was used to standing straight and firm needed no crutch.

As the weeping ebbed her words came, one by one, the sentences broken by sobs: "I have never felt such regret as I feel now, that I was soiled by the touch of his body. That I gave birth to his children. Bastard, bandit, scum! That I ever served him: cheater of peasants, creator of poverty, oppressor, blackmailer."

"Ma, forgive me for writing that story."

"Murdered. That camat was murdered on his orders. They said he was gored to death by a buffalo, but it was Mellema who killed him. Mellema!"

"Ma."

"Surati did the right thing, killing that man. She killed him.

That's what I should have done, not with smallpox, but with my own hands. Dog! Crocodile!"

"If I hadn't written about Trunodongso—"

"You have done nothing wrong at all, Child. Mellema is lucky he is dead."

"Ma."

"Otherwise, I could do the worst and have Darsam kill him, so that he would die before my very eyes!"

Nyai Ontosoroh covered her face with both hands.

I could see Darsam out at the back, walking about with his arm in a sling, wanting to come inside and report. I signaled to him to go. He turned off to the right and disappeared from view.

"What is my situation now? For twenty years I have developed our capital, evilly gained capital, won by cheating those without power."

"It's not all from deception, Ma."

"Who knows? I don't dare have such hopes. How dare he! How dare he! Barbarian! Animal!" Once again she burned with fury and disillusionment.

"I'll get something to drink." Without waiting I went off to the kitchen.

I found Darsam sitting at the table. A cook was making coffee for him.

"Cold water, please, cook, one glass."

"Good, Young Master, let me take it to her."

"I'll take it myself, cook."

Darsam stood up, paid his respects, and asked: "Is there still something important being discussed, Young Master?"

"Perhaps you won't be able to make your report tonight, Darsam."

"Perhaps or definitely not?"

"Perhaps."

"Let me take the drink in, Young Master."

"No."

I took the water in myself, leaving the two in the kitchen staring at each other in amazement.

Mama took the glass and drank it all down at once. She seemed to have calmed down.

"Life seems so empty, futile, knowing where all our money has come from."

I could understand her feelings: She had devoted herself to the business, always doing things the honest way; now it turned out that the business itself was born of tainted capital.

"Have you ever heard of or read about anyone having to go through what I have? Accursed experiences like these?"

"No, Ma."

"Don't write about this last thing. Now talk to me. How lonely it will be if you're not here, Minke."

"Ma, even if there had been more capital, if Mama hadn't worked, this business would never have grown."

She looked at me for a moment. Her lips were taut as she held back another explosion of anger. Then slowly the tension disappeared, and she was calm again.

"What do you really mean, Minke?" she asked, seeming unsure of herself.

I told her what I had been taught about Robinson Crusoe.

"Yes, I've read that book," she cut in. "He was marooned on an island by himself."

"True, Ma. It wasn't his money that enabled him to live, but his labor. Gold and coins were of no use to him on an uninhabited island. A mountain of gold and three mountains of coins would have been of no use to that Robinson, Ma. Without the labor of humans, nothing has value. Under the ground, under our feet, Ma, there are many things to be found: gold, silver, copper, iron, coal, salt, and gas—wealth beyond our imagination. But it is all useless without the labor of human beings; valueless, until people dig it out from the womb of the earth, to use it."

"You mean you value what I have *done,* Child, rather than that accursed capital?" she asked, somewhat comforted, a little childlike.

"I value all that you have done rather than the things you have accumulated as your property."

She let out a long breath. She was confused as to how she should look upon all her successes.

"Everything that you have come to own," I said, daring to offer her advice, "is not tainted. Not all the capital came from conspiracy and deception."

"That's where the problem lies, Child. We don't know how

much of the money is tainted and how much isn't. If I knew, then it would be easy enough to separate them."

"There's no need to know now, Ma."

"It must be returned to them, to those peasants and farmers. And even that is not possible. We only know Trunodongso, and it would not be right to give it just to him. To share it out isn't really a possibility either. To hand it over to the government would be folly. And how much each farmer has a right to—that isn't clear either."

"You don't have to think about it now, Ma."

"Yes, it doesn't have to be resolved now. But then again at any moment now, Engineer Maurits Mellema could turn up to take over the business. Everything must be arranged before he arrives."

Then I remembered what a teacher had once said about the differences between rich Europeans and rich Natives. The Natives collected wives with the excuse that they were doing it to help out the women they married. Europeans gave a part of their wealth to help with projects in the public interest: schools, hospitals, publishing, meeting halls, research.

"You have an idea, Child."

"Yes, Ma," but I was unsure.

"If there were teachers . . ." began Mama.

"Yes, Ma," I agreed, "we could found some schools for the children of those who were cheated."

That idea of using her own wages from the business, which she had saved, became a medicine that settled her spirits. Her anger began to subside, as did her regret and melancholy.

"Darsam!" she called out suddenly. She had recovered herself.

Darsam was already waiting between the back and front parlors. His unslung hand twiddled his mustache. I waved, signaling him to come closer. He saluted Nyai with his good arm.

"If Nyai isn't too tired, I want to make a report tonight," he said.

"Fetch a chair!" Nyai ordered.

He pulled a chair across with his left hand. With his left hand too he apologized for sitting on a chair that made him higher than Nyai. He let out a long breath, releasing the tension within.

"What must you remember when reporting?" Mama asked in Madurese.

"Smoking is not allowed, Nyai."

"Good. You may begin."

"Not just yet, Nyai. There is one other thing." He took a thick wad of paper from his pocket, a letter, and handed it over to his employer.

Mama read it for a moment, then pushed it over to me.

"I can't understand it. Read it," she said.

The letter was in English, badly written in large, round letters. The address wasn't clear. But from the first lines it was clear that the writer was Khouw Ah Soe. I translated it into Dutch for Mama.

My beloved and honored Mama, I began.

"He calls me Mama?" asked Nyai. "Your translation isn't wrong?"

"Exactly as written, Ma. I'll read on."

I cannot tell you how grateful I am for all the help you have given me. And that help means even more because it was given at a time when your own child was in such great difficulties. In the end, in all of Surabaya you were the only person to hold out your hand in aid, while my own people cursed me, abused me, derided me. They let themselves go on embracing the old beliefs that the Heavenly Kingdom cannot fall into the hands of foreigners. They forgot that Hong Kong, Kowloon, Macao have already long been in the hands of foreigners. Canton, and even Shanghai itself, the biggest city in China, in the world, has been cut up into concessions for the foreigners. More than ten foreign nations, Ma. And their rotten influence makes itself felt more and more as every moment passes. In those cities my people are abused and insulted in their own country. They blind themselves to reality. While you, my beloved and honored Mama, a foreigner and stranger, not understanding my language, it was you who were able to understand what I wanted to do. In you I found a true mother.

For the past few days I have been staying here. Darsam looked after me very well. He always left the door open for me whenever I came home around dusk. I lacked nothing, and I was able to lay my body down in its weariness and get rest without ever being disturbed. He looked after my safety, and took care of my every need. He did not understand at all what my secret was, nor did I understand him. We spoke to each other with nods and shakes of the head, but our hearts spoke much.

I shouldn't really be writing such a letter. But other considerations have forced me to do so, Mama. Over these past few days my room to maneuver has been getting smaller and smaller, even smaller and narrower than the freedom allowed by the identity and residency regulations enforced among the Chinese of Surabaya. And it is only Mama's house that has provided me with protection and sustenance. It is because of the ever-narrowing room to move that I write this letter.

Yes, the thanks I wish to pass on to you should not be in a letter but should be spoken to you, face to face, coming straight from a clear heart. But who knows, my beloved and honored Mama, I may not have the chance to speak to you again.

Thank you, a thousand thanks for all your sincere help and protection. From your son.

And beneath was his name written in Latin script.

There was another letter in the envelope, addressed to me. I translated it also for Mama:

My good friend Minke,

Perhaps this is the only way I can pass on my message to you. I very much need your help. My situation is desperate. Perhaps soon they, my own people, will succeed in having complete control over me. . . . My mission in Surabaya was too difficult. Now that I will never be able to meet you again, please take the letter which I enclose in this envelope to a man in Betawi, named [and he gave a name]. My apologies, you'll have to obtain the address from someone else, a man called Dulrakim in Kedungrukem. I don't remember the address and I can't get in touch with Dulrakim himself because he's a sailor and hasn't been in Surabaya for a while.

Another thing, my friend—don't send this letter through the mail. You are going to Betawi soon, aren't you? This person lives there. Say that, right up until the end, I never forgot.

My profound thanks to a friend whom I will never be able to repay for his kindness.

Then I saw the other letter, written in Chinese.

"It seems he knew it was coming, Child," said Mama in Dutch. "There's something I didn't understand though, Child. What is a concession?"

"I'll look it up in the dictionary later, Ma. I don't know either."

Darsam's eyes went back and forth from Mama to me as he tried to understand what was being said.

"Your guest, Darsam," Mama said in Madurese, "was forced to write this letter because he could not speak to you. He expressed his great thanks to you. You had been so good to him."

Darsam's eyes shone and blinked slowly as he savored Nyai's words.

"In this world and the next, he would never forget you."

"That young Chinese, Nyai, he could say that?"

"Why wouldn't he be able to say something as simple as that, Darsam?"

"He wore a pigtail, Nyai, and would cough his phlegm up and spit it on the ground."

"And what's the matter with a pigtail? Anyone with hair can grow one. Cough up and spit out phlegm? Everyone has phlegm. The only difference is that he spits it out, making a noise, and you swallow it secretly."

"But he mentioned something about the next life," Darsam protested.

"He was only saying he owed you a thousand thanks, Darsam, in this world and the next."

"He was just a Chinese, Nyai."

"Yes, like me—I'm just a Javanese. And a Dutchman is just a Dutchman."

"He won't be coming back, Nyai?"

"He won't be coming back. And so he says his final thank you."

"Returning to his country, no doubt."

"To his ancestors."

"By boat, naturally."

"In every kind of boat, by every kind of vehicle that is available. Now Darsam, let us hear your report."

12

Darsam's report turned out to be quite long. He told it all in Madurese, so I had to get Mama to help me put it down in written form, as it is given here:

The second day after Nyai Ontosoroh's departure for Tulangan, Mr. Dalmeyer arrived.

As Nyai had ordered, I invited him to work in Nyai's office. The books and papers that Nyai had prepared I took from the cabinet and put before him on Nyai's desk. Food and drink were prepared for him and set in the office too.

He read everything, examined the papers page by page.

At four in the afternoon he asked to be shown the cattle pens. I took him out to the back. He counted all the dairy cows and noted the figures down. It shouldn't have taken long just to count how many cows, how many bulls, how many calves. But he ended up staying there for quite a while after meeting that other "cow."

Nyai must know who I mean.

So I left him with that saucy Minem girl. What can one do?

They had met and got to chatting. Even as master of the house, I was no longer relevant. I left them at the cattle pens.

That girl Minem used to harass Miss Annelies, pressing Miss to make Minem a supervisor over the milking. As soon as Miss left, she began to try to win me over. And she is indeed clever at cajoling, that saucy one. If it hadn't been for her ever-enlarging stomach with that child inside it, and then not being able to work, and giving birth, she would have kept on harassing Miss forever.

Nyai herself knows what happened: She had her child several months before Miss Annelies went away. Working while she carried and suckled her baby meant that her output fell. There were no grounds to make her a supervisor. But even so, without any hesitation, she began again to press and cajole Miss to make her a supervisor. Miss might even have given in and made her one if she had not gone away all of a sudden.

But that daughter of the devil really has a devil's tongue. When she saw Nyai and Young Master go off to Sidoarjo, even before anyone had left for work, she came to my house. She paid no heed to my wife and my children, who hadn't yet been got off to school. She carried her baby with her.

"Look, look at him, Darsam," she said, pointing to what she was carrying. "Is it right that this baby should be in such a condition when his grandmother is so rich?"

Impudent. Insolent. But even so, it was a startling statement.

"And I'm not even considered worthy to be a supervisor of the milking."

"Why don't you hand the baby over to its rich grandmother then?" I asked, pretending not to understand what she was getting at.

"If his grandmother would acknowledge him, that would be easy. But if she won't?"

Minem had no husband. People said she was a widow. Others said her husband had left her or that she had left her husband. Nyai must still remember her, the one who flirted with the men all the time. The big problem was that she was pretty, her body was quite good, her skin wasn't too dark. She was very attractive. If she were a good dancer, she would be in demand for sure.

"So who is the child's father?" I asked her. She smiled coaxingly.

"That's what happens if you accept just any man," I went on. "Now the child is an excuse."

"Not just any man," she denied, still smiling invitingly. "The father of this child is none other than the son of my employer. Now say it's just any man."

"Don't try any blackmail here," I warned her.

"Who would dare blackmail Darsam? This is truly Sinyo Robert's child."

Nyai, another problem. Actually I didn't want to tell you. But as I thought it over, I knew I must tell you. Yes, if she was lying, all right, but if she was telling the truth? Whatever else might be the case, if she wasn't lying, then perhaps indeed that child might have Nyai's blood. I had to tell you, Nyai.

"Give the child here!" I ordered, and I took the baby from her.

She didn't object. The baby was dirty with snot and spittle. Seeing how disgusted I was, she wiped the baby with her sash. A boy, Nyai, healthy, plump, but not looked after properly. I somehow felt there was some of Nyai's blood in him. The face was like that of Miss Annelies. His nose was pointed but the skin was like that of Sinyo's.

The baby cried when I lifted him from Minem. His eyes were big, Dutch eyes. I became suspicious. Was it true that this was Sinyo's child or—forgive me, Nyai—Tuan Mellema's? I asked.

"Sinyo's!" she maintained.

"There are many sinyos and tuans in Wonokromo," I said, though unsure of myself, because no sinyos and tuans came visiting the villages around here. And Minem spent her days working with the dairy cows. She'd be too tired to travel away from the village at night. She had never taken holidays. Whenever I visited the village, I never saw anything suspicious. The men who did the patrols never reported seeing any sinyo or tuan.

A few weeks before Nyai went away, though, the patrols did report seeing an outsider visit Minem's house several times. But they said there was nothing suspicious. Just a guest, not an outlaw or anything. Perhaps he wanted to marry her. We had no right to stop him.

So I had never paid any attention to him, as he was not making trouble. But remembering those reports of her guest, I then asked Minem: "Minem, you've never spoken about the

215

child's father before. Why all of a sudden, after being visited regularly lately, do you begin to bring the subject up?"

"There's no connection with him," she answered, becoming even more cheeky. "The thing is that I've been waiting for Sinyo to come back, but he never has. So what will become of the child? Sinyo Robert promised that when the child was born he would acknowledge him."

"But he never has."

"That's why I have come to Darsam."

"You want me to help you to convince Nyai to accept him?"

"Why not, if he is indeed her grandson? On my death, I'd swear anywhere, this is the child of Sinyo Robert."

I sent my wife and children out, but they had already heard part of the story. I think Minem indeed planned that they hear, so the story would spread. Soon all of Wonokromo will hear, Nyai. That is one reason why I thought I had better report to you as soon as possible. Perhaps already she has begun to tell her story to her friends, with the intention of trying to squeeze something out of you later.

What I thought then, Nyai, was that a simple girl like Minem surely wouldn't know how to go about blackmailing someone. Then it occurred to me that she might have been encouraged by the man who has been visiting her lately. Perhaps he has been inciting her to try to make some profit out of the affair, squeeze something from Nyai. Was I wrong to think that, Nyai?

So I gave the baby back to her. He looked as though he would become a tall boy.

"Darsam, you can see for youself. His father isn't Javanese," said Minem.

"Who is this man who has been visiting you lately?"

"*Babah* Kong," she answered without shame.

"Perhaps this is Babah Kong's child," I said.

"No. I've only known him for a little while."

"Babah Kong wants to marry you?"

"No."

"Take you as his concubine?"

"He only comes to chat."

"Liar," I said. "As if I don't know what you are. Come on, say it again: He only comes to chat. Come on, say it."

Minem didn't repeat her statement.

"Now if you have another child, you'll be accusing someone else of being the father."

"No, Darsam. This is Sinyo Robert's child."

"What does your guest talk about?"

"This and that."

"What does he say about this child?" I asked.

"He did once ask who the child's father was: Sinyo, Tuan, or Young Master. I answered: He's Sinyo's child."

"How could he know there was a Sinyo, Tuan, and Young Master. You're the one who has been running off at the mouth!"

"No, I didn't tell him anything about Nyai's family."

"Good. So he knew before he met you. So it was he who told you to come to me now."

Minem denied this ferociously, with all her being. But I don't know, Nyai, if she was telling the truth or not. She was always smiling, flirting, pinching me, and things.

"Why don't you claim that his father is the Tuan Resident, or the Governor-General?"

She didn't know what a resident or governor-general was. She answered like this: "His father really is Sinyo Robert. I will always say so, Darsam, because Sinyo made a promise to me. He said he would take me as his nyai and that we would live in a building and I wouldn't have to work but would be an employer instead."

"But Babah Kong wants you as well. What are you up to?"

"I've already said no. I'm still waiting for Sinyo. And he still hasn't come home. Help this child, Darsam. Talk to Nyai. Could you stand to see her grandson going without like this?"

"Is it the child who needs help, or you?"

"What would be wrong with both of us receiving some help?" and she pinched my thigh so hard I let out a yell. I pushed her out of the house.

So I have told you the beginning of the story, Nyai. I mean about the matter of Minem's child. In Darsam's opinion, Nyai should examine both the child and his mother. I don't know what that girl, that Minem, really wants. She has the tongue of a devil. And even on the first day that Mr. Dalmeyer arrived here, she was flirting with him—it was incredible. And Mr. Dalmeyer responded to her flirtations. He worked here for four days, and every evening he disappeared into the barn. Everyone saw what was going on. Even though the two of them always talked in whispers, in the end they were overheard. I won't tell you what they said, Nyai; it wouldn't be proper.

Then one day, after Mr. Dalmeyer's work here was finished, a watchman reported to me: Babah Kong had arrived to visit Minem. According to the schedule Minem shouldn't be at home yet. But she was. So I went after her, to her house. From a distance, I saw them go inside the house. I could see Babah Kong. Nyai, it was someone we all would recognize: Fatso!

But I only glimpsed him for a moment. I had to have another look. I went up closer to Minem's house. It seemed they knew I was coming. Minem came outside to greet me.

"Who is your guest?" I asked.

"I have no guest here," she answered. She was carrying her baby.

I went inside. The only person there was her old mother. I checked under the sleeping benches. It was true; there was no guest. Minem went off again, back to the cattle pens to get on with her work. She paid no heed to me. But I had seen Babah Kong go into the house; I had seen him with my own eyes. He must have gone out the back door. I went out to the back of Minem's house. Yes, I was right; there he was, walking off quickly between the thickets of banana trees and taro bushes.

I was not mistaken, Nyai. There was nothing wrong with my sight. Babah Kong was none other than Fatso.

I pulled out my machete and set off after him. He knew I was chasing him and he began running too. He was fat all right, but there was still a lot of briskness in his stride. He ran fast, like a devil.

"Hey, stop, you, Fatso!" I shouted.

He paid no heed, so I kept chasing him. He tried to get out of the village and make his way into the fields. I kept after him but he ran very well, that fat body of his bent over; he looked rounder, like a marble. Run! You will not escape me. You do not know these fields as I do.

I wanted to make sure he could not lose himself again in the compound of Ah Tjong's brothel. He must die unwitnessed at twilight in these fields. His sins against us have been too many. His reappearance was the omen of some new disaster. He must die.

It appeared he was indeed trying to get to Ah Tjong's brothel. I moved to cut off his path. He turned left. The distance between us seemed less and less. I saw his face was already scarlet when he turned to get a glimpse of me, and his chest was heaving and panting. Three people are not needed here—you will not escape Darsam, one man alone. Fatso! Ayoh, use up all your breath before this machete sweeps through the air to split your chest.

He finally reached an area that has never been planted, because the ground is bad, too low and full of potholes and roots. Miss Annelies had once ordered it leveled and covered with peanut-shell waste. Some work had been carried out. The compost had begun to rot away and the potholes had reemerged. We really didn't put on enough in the first place.

Fatso ran in that direction. Several times he fell, but he easily recovered himself. I also fell. I was having a hard time as well. Once I dropped my machete. It took quite a while to find it amongst all the dense bracken. Fatso ran on happily, even stopping to look while getting his breath back.

"Fatso!" I threatened him. "Don't enjoy the dusk air for too long. In a moment I will catch up with you again."

Once I found my machete, I mobilized all my strength. The distance between us narrowed again. He began to run out of breath and strength. Now I've got you! "You!" I shouted. Fatso was cornered in a dry canal. He had toppled into it and hidden himself there. His whole body was hidden from my view.

When I reached the dry canal I found him trying to free himself from an overgrown vine. His eyes showed no fear—this madman.

"Now you die!" I hissed.

"Don't kill me," he said, panting softly. "I'm not an enemy."

"Shut your mouth!"

"Truly, I'm not an enemy."

I raised my machete to scare him into admitting who he was.

"I'm a friend," he said, and he remained calm and unafraid.

I attacked with my machete, intending to cut off his head. He adroitly stepped aside. Although fat, he was tremendously fit, quick like a deer. That alone was enough to confuse me. I jumped into the canal to finish him off once and for all. I heard him still panting. I heard my own breathing too.

"No!" he shouted, seeing I was truly out to kill him. No

matter. In a moment his neck would be sliced, as soon as he was no longer able to sidestep the machete, which was already whistling in the air. He rolled over quickly. My machete missed again, hitting a clump of clove plants. I raised it once again.

All of a sudden there was an explosion. My hand, holding the machete, bent back. The machete snapped and the broken piece disappeared into the overgrowth.

I stopped in my place, Nyai. The machete did not cut through his neck. I glanced up at my weapon. All I could see was the top of a tree. All that was left of my machete was its stump. Fatso seemed to think I'd be worried by that. He smiled, that madman! He obviously didn't understand who Darsam was, Nyai.

Fatso leaned against the bank of the canal. My shortened machete was once again raised, ready to smash down on his face. His fat lips and narrow eyes would disappear from his face. I no longer heeded the pistol in his hand.

"Don't go on," he warned.

I paid no attention. The pistol exploded again. Now what was left of my machete fell to the ground amongst the weeds and ferns of the unused canal. Nyai, my hand felt hot. My fingers were unable to grip. He had shot me; I could do nothing.

"What did I say?" he said in Malay. "I'm not an enemy. What could I do? You forced me to shoot." He stood up straight. The pistol still pointed at me.

If he had shot once more, I wouldn't be here reporting today. I'd have preferred to be shot dead. But he didn't do it. The injury to my hand left me helpless. I wanted to attack with my left hand, but I realized in a moment that it would be useless. I stayed silent.

"Had enough?" he asked insolently. "Not going to attack me again? Learned your lesson?" I was silent, ashamed, fuming. "If you're not going to attack again, I'll put this pistol away and help you. Well? Agreed?"

How insolent he was! I still said nothing; I was clenching my teeth. He only shook his head, smiling, perhaps in insult, perhaps in pleasure at my condition.

"What's the meaning of one person with one machete?" he said. "Come on, out of the canal. I'll help you out. Out of there first."

I performed that shameful act. I climbed up the bank of the

canal. He heaved me up from below, pushing my buttocks. Insolent. Once I was up, he climbed up nimbly, that jungle cat.

"Let me stop the bleeding," he said. "If you lose too much blood, that'll be the end of you. Lift your wounded hand right up in the air. It hurts? Of course."

He was so friendly, I don't know whether to make fun of me, or to rub in the shame, or whether it was sincere. I don't know. I raised high my wounded hand. He put away his pistol. He could have killed me, but he didn't. His attitude was not that of a troublemaker. I didn't know what to do. Carefully he put his hand into his pocket and took out a handkerchief. He twisted it around until it became like a piece of cord and he tied it tightly around my wrist. The blood stopped flowing.

"Let me take you home," he said again.

It was true—he didn't want to kill me. His hands were well muscled and strong. He wasn't just any fat man. I had underestimated him. It was lucky there were no villagers about. When they heard the shooting, everyone had shut themselves in their houses, locked their doors. How ashamed I would have been if they had seen me being escorted along by the man I was going to cut up! There was no patrol about either. The sun had set. Dark. No moon, Nyai. My own house was locked from the inside.

In front of the door, he said: "Tell your wife to take you to the hospital at the palm-oil factory at Wonokromo. Don't say you were shot. Don't go to the police. Say you've had an accident."

And before disappearing into the darkness, he added again: "I am not an enemy. Don't get things wrong. Behind all this, I'm your friend, only you don't know who I am. Go to the hospital straight away."

After I shouted and banged on the door, my wife opened up. She took me to the hospital. Marjuki drove the buggy. I was lucky there were people still on duty. And, yes, they did ask what had happened.

"I fell, Tuan, and was stabbed by some bamboo," I answered.

The Dutch doctor treated me, washed and bandaged my hand himself, and put it in this sling here. He didn't let me go home. The three of us were given coffee and told to wait a moment. We sat on a long bench.

Disaster, Nyai. It wasn't long before the police arrived. We were taken away to the police station. We were interrogated that night. They didn't believe my wound came from falling on bamboo. They said there were no signs of bamboo around the wound, but there were signs of a bullet passing through. I don't know how they could tell. But I still didn't admit anything. They threatened to detain all three of us until we confessed what had happened. I had to tell them, Nyai. If I didn't and they kept us, who would look after the business?

That night too a detail of policemen took us home. They took lamps to the canal and examined the place. They found not only the shell of a bullet but plenty of signs of a fight. They took away the spent shell and also the pieces of my broken machete.

That's what happened, Nyai. Once I started to tell what happened, the whole story came out. Minem was interrogated that night too. She didn't know where Babah Kong lived. She admitted to sleeping with him a few times and said he had promised to make her his concubine. But Minem didn't believe him. Babah Kong wasn't very generous, according to Minem, so she wasn't sure about the idea.

It was all taken down. And you can see, Nyai, I wasn't arrested. Neither was Minem. Now it's Babah Kong who's being chased by the police on some other charges. It seems, Nyai, maybe we'll end up in court again, if Babah Kong is caught.

I thought, at that point, that Darsam's report was over. Mama didn't ask him anything, though she must have realized there were a lot of issues to follow up: Minem's baby, Mr. Dalmeyer's work, Dalmeyer's relationship with Minem, Fatso still being around the place, Darsam's new troubles, the upcoming trial . . .

This woman had so much to face.

But Darsam hadn't finished.

He put his bandaged hand on the table, having taken it out of the sling.

"Nyai," he said, his voice taking on an even more serious tone. "I have carried out Nyai's orders as well as I could. If I have made any mistakes, done anything incorrectly, I would like Nyai to say so."

A tense silence followed. Nyai still said nothing.

"Have I done wrong, Nyai?"

Nyai Ontosoroh let out a big breath; both her cheeks sagged

a little. She rubbed behind her ear with the finger of her left hand, then said slowly: "You have made no mistakes, Darsam. You have not been in error in anything. Everything has been handled correctly."

"In dealing with Fatso too, Nyai?" asked Darsam, childlike.

"You weren't entirely right there. The same as the other time, you wanted to go too far. If Babah Kong hadn't been armed with a pistol, would you have killed him?"

"No, Nyai, I just wanted to frighten him."

"Don't lie! Fatso wouldn't have taken it so seriously if you hadn't been serious as well," Nyai replied. "How's your hand now?"

"Nyai," he said sadly, "my fingers no longer have the strength to carry a machete—to swing it, or to spin it. I can't even hold it. I understand now, Nyai, how my livelihood has depended so much on these fingers of my right hand. With them I carried out all of your orders, Nyai: Removed trespassers, escorted the milk wagons, taken up my machete, collected debts, taken care of security, maintained authority over all the workers. Now these fingers are of no use. I have thought about this for a long time, Nyai, yes, these last few days; without these fingers Darsam is no longer of any use to Nyai. I'm no longer of use even to myself. I'm unable to work. I must admit it, Nyai: My service to you is at an end." His voice slowed, serious and sad. "Darsam will go home to his village, Nyai, home to Sampang."

"And what will you do there? Make salt? It'll be no different. You won't be able to work there either, without those fingers."

"That's the trouble indeed, Nyai."

"Go and see Dr. Martinet tomorrow. You can't be sure your fingers are damaged permanently."

"And if they are, Nyai?"

"Get them checked first. Dr. Martinet will do all he can."

"And if they are damaged permanently, Nyai?" he repeated.

"Ah, see the doctor first."

He didn't want to go. He remained motionless in his seat, waiting for his employer's decision.

"What are you waiting for now?"

"Will I be dismissed, Nyai?"

"Even if nothing can be done for your fingers, Darsam, you will stay here. Your children graduate from the local primary school this year, and must learn to work. They can begin to learn Dutch. Who knows, Darsam; your children may not be as ignorant as you. And what does it matter that your right fingers are broken, if your heart is strong? Go, get some sleep."

"But Darsam will never hold a machete again."

"Go to bed!" shouted Nyai.

Very hesitantly he rose, raised his left hand in salute to Nyai and me, put his chair back against the wall, then went. He walked erect, not looking back. He disappeared down the stairs.

"Do you know what has happened tonight?" Mama asked me.

"The police are out after Fatso, Ma, who is really Babah Kong."

"That's not important."

"Thre will be another trial, Ma, and more abuse and humiliation."

"That's not important either. The case is over, although there are still loose ends. It's this, Child. Darsam and others like him only realize now: All this time life has depended on those right-hand fingers. Life comes from those fingers. All of a sudden those fingers cannot be used. He only realizes it after his capital is damaged, the living capital of his fingers. Others pretend they work with their brains. For years and years, they study, they learn to think that they might live properly and as they wish to live. But a person's brain can be damaged too; remember Tuan Mellema. Years of learning and practice disappear in one moment—decades of learning disappear. Wandering at night like an animal, forgetting he is human . . ."

"Why, Ma?"

"And there are others who put their lives in the hands of money capital. For decades too, they make their capital grow, from a small seed to a banyan tree thick with foliage. Then, suddenly, they realize that the money was obtained immorally, the fruits of deception—"

"Ma!"

"So it seems we are all the same, Child: Me, Tuan Mellema, and Darsam. What we thought to be solid, strong, trustworthy, something we could hold on to, turns out to be no more than a speck of sand. Perhaps this is what they call the tragedy of living. How fragile we are! And Khouw Ah Soe, young and intelligent, is now dead, killed by his own people—a people he was working to help. Perhaps his murderer knew who he was—a killer paid just one rupiah or perhaps two."

"If they knew him well, they would never have killed him," I objected. "Maybe they would even have helped him."

"That's what happens in the shadow puppet stories, Minke. In real life, people are killed precisely by those who know and understand them. And the Acehnese, Minke—how many of them have been killed by Europeans, who have made it their business to know all there is to know about them? And your story about Trunodongso—who do we see there, impoverishing him and forcing him off his land? Those who know more, more about farmers and farming. I'm sure Tuan Mellema was involved not only in deceiving those farmers, but in oppressing them and using force against them as well. A conspiracy to embezzle rent money must start with cheap land to rent."

Mama wasn't really talking to me. She was testing her own thoughts. She was looking for something to grip hold of, some truth that had its very roots in truth. She was trying to face and not give in to the tragedy of life.

Slowly it was becoming clear that my own and the world's joyful greeting to the modern age was an act of folly. Only the tools and the methods were modern, Mama said. Man remained the same, never changing, on the sea, the land, at either pole, amongst the wealth and poverty that he himself makes.

"While listening to Darsam's report, I decided how much money I would return to the peasants, Child. An amount equivalent to all the capital we used to set up this business. I will build schools. I will employ one or two teachers. I will tell them to teach Dutch and arithmetic."

"That will be good, Ma."

"If they knew Dutch, they wouldn't be so afraid when they had to deal with the Dutch. And if they knew some arithmetic, how to count, they wouldn't be tricked so easily. If you decided not to leave Wonokromo and Surabaya, you could visit there once a week. You could tell the children about the evil doings of the colonialists."

"They'd arrest me and put me on trial, Ma, and accuse me of agitation and incitement. They even expelled Magda Peters."

"So who must begin, if not you? Do you too want to go to

sleep, like in that story of Kommer's about Kartini, and wake up with the modern age already here?"

To be honest, I shook with fear as I heard that challenge.

"You're not saying anything, Minke, Child. Who must begin? Must I do everything myself?"

"Of course not, Ma."

"Then who must do it? Yes, indeed, hundreds of people will carry out this work. That is in the future, I don't know when. But who will begin?"

Indeed I was afraid of that idea—just an idea. I didn't have the courage to answer. I was ashamed to listen to my own voice, fearful that I might be exposed by that challenge to admit what I really was.

"Oh, yes," Nyai Ontosoroh abruptly changed the subject. "I forgot: You want to continue your schooling at the Medical School in Betawi." Her voice held the hint of a sneer.

"Yes, Ma. I will leave as soon as Panji Darman arrives."

"But still it must be you who begin, Child, wherever you are, whatever school you attend. You were the first to suffer all these things, you know how things really are, and the reasons, and how things are connected."

"Ma—" I tried to defend myself.

"If you don't, you will be running away, Child. Do you remember that letter from your mother you once told me about? To run away is to admit you are a criminal. All your education and experience will be in vain. I know you are not someone who runs away."

13

But still we couldn't close the book. Events kept pursuing us, one after another.

A newspaper story reported that a peasant rebellion had broken out in the region of Sidoarjo. The police were unable to handle it and had to call in the army. It took three days to quash the outbreak. Kyai Sukri, who was thought to be the mastermind, was arrested and brought in chains to the Tulangan sugar factory. The Tuan Besar Kuasa Manager was furious that the disturbances had held up production. He ordered Kyai Sukri punished with eighty lashes before being taken to stand trial.

The Kyai suffered his punishment, witnessed by all the factory employees, foremen and coolies. He let out his last breath with the seventieth lash.

"If your article had been published that time . . . " Mama began.

"Yes, Ma; without wanting to, I've ended up betraying them."

"Your article would have made Nijman smell that there was something going on. You have been in the position of a spy working for Nijman—and unpaid to boot—and you could still be in trouble yet."

I felt so ashamed to hear her sum up my situation that way. I saw Trunodongso, and little Piah, and Mama Truno. I had told Trunodongso that not all problems can be solved with machete and anger. Did they tire of waiting to see my promise carried out? Yes, surely they must have hoped they had an ally in me.

"It is good that you destroyed your article. But you are still in danger, Minke. Nijman knows now who you are. Sastro Kassier and his family know you stayed overnight in Trunodongso's house. Jean Marais and Kommer know too, from the story you told them. I know. Jean Marais probably wouldn't have said anything to anybody. But I don't know about Kommer and Sastro Kassier and his family. If Trunodongso is caught, and mentions your name . . . " She sighed deeply. "If he is dead, then you should be all right, or at least things can't be too bad for you."

I knew I had to get away from this house, from Wonokromo, from Surabaya; I had to disappear.

"And me too, Minke, Child, because you were always with me. We have been involved together in another case. And there is the incident now with Darsam. Our situation is getting worse and worse."

Yet again we were bound together by an unhappy matter. I felt even closer to her.

"It's lucky you didn't take up the Tuan Manager's invitation while you were there, Ma."

"Someone as young as that, well educated, just out from Europe, how could he be so heartless to order that Kyai Sukri be whipped—and eighty times too. The Kyai was already old and bent, perhaps with arthritis."

And with the words she spoke next, I felt orphaned: "Yes, Minke, you must go. This house is not good for you. You are still young, you have the right to some joy, as Kommer said. I can handle these troubles. No need for you to stay with me through all these difficulties. But I cannot help thinking now: Trunodongso will remember your promise."

"I could never leave Mama at a time like this. Even though it has been only for a short while, Ma, I have been very happy as your son-in-law, and that happiness binds me to you. I could never leave you in a situation like this."

"No, Minke; you must have some joy in your life. But remember Trunodongso. You owe him a promise."

"I told him once, Ma, not everything can be solved with machete and anger."

"He will always remember the help you promised him."

The conversation was brought to a halt by the arrival of a carriage. It would be Marjuki bringing back Panji Darman alias Robert Jan Dapperste from Tanjung Perak harbor. We had told Marjuki to convey our sincere regrets that we were unable to meet him ourselves.

As the carriage pulled up noisily outside the front door, we heard someone announce himself with a formal greeting. From behind the thick beard and mustache I recognized him: It was Trunodongso, about whom we had just been talking.

"Who is it, Child?" Mama asked, seeing me go pale.

"Trunodongso, Ma," I whispered.

"Ha?" she rose from her chair and ran to meet her guest.

We went outside to help him. He looked filthy. He had covered himself with a horribly dirty sarong, all torn; he looked like a beggar. Behind the beard and mustache his face was pallid.

Without talking, Mama led him inside and into her office.

His eyes still fixed on me, the one person here whom he knew, he said very slowly: "Yes, Ndoro, I come to seek your protection."

"You've got a fever, Truno," Nyai Ontosoroh said to him.

"Ya, Ndoro, I am sick. Fever. Not *harvest-time fever*. I made myself come here even sick like this."

Mama sat him down in a chair, unable to say anything more. Her eyes shot nervously about. Seeing her do that, I closed the office door. From the middle parlor came the sound of shoes heading our way. I jumped up and locked the door that led to the parlor.

"I have come, Master, Ndoro, to surrender my life into your hands, and that of my wife and my children."

"Where are they?" asked Mama.

I hurried over to the window to make sure no one was trying to peer inside.

"Still on the other side of the river, Ndoro."

"Why are you covered in a sarong like this?"

He opened his sarong. He wore no shirt, and on the left side of his back was a wound six inches long.

"From an army sword, Truno?" hissed Mama. Seeing the wound seemed to make her even more nervous. "Pull up your sarong. We'll call a doctor soon."

229

"I am afraid of doctors."

From the window I saw Panji Darman walking towards the house. He waved, so pleased to be seeing everyone again. His face was bright, having lost some of its darkness while living in Europe. His cheeks were flushed, fresh, healthy.

"Hai, Minke."

"Oi!" I answered. "Welcome, Rob." I was still reluctant to call him Panji Darman. "We were too busy, we couldn't meet you."

"Ah, doesn't matter. Where's Mama?" He came closer to the window.

"She is well, well." He reached the window.

"We're busy right now, Rob. Can we get together tonight?"

He looked disappointed, nodded, and moved away.

"So you left them all, Truno, paddy, dry fields, your house?" asked Mama. "Minke, get someone to fetch Dr. Martinet. Tell Darsam to prepare a place in the warehouse."

But Trunodongso didn't feel safe without me. His eyes called out to me. I explained: "Wait here, Pak. Don't worry. You are safe here as long as you don't speak. Understand?"

"Don't call a doctor for me."

"Silence, you, Truno," whispered Mama. "It's all to help you."

His head dropped in pain, and I went.

The grain warehouse was almost empty. Mama had ordered everything sold. Grain was being sold every day. Usually she waited for buyers to come looking, but not now. She was selling everything she could.

As I walked off looking for Darsam I could still see Trunodongso covering his body with the sarong. As he lifted the sarong to cover his back, we could see his swollen feet. He was no longer the Trunodongso who dared stand and challenge everybody with his machete. He was more powerless than a wooden doll.

I found Marjuki unharnessing the horses from the carriage. Frowning, he protested the new orders to go and fetch Dr. Martinet. "The horses are still tired, Young Master."

"Take another horse."

"They're all being used at the moment."

"Then hitch up these horses again."

"They're still tired," he answered back.

So we had to argue. Darsam came along to help. Marjuki, with a very unwilling heart, harnessed his horses again. Darsam went off to carry out some other order.

When I got back to the office, I found Mama talking with Trunodongso. They were whispering to each other. As I came closer, I heard Mama say: "You're ill; you can't go to get your family yourself."

"They won't know how to get here," he said.

"Minke will fetch them. Tell him where they are."

"They won't trust him," answered Trunodongso.

"Minke will be able to make them trust him. They have seen him and met him before."

"They still won't believe he's there to help them."

"You must go, Minke. Don't use one of our carriages; hire one. Truno, tell him where they're waiting."

So I set off in a hired carriage for the address he had given me: a ferry crossing along the Brantas River. I had never been to that area. The driver had to tell me where to start walking—for one mile to the south. I had to walk through villages. The carriage had gone on one mile past the Brantas Bridge. The driver had agreed to wait for me.

While I walked I tried to think why Mama had ordered me to fetch Trunodongso's family. She could have sent anyone from the business. I was very tired and didn't know this area of Wono-kromo well at all.

The village lanes were dirt tracks, still and quiet, overgrown with grass, and looked as though they were never cleaned. There were no drains along the path's edges, which were lined with shady dadap trees, cactus, and dead thorny branches. A number of people I passed moved to one side, hugging the edge of the path, because I wore European clothes and shoes, Christian clothes. Perhaps they thought I was some black Dutchman out looking for trouble.

As I got closer to the ferry crossing, it suddenly came to me: Perhaps Mama was deliberately sending me away from the house—from Trunodongso. If he had been followed by spies, only Mama would be arrested. I would not be there. If this were not the case Mama must have had something else in mind. And it was all a result of my own actions. Mama, ah, Mama, you have nothing to do with all this, but still you hold out your hand to help, involving yourself in new troubles.

The ferry crossing was quiet—no one about except the ferryman himself, poling his way across the Brantas. I had no choice but to wait for him to arrive at my side of the river. There were no signs of Trunodongso's family.

Seeing me waiting on the riverbank, the ferryman stopped his work. Indeed, he started to pretend to have some trouble with his raft. You! I shouted in my heart, you're just pretending, you're afraid of this black Dutchman too!

"Hey! You! Quickly! Over here!" I ordered in Javanese.

His eyes darted about, startled. Fear was written all over his face. Yet he brought the raft over to the riverbank and tied it to a wooden pole. He threw the rope over to the shore. He came up to me, bowing again and again, and stood, hands clasped in front of him: "Ndoro Tuan, Master."

"Where are the people who were here a while ago, the ones not waiting for the ferry?" I asked.

"There's been no one who hasn't been waiting for the raft."

"A woman, two boys, a girl who had little sisters?"

"No, Ndoro Tuan, no one like that."

"Look out! Tell me quickly, or . . . "

"Ah, oh, ah . . . "

"No need for 'ah, oh, ah'—do you want me to take you to my office?"

"No, Ndoro Tuan. Truly, there is no one here." He bowed his head and eyes; he didn't even dare look at my shoes.

"Is that true?" I asked threateningly.

He said nothing.

"Ayoh! to the police station."

"Please, no, Ndoro Tuan. My children will be waiting for me at this time of day, Tuan."

"Where is your wife?"

"I have none, Ndoro Tuan; I am a widower."

"Who cares? Come along with me."

"Mercy, Ndoro Tuan, I have done nothing."

"No mercy for you. Come on." I made a move to leave and he followed.

From the great fear he showed, I guessed he was indeed hiding the people I was after.

"Where's your house?"

"I have never stolen anything, Ndoro Tuan. There's nothing in my house."

"Walk in front of me. Show me your house."

He walked along slowly before me, every now and then turning to see if I was still there. I began to feel badly about the way I had treated him, about coming here wearing European clothes and shoes—symbol of the bogeyman, enemy of the little people. They would all think I was here to steal their freedom or their possessions.

One behind the other we walked along a narrow path under thickets of riverside bamboo, passing fields of neglected banana trees.

"That's your house?" I saw a bamboo-thatched hut emerging from behind the thicket. Smoke formed clouds as it passed through the roof, only to be dispersed by gusts of wind.

"My hut, Ndoro Tuan."

"Who's doing the cooking?"

He kept walking, his head bowed, pretending not to hear. Seeing that, I quickened my pace, passed him, and ran on alone to the hut.

The bamboo door was open. It was dark inside, full of smoke. I saw Piah boiling something in an earthenware pot; she squatted facing the fire. Beside her squatted two smaller children.

"Piah!" I called.

She was startled when she saw me. Afraid. Her arms trembled. Her two younger sisters hugged close to her.

"You haven't forgotten me? Are you afraid of me?" She kept her eyes on my shoes as she stood up. She placed her shaking hands on her sisters' heads. "Where's your mama?" I asked.

She still wouldn't answer. Her eyes wandered to the bamboo sleeping bench. There Truno's wife slept, beside her two boys.

"Tell your mother I've come to fetch you all. A carriage is waiting at the main road."

As I came out of the smoke-filled hut, the ferryman arrived. He kept his eyes to the ground, still afraid to look at me.

"Those little children are yours?"

"Yes, Ndoro Tuan."

"You said you were a widower. Who's that woman in there?"

Trunodongso's wife came outside and up to me. Her eyes

233

were still red. Obviously she hadn't had enough sleep. Her clothes were a mess. Like Trunodongso, she had swollen feet. Then came her two sons. Their feet were swollen as well. They wore shorts that went down to their knees, and their torsos were wrapped in sarongs. They stood, hands clasped in front of them.

"Still tired?"

"No, Ndoro. How did Ndoro know I was here?"

"From Pak Truno. He's at my house. He told me. Are you strong enough to walk another few hundred yards? There's a carriage waiting."

They all looked exhausted. Perhaps they hadn't eaten for a long time. Truno's wife looked at the ferryman, seeking some kind of advice. The ferryman said nothing. He kept his head down, still afraid and suspicious.

"Good, have something to eat first. It's already afternoon."

I waited outside the hut. The two boys came and waited with me, sitting on the ground. I sat on a felled banana-tree trunk. Neither said a word, neither looked me in the face. The ferryman went inside and didn't come out for a long while.

Five minutes later Piah came out carrying an earthenware dish containing three yellow sweet potatoes in one hand and a jug of water in the other. She put the dish down on the banana-tree trunk and the jug of water near my feet. She invited me to eat, ignoring her brothers.

I guessed this was the ferryman's daily meal—now it was being given to his guests. I pushed the dish across to the two boys.

"Eat. We will be leaving soon," I said.

They didn't eat.

"Don't worry about me. I've already eaten. You still have to walk another mile or so."

Unable to restrain their hunger any longer, they devoured the sweet potatoes, skin and all. Then they gulped down the water in the jug.

The ferryman had given them all he had, these guests on the run: A roof to shelter under, sweet potatoes, sleeping-bench, and even his own safety—he was ready to give them that too. In another place, Engineer Mellema, educated and quite well off, wanted to obtain other people's property. And it was none other than the late Herman Mellema who had turned families like Trunodongso's into vagabonds.

Trunodongso, this time I failed. But one day, you will still become one of my characters—you, who knew nothing of this modern age. No schooling, illiterate; merely the sight of someone in shoes makes you tremble! And you too, ferryman, you too will become a character in my stories. Perhaps you too are a farmer who has lost his land, and now hoes the waters of the Brantas.

I cannot do it now. Later, later when I have learned more about my own people. The thing to do now is get them away from here. I myself may have to leave quickly, leave Wonokromo and Surabaya.

Still the ferryman didn't come out of the hut. Perhaps he was advising Trunodongso's wife not to trust me.

"We must leave now," I said to the two eldest, the boys.

They went inside the hut. I waited a long time. They didn't come out, all apparently agreeing not to trust me. I went in. They all watched me, strange looks in their eyes.

"Quickly. It's already late. Do you want to keep Pak Truno lying there in pain waiting for you?"

Surely it was the ferryman who was making things difficult for me, but I was not angry. I must respect him, no matter what. He himself didn't try to look at me, just kept his head bowed. Perhaps he avoided looking even at my dirty, dust-covered shoes.

"So you and your children don't want to come with me?" I asked. "Then I will return by myself. Pak Truno can't come to fetch you until his wounds have healed."

I went out, and walked away slowly, giving them more time to decide. I looked back, and still they hadn't come out. I began to quicken my pace. Only after about fifty yards did I hear Piah shouting. I pretended not to hear, though I slowed my pace to let her catch up.

I could hear her footsteps as she got closer.

"Ndoro! Ndoro!" she called.

I stopped. Now I could hear her panting breath. I looked back. Extreme exhaustion was painted on her face—a face that looked so old and yet so childlike.

"Ndoro won't arrest us?"

"Your father is waiting for you and he is hurt. If you don't want me to take you to him, that's up to you, Piah. If you want to come, good, you can all catch up with me. I will walk slowly to the main road. It's still quite a way from here."

Who wouldn't feel sorry for that most exhausted member of the group? Even in these circumstances, they still held important the ideal of freedom—just a tiny bit of freedom—without ever having heard of the French Revolution. But I could do no more than offer them my help.

She stood there, bewildered.

"If it's only you that is to come, then let's go."

"I will go back first, Ndoro."

"Yes, go back first. But I can't stop. I will keep on walking slowly."

The child went back to get her mother. I kept walking, without looking back. It seemed a long distance I had to travel. The trust I had won from them in Tulangan was now lost. How many months ago was that? Two? Had things changed so much since then? I wore Christian clothes, I wore shoes, I was closer to Europeans than they were. And it was Europeans who wanted to catch Trunodongso, husband and father. They were people on the run, afraid, hungry, and tired.

They will give in to me too, I decided in my heart. On the run, in other people's villages, without Trunodongso, they will have nothing. They will surrender to me.

When I arrived back at the main road, I found the driver sound asleep, snoring. I climbed aboard and sat beside him. His head was uncovered and his mouth open. His headband had fallen to the floor; I could see his hair was graying.

For five minutes I sat there beside him. The carriage swayed every now and then as the horses, worried by swarms of evening flies, kept shaking their bodies. The driver still didn't wake up. And Trunodongso's family still didn't appear.

I cleared my throat and he woke up. He blinked his eyes several times, startled, looking at me in great embarrassment. His hand groped about his head looking for the band of his destar. He became even more nervous when he realized his head was uncovered—very impolite according to Javanese custom. I picked up his fallen destar and gave it to him. He bowed again and again as he climbed down from the carriage, all the while thanking me, feeling he had been too much honored, that I had been too considerate in my actions.

"Forgive me, Ndoro."

"It's all right."

"Do we leave now, Ndoro?"

"We'll wait a bit longer."

He didn't protest. The sun had almost sunk below the horizon. He asked nothing, said nothing. It was not yet an age when someone barefooted could start up a conversation with someone who wore shoes. In the stories of our ancestors only the priests and gods wore slippers and shoes. And these simple people equated shoes with the power of Europe, of the same essence as the army's rifles and cannons. They were more afraid of shoes than daggers or machetes, swords or spears. You are right, Herbert, Sarah, and Miriam de la Croix: They have been made to abase themselves so low by the Europeans, by their own Native leaders. They have become so full of fear: The wages of continuous defeat in the battlefield of confrontation with European civilization.

Kommer, do I still not yet know my own people? Will people still think of me as incomplete, laugh behind my back, because I write only in Dutch? Now I can answer: Even if only a little bit, I have begun to know my people, a peasant people.

Just watch, the Trunodongso family will be forced to overcome their fear and suspicion, called to Trunodongso, the center of their family. That is the way of things in Java. They must come and will come. I know the Javanese way. I will wait. My efforts must succeed.

As twilight reached its climax they became visible in the distance, walking one behind the other. Slowly, hungrily. The two boys carried their little sisters on their backs. Little Piah walked in front.

I climbed down from the carriage to greet them. They seemed unsure. The hope of seeing the center of the family again shone a little in their faces. The ferryman followed behind, a little way in the distance.

"Climb aboard, everyone."

They climbed up silently, surrendering to whatever might befall them as long as they could see Trunodongso again—but not surrendering from hunger or exhaustion.

The ferryman stood watching us from a distance. I waved to him. He came closer, bowed his head.

"Thank you for looking after Trunodongso's family. When you go home, you'll be lonely?"

He just spat.

"Come here, closer."

He took a step forward, but didn't dare come too close.

"For the hospitality you gave them, and for the sweet potatoes you need yourself, take this talen."

He took it silently.

"There's nothing else you want to say?"

"Can I come to see them soon?"

"They will come to see you, once things are all right."

The carriage began to move. I sat beside the driver. Looking over my shoulder, I examined them one by one. How many miles had they traveled, circling to avoid the soldiers? I won't ask them here. I saw how their gaze wandered everywhere without fixing on anything in particular, as though they had no interest in the difference between their one-hut village in the middle of the sugar cane and the town with all its factories and street lighting. Perhaps the town's activities were no more to them than the rustling and swaying of the cane leaves.

"Have you ever seen a train, Piah?"

"Yes, Ndoro," she answered tiredly. But she wasn't really interested. Neither were the others. It was as if Stevenson, the inventor of trains, had never harnessed steam to move a locomotive engine, which then carried the products of cane workers' sweat to Tanjung Perak harbor.

"Have you been on one?"

"No, Ndoro."

"Wouldn't you like to?"

"No," she answered slowly, paying more attention to the actual question than to the presence of a train in either her imagination or on this earth of mankind.

"Look at the train." I pointed to a string of carriages with its engine puffing and hissing along from the south. "Isn't it fantastic?"

They all shifted their gaze to the horseless iron carriage. Not one of them held it in particular admiration. It was not part of their world. Perhaps their own dreams were more beautiful.

The carriage was being overtaken by the panting, breathless train, which puffed out clouds of smoke and ash like a dragon in the myths of bygone peoples. But my fellow passengers were still not interested. Perhaps they were exhausted by the uncertainty of their fate. Perhaps, too, Trunodongso, the center of their lives, was the only grand thing in their thoughts.

"Do you know that Pak Truno's sick?"

No one answered. They knew; better not to speak out.

"You can work at Wonokromo," I said to the two eldest children.

They didn't answer.

"You've never been to school?" I asked again.

"It's enough they know how to hoe the ground, Ndoro." Now it was their mother who answered.

"Perhaps Pak Truno has already been seen by Tuan Doctor."

In the glow of the streetlights I could see them become anxious: A doctor had entered the life of Truno. Ah, how much everything European torments their peace of mind. I didn't feel able to keep the conversation going. I realized there was a centuries-wide gap between them and me. Centuries! Perhaps this was what my history teacher meant when he talked about the social gap, or maybe, better still, the historical gap. In one nation, where people eat and drink the same things, in one country, yes even in one carriage there can be such a gap, not yet or not at all bridged.

All of us in that carriage sat silently, each with his or her own groping thoughts.

Our vehicle entered the *Boerderij Buitenzorg* long after the sun had set. Mama ordered that they all be taken straight into the warehouse. Trunodongso was sitting on a bamboo mat being examined by Dr. Martinet. Seeing a European present, Truno's wife and her children stopped, each gripping hold of the other.

"It's all right," I said, encouraging them. "Go on in."

I set an example, and they moved forward, their feet dragging along the floor, bowing again and again, keeping their gaze away from the white person in front of them.

Mama followed behind them.

"Ayoh, don't be afraid." She too encouraged them, passing them and going up to the doctor.

"The wound is somewhat old," said Dr. Martinet in Dutch to Mama.

"A villager, doctor," answered Mama.

"It's not a wound from being pierced by bamboo, Nyai," he spoke again. "A wound from a sharp weapon, perhaps a week ago. Has there been another fight here since the incident with Darsam?"

"No."

"Remember, Nyai, what you say now I'll have to report if there is any investigation."

"Of course, Doctor."

"I know he didn't fall on any bamboo," Dr. Martinet pressed.

"What does it matter, Doctor? It's all the same. He is wounded and must be treated."

"It might be a different matter before the law."

"There's no need for a trial, Doctor," answered Nyai Ontosoroh patiently.

"Very well. It was an accident with bamboo. Make him understand, Nyai. If he doesn't, he can get a lot of people in trouble."

"Thank you, Doctor. You are always so good to us."

Dr. Martinet went home without joining us for dinner.

Only then did Trunodongso's wife and children sum up enough courage to approach. As quick as lightning Mama shifted her attention to her new guests: "Stay here with your husband, you and all your children. Don't think about what's happened. Look after him well. There are more mats over there. Roll them out on the floor when you want to sleep. The warehouse is big. Don't talk to anyone. Don't tell anyone anything. Just one story to someone, and you could bring disaster upon us all. Do you understand?"

"They all understand, Ndoro," Trunodongso answered from his place on the mat.

"Come on, Child," Mama said.

As we walked away she put her hand on my shoulder and whispered slowly: "After you left to fetch them I sent Panji Darman off to the shipping agent. There's a ship leaving for Betawi tomorrow. You must leave tomorrow, Child, Nyo. You must act as if nothing has happened. And don't speak to anyone."

I took Mama's hand and clasped it. "Your child will go, Mama. Mama has done so much for me. Thank you, Mama. Will I not be sinning to leave you here alone to face so many difficulties, Ma?"

"I've thought it all out, Minke."

"Bless me, Ma, that my journey be a safe one, and that I will do well at medical school."

"You will do well, Minke. You have gone through so much with me. I understand the problems you face being so close to me.

240

Go tomorrow, leave before dawn. Hire a carriage. No one will go with you. Don't ever be afraid or discouraged."

"I haven't been inoculated yet, Ma."

"Panji Darman had his on board ship too. The shipping agent will arrange everything."

I kissed the hand of this compassionate and loving woman, my mother-in-law. After tomorrow would I ever see her again? She let me kiss her hand.

As we came closer to the house she whispered again: "And don't forget the task your dead friend gave you."

"Who, Ma?"

"Khouw Ah Soe. You haven't forgotten, have you?"

"I'll make sure his letter is delivered."

"And so you must. A task given by someone who is dying, Minke, is sacred."

"I've got a request too, Ma."

She stopped. The night was black. The sky was thick with clouds. Not one star was to be seen. Darsam could be heard coughing some distance away.

"What, Minke? I will help you in your difficulties. You have the right to ask that."

"Not that, Ma. Trunodongso and his family."

"Don't worry about him. He has a claim on this business. So too do all the other farmers who were cheated by Mellema."

"And what about Mama herself?"

"Everything will be all right. And another thing—don't take your wife's portrait with you."

"I miss her, Ma."

"No. Your schooling—that picture will only hinder you. Forget her. Mix with other girls, Child, and be proper too. And when you are in Betawi don't forget about your Mother. You forget that wonderful woman too easily."

Darsam coughed again. Mama called him over. "Darsam, look after that man and his family well. When you're ready, give the two boys some work. Whatever you think is suitable. Put the woman to work in the main kitchen."

"Who is he, Nyai?"

"Your faithful comrade in days to come."

Mama went inside and I followed. She sat down in the front parlor where Panji Darman had been long awaiting her.

*　　*　　*

He had only been away a matter of months carrying out Mama's instructions, yet Panji Darman now looked fully grown up. He stood up as we walked in and bowed to show his respect to Nyai Ontosoroh.

"Ya, Rob, you may begin."

The youth nodded to me, sat down again, and began in Dutch: "My Mama." He stopped for a moment, watching for something in Mama's face. "Please forgive my letters. I am not able to write any better than that."

"Well enough," answered Nyai.

"And not clever at talking either."

"You're quite clever there too."

"Minke, please forgive me. You look very tired. Please don't be angry if I say the wrong thing."

Humbly, carefully, avoiding any chance of offending or hurting our feelings, he began to make his report. He first expressed his gratitude that Mama should trust him enough to send him to Holland as Annelies's escort. He asked forgiveness for all his deficiencies. I don't know how many times he asked our forgiveness.

"You have carried out your task as well as you could, Rob. No one could have done better. You have represented Minke and me perhaps even better than we could have ourselves. It is we who are grateful to you. There's no need to repeat what you have told us in your letters. About my late daughter, there's no need to mention her again. Your task is over, and so too is that whole affair."

Panji Darman looked at Mama, amazed and bewildered. He asked quietly, "Is Mama angry with me?"

"What about your reports on other matters, Rob?" I helped him.

Panji Darman understood. He went on: "No, Mama, Minke, I must finish my report. I have not written to you everything that happened. It's not that I want to remind you of all that past sadness. My task isn't over until I have finished my report," and, ignoring what Mama and I had said, he went on.

Only Panji Darman escorted Annelies to her final resting place. A funeral parlor took care of all the arrangements. The preacher refused to carry out any service because he was unsure about my wife's religion. Panji Darman himself performed a little Javanese ceremony.

"My Mama, forgive me if I did wrong."

Mama's countenance didn't change. I bowed my head deeply as I listened. His words were clear and pure, from a heart that knew no self-interest.

"Even now I don't know what Mrs. Ann's religion was. If it was Islam, please forgive me. I thought it was better to have some ceremony rather than none. I join in the deepest sadness with my Mama, whom I love so deeply, and with Minke, my truest friend. I know better than most just who Mama, Minke, and Mrs. Ann are. All people of character, to whom I owe so much."

The more he spoke the more formal it all sounded. And too much trivial detail. Mama cut in: "Thank you for all your kindness, Rob. Minke also thanks you, isn't that so, Minke?"

"Yes, Rob."

"Now, about the other things."

Panji Darman, alias Robert Jan Dapperste, for the millionth time expressed his gratitude for Mama's offer of putting him through school in the Netherlands. Then there was another request for forgiveness because of his lateness in returning to the Indies.

"An unnecessary extra expense," he went on. "The thing was, while I was in Amsterdam I saw a report about preparations to publish a Malay journal. Its name was going to be the *Pewarta Wolanda*. The report said, Ma, Minke, that this magazine was being published especially for people in the Indies, and that it would use good Malay. It was going to try to develop Malay into an appropriate administrative language and a language of polite social communication. But the most interesting thing was that they were looking for articles about life—real life—in the Indies. So I decided to visit the magazine's office. And who should I find there? None other than Miss Magda Peters."

Panji Darman was sitting in the reception area. Magda Peters was arguing with some Indisch. With all the racket from the printing, he couldn't make out what they were disagreeing about. As she came outside she quickly recognized Panji Darman, but because he was then asked in to see the editor, she only had time to give him her address.

The editor turned out to be a veteran of the Aceh War who knew a great deal about the Indies. He had been a lieutenant in the army. He was very happy to have Panji Darman visit him. He was assisted by a Sumatran, Abdul Rivai, a *Java Doctor* who was continuing his studies in Holland.

"Forgive me, because I can't remember that Dutchman's name now," said Panji Darman. "He asked me to write about my experiences in the Netherlands, in either Malay or Dutch. I was willing. And in a flash I was thinking about all that had happened in those last few weeks. I would tell the story of the unjust way Europeans had treated Mama's family. I said I'd be back in about two weeks. The only trouble was that he asked that I write it in proper Malay, not in the uneducated Malay of the marketplace. I wasn't able to say yes to that. I said I could only write in Dutch. He gave in.

"Before I left he showed me sample copies of coming editions. They were going to be very beautiful, Mama, Minke, full of attractive photos—just like European magazines. I went back to my lodgings and began to write. That's why I was late in returning home."

Then one day Rob went to visit Miss Magda Peters. Our former teacher was renting a room in a very austere area. There was no carpet in her room. Her fireplace was an old iron stove. Her furniture comprised a bed, a wall cupboard, and a table with two chairs. How different was her situation here compared to how she lived in the Indies—in a nicely furnished house, all to herself. But she didn't seem ashamed of her poverty.

"I'd come to ask advice about my article. I'd changed the names of the people in the story. She said that an anticolonial article like that could not be served up to the readers of a colonial magazine; that the magazine was to be published to help broaden the knowledge of those loyal to colonial power, so that the colonial masters would be able to converse occasionally with them."

"You are always so well-intentioned, Rob," Mama cut in, "but you needn't have done all that."

"I felt it was my duty, Mama. I had to do all I could."

"You've done so much for us, Rob," I added.

"If I didn't finish my tasks properly, I thought, I will live in shame forever, Minke; I would never be able to finish another task ever."

Tears glistened in Mama's eyes as she watched Panji Darman, moved by the loyalty of this simple young man.

"I didn't understand what Magda Peters meant," he went on. "I didn't get the chance to talk with her again. I excused myself and went to the editor's office. He read what I had written, not saying a word, and he gave me three guilders as payment."

"I've never seen that magazine," I said.

"Neither have I. I asked him to change the names in the article and use the real ones. He said there was no need. He didn't ask my address either."

"They won't publish it, Rob," said Mama.

"However that might be, at least I tried," he answered.

"Is there anything else, Rob?" asked Mama, beginning to get impatient.

Panji Darman then reported on the use of the money he took with him, including the three guilders he earned from the article. Then: "Now about the business side of things, Mama."

The orders were for the cinnamon to be sent unpowdered by Mama's spice business, Speceraria.

"Good, Rob. As soon as you're ready to work, you can contact the cinnamon collectors. Now go and get some rest." Mama stood up and went upstairs. She seemed very tired.

"Good night, sleep well, Mama."

She didn't answer, but disappeared from sight.

"We'll meet again tomorrow, Rob. Rest now." I didn't give him a chance to speak. As soon as he left, I locked the door. Then I went out to the back and locked the back door from outside.

The clouds had disappeared from the heavens. The scattered stars sparkled peacefully. I went to the warehouse to have one more look at Trunodongso.

The children and his wife were asleep. Truno himself was lying in a somewhat uncomfortable position, not yet asleep. As the light from a wall lamp struck him, his eyes blinked open and shut. He didn't see me approaching. As soon as he saw the shadows, he became vigilant; then: "Oh, Ndoro," he said, and sat up with some difficulty.

"Feeling better?" I asked.

"My land, Ndoro," he said anxiously. "They will have taken it by now."

"Hush, don't think about that. Get better first. Nyai will look after you all. You and your children will be able to work here until you want to go back to your village."

"Ndoro promised to help me."

"You were too impatient. I hadn't succeeded yet, and you were already up to all kinds of things. Didn't I warn you before?"

"I was bound by an oath, Ndoro."

"My promise to you is still in force. But your oath, your promise to these other people, has only brought disaster. All right now, get some sleep. Don't worry about these things now. Nyai will take care of everything. Don't ever talk about Tulangan. Don't say that you've ever met me. Don't go anywhere without Darsam's permission. They will still be looking for you. Your mustache and beard—shave them off—everything."

"Good, Ndoro."

As I came out of the warehouse I bumped into Darsam, who never seemed to sleep.

"Not asleep yet, Young Master?"

"And you, why aren't you asleep, Darsam?"

"Young Master, I don't know, I'm always restless, ever since my hand's been like this."

"Nyai has said you will stay here."

"But what work can I do like this? I just end up wandering back and forth like a hungry mouse."

"What do you want to do?"

"To work, Young Master, but I can't. Must I be just like a tree, doing no work but forever sucking strength from the earth?"

"You'll slowly adjust to your hand, Darsam. You'll be able to work again. Dr. Martinet says not all your fingers will be useless. Some of them won't be able to move, but not all of them."

I grabbed his shoulder and ushered him towards his house. We went inside. Everyone was asleep. He turned up the light.

"Darsam," I called him softly.

He didn't hear me. He fetched a rag and cleaned the seat where I was to sit.

"Darsam," I called again. "No need to sit. I want to talk to you standing here like this. Darsam, I don't want ever to forget all the help you have given me during these difficult times. I don't really know whether I should consider you my brother or my uncle."

"You're very strange tonight, Young Master," he said, amazed.

I took out the gold pocket watch that Mother had given me. "Look, Darsam, you can read and write now. You can read the time? Here, what time is it?"

"Twelve o'clock less fifteen minutes, Young Master."

"Very good." I opened the back of the pocket watch and showed it to him. "Can you read that writing?"

He tried and tried, but couldn't.

"No. You can't. It's Javanese writing. It says: 'To my beloved son on his wedding day.' Darsam, this was made by the best of the goldsmiths at Kota Gede, Yogya. From my mother. Try it on. It looks good, doesn't it?"

"No, Young Master, no."

"Hush; don't wake anyone." I put the watch into his shirt pocket and hung the chain on the second button from the top of his shirt. "Very good, Darsam; it suits you. This watch really suits you. Take it as a remembrance of a young man who can never forget the thanks he owes you."

"Young Master," he protested.

"Don't refuse. This is an order. Take that watch wherever you go." I took his left hand and I shook it, trembling.

He became even more amazed. And in that condition, I left him.

The pendulum clock in the front parlor rang out twice. All my things were packed in my suitcase. My briefcase was full of writing paper. I had resolved not to sleep. I walked back and forth in the front rooms and the back, making sure I would remember all these things that I was about to leave behind for who knows how long, perhaps forever: the furniture, the phonograph that had not been used for so long, not even for recording, the ornaments on the walls, and the shiny, newly polished parquetry, all glowing in the light of the gloomy oil lamp.

For quite a while I gazed at the portrait painted by Jean Marais—the picture of Nyai Ontosoroh. In the dim light of the lamp it seemed more alive than even Mama herself. All her strength was there, as if she were a goddess immune from pain and death, remaining strong in all weather and situations. Yes, even the clouds in the background seemed to be running away to avoid her head. If she had lived ten or maybe thirty centuries ago, the painter would have had the right to paint her with a halo. In the future, if I am given a long life, long enough to become senile, this woman will still never leave my memory. Her face, her kindness, her wisdom, her patience and resolve, her strength, I will take them all with me to my death.

I went back into my room and took out from its wine-red velvet cover Jean Marais's painting of Annelies and stood it near a lamp.

Ann, you are still smiling. It was you who first brought me into this room, and into the garden beside it. I am still here now, Ann, even though for the last time, and you left it before me to go who knows where. I know I will never see you again in this life. Nor will I ever meet a woman like you.

"Put the picture back!"

Mama was standing behind me. She was a carrying a bamboo bag, which she put on the table.

"Here is some bread and drink; you must breakfast before you board the ship." From the basket she also took an envelope, and gave it to me. "This is what you have saved while you have been working here. One hundred and fifty guilders. A carriage is waiting. Leave now. You must carry all your things yourself. No one must see you. Good luck, Child, Nyo. Good luck."

She embraced me. She kissed my forehead. She helped me carry my things to the door. Before leaving the house I asked for her prayers for my safety and for her blessings. She gave them, then said once again: "Good luck, Child. Live up to your ideals."

She turned and went inside. I stood in a daze on the steps. It was here that I first met Annelies and came to know her, then became a member of this family. My breast felt heavy. What more could I hope for from this beautiful house? There is no longer anyone waiting for me to come home, waiting for my caresses. A tear dropped.

The cold wind struck my face. The basket and bag and suit-case I carried all together in my two hands. I had taken just a few steps.

"Let me help you, Young Master!" My bag fell from my hands. It was Darsam.

"You won't talk to anyone!"

"Where is Young Master going?"

"You're the only one who knows. Keep quiet about it."

We stealthily made our way to the road. Seeing us approach, the driver lit the carriage's lamps.

Silently Darsam lifted my things up onto the carriage.

"A safe journey, Young Master, wherever you are going." From his waist he took a dagger in a leather sheath and handed it to me. "Take this, Young Master." He pushed the weapon into my belt.

"Come on, driver!"

Good-bye to you all: Wonokromo, beautiful and sorrowful memories, Mama, Darsam, Trunodongso and your family. Good-bye; I will not return. Mama, the woman I admire most in my life, you, in whose hand I was no more than a lump of clay to shape however you wished, who can explain the great issues, who can dig deep into many things at once, who is intelligent and educated, who is ahead of your times, good-bye. All your hopes for me will be realized, Mama. All of them.

I sobbed in the darkness of the morning.

The carriage traveled slowly through the stillness, farther and farther away from Wonokromo. I ordered the driver to drive around Kranggan, past my old boarding house and Jean Marais's house. Maysoroh was no doubt still asleep under her blankets. Good-bye everybody, good-bye to you all. And to you too, Mr. and Mrs. Telinga! I had to use all my strength to resist the urge to see Maysoroh. That sweet child! How clever she had been in keeping her father's friendships alive! How deeply she loved him! All her father's hurt and pain became her hurt and pain. So young a little one! Good-bye May!

Good-bye to you all.

I instructed the driver to fill in a few hours traveling around, visiting the places I used to like, and also my old school. The building was still blanketed in darkness—no light, either in the compound or along the street outside. Ah, you, my school, are you afraid to look me in the face? Because what you gave me has turned out to mean so little?

The carriage kept moving. Good-bye to you all. I will never return to see any of you again. I am on my way to become my own person, to become what I was meant to be.

Good-bye.

14

The ship *Oosthoek* set sail from Tanjung Perak.

The crowd that had come to say last farewells dwindled in the distance; the people now looked like ants swarming over the wharf. I knew not one among them. No, I was afraid, not discouraged. Good-bye to everything, to men and their earth.

The sea took me farther and farther away from the land. I needed to become complete, not the shadow or image of someone else, no matter how much I respected and admired that someone else. I must not see this parting as a sad event. There was nothing more I could expect to gain or learn in Surabaya and Wonokromo, the places that had swallowed up my youth. As time passed, the crowd on the wharf became a blur. In the end all I could see were the mountains to the south.

Though I hadn't slept at all the night before, I had no desire for sleep. This was the first time I had traveled by boat. My first view of the island of my birth from the ocean: A white line of beach pressed by heavy layers of green growth and mountains, looking like rows of gray-blue waves—Multatuli's "Emerald Horizon."

"Something wrong?" I heard someone greet me in Dutch.

Beside me stood a European—young, friendly-looking. His face was adorned by a smile. His lips were pale. His teeth were somewhat yellow from smoking. He was tall and slim. On his little finger he wore a gold ring with a small diamond, less than a carat. His clothes were all of white cotton.

He held out his hand by way of introduction: "My name is Ter Haar, Mr. Minke, or is it Mr. Max Tollenaar." He knew my old pen name.

"Oh, Mr. Ter Haar—have we met?"

"I'm a former subeditor at the *Soerabaiaasch Nieuws*."

"I don't think I ever have seen you before."

"Of course you have not. Mr. Nijman does not wish others on the editorial staff to deal with Asians, especially not with Natives."

"May I ask why not?"

"Especially in your case, Mr. Minke. He did not want you to be influenced by anyone else."

"Influenced? How?"

He laughed and slapped my shoulder. He took off his glasses and cleaned them with a handkerchief. After he had put them back on, he offered me a cigarette. I said I didn't smoke; he nodded: "It's best you never take it up, Mr. Minke. Once you try you'll never be able to give it up. But my smoking doesn't bother you?"

"Please, go ahead, sir."

"It is good that you graduated from H.B.S. Too few Natives receive an education as good as that."

How many times had I heard that? It was a signal: Get ready to discuss a European-type matter. Like a mechanical voice-box I automatically produced from my mouth the usual ever-so-polite response: "I will try to follow what you say as well as I can, Mr. Ter Haar."

He nodded, focusing his eyes on me. The lecture was about to begin.

"In these times we live in, Mr. Minke, there are different ideas floating about the place. Mr. Nijman doesn't like people who don't think as he does." He coughed several times and threw his cigarette into the sea. "Ah, this is how it is for cigarette addicts. If you don't have a cigarette you must have one; once you get one your throat's hot and sore. You're lucky you don't smoke."

Perhaps he threw his cigarette away not because his throat was sore, but because he needed time to make up his mind whether to tell me what Maarten Nijman was like.

"Mr. Nijman doesn't like radicals," I said.

"Ah, you have sharp insight. You are right. And more than that, he is actually an Indo. He is a member of the *Indische Bond*."

"You're a radical?"

"A good guess, Mr. Minke."

I remembered Miriam de la Croix, who had joined a political party, so I asked: "You're a member of the *Vrizinnige Democraat* party?"

"That's about right."

"And you mean that Nijman doesn't approve of it?"

"Oh, he's a shareholder in TVK." He scratched his neck. "So people say, anyway. It seemed he didn't like my thinking. We often argued, even when it wasn't necessary. I had no involvement with the TVK. You know about the TVK, the sugar company?"

"Of course. The Madurese call it *te-pe-ka*."

"It'd be strange to find a Surabayan who didn't know of it." He whistled, his cheeks collapsed, and his lip shook. "We had so many fights, I gave in and left."

"That's what you're doing here?"

"Yes."

"Where are you heading?"

"Semarang, Mr. Minke. I'm going to work for *De Locomotief*. Have you read that paper?"

"Not yet."

"A pity. The oldest paper in the Indies. It has a long and brilliant history. It's read in the Netherlands too."

"A strange name for a newspaper—*De Locomotief*."

"To honor Mr. Stephenson. The paper was founded at the time the very first locomotive was put to use on Java—thirty-six years ago."

"How would you compare it to the *Soerabaiaasch Nieuws*?"

"There's no comparison, Mr. Minke. The *Soerabaiaasch Nieuws* is no more than an extremist colonial paper."

"So it is a sugar paper."

"Yes. Many of its younger reporters have been let down, disappointed. They're sent off to do jobs that aren't really work for journalists at all."

Ter Haar did not go on with his comments. Having heard about Kommer's experiences at Tulangan, it was easier for me to understand what he was saying.

"While nothing adverse is being said about sugar, it looks like any other neutral paper, but as soon as sugar interests are offended, it appears in its real colors. I heard you've had some bad experiences of your own with Mr. Nijman."

"No."

"Even so, you should write for *De Locomotief* instead. It's more famous, has a bigger circulation. I'll try to get your writings published. The paper is read not just in Holland but in South Africa—the Transvaal and Oranje Vrijstaat—and wherever Dutch is understood: in Surinam, in Guiana, in the Antilles. It gives a realistic picture of the Indies to the world."

He talked with great enthusiasm about the world of the press. I listened like a little boy being told a bedtime story.

There was virtually not a single neutral paper the world over, he said. In the Indies nearly all the papers were colonialist in the extreme. The plantation papers were even worse. Their job was to give indirect orders or make suggestions to government officials that suited the plantation owners. The news reports were merely a formality, so they could call themselves newspapers.

"Your pieces, for example, were published just to keep the readers entertained, humored—to assure them that nothing was wrong in the Indies, that all was safe and secure—safe and secure for the sugar mills, so that the shareholders in the sugar companies would feel at ease, and the share prices back at the exchange in Amsterdam would remain stable."

I felt he was accusing me: My writings were no more than a way of making the mill owners happy. But I had written those articles in full seriousness, mobilizing all my abilities, all my emotions, and exhausting both in the process.

"And if I had written negatively about the sugar interests?"

"There would have been no space in the paper for your work. On the other hand, everything must be done to keep the confidence of the shareholders, for example, if there were a sugar crisis because of a fall in prices."

I didn't understand. How stupid and ignorant I was! A sugar crisis! Fall in prices! How much I did not know. And I was ashamed to ask—an H.B.S. graduate who doesn't know anything about sugar, who tried to make contact with a cane coolie and was laughed at by Nijman.

As time went on his lecturing became more and more overbearing. He became more enthusiastic—the enthusiasm of an unpaid teacher. It was killing the enthusiasm of the student, who had never paid his fees anyway. What I had heard and understood from Kommer's story about *Soerabaiaasch Nieuws* was no longer enough to help me. I couldn't understand. Couldn't understand! Who can fault someone who simply doesn't understand?

"So now you know why Nijman could get so upset about a peasant farmer."

He became more and more carried away. Lustily were the wolf's teats pushed towards me. In anger and frustration my throat was seized and the nipples jammed into my mouth.

And that sugar-owned man, Nijman—his hands have never held cane, his trousers have never brushed the earth of a cane plantation—why must he become so savage just because of one farmer? Doesn't the government have enough soldiers and police?

Ter Haar nodded in his knowing-teacher fashion. He raised his head and lit a new cigarette. His sucking made the cloves in the cigarette crackle. The dirty white cigarette paper caught alight, curled, and turned into ash. His threw his gaze towards the deck tower.

"Take this ship, Mr. Minke. Listen to the engine. This is not owned by the government. The Dutch company KPM owns it. Yes, people say that most of the capital comes from the queen. And that's why they can use the word *koninklijke*—royal—but it's not owned by the government."

His talk became even noisier, the milk from this wolf was becoming thicker and thicker, too sticky to swallow. His lips moved quickly, sometimes sucked in and almost disappearing, but his voice lashed out, overcoming the power of the wind that was crashing into my ears. "Surprised? That there is a company owned by the queen but not government property? That's called a phenomenon, sir, a phenomenon of our age. Don't ask me. I know what it is you want to protest. Ah no, you already know."

I shook my head in a panic.

"No? Truly?" He gave a short, biting laugh. "It is the government that guards, that guarantees the security of the queen's ships, the profit that comes from each trip. It is the same with all the sugar mills and plantations, all the private businesses."

He went on to tell me all about all the giant businesses in the Indies: figures, protozoa spread throughout my land, growing and multiplying, making the people of this land dance like marionettes.

He flung his cigarette into the sea. It didn't sink, but bobbed with the waves as they broke against the ship's sides.

"Any kind of capital can enter the Indies. The government has opened the door. The government guarantees the security of that capital. A bitter thing to know, Mr. Minke, where all that capital comes from. Mostly from the Netherlands, sir, but lately there has been more from the peasants of Java themselves. Have you read about this year's sensation?" He stared at me like a devil about to pluck out my eyes. "No? Of course not: It hasn't been reported in the papers here. An incredible story, Mr. Minke. Something uncovered in Holland and exposed to public view in the Parliament. N. P. van den Berg and Mr. C. Th. van Deventer have made the accusation that the royal family has taken from the peasants of Java the amount of 951 million guilders. Have you ever seen a thousand guilders?"

The wolf's thick milk was gulped down in one clot.

"The royal family misappropriating the wealth of the Javanese peasants! Farmers, just farmers! That's what they have alleged—van den Berg and van Deventer."

Ter Haar stared at me once again, as if he wanted to lift me up and fling me onto the deck. He was angry, frustrated. "We here in the Indies have been waiting and waiting for something more to be done about the matter in Parliament. But no, that was all, Mr. Minke, nothing more. I don't know how many mouths the palace gagged with wads of money, but all of a sudden the members of Parliament went mute."

I didn't understand, but I nodded. Even how one thing related to another I didn't understand.

"But the greatest outcry in Holland is over the debt the Indies accumulated—one hundred million guilders in six years—to finance its lust to conquer Aceh."

The image that appeared before me was of Jean Marais. And

a question: Who was this man that I have called Ter Haar? As he watched me—perhaps I was standing open-mouthed in confusion—he laughed boisterously.

"What can one do? Your eyes must see these things clearly. Ignorance is shameful. Allowing someone to remain in ignorance is betrayal. I'm free from accusations of betrayal now."

He slapped my shoulder. "What a *De Locomotief* man says is different from what a *Soerabaiaasch Nieuws* man says."

"Do you know Kommer?"

"Kommer? The reporter from the Malay paper? I've heard his name."

"He's never spoken as you have."

He didn't react. Instead he bent his tall body over so he could bring his lips close to my ears. "And Governor-General Rooseboom, famed for his liberality and gentleness, no less a fraud—the deceit of a mousedeer, Mr. Minke." Abruptly, he straightened his body. Leaning against a ship's ladder, his head thrown back, he broke into cascading laughter. And when he finally stopped laughing, he bent down again, his lips near my ears: "You read the newspapers." And like Nijman: "But not everything is printed in the papers. Have you heard about the decision to grant the Japanese equal status with Europeans?" I nodded. "Russia is furious with the Netherlands Indies."

"Russia?"

"Yes, Mr. Minke, the czar. You know why?" I shook my head. "Well, isn't Russia at odds at the moment in Manchuria with Japan? Several weeks ago"—he tried to count it out on his fingers but was unsuccessful—"the Russian fleet turned up at Tanjung Perak harbor, Mr. Minke, at Batavia itself. Old Governor-General Rooseboom, Mr. Minke, he was rushing about everywhere looking for ways to make the Russians happy. Yes, Mr. Minke, the crown prince was with the fleet. He was on his way to Port Arthur." He let out a breath. "Do you know where Port Arthur is? In the name of neutrality of the Netherlands Indies, the crown prince was entertained with a hunting trip in the forests around Priok. And so there would be no complaints, Rooseboom ordered that some of the deer from the governor's palace at Bogor be caught and let loose at Priok." He broke out into that boisterous laughter again. "Just imagine how happy the crown prince must have been to make those half-tame animals topple to kiss the earth.

And the flattery from the Dutch officers, already prepared: What a great hunter is His Highness, the noble crown prince of Russia. It was the first time in the history of the Indies a hunter could down three deer in one strike."

Now his voice slowed down.

"That was during the day. At night the daughter of a bupati was brought to him. God! In the name of the neutrality of the Indies! How old was that girl? Almost fourteen! God! In Europe, in the Indies, the lies are the same."

I wasn't capable of following all his chatter and all his laughter, his bendings and straightenings. Now a new cigarette inhabited his mouth. The previous one had been elegant; this one was of corn husk, tied with red thread.

"And that neutrality, Mr. Minke, is all for the sake of big business in the Indies."

It seemed he was relieving himself of some burden that had nothing to do with me. Now that he was released he was silent. I used the opportunity to question him about where he came from and where he received his education. He seemed so young. He laughed. He did not avoid my questions, but neither was he clear in his answers. From his sparse replies I gathered that at twelve he had become a cabin boy on a ship bound for the Indies. In Surabaya he had jumped ship. He then became a general run-about at a factory. Later he went into the interior of Borneo, and the land of the Torajas in the Celebes, and the Batak lands in North Sumatra—perhaps then too as general servant—with a research scholar. Since that time many researchers had sought to hire him as an assistant, especially people from the churches.

Humbly he acknowledged: "It was from them I gleaned what knowledge I have of the world. But it was with my own eyes, my ears, the soles of my feet, that I gathered a few clumps of knowledge about the Indies themselves."

"What you've just been telling me—it's not about the jungles, is it?"

He laughed again, but not so boisterously this time. He was no longer smoking; his stock had been wiped out.

"What's the difference? All these great cities are just jungles, places to wield power over others, to get whatever life-essence can be sucked from people's bodies. Yes? Isn't that so?" His laughter was less and less convincing. Then, abruptly: "Mr. Minke, the government is not as it used to be. Your people, Mr. Minke, there's nothing left of them but the dregs after their bodies have been squeezed by forced cultivation. The great companies pay the fattest tribute to the Indies state now. So, if necessary, the government will mobilize army and police, civil service and village officialdom to make sure their will is done."

So we returned once again to that issue. I could find no way to escape the harangue.

He talked on and on about a dozen things of which I had never heard before. The *Oosthoek* sailed calmly to the west. Everywhere there were sailboats of the fishermen, and of the Bugis and the Madurese.

"I don't know how long these Buginese and Madurese boats will be able to hold out against the Dutch ships. There used to be many more; I myself have witnessed how the steamships—first the Arabs and then the Chinese—started to push them aside."

"That's never been taught at school."

"Sorry, Mr. Minke, I've never been to school. And anyway, what would be the point of teaching things like that? Truly, I am so happy to hear a Native say something like that. These times, Mr. Minke: Like a perforated rice-steamer, this age can never be filled up, no matter how many different questions are asked and answers given. Deceit is flourishing everywhere. Not the deceit of people who only want a dish of rice—that's no more than the cunning of a people already at the same level as the mud of their homeland—but deceit and falseness that ride the wind, Mr. Minke, deceit as the legitimate child of excessive power. I'm sorry, Mr. Minke, this person you speak to here is no more than the illegitimate child of one mother and who knows how many fathers."

His confused talking, as if he were being hunted by some devil, ended abruptly. His hands groped in his pockets, left and right, but he couldn't find a single cigarette.

"Why would the queen invest capital here?" A question flew from my mouth to mask my stupidity.

"What for? Ah, Mr. Minke, what does it mean to be a queen in these mad times? Without capital she too would be the servant of capital. Even a king is best off being a king of capital."

"But the teachers all say we are entering the age of modernity, not the age of capital."

"They only half know what's going on, Mr. Minke. The

journalists know more about what's actually happening. And to half know something is not necessarily to know it all. Look, Mr. Tollenaar, didn't you use the pen name Max Tollenaar to conjure up the image of Multatuli's *Max Havelaar*? From that alone people will know you are the spiritual child of Multatuli. Your humanity is great; even so, Mr. Minke, such humanity, without real knowledge of life in the Indies, could miss its mark altogether. What people call the modern age, Mr. Tollenaar, is really the age of the triumph of capital. Everybody alive in this modern age is ordered about by big capital; even the education you received was adjusted to capital's needs, not your own. So too the newspapers. Everything is arranged by it, including morality, law, truth, and knowledge."

As time went on Ter Haar's talk became more and more like a pamphlet. (I myself had some doubts about including all this here, especially as I wasn't really able to fathom it all. But not to include it would also not be right; Ter Haar took me on a journey to new continents that I had never encountered in my geography lessons. So if these notes read like a pamphlet—yes, that was the situation in which I found myself. The ship, the past, Surabaya and Wonokromo back there—they all became the pages of a pamphlet, splinters of an incomplete knowledge.)

And it was still difficult to accept the notion of the absolute sway of big capital over people's lives. In the villages people weave, spin, make batik, plant their fields, marry, reproduce, die, and are born—and none of this is because of capital. And early in the morning people leave their beds, ritually wash themselves, and face God—and is that because of capital?

Now I was beginning to understand what Jean Marais had said about the power of capital in the Aceh war. Ter Haar gave more than a glimpse: It was a flash of lightning. Marais had said that the Netherlands Indies was jealous of English capital, which could fondle and control Andalas through Aceh, a buffer state. The independence of Aceh was violated by the Dutch, even though Holland always said that the Netherlands violated Aceh with the agreement of England.

"Yes"—Ter Haar spoke again—"but what people call capital is more than just money, Mr. Minke. It is something invisible, abstract; it has a supernatural power over real objects; it causes everything that is scattered to collect together, that which is together to scatter, that which is liquid to solidify, and that which is solid to turn into liquid. Once in its grip, everything changes shape. The wet is made dry and the dry made wet. A new god has the world in its fist. Yes, it's a boring thing, but a fact. Production, trade, the sweat of the people, transport, communications—no one, not one person, is free from its power, influence, and instructions. Also, Mr. Minke, the way people think, people's ideals, they too are approved or not approved, blessed or not blessed by it."

The longer he spoke the more fantastic his story became, contradicting everything I had ever been taught at school. It burst from my lips—an attempt to restate a classic issue: "Would it be as true to say that everything is ruled by science and its laws?"

He laughed amiably. "Science and its laws are now no more than just an empty swelling, powerless. . . ."

And Mama reckoned everything was ruled by authority, by power. Ter Haar broke into that uncontrollable laughter again. His tall body shivered. At that moment I reckoned he must have a nervous disorder. Neither he nor his rhetoric could be completely accepted.

"There is no power that does not stem from massed capital, Mr. Minke, not these days. That other kind of power is to be found only among shepherd peoples wandering the grasslands, or other nomads in the deserts, jungles, and savannah. The cleverest of people, and even Stephenson, the hero of the century, would never have been able to give the locomotive to the world with no capital. It is only with capital that he was able to order the clouds of steam to make those carriages move hundreds of feet. Without capital people could not make light or bring to life the telegraph. Without capital, those big men would be nothing more than leather shadow puppets with no backbone to keep them from flopping. Isn't that so?"

The wild wolf had spoken too much. It was too complicated to digest.

That afternoon I slept well. I used the evening to note down all his babblings and to think a little about the truth of his words. Everything my teachers had taught me was now threatened with being turned upside down, thanks to this Capital. What had Ter Haar said? Everything is subjugated by it: individuals, societies, and peoples. Those who don't wish to be subjugated remove themselves, run away. Kings, armies, the president of the United

States, France, even the beggars by the roadside stalls or the churches, all, he said, are in its grip. Peoples who reject the power of capital will languish and die. Societies that run away from it will return to the Stone Age. All must accept it as a reality, like it or not.

I was on my way to Betawi to continue my schooling. After I graduated I would become a government doctor, curing the sick employees of the state. They must be able to carry on their work for the government. And the government, in its turn, would ensure the health of the capital. Is that all that will become of me in the future? An insignificant expender of energy in the interests of capital?

I had not finished with my thoughts. The writing still stood on the paper, gaping open-mouthed. I had not closed it with a full stop when he came to my cabin. He invited me to eat with him.

On leaving the cabin I realized it was already night.

Dinner in the second-class dining room was all European. My appetite died. Ter Haar, on the other hand, ate happily and lustily.

"You don't like European food very much," he said. "Yes, food is a matter of habit. I still to this day prefer pears to bananas."

Back up on the deck, however, it was I who began: "Mr. Ter Haar, why did Mr. Nijman and his paper treat Khouw Ah Soe as an enemy?"

"You mean the Chinese immigrant murdered at the Red Bridge?"

He didn't know what had happened, so I told him.

"Mr. Minke," he began, "the situation is now safe, calm, and orderly for big capital. People can get on with their work without any significant disturbances. Khouw Ah Soe and his Young Generation might have influenced the Chinese in the Indies, might have had some influence generally. If society is disturbed, then trade will most surely be disturbed as well, and prices too."

"But there are always disturbances." I told him about the troubles of the peasant farmers in Tulangan, about which he already knew.

"Peasant rebellion is meaningless, Mr. Minke."

"But the situation is disturbed too."

"Such small upsets are already calculated as part of general production costs." Now he seemed to try very hard not to lecture. "What kind of power do those peasants without capital have?

How much damage can they do? It won't cost the companies more than twenty sacks of sugar to put things back in order." He laughed. "What's twenty sacks compared to five thousand? The peasants will be put down. It takes a week at the most. Then they return to their original state. But, Mr. Tollenaar, if the people themselves change . . . things will never be the same. The conditions of life will begin to change also, slowly moving further and further away from the original situation."

"But it wouldn't be the farmers, but the Chinese that changed, that is, if Khouw Ah Soe had indeed succeeded in his efforts."

"It's not as simple as that. All kinds of people influence one another—even into their kitchens. Perhaps you yourself are already a lover of bean curd, and noodles without ever feeling you have been influenced by another race. And not just the Natives of the Indies, but the peoples of Europe too. People use spoons and forks, eat spaghetti and macaroni—all influences from China. Everything that gives pleasure to mankind, everything that does away with mankind's suffering and boredom, everything that lessens his fatigue, will, in these times, be copied by the whole world. That young sinkeh too. He and his friends were only trying to copy the United States and France. In the end so too will the Natives of the Indies. And if the Natives started on that path, then soon there would be no more comfortable place for big capital in the Indies."

This last exposition of his was easier for me to follow and helped explain what had been said earlier. A spot of light appeared to expose the way ahead so I could travel it without the aid of others.

Before us, the island of Java was swallowed up by the darkness. Here and there were lights like yellow-reddish fireflies. There was life there, the greater family of my people. They were not allowed to copy America or France, either directly or through the influence of others; they have to stay in their present state forever.

"They are the source of earnings for big capital," Ter Haar went on. "Everything must be turned into a source of profit. From every inch of thread that is sewn into a torn garment, from every stride that makes itself felt on the earth. And in the towns of Europe and America, from every mouthful of water. Maybe in the future they will take profits too from each cubic inch of air we breathe."

Abruptly the tone of his voice changed. Stingingly: "Do you know anything about the Indies' close neighbor, the Philippines?"

"A little. They rebelled against the Spanish colonization, then against America."

"Where did you hear that? It has never been reported here in the newspapers."

"Just by coincidence, Mr. Ter Haar," I answered. I could not say anything else, not because of the subject itself but because my source was Khouw Ah Soe. I still had his letter in my suitcase.

"News from the Philippines is very scarce. It seems the government feels it has to restrict such reports." Ter Haar's words came forth more and more quickly, more enthusiastically; he seemed now to be expounding his own beliefs: "The government is afraid that if the Indies Natives find out a lot about what's happening, about how far the Filipino Natives have progressed under Spanish rule, they would be ashamed.

"Many Filipinos are educated, really educated," he went on. "Already some are graduates. And the Indies Natives? Just a handful sit on the benches of universities in Holland. There is still not one graduate in all of the Indies. Public schools are not even three-quarters of a century old. In the Philippines, they have been going for almost three hundred years. In the Indies ninety-nine percent of Natives are illiterate. In the Philippines it is ten percent less than that."

Such progress. The Filipino natives were closer to European science and learning, closer to understanding the power that rested with the European peoples, to knowing how to use that power, and so they rebelled. They had changed as human beings because of European education. They could never return to being the Natives of earlier times. And the government of the Netherlands Indies was worried that the educated Natives of the Indies would find out that the Filipino rebellion against the Spanish was led by educated Filipinos and was no mere peasant disturbance like that in Tulangan.

Before the rebellion itself took place, he went on, the port workers in the Philippines harbors refused to work. Coolies refusing to work! I thought, amazed. In a flash I remembered something like that being reported in the newspapers here, something they gave the name of "work desertion" and in Holland "striking."

"The Filipinos have already carried out strikes," said Ter Haar. "But their rebellion is even more interesting; it rocked all of Europe, including Holland, Mr. Minke." He hurriedly lit another cigarette. "They're all busy studying why it happened so they can make sure nothing similar occurs in their own colonies. A friend of mine knew one of the Native leaders there, someone called Dr. José Rizal. My friend met him in Prague. Rizal was a poet, very brilliant, and a fiery lover also. The Spanish caught him in the end. A great pity—someone as outstanding as that. His faith wasn't strong enough. A pity." He smacked his lips. "Of course there can be no doubt now about his fate: The death sentence ended his life story. Someone as cultivated as that, writing poems in Spanish, just as you write in Dutch. A doctor, Mr. Tollenaar, and you too intend to become a doctor. Perhaps that is no coincidence."

"Somebody educated, a doctor, a poet . . . rebelling . . . "

"Maybe the Dutch are cleverer than the Spanish. There has never been any rebellion by educated Natives against the Dutch here. Here the educated Natives always follow the Dutch. The Indies is not the Philippines, Holland isn't Spain."

"And he was sentenced to death?" I was reminded of Khouw Ah Soe.

"That's right. The Spanish military are famed for their viciousness."

An educated person had rebelled against his own teachers— indeed there had never been anything like that in the Indies.

"And then even when isolated from his comrades, José Rizal did not stand alone. So many, so very many people loved him, because with all his knowledge and learning, he loved his own people so much. Many prominent people, clever people in Europe pleaded with the Spanish government to pardon that brilliant, educated Filipino."

"What did he want to achieve with this rebellion?"

"You don't know? He wanted his people not to be ruled by the Spanish. He wanted them to rule themselves. A pity"—he made noises with his lips again—"that inexperienced people in the end became the victims of an alliance between Spain and America."

264

"I don't really understand, Mr. Ter Haar. How could they rule themselves? You mean the educated Natives would replace the Spanish and the Americans to govern their own people?"

"Of course, that's what they wanted. National independence."

I conjured up in my imagination the kings and bupatis of Java, mad with their lust for power, making people bow down and crawl before them, give obeisance to them, do their pleasure. And no guarantee that they would be better educated than those they ordered about. I shook my head. Even to imagine the Filipinos governing without white people was beyond me. And here, on my own earth to think of such a thing! To make any sense of it at all was impossible. Without the power of the whites the kings of Java would soon be mobilizing every single inhabitant in the effort to annihilate each other, each trying to emerge the sole triumphant ruler. Wasn't that our history for centuries?

"What's the matter?" Ter Haar reacted to my brief silence.

"And what would happen if the Native kings held power again? Imagine how the educated groups would suffer, Mr. Ter Haar."

"No. The Filipinos intend to govern along American and French lines: a republic—that is, if they won. In such a great awakening as that there were of course many leaders whose thinking was European, and a modern organization also. Not like the peasants of Tulangan. There was an organization that was the engine of opposition."

"A modern organization?"

"So you are not familiar with the idea of a modern organization?" Now it was he who shook his head.

I couldn't see his face clearly. The evening darkness provided him with a good disguise. Perhaps he was pitying me, a graduate who didn't know about modern organizations! Probably Nyai Ontosoroh would have understood and been able to explain it clearly. But truly, I didn't understand. I stayed silent, no more questions; shame and embarrassment enveloped me now.

The drumming of the ship's motor shook everything inside my body, even my thoughts.

"In the end," Ter Haar went on, "the more European science and learning Natives obtain, whatever their race or nation, the more it is certain they will follow in the footsteps of the Filipino

Natives, trying to free themselves from European rule. The Filipino Natives wanted to stand up themselves as a free nation, as Japan does now, acknowledged by all the civilized nations of the world."

"And you include the Indies in this prediction?"

"Of course, though who knows when? And to prevent such a thing from occurring, or at least to postpone it, the government here is especially miserly in handing out European education. Science and learning are sold at the highest price. But there can be no doubt that the Netherlands Indies will arrive at that point one day, as the numbers of educated grow. That day will arrive, perhaps as predicted by Sentot. You know that name?"

"You mean Multatuli's friend?"

"Yes. Let's walk. Standing here is not healthy, especially for a smoker like me."

Perhaps he thought I wasn't following him; he moved on to another subject, but then turned back: "One day when you have read and studied more, you will understand better than you do now."

"The Indies, Mr. Ter Haar," I said, because I didn't feel comfortable just listening and never contributing any words, "has been confronted with the rifles and cannons of the Dutch army for three centuries and has always been defeated." All of a sudden I remembered the story of Untung Surapati, who had won. "Only a few times have we won, but then only momentarily."

He laughed affably. "Naturally, because those Natives were still back in the Middle Ages, or perhaps even earlier—maybe you could say the Stone Age. But if the Indies Natives—just one percent—could master European science and learning—even less than one percent, one tenth of one percent—those changed human beings could start changing their society; then their whole people would change. Especially if they had some capital as well. The rifles and cannons of the army do not have the power to hold back change, Mr. Tollenaar. Even if their numbers are small, if one class rises in rebellion, even the smallest nation will rise up along with them. You remember the Eighty Years' War, don't you? What was Holland compared with Spain at that time? But once Holland had risen, even Spain had to admit defeat. Do you know about Mexico?"

"No."

"The first conquered people to defeat their masters, the Spanish. What was the significance of the Mexican Natives compared to Spain then? But once a group rises up, once a nation rises up, its power cannot be dammed up any longer. It cannot, Mr. Minke."

"You seem to believe the same thing will happen in the Indies too."

"I'm not talking to you like this without reason."

"Such a thing won't make the Dutch nation happy, including yourself," I said.

"I believe in the French Revolution, Mr. Tollenaar: Liberty, Equality, Fraternity—not just for ourselves, as is now the case on the European continent and in America, but for everyone, for all nations upon this earth. The true liberal point of view, Mr. Minke."

"But France herself has colonies in Africa and Asia and the Americas."

"That is France's, and Europe's, wrongdoing. But the shout of the revolution remains as grand as always. It was created from French blood, tears, and pain, and French lives."

"You amaze me, Mr. Ter Haar."

"I'm proud to be a liberal, Mr. Minke, a liberal who sees things through. Yes, others call this sort of view 'extreme liberal.' Not just disliking being oppressed, but also disliking oppressing. And, indeed, more than that: disliking oppression anywhere."

It was far into the evening when I returned to my cabin. I noted down only the main points Ter Haar had discussed, including those I didn't yet fully understand. Totally exhausted, I laid myself down on the upper berth. The others in my cabin had long been asleep. And I was absolutely sure that in a moment I too would be blessed with a health-giving sleep.

When I awoke it was light. The day was visible through the porthole. Two small fishing boats with small sails were attacking a wave. The howl of the ship's motor shook everything, including me. Washing my face in the basin, I went outside. And Ter Haar's words were still there, swooping down, attacking me, pursuing me. How could a Native become president? Would he not just fall back into the ways of the kings, which he would know from legends, and which he could see for himself in the bupatis? And then would not others emerge who wanted to be like him? Then wars would rage continuously, just as in the classic history of our rulers. War without end—each person pitted against the other, all against all? What would come of it?

We have had hundreds of years of experience of war, Mr. Ter Haar. Defeat, always defeat. And according to Miriam—who knows whether it was her own opinion or just picked up in one of the alleys of this world—it is Minke, and Minke's race that is perhaps the cleverest in the world at turning its back on reality, at drugging itself into sleep, at humoring itself with the fantasy that they have never been defeated.

That maiden had the hope, whether a just or an insane hope: Don't be like your fellow countrymen, Minke. There must be one person who is aware, who can be their brain and their senses. Another wolf, that Miriam.

And the Philippines—salute! Defeated? Defeated in its fight against America? At least this mighty people had defeated Spain. It's a pity, Mr. Ter Haar, but we are not Filipinos. I could not imagine it: The Indies without the Dutch! We must draw as deeply as possible on the well of European knowledge and learning. Just as Japan is doing. There is no honor without European science and learning. Mr. Ter Haar, you are truly a spirited coaxer, leading me astray.

With that last thought I went into the bathroom. But none of these things wanted to be shaken loose. They kept popping up, pursuing me and hopping up and down crazily everywhere. What torment such a little knowledge can wreak . . .

Private capital began to enter the Indies . . . yes, at the end of the *Culture System*. The minister of colonies, de Waal, legislated for the expropriation of land which was to be set aside for capital interests born of the corruption during the Culture System. And these interests wanted guarantees from the governor-general of the Netherlands Indies, not against the possible depredations of Native rebels—they were considered insignificant—but against the incursions of the English, who were biding their time and quietly keeping their eyes on the situation from Singapore and Semenanjung. What was the meaning of the London Treaty of 1824? It was just a piece of paper. The English could use Aceh as a bridge into the Indies. Aceh had to be brought totally under Dutch control, to dispel the fears of big capital.

And Aceh proved to be unlike Java. The Dutch fell into a trap. The Acehnese War raged, the most costly during the whole of colonial history. Ninety percent of the armed forces and seventy percent of the budget were siphoned off to win that war. It went on for almost a quarter of a century! The commitment shown by the Netherlands Indies government in subjugating Aceh acted as a guarantee for capital. More and more capital made its way to the Indies. . . .

In the dining room Ter Haar was already waiting. He went on with the stories from yesterday. He tried to explain the power of big capital in our times, the modern era. He never mentioned the Acehnese War. All this talk he came out with now was almost a repetition of what was in that anonymous pamphlet that Magda Peters had given me.

I asked him whether he had ever read an anonymous tract on this subject. He asked in turn, amazed: "Do you mean *The Cesspool of Our Colonial Policies?*"

"Exactly," I said.

"So you have read it. Do you know that pamphlet is a banned publication?"

"I never knew there were banned publications in the Indies."

"Be careful not to get caught with it, Mr. Minke. There was an earlier banned book too, *Women of Jayakarta,* but it is nothing compared to that pamphlet. If you have already read it you should be a member of the Radical Group. I'll try to arrange it, if you agree. But keep away from the Indies Union."

"What is this group?"

"Just a discussion group. You agree?"

What was wrong with being honored with membership? Discussions about the current situation, no doubt more interesting than school discussions. I agreed without thinking about it any further. Anyway, he knew more than I did.

He invited me to walk with him on deck. He was becoming more and more friendly and open. He went on with his story:

These days the big capital that came into the Indies was not active only in agriculture. Capitalists had their fingers in mining, transport, shipping, industry. The small Chinese tin miners on Bangka Island had been swept aside by big investors. The small sugar business of Java had been stamped out by the sugar factories.

These small businessmen were now just coolies belonging to the new, powerful tuans.

"You know about de Waal's Agrarian Laws?" I shook my head. Another new continent.

"And you must know that it was former Minister of Colonies Van de Putte who was the brilliant mind behind them, and the cleverest of all the devils of heaven and earth. A sailor, Mr. Minke, who came to the Indies and became a Tuan Besar Kuasa in charge of a sugar mill. It was he who drew up the sugar laws when he later became minister for the colonies. Now it has been revealed: All this time he was the owner of the biggest sugar-cane plantation in the Besuki-Bondowoso region. Him! While your people, Mr. Minke, who lived all around those plantations, had nothing! That is the sort of thing you will find out by joining our discussions."

What a huge range of things this one wolf knew! Perhaps there wasn't a grain of truth in any of it. But he did seem to know.

"Do you know the story of how the big farmers of Priangan were robbed of their most fertile lands?"

It had happened not long ago, he told me. The big farmers or rich villages had their own forests, rice lands, other fields and crops. They owned hundreds of buffalo, which roamed freely in the village or on private land. In order to seize those lands for the big capitalists, the government only had to issue land regulations. But in order to take the lands over without creating suspicion, Native agents were set to work. They put poison in the water holes where the buffalo drank. In one month ten thousand buffalo died. The villages stank of rotting carcasses. Disease was rampant. So it was announced: No cattle were allowed to roam freely in the forest lands or in the jungle. With army troops as their bully-men, and facing little resistance, the government forced the villages and big farmers to give up their lands. Now it was all planted with tea. Not a single relic remained of the great cattle farms. Destroyed, totally annihilated.

"You would never find out such thing without joining the Radical Group, Mr. Minke. Please, don't look at me like that. Our group is only a vehicle to collect information about all the dark, illegal goings-on in the Indies. And then there is the gold rush around Pontianak. You surely wouldn't have heard about that. Isn't that right? Yes? And the secret societies of illegal immigrants from North Borneo."

His words kept swooping down without a pause. I don't know when he had the opportunity to wet his throat and lips. Perhaps he had finished five or seven cigarettes. You could even smell the cigarette smoke on my clothes. He talked and talked:

Capital wanted to turn all the Natives into its coolies. The Natives' land would become its own land. So the capitalists resisted with all their might any moves for European education to be given to Natives. They were afraid the source of their power, cunning and evil, would be revealed. But capital needs more than just coolies; it also needs foremen who can at least read and write. So schools were set up to teach a few people to read and write. Then that too wasn't sufficient; they needed some who could count. And those schools needed teachers, so a teachers' school was set up. Then they felt the need for a few people who could speak a little Dutch. The primary schools that were operating were divided into grades I and II; students in first grade received a little tutoring in Dutch. So, as things developed, capitalist interests in the Indies found they needed educated Natives for their own enterprises. And so on and so on. More advanced schooling, at high-school level, in special subjects, was instituted for Natives: agriculture, administration, medicine, law. It could not be avoided. It was necessary because of the growth and development of capitalism itself—including the medical school I myself was about to enter. And I will be given good money to stay with the government, to make government service attractive.

And the most powerful of all capital was sugar capital. It was on behalf of sugar that the liberals in the Netherlands, calling their policy the Ethical Policy because they wanted to pay the Netherlands' debt to the Indies accrued in the days of the Culture System, waved the banners of education, emigration, and irrigation for the Indies, and prosperity for the Natives. But in reality it was done in the interests of sugar. Education: to produce the literates and numerates and technicians needed for the sugar industry. Emigration: to move more Javanese off Java, providing much-needed labor in Sumatra and opening up more land for canefields in Java. Irrigation: Water for the cane plantations, for sugar.

"And that's not all, Mr. Tollenaar," Ter Haar went on.

"One need gave birth to another, because that is the law of life. Willing or unwilling, capital will bring Natives more and more into contact with Western science and learning whether they want that to happen or not.

"And Mr. Tollenaar, you yourself want to study to be a doctor. Yes, there must be doctors, so that the plantations and factories aren't disturbed with people falling ill."

"If in the future I graduate as a doctor, it won't be my intention—"

"Willing or unwilling, you will become a part of the cane-crusher machine—like the sieve, or a cog, or steam kettle."

"But a graduate of the medical school becomes a government doctor."

"It's all the same, Mr. Minke."

He had succeeded in making me understand.

"The government would not provide education and training if it weren't in its own interests. Remember what happened in the Philippines. But they have no choice."

I understood now why Jean Marais was so sickened by the Aceh War, something he experienced himself.

Another ship came into sight as it passed us from the west.

"Look at the ship, another KPM ship. The queen's capital is behind it—just like this one. Both made by clever engineers and tradesmen. The motors made by the best inventors. But it all belongs to capital. Those without capital are no more than coolies, no more than that, no matter if they are more brilliant than all of the Roman and Greek gods together."

Now I thought of Nyai. She too was able to employ Europeans to do her business. They came when she called. And Mr. D——. L——., that incompetent lawyer, was tossed out of the house in front of everyone because he was no longer of use. A Native throwing out a Pure! What a lot Nyai had learned from Mr. Mellema!

Ter Haar began again to discuss the Philippines, but this time choosing material he thought I would understand. Now he used a new term that was even more difficult: nationalism. He himself had great difficulty in explaining it.

Then he stopped. Like somebody who had just remembered something, he took out his pocket watch: "I have an appointment, Mr. Tollenaar. You must be bored with this endless chatter of mine."

"Not at all," I said, though in fact I did feel more than a little full.

"Then we'll take this all up again another time."

"I have never met a European like you, Mr. Ter Haar."

"Not all Europeans are rotten."

"You remind me of Miss Magda Peters."

"Quite possibly. I only heard her name after she was expelled from the Indies." He nodded, excusing himself, and walked off, disappearing down some stairs.

Back in my cabin, I opened the dictionary. But its explanation of nationalism was just as unenlightening as Ter Haar's. Nothing in the dictionary equated this nationlism with the greatness Ter Haar attributed to the rising up of the Filipinos against Spain and America.

I had not been long scribbling down the outline of Ter Haar's discourse when his servant arrived with two magazines: *Manual of the Indies* and *Research and Experiment,* a German magazine. It seemed this was how he wanted to continue our discussions.

Only because I had never seen it before, I opened the German magazine first. There wasn't a single picture. My German was terrible, but there was an article about the Philippines. I felt I had no choice but to force myself to untangle its meaning. And it was more than just difficult. Knotted up and entangled by all my own recent experiences, my mind turned the article's complexity into complete confusion. On the other hand, it was those very experiences that enabled me to understand some things. Aided by those experiences, I came up with this picture of the situation.

The educated Natives of the Philippines put their hopes in the Spanish liberals back in Spain, just as I had put my hopes in the Pure Dutch liberals back in the Netherlands. Yes, in Europe, the land where the peak of human achievement and brilliance was stored as in a museum. And the Natives had beautiful dreams: One day the Spanish would, in their generosity, make them members of the parliament in Spain and give them the full civil rights of subjects of Spain, and they would be able to feel they could do some good for their own people in their own land.

One thing I learned, a basic piece of knowledge: that a small group with this dream tried to bring it to reality, inviting others to dream the same way. They set up a newspaper. A newspaper!

Filipino Natives publishing their own newspaper! And the educated Native Dr. José Rizal was one of its leading figures.

I had never seen a picture of him. But I imagined him as someone tall and slim, with big side-whiskers, mustache, and heavy eyebrows. But that's not so important. What was important was that the authorities in Spain cursed him and took action against him. And I was forced to think about how things were in the Indies. There had never been anything like that Filipino group here. Never. And the indications were that there never would be. Poor Trunodongso; with machete and hoe he wanted to fight them, while even Rizal had been trampled so easily.

Still fortified by his hope in Spanish charity, he carried on with his attempts to make his dream a reality: He founded the Filipino League. But the Philippines colonial government continued their attacks upon him.

I know these notes won't be of much interest to anyone, but I have no choice but to include them. Why? Because these thoughts are so much a real part of my environment, the world I inhabited. Ah, knowledge: Trunodongso would never know that there is a nearby country called the Philippines. And knowledge, the result of my reading this article, made the Philippines a part of my own world, even though only as an idea. The wonder of knowledge—without their eyes ever seeing the world, it makes people understand the breadth of the world: its richness, its depth, its height, and its womb, and all its pests and plagues as well.

And Rizal still dreamed of the honor and nobility of Europe. But European power was a monster that became hungrier and hungrier the more it gobbled up. I found myself thinking of the greedy ogre in the wayang stories of my ancestors.

But other groups of educated Filipino Natives had long lost their faith in Spanish colonial power. They took up arms and rebelled. Poor Trunodongso and his friends: They knew no geography; they thought that if they could rid Tulangan of the sugar mills they would win an eternal victory. But Rizal was even more pathetic than Trunodongso. When his comrades took up arms, he was still dreaming of the generosity of the Spanish governors of the Philippines, even after he was arrested and exiled. And a few days before he was executed he was still urging his fellow Filipinos who had taken up arms to stop fighting. He was more pitiful than

Trunodongso. Him—Rizal! Truno was defeated because of his lack of knowledge, Rizal because he did not believe in what he knew . . . in his intellectual conscience.

The Filipino revolution broke out. The goal was to run the Spanish out of the Philippines. In my soul's eyes I could see the educated Filipino Natives rising up, leading their fellow countrymen, uneducated like Trunodongso, in attacks against the Spanish garrisons—a war that could never be depicted on the wayang stage. Even in my fantasizing I could not imagine it. They weren't led by individuals, but by a spirit of resistance, represented in that organization of theirs. Represented too in its top leadership: Andres Bonifacio. Seven years ago. Poor Trunodongso—he knew nothing of such leadership. Poor Minke—I had only found out a few hours ago. Tens of thousands of Native Filipinos mobilized the whole people into resistance. And they did resist, they did fight back. The whole land seethed with rebellion, marching out of the houses to take part in the fighting, to live or to die. The Spanish in the Philippines were pressed hard and then pressed even harder. And the Filipino Natives chose their first president: Emilio Aguinaldo. In 1897! The first republic in Asia.

And they built their own government on the French model! No wonder Khouw Ah Soe was so excited about the Philippines! He was still at the stage of crying out to his people like Rizal, at a time when his own country was suffering under the Americans, the English, the French, the Germans, and the Japanese, as well as being parched by drought, the whole country, north to south, east to west. He too died, just as Rizal did. And this Javanese—he is still nothing. He is nobody.

The Filipino revolution was thrown into turmoil by traitors who loved money more than freedom for their country and their people (another piece of basic knowledge for me). The rebels, in their defeat, accepted the hand of friendship from America. The warships of America sailed to the Philippines and surrounded the Spanish armada. On land the Filipinos worked together with the American marines. No different from the wayang stories.

I have heard the explosion of a cannon on Queen Wilhelmina's coronation day. But in my soul's eyes thousands of cannon explosions tore apart the garrisons and the earth of the Philippines. The sky was dark with cannon smoke. Death arrived to the sound of tumult. Not like the death that silently throttled the people to the south of Tulangan which Surati witnessed. How different is killing to the sounds of shouts and cries, from the strangulation of smallpox.

But the Filipinos, still inexperienced in these things, were finally deceived by the Americans. In the battle of 13 August 1898—a show battle between Spain and America, like the show battle between two ancient Javanese kingdoms—Spain was defeated, America won. The Filipino patriots were the real losers; they were freed from the Spanish, but fell into the hands of the United States, which became their new master.

So far I had learned one thing clearly: White power was equally greedy everywhere. Greed. No longer just a word, its meaning fused in my mind as the starting point for all understanding. Greed. But that was still better than war, killing, destruction. Especially a war where there is no hope of victory, as in Aceh, in the Philippines, like the one Trunodongso wanted to wage. No, Ter Haar the Coaxer, I still need Europe as a teacher, including you yourself. Only through your own strength can we confront you, Europe.

Oosthoek's chains clashed and clanked as the anchor was lowered into the waters off Semarang. Night had fallen. Lamps flickered on land and sea. Stars twinkled in the sky, and the surface of the sea glimmered in shining yellow waves. Ter Haar was to be seen neither on deck nor in the dining room.

I went to his cabin. Not there either. His things were already tidily packed.

From the loudspeakers came an announcement: All passengers not leaving the boat at Semarang could make a four-hour visit beginning at eight o'clock the next morning. Passengers for Semarang were asked to disembark now.

I used the time to walk around watching the people disembark. I found Ter Haar speaking to another European near the gangway. It was he who spotted me first: "Mr. Max Tollenaar, may I introduce you to my friend from *De Locomotief*."

"Pieters," he said.

Ter Haar explained who I was and about the *Soerabaiaasch Nieuws*.

"Oh, Mr. Max Tollenaar is really quite young. I thought

you'd be middle-aged at least. There is much wisdom in your writings."

"We will be going ashore in a minute," said Ter Haar.

"You will be visiting ashore tomorrow?" asked Pieters.

"Of course."

"Good. Don't head off before we come to fetch you," he said. "You must come and visit our newspaper offices. Who knows?"

They boarded a small rowboat and waved good-bye. Not long after, the few passengers for Semarang went ashore.

"Eh, Mr. Minke." Someone spoke to me. Beside me stood a Pure European—a police officer.

"I'm not mistaken, am I?" he asked. "*Tuan Raden Mas* Minke? Officer Van Duijnen. How was your journey? Enjoyable?"

"Very much so, sir—my first trip by ship."

"Not seasick?"

"The weather has been beautiful and the sea calm."

"Very good. You're not going ashore?"

"Tomorrow, sir, in accordance with the ship's announcement."

My heart beat with suspicion. There had to be some reason for his approach. Perhaps Trunodongso had opened his mouth under interrogation. Truno, yes, that Truno. Who knows what stories he came up with.

"I think it would be best if you went ashore now, sir," he advised me. I became even more suspicious.

"A pity, sir, but I still need some rest."

"You can rest in the hotel."

"Thank you, but no."

"I'm not joking, sir. Let's go ashore. Where are your things?"

Yes, Trunodongso had betrayed his promise. The policeman was obviously arresting me. I headed off to the cabin. He followed me. I packed all my things. He helped me.

"You got around to making notes even on this journey?"

"It seems you need me ashore?" I asked.

"Yes, sir." He presented me with the order. "There's no need to worry. You can see for yourself that it is an official order. I'm not here to kidnap you."

"My destination is Betawi, not Semarang."

"There's plenty of time to go to Betawi. Why didn't you go by train? The trip through the south is much more interesting."

He was suspicious of me. I didn't answer, pretending not to hear. I picked up my suitcase and bag. I left the food basket behind.

"Let me help you," he said. He carried my suitcase. "You don't have anything stored in the hold?"

"Nothing, sir."

We descended the steps under the gaze of many eyes. A young criminal had been arrested on board.

"What have I done wrong, sir?" I asked.

"I don't know. Don't be anxious. I don't think there is anything to worry about."

"How can I be detained like this? I'm a *Raden Mas*. You know that."

"Precisely. That is why a district police chief has been assigned to meet you."

"Meet me?" My mind raced, trying to make sense of it all. In the end I couldn't escape the thought of Trunodongso. New troubles hovered before me. More newspaper reports. More suffering for Mother. I still have given you nothing, Mother. It seems I can only fall into predicaments like this.

The last time I was met by a police agent, Father was made a bupati. Now it is a district police chief, but certainly Father has not been made governor-general of the Netherlands Indies.

A special boat took us ashore. A government carriage was waiting to take us.

"Where to, sir?"

"No need to worry."

The carriage took us to a hotel. "The best in Semarang, sir," he said.

Semarang was fast asleep in the light of the gas street lamps. He was not joking; it was indeed the biggest hotel in town. People looked after us very politely. I was given a big room, for two people, a bit too beautiful.

"*Tuan Raden* Mas Minke, just stay here and be good. Don't go out. Don't leave the hotel until someone comes to get you."

"What's really happening? Why am I being detained like this?"

"Have you been treated improperly, Tuan?" It was exactly as the police agent had behaved the last time.

Before leaving, he repeated his warning. Once again I was a pawn in a chess game. Certainly, Father had not been made a governor-general. Perhaps he had been awarded the Lion Cross for his services to the state. Well then, it was Trunodongso I had to think about. Or Robert Suurhof?

Dinner was brought by a waiter. And the way he served me—how careful he was, as if he were afraid. All my questions went unanswered. Perhaps outside the door there was another policeman?

How I missed Ter Haar now—that broadcaster of ideas. His whisperings still buzzed around me: They, those people, Mr. Minke, build their power upon the ignorance and backwardness of the people of the Indies. Who are you, Ter Haar? A police spy? My suspicions were set in motion again. Maybe that's it. That school report of mine—that my moral character was wanting—that would be noted down in all the books of the offices that administer candidate civil servants for the bupatis. As an individual, I could do nothing to defend myself against those books, or the silence of the police chief.

For the rest of the night I lay with my eyes blinking open and shut, on that incredibly soft and comfortable mattress.

At four o'clock in the morning knocks on the door startled me awake. My heart beat like the mosque drums at festival time. A first-class police agent, a Mixed-Blood, was standing beside my bed. A short nod from his apparently wooden neck informed me it was time to get ready, to bathe, eat, and depart, though not a sound emerged from his mouth. Like a lamb who had lost its mother I did everything those preemptory gestures seemed to order.

Then District Police Chief Van Duijnen came to take me. Without much talking we left for the railway station. Five in the morning, and the train left for the southeast on my first journey into the hinterlands of central Java. Dry and bare. Gray-colored earth. Long bridges, wide riverbeds, yellow water, mountains.

The locomotive huffed and puffed wearily towards the central Javanese kingdom called *Vorstenlanden,* past indigo warehouses, coconut, sugar, tobacco, rice, cinnamon—all property of the European landlords.

Locomotive! Locomotive! Locomotive! It announced itself constantly with its own incessant rhythm. Lo-co-mo-tive! Hissing crazily along the rails, spouting black smoke into the sky, screaming with its whistle, it woke the people from their dreams, declaring itself the mightiest being on earth.

Ter Haar had not repeated the clichés of others. "It was this locomotive that inspired the *Semarangsch Nieuws—en Advertentieblad* to change its name to *De Locomotief.* Everybody remembers the year: 1862." No, it was different with this person Ter Haar; he had had his own story.

"Mr. Minke, after Prince Dipanagara was defeated, the Culture System went on to great successes in the Vorstenlanden. Yes, isn't it so, Mr. Minke; it is only in the Vorstenlanden that peasant farmers can be squeezed clean of everything and end up as dregs. It was to there that Dutch capitalists migrated to steal the peasants' land and to become great landowners. Isn't it so? Yes? And when their warehouses could take no more indigo and sugar for export to Semarang, and the aristocrats' warehouses were full too, then the matter of transportation to Semarang became a problem. You couldn't ever have heard this story. I say couldn't, Mr. Minke— why? Because it involves another bigwig. Another minister for colonies, that lawyer Baud. He sent camels to Java. Real camels, truly, Mr. Minke. Almost four dozen. And the thing was, in the experiment of transporting the indigo, there was no trouble. From the Vorstenlanden to Semarang, those animals with their serious faces, like a caravan of philosophers, walked along in a line doing their duty.

"But then the forts at Ungaran and Semarang ran short of rice. Now the behavior of the camels from Tenerife was different. You know where Tenerife is? Over on the west coast of Africa. After carrying the rice for a week, these immigrants from the Canary Islands lost their seriousness. They all began crying and howling; they couldn't stand the smell of the rice they carried. Every few moments they were turning around, scratching at the stones on the road, then knocking into each other and falling down. After two weeks of carrying rice there wasn't one that could stand. Some dropped beside the road; others died in their pens.

"The kings of Java owned nothing but their grandeur and

their harems. They had no horses, no cattle, no buffalo—nothing to use as beasts of burden. So Minister Baud sent donkeys to Java, ten times more than the now-dead camels. The battalion of donkeys put on a different act, Mr. Tollenaar. During the first month they grouchily made their way along the Vorstenlanden–Semarang road with the sacks upon their backs. In the second month, their tongues hung out as they carried the sugar. Then, as they carted the indigo, they began to sneeze. In the end, they all died as well of infection. And there was nobody fuller of spleen than the European landowners of the Vorstenlanden. Finally, in the end, Mr. Minke, it was the iron horse that they decided upon, the locomotive. And more and more land was stolen."

Now that first locomotive in Java, in the Indies, was hauling me in my carriage towards the Vorstenlanden, the source of the indigo and the sugar and all the other commodities needed for the comfort of Europeans.

Van Duijnen didn't speak. He was reading a poetry book in Malay: "A Poem on the Arrival of Prince Frederick Hendrik in Ambon" by Ang I Tong. The Malay newspaper on his lap remained untouched, and he did not offer it to me. Now I saw for myself a Dutchman reading Malay books and newspapers. My thoughts didn't want to focus. I had no desire to read. My mind kept wandering, groping to discover what was about to happen to me.

That evening Van Duijnen was kind enough to pick me up at the hotel. He took me around in a luxurious carriage to see Surakarta. He spoke a lot about this center of Javanese culture. He liked it here.

I think I knew why he liked it so much. Ter Haar had also said, "Surakarta is the center of your culture, and of a hundred and ten large European-owned plantations. Imagine! Where could the peasant farmers possibly find land for their own needs? Just imagine! Do you know what that means? Heaven for the European planter, for every white person, like me." His laugh boomed. "Isn't it so? Yes? True, heh? And your people, Mr. Minke, except for the aristocrats and a few successful traders, they got nothing. They had to crawl like worms to get a bowl of rice."

It was as if Ter Haar's finger were pointing at my forehead:

281

To whom should you speak now? Still to people like Van Duijnen, who can lounge on the cushions of your culture, your civilization?

The streets were lantern-lit—lamps at the mouth of every alley, peddlers' kerosene lamps along the road, everywhere, tiny, flickering, dim. Forgive this son of yours, Mother. I have not answered your letters. I have given you nothing you desired, even though your hope was simple, that I write in Javanese. Speak to the Javanese, said Jean Marais. Kommer too. But it is only the little lamps I see, Mother.

The train was headed back to Surabaya. Van Duijnen was silent again. His head lolled, then he jolted awake.

"You look pale. Ill? A chill?" he asked.

"No," I shook my head. "Perhaps it's just that I'm so tired."

"Is that why you took the boat?"

"At least on a ship you can walk about, and bathe."

"For a long journey it's true that ships are still superior." He became more friendly.

But I had lost the desire to respond. I deliberately exhibited my tiredness and kept my eyes closed. I curled up in the corner.

At five o'clock in the evening we arrived at Surabaya station. A government carriage picked us up. Where were we heading? Wonokromo? I knew all the countryside; I didn't need to look.

All of a sudden there was a crowd of people on the road, blocking the traffic. The carriage had to stop. Van Duijnen stuck his head out, amazed to see this crowd cutting off the roadway. Our carriage bell rang out. The people wouldn't move out of the way. Van Duijnen rose to his feet, his face glowing.

"Look, Tuan Minke!"

Out of politeness I did what he wanted. In front of us were . . . what were they? Ya Allah, the velocipede, the bicycle! There were four Europeans spread across the road holding each other's shoulders. Each was slowly pedaling his own bicycle. I had seen these magical two-wheeled vehicles many times now. They looked so fragile, as if they could be taken apart, folded up, and thrown anywhere you liked with one hand. They looked thin and tall and frail.

The onlookers were astounded that the riders did not go flying onto the ground.

The four Europeans seemed quite young. They raised their

hands into the air—"no hands!" Now while their feet pedaled they all began to sing. And they didn't fall! Once again Europe showed its magic.

Walking in front of the performing youths was a Mixed-Blood who shouted through a loudspeaker, in Malay: "This is what they call the *keretaangin,* sirs, the velocipede, the bicycle. Genuine German-made. Speedy, as fast as the wind. The Lord Wind gives his aid to the riders so they do not fall. You sit safely in the saddle. The feet start pedaling slowly . . . and rider and vehicle shoot off like an arrow! Anyone can buy! Cash or time payment with the Kolenberger Company, Tunjungan Street. And it is not expensive, sirs.

"Runs as fast as a horse. Needs no grass, needs no stable. Just takes a quarter of an hour to learn how to ride, and you can travel anywhere. Far more comfortable than a horse. This vehicle never farts, never needs a drink, never drops dung. Genuine German-made. You can take it straight inside the house; it never sweats."

The government carriage we were traveling in moved to the side of the road, making way for the slowly advancing bicycle riders.

The pedestrian announced again: "The Firm Kolenberger also gives lessons. Only on *tali* for as long as it takes to learn to ride. Don't miss this chance! The most dependable of all modern vehicles. The missus can ride at the back and a child at the front. Three people can set off together and pedal all around the town—no exhaustion, no cost."

They passed us and our carriage turned back into the traffic.

"Crazy!" whispered Van Duijnen. "The world's gone mad!" Suddenly he laughed. "Two wheels. Just think, two wheels! There's more and more of them nowadays too. Crazy! Just one bump and husband, wife, and child would be over and injured. Who'd buy a thing like that? Like a mantis! It'll just end up messing up the traffic." He laughed again. Perhaps he was imagining the victims of the bicycle falling in the middle of the road. "And did you hear what he said?" he exclaimed. "Better than a horse. Can that thing jump over a gully? Can it climb a mountain? Can it swim? Can it have children? Crazy! Yes, it's superior if all you worry about is that it doesn't drink or eat or drop dung." He laughed again. "It can't neigh either!"

I sat down and rested my body against the seat. A number of

Dutch magazines had begun criticizing young women who rode bicycles. It wasn't polite, they said. If the wind blew, all eyes looked the girls' way, so not only was sin being encouraged, but accidents as well. The problem was that people had to stare bug-eyed at every new thing. But once things got started, the world lined up behind. And these young women had begun riding around in public, just for the fun of it, without any real purpose! The Netherlands and Europe were being attacked by bicycle fever.

I remembered an article in another magazine: To oppose progress was no different from Don Quixote's attack on the windmill. If women now liked to ride the bicycle, why wasn't a special version made for them so that the wind couldn't be made the scapegoat? Did people think the world belonged only to men?

The bicycle of my imagination was in the Netherlands, and so my thoughts went to Annelies. She now lay in the earth. She never had the chance to see the two-wheelers proliferate in the land of her father. Had her heart not been broken, this year she would have been free from her guardianship, able to return to Java, and we could have been together again.

Must I keep remembering her? And why do thoughts of the Netherlands always link me with her? She chose extinction without me. She made her own choice. And in the embrace of the earth of the Netherlands she would never witness the wave of women's emancipation that was roaring through the land: emancipation on bicycles.

Now my mind, leaving Annelies alone in her grave, concentrated upon the wonder of this emancipation. You will never hear the famous Dutch feminists, Ann. Humanity would collapse without womankind, they said. Why must women be just the substratum of life? Why do their own children, who happened to be born males, have such extraordinary objections to women appearing in public? Why does the Netherlands even today deny women the opportunity to become ministers or members of parliament, even though twice consecutively it has been ruled by female monarchs?

This modern world! What blessings have you really brought us? The rotten heritage of the past still has not been flushed away: Natives are not allowed to be equal, let alone superior, to Europeans, and must always be defeated. Europeans are against each other too, liberals opposing nonliberals, liberals opposing liberals. And now there was the women's movement for emancipation:

women fighting men. Is the modern age the age of the victory of capital? Machines and new discoveries cannot answer, cannot say anything. Humanity stays as it always was, complex and confused by those same old passions, just as in the wayang of ages past.

I had fallen asleep in the government carriage. I awoke when it came to a stop. As soon as I climbed down the surroundings felt familiar. Yes, it was so: We had stopped in front of Nyai Ontosoroh's house in Wonokromo. What was the policeman doing? My heart beat strong and fast: Trunodongso! It was the Tulangan affair after all.

Nyai Ontosoroh came out, greeting me with a smile. No, that smile could not have anything to do with Trunodongso.

"Nyai Ontosoroh," said Van Duijnen, "I have brought Tuan Minke back. I will leave now. Tuan Minke is not to leave this place, as ordered by the prosecutor. My respects!" Having said this, he left in the carriage.

"Come in Child. Let someone else look after your things. Don't be angry, don't be disappointed. You look so tired. I understand what you've been through. You want to forget your past as quickly as you can," said Mama, "and now it turns out things still have not finished. Even so this house and I are a a part of your past. Smile, sit down."

"What is it this time, Ma? Trunodongso?"

"He's caused no problems."

"Robert Suurhof?"

"No."

"So what now, Ma?"

"Don't be so depressed, Child. You are not the only one who has experienced these new troubles. I too, and all those we love. I hope this will be the last incident. Forgive me, Child, a thousand pardons. We all want some happiness. If the other has come instead, forgive me. Have a bath first, then we can talk properly about all that has happened."

Nothing had changed in the front parlor. The picture of Nyai still hung in the place of the picture of old Queen Emma.

"You've only been gone a few days. Why do you look so foreign now? I'm sorry. A thousand pardons," she said again.

She went into the office.

15

Something had happened in the household: Minem, that saucy girl, was now living in the main house. Minem, the milker of cows! She was sweeping the floor. Even from a distance I could see her eyes wandering.

As I passed I heard her soft greeting: "Young Master has arrived," like the whispering of seduction.

I pretended not to hear and kept walking to the bathroom.

Poor Mama. It seems you became so lonely after I left that you gave in to Minem's desires. Or is it that you want to be close to your grandson? At peace with your fate?

Close to dinnertime, when I was reading the paper, Mama came in carrying Minem's baby: "This is Rono, Child."

"Minem's son, Ma?" I put aside my newspaper.

"Robert's child, my grandson." Her eyes shone. "So my line will not be broken, Child. It was your child really that I hoped for."

Seeing that I was still confounded by it all, she began to explain: "It is Robert's child. See his eyes! The eyes of his grandfather. Rob himself has confirmed it."

"Rob!" I cried.

"Yes, his last and concluding letter."

"Last and concluding?"

"He is dead, Minke. Rob is dead. Venereal disease. In Los Angeles."

"The United States?"

She nodded.

"So far away."

"This child will never see his father." She was speaking to herself rather than to me. Her voice was lonely, heavy.

I understood and bowed my head. Both her children had died in their youth, within months of each other. And before Robert, Annelies's beloved horse Bawuk had died too.

For a moment I remembered the horse's death. The stable hands had not been able to humor its heart. Every day Mama spent two or three minutes chatting to it, just as Annelies had. It ate its favorite sweets, but lazily. Slowly it became thinner and thinner. Finally the veterinarian announced there was no hope.

The animal could no longer stand, perhaps just like Annelies. It lay on the stable floor, without the desire even to raise its head.

Then, one day before we went to Sidoarjo, Nyai and I were working in the office. Nyai asked the time. It was ten past nine. She covered her ears. Half a minute later there were two shots. Mama uncovered her ears and went on working. "What was it?" I asked Mama. She answered: "Bawuk, Bawuk has been put to sleep."

Bawuk had made itself a member of the Mellema clan.

And now there was Rono.

"It's over with my children. I need Rono, this child."

I looked at Nyai with questioning eyes. She started to tell the story, slowly, like someone groping through the darkness of the night. It was not straightforward.

While the *Oosthoek* was carrying me to Semarang, a letter had arrived from Robert Mellema in Los Angeles. That afternoon Nyai took the letter to the prosecutor's office as evidence in the Ah Tjong case. She was received politely. The letter was copied by two clerks. Mama was asked to check that the two copies were the same as the original. She received a copy. The original was kept by the prosecutor.

Then Mama had gone to the police to ask for help in contacting Robert Mellema. Darsam had driven Mama there in the buggy. Then something had happened in the police-station court-yard. Like a plot devised by a playwright, Fatso, alias Babah Kong, appeared in the yard.

"Fatso!" Upon hearing his name in Nyai's tale, I stood up from my chair.

"It turns out he is a first-class police agent."

"What did Darsam do?"

"It was Fatso who quickly told Darsam not to say anything about the earlier shooting."

"And Darsam, what about Darsam?" I asked impatiently.

"Darsam ran inside and reported everything to me. The po-lice looking after me were surprised too, so they summoned him—his name is not Babah Kong, it is Jan Tantang."

I couldn't picture how confused Mama must have been at the time, as though she were watching a complicated melodrama un-raveling on a stage.

"Jan Tantang was questioned in front of us," Mama went on. "And it turned out he isn't a peddler, he is a police agent, first class. But he wasn't doing official work, so he is in trouble for that. He's a Manadonese-Dutch Mixed-Blood."

"Did he admit everything, Ma?"

"From the very beginning, as soon as the questioning started."

"Another trial, Ma?"

"Of course."

Rono gurgled. Minem came and took him, leaving behind sharp glances.

"Yes, Child. A lot has happened. Yesterday the police came with a telegram from Los Angeles. They had found where Robert was living, but that's all they found; Robert himself had died four months earlier."

"Ma!"

"Yes. So be it. That's what had to happen and indeed has happened." She told me the month and day—exactly the same day Bawuk had been shot by the vet.

"I am sorry, Ma."

"He has reached the destination he set off for. I think that's for the best. At least his dreams were fulfilled: to be a sailor, to sail the world."

This extraordinary woman showed no signs of sadness; but I knew her heart was torn apart. It would not be long now before she had to lose the business as well—which had always been her first child, her honor, the crown of her life.

She turned the conversation. "Isn't it amazing, Child, all of a sudden, out of the blue, I have a grandson."

So now I knew with more certainty: It wasn't because of Trunodongso that I had been brought back here, but because of the arrival of Robert's letter and the discovery of the identity of Fatso alias Babah Kong alias Jan Tantang.

"You must read Rob's letter, Child; here's the copy."

"It's not for me, Ma. I don't think it's necessary."

"The trial will involve you, Minke. You must read it."

After dinner Mama gave me the letter. I don't remember now exactly what was in it as I only read it once, and there were so many errors of language. But I have written it up again to read like this:

Mama,

I know you have not forgiven me. Even so I ask again for the thousandth time: Forgive me, Mama, forgive this son of yours, this Robert Mellema, whom you yourself brought into this world.

Ma, my Mama, as I write this letter I feel so close to you, as when I was a child who suckled at your breast. But it seems now that there is nothing for me in those breasts. The water of life, Ma, the water of forgiveness no longer flows. I know I will die young, Ma, without your forgiveness. With my head splitting, aching, throbbing, all my joints stiff and pained by any movement, I forced myself to write you this letter, Ma, news from a lost child. Fever attacks me again and again, my vision is almost gone, lost in the haze. I no longer know if I write in a straight line. But I must finish this letter. Perhaps it is my last. I will keep writing for the next week, until I can write no more.

The nurses here have been so good to me, giving me paper and ink and pen. They have promised to post it to you and even to pay for the stamps. They have promised to post it only after disinfecting the paper.

Now that I'm writing this last time, it is not to ask for

your pity. I only ask forgiveness. I will face everything with resoluteness just as you have faced everything. So you must not feel at all sad if I talk about my illness. I only want to tell you what has happened, as a son to a mother. No more than that.

My illness spreads, each day becoming worse. My body is no longer of any use to me, let alone to anyone else. There is just a heap of rotting flesh and bruised bones. I have no pity for myself, Ma. I have more pity for you, who suffered so much pain and spent so much energy to give birth to someone whose fate is no better than this.

Mama, it is best that first of all I tell you from where I caught this disease.

I have a disease of pleasure. After thinking about it I am sure it was in Ah Tjong's place. May he and all his descendants be cursed. I was still very young and inexperienced. He invited me in and provided me with a Japanese woman. And it was because of that woman that I lied to Mama for the last time, the biggest lie I ever told.

There is no one here in the hospital who can treat this disease. They never talk about my illness, but I know what their silence means.

Because all this goes back to Ah Tjong, let me talk first about him. Cunningly, using a thousand tricks, he got me to sign a letter confessing to living in his house and that all my food, drink, accommodation, pleasures, and everything I needed were provided by him. The next day he started a long conversation with me:

"If Tuan Mellema dies, Sinyo Robert will be the sole heir."

"No, Bah, I have a younger sister."

He nodded, then went on: "You are discouraged just by a little sister?"

"And there is a stepbrother from Papa's legal marriage."

"A stepbrother? What's his share in Sinyo's family in Wonokromo? He has no rights. I can help Sinyo get good lawyers to arrange everything. It'll all be fixed. Sinyo will be the sole heir."

"It can't be, Bah."

"Your only problem is your sister, and that can easily be fixed. Ah, she's only a sister anyway."

"Maybe Papa's already made a will."

"No," he said, "your Papa hasn't written anything."

"How does Babah know that?"

Babah just laughed.

"How do you know that?" I repeated.

"Ah, don't worry, it'll all be fixed without you doing a thing. Sinyo will be sole heir."

"Maybe my sister will soon marry this student. He might want to demand his wife's rights."

He went silent. He asked who it was and where he lived. I told him that the person in question was staying at our house but that at the moment he was involved with the police. He asked me whether I liked my future brother-in-law, I said: "He's just a disgusting Native. From the moment we first met I didn't like him."

"Look, Nyo," said Babah, "if Sinyo becomes sole heir, Maiko can be Sinyo's concubine. And you won't have to do any work. Babah will look after the business. You will have no problems."

"Mama wouldn't allow it."

He nodded, then he spoke like this: "Your sister is just a girl. Your mother is just a Native woman. What are they compared to Sinyo? Nothing. They're no more than banana-tree stumps, Nyo. Believe me. If I say Sinyo will be the sole heir, it means the two of them will be gone."

"But they're not gone," I rebutted him.

"Yes, now they are here. But who knows about tomorrow or the day after? But the business, it will all be Sinyo's alone. And no need to work. Just take pleasure, while the profit rolls in by itself."

"There's still Papa."

"Sinyo's Papa is no longer a factor in anything. He's dead in life, alive in death. Neither his mouth nor his heart have any value. Everyone knows that. It's sad, but that's how it is."

"Yes," I admitted.

"How much pocket money do you get from Nyai?"

"Nothing now."

He clapped his hands and smacked his lips reprovingly. But I know now why Mama never gave me any money. Mama wanted to teach me to earn money from my own efforts, and I *didn't like working. How happy must Annelies be, wanting nothing and understanding what you wished to teach us. It was I who was in the wrong, Ma, and it's no use being sorry now. And yes, you were right, Ma, it is only from their own efforts that people know happiness. At least, Ma, it is certain that you have obtained some happiness from your work. Ah, what's the use of talking about my own feelings, feelings that will have no value in your eyes, Ma?*

But let me go on with this chat between the two of us, Ma.

It was clear he was proposing some possibility of inheritance for me. And how stupid I was; I was happy to hear those poisonous suggestions.

"About the possible brother-in-law, Nyo . . . easy, especially if he's living there. What's the price of a brother-in-law?"

"Darsam will guard him," I said.

"Darsam? He's just a hired fighter. How much does a hired thug earn? Three ringgits?"

"I don't know, Bah."

"Just say it's three ringgits. At the most it'd be thirty guilders. If you give him fifty, he'll do whatever Sinyo wants."

I said he was right. He told me how to approach Darsam. "All these men are the same," he said. "Pay them more and they'll betray their own employers. A hired killer from anywhere. Give him ten guilders as a deposit. Here's four ringgits. Sinyo doesn't like his sister or Nyai, do you?"

"I hate them both," I answered.

"Easier still. But the candidate brother-in-law has to be taken care of first."

Satan had entered into my heart. One evening I met with Darsam at his house. I invited him down to the warehouse and he came with me but was suspicious. I lit a match and put down the four ringgits before him.

"Four ringgits, genuine, ten guilders altogether, new and shiny," I began.

He gave a short laugh.

"For you, Darsam."

"You've become rich very quickly. Where's the money from, Nyo?"

"Ah, don't worry. Put it in your pocket. Next time I'll give you ten times four ringgit more."

"Forty guilders more?" he asked. *"Sinyo's not fooling around this time, hey?"*

I put out the match so he wouldn't be embarrassed to take up the money. *"How much do you get each week from Mama, Darsam?"*

"Ah, Sinyo's just pretending not to know."

"Anyway, if you join with me, you'll be much better off."

"Where did Sinyo get all this cash?"

"All taken care of, Darsam. Hey, people say you once killed a thief here."

"Easy, Nyo, if only a thief and only one man."

"Of course it'd be easy for you, Darsam. What isn't easy for Darsam? Hey, if there was another thief, would you still dare fight him?"

"I'd have to check first who he was Nyo. If the thief was Nyai's own son, it'd be best if I didn't interfere."

"You mean me, Darsam? I've never taken anything that didn't rightfully belong to my father."

"That's why I'd have to see who the thief was first."

That answer not only took away my confidence but scared me as well. Remembering Ah Tjong's assurances, I put aside those feelings and went on: *"There is a thief here again. He doesn't carry a rifle. Forty guilders more if you take care of this other thief and leave no trace."*

"What thief, Nyo?"

"Minke."

I couldn't see his face in the dark, but I could tell he was furious. He growled like a leopard.

"Take back your money, Sinyo," he shouted viciously. *"Darsam has never taken blood money. Don't go yet, before I say my piece: If you take another step before I have spoken, I'll cut you down right here and how, unwitnessed by anyone. Listen: My employers are only Nyai and Miss. They like Young Master. Look out! If anything happens to any one of the three of them, I'll know who did it. Look out! It'll be you I'll kill. Go, get! Don't trifle with Darsam!"*

Frightened by his threats, I ran all the way back to Ah Tjong's house. Babah shook his head but didn't say anything. I tried to forget the incident. I was afraid to meet Darsam. I had thought of him as a hireling but he had frightened me into total collapse.

Babah ordered me to live secretly in his house. I lived in the midst of unlimited pleasure. Everything was made available to me. I didn't have to think about a thing.

Ah Tjong has some plan for our family, Ma. I feel so guilty now that I not only didn't resist letting him do whatever he wanted but, worse than that, I actually agreed to all his plans. It's only proper that Mama is unwilling to forgive me.

Everything is catching up with me; I must look upon it all as a punishment that I must undergo to redeem myself. I don't want pity from anyone. Don't pity me, Ma. Don't remember and miss me, Ma. Forget me as if you had never given birth to me. As if the milk from your breasts had just spilt onto the ground. I'm too low to be your son; even the offspring of a dog knows how to be faithful and return kindnesses. I'm too low a person to be the child of anyone. Even so, once again, Ma, I say I need your forgiveness. And Annelies's and Minke's, even though I know they won't give it. At least I have done my duty and asked for it, petitioned for it.

Be careful, look out for Ah Tjong. Now I understand better: He wanted to gain control of Boerderij Buitenzorg and its land by means of murder and evil, cunning tricks.

Let's leave this horrible matter, Mama.

Does Mama remember a dairy herder called Minem? Annelies will know her. When Darsam, Mama, and Annelies and Minke came to Ah Tjong's house, I had to run away. I knew how furious Mama felt towards Ah Tjong and towards me. I ran, Ma. It was then, Ma, that I left my seed in Minem. I mean: Minem is pregnant because of me, not because of anyone else. I don't know if she aborted the pregnancy or not. If she hasn't, Mama, that is my child, your own grandchild.

Ma, my request to you is to look after that child, boy or girl. I hope she is a girl. Whatever else, she is your own blood; she has never sinned against you. Give the baby my name: Mellema. If she is a girl, call her Annelies Mellema, because she too will be wonderfully beautiful.

Don't let Minem keep on working in the dairy. Bring her into the house, because that is what I promised her. It's up to you, Ma, how you arrange it.

Mama, it's been a week now that I've been writing this letter. By tomorrow I will not be able to write anymore. Live your life in happiness, Ma. . . .Good-bye, my great Mama. May you stay healthy and safe as long as you live. May you live long to see your grandchildren and great-grandchildren. May no one ever make trouble for you again. May there be some among your grandchildren that make you very proud. Best wishes too for Annelies and Minke.

Once again there was a trial. The court wasn't packed this time The public's interest in the case had waned. But one extraordinary thing did happen: For the first time the *Soerabaiaasch Nieuws* printed a photograph on its front page, a photograph of Annelies wearing her diamond necklace. But it was a great pity the caption was so sensational: THE BEAUTIFUL VICTIM OF A STRUGGLE OVER AN INHERITANCE.

What fantastic events and experiences lay behind that photograph. And how beautiful was all that had tied the two of us together for those months. So little was contained in that caption. And it hurt even more when Maarten Nijman came to our house to gloat over his success.

"Ah, we can't keep up with our orders from other publishers, magazines and papers, from outside Surabaya as well. They all want to hire the negatives." He didn't bother with our feelings; he was too involved with the photo's success. He went on: "The royalties I'm charging are way too low; there are so many orders. Some would even pay three times as much.'

I no longer just hated but was now sickened by this man who once was a god to me. The more pictures of my wife appeared in the press, the more I was sickened by the behavior of all the press. They were concerned only with trading on our feelings. Their profits and their success made them forget there was somebody who didn't like what they were doing. But there was nothing we could do.

Even with all the publicity, the trial did not attract much interest. But on the other hand, the pictures of my wife started to appear in people's houses, in the road-stalls and restaurants, even in the hotels. Anyway, that's what one Malay-language paper reported.

In this sickened mood we faced the trial.

The trial became convoluted and went on and on. The judge was Mr. B. Jansen, the same one as before.

Ah Tjong looked thin, pale, and bent. His pigtail had gone white. He wore silk clothes that were already far too big for him. His eyes were sunken and he hardly ever lifted his face.

Ah Tjong's platoon of prostitutes was paraded out again as witnesses, including Maiko. Fatso alias Babah Kong alias Jan Tantang was also a witness.

I'm not, of course, going to cover the whole course of the trial, which went into the same trivial details as the earlier one. Just let it be said that the proceedings became so caught up with detail that the court had to adjourn several times. And it got even worse.

But the adjournments didn't spare me from the courtroom. For me there was another trial. I was a witness in a new case, that of Robert Suurhof.

He sat in the dock with the proprietor of Ezekiel's jewelry shop. Myself, Robert Jan Dapperste, and a few other school friends were witnesses to his putting the stolen ring on Annelies's finger at our wedding. The family of the corpse whose grave was robbed were also witnesses. So too was the graveyard watchman who suffered Suurhof's thuggery.

The trial went smoothly, even though Suurhof gave the most indirect and complicated answers. But he couldn't escape from admitting his own deeds.

And behind me, Mrs. Suurhof never stopped crying and sniffing. Her sadness was swept away by laughter in the courtroom, caused by the question and answer about the reason Robert Jan Dapperste changed his name to Panji Darman.

My friend frowned sullenly, his honor offended, sickened by the behavior of the court. And the laughter and giggles were silenced by his challenging answer: "It is my right to change my name to whatever I like. It did not cost you gentlemen one cent."

I liked his answer.

Robert Suurhof's trial lasted only an hour and a half; he was sentenced to eighteen months in jail on top of the time he'd spent on remand. Ezekiel was sentenced to eight months for receiving stolen goods.

As soon as the trial ended everyone stood except Mrs. Suurhof. My eyes met Robert's; his shone with revenge. He let me see his hatred. He even bared his teeth at me. He showed the same hatred to Panji Darman.

Mrs. Suurhof called out to him again and again. He pretended not to hear and walked off quickly with the police guards to Kalisosok jail.

On the way home to Wonokromo Panji Darman began: "He wants revenge, Minke."

"I'm going to Betawi as soon as possible, Rob. And you'll be protected by Darsam."

"Even so, Minke, he's still dangerous."

"He's not the only one who is a man, Rob."

The conversation ended but our hearts remained anxious.

"Yes, we must be more careful," I said soon after. "People like him can be nasty and treacherous. Rob, I liked your answer in court. I felt offended too."

"Yes. I had to take a stand against those honorable tuans."

"Good for you, Rob. All the best to you." I held out my hand. He took my hand, and without realizing it, we were embracing each other like little children taking an oath for life.

In the trial sessions that followed in Ah Tjong's case, the proceedings concentrated on Jan Tantang, Minem, and Darsam.

Jan Tantang explained that he had never met Ah Tjong. He had never even laid eyes on him. He was confronted with Ah Tjong's prostitutes but they all denied having met him or knowing him. Ah Tjong's gardener said he did see a fat man walking calmly through Ah Tjong's garden on the day of Herman Mellema's murder. The man did look like Jan Tantang, he said, except he only saw him from behind. He thought the man was just another customer out getting some fresh air. The man was wearing European clothes and had no pigtail. The gardener thought he must have been a Chinese Christian, perhaps the family of the head of the local Chinese community. Not only had he no desire to speak to the fat man, but he would not dare to do so, so he didn't pay the man any more attention.

The questioning then went to the matter of relations between Robert Mellema and Ah Tjong on the one hand and Mellema's relations with Jan Tantang on the other. Jan Tantang explained that he did not know Robert Mellema, though he had heard the name. He admitted he had been on Ah Tjong's property on the day of Herman Mellema's death, but claimed he had never set foot inside the house.

"I ran into Ah Tjong's yard to escape from the machete of a certain Madurese," he said, "a Madurese that people say has the name of Darsam."

"Who told you that was his name?"

Jan Tantang thought for some time, trying to wriggle out of the question. The judge's persistence forced him to admit: "Minem told me."

The questioning about Minem caused some laughter.

Darsam admitted he wanted to teach the fat man a lesson because he thought he was killer paid to murder Darsam himself.

"My duty is to guard the business and the family," he said, "and I have always tried to carry out that task to the best of my ability. I am paid to do my job."

He was pressed on the question of whether he intended actually to kill Jan Tantang, because hadn't he already killed a man, and wasn't he also suspected of being involved in the fighting against the Marechausee and police on an earlier occasion? He answered: "I only wanted to find out who was his boss; and if he was out to kill, then I would have done him in on the spot. That would be the fate of any hired killer."

"And why were you suspicious of Jan Tantang?"

The convoluted questioning finally made its way to me. I told the story of being followed from Bojonegoro railway station to Wonokromo. My suspicions, I said, were passed on to others as well. Jan Tantang confirmed what had happened as a result, in front of the Telingas' house.

The trial had been going on a week already. Medical school would be starting in only six weeks' time. The questions and answers went on as if they would never end. I waited expectantly for Robert Mellema's letter to be read in court. It seemed I would have to wait even longer for that hoped-for event.

Days came and went. Still there was no sign that the trial was nearing an end. The whole issue of Herman Mellema's death was still not getting closer to any kind of resolution. Instead the court headed off once again in the direction of the internal affairs of Nyai Ontosoroh's family: How did she treat her children? Straight away

Mama refused to answer all such questions and proclaimed that how she brought up her children was her own affair.

Then abruptly there came a question like a clap of thunder: "Mr. Minke, what are your feelings towards Nyai Ontosoroh alias Sanikem?"

My blood boiled. Mama went red as she watched my lips. But they did not succeed in making us the object of more laughter. The trial seemed to be trying to paint a certain picture: There was indeed no connection between Jan Tantang and either Robert Mellema or Ah Tjong. And so, precisely because of that, the questions were now being fired off in our direction. And Robert Mellema's letter still did not appear. The prosecutor did all he could to discover what orders Nyai had given to Darsam.

Mama steadfastly refused to answer any questions that were intended to reflect upon her policies as manager and owner of the business. She restricted herself to answering that she had never given any orders to anyone to act against people, and she certainly had never ordered that trespassers into the villages on company land be killed.

A month had passed. Then a month and a week, two weeks, three weeks. I would not be able to start medical school that academic year.

Then I was asked: whether I had ever received an order to take action against someone I was suspicious of while working for the business.

"What does the prosecutor mean by 'someone suspicious'?"

"Someone who was going to do harm to Nyai and you yourself."

"So far I have never seen the person who has done harm against us," I said.

"So there is such a person?"

"Yes, there is."

"Where is he?"

"I don't know."

"And what harm has he caused you?"

"He took my wife away from me."

It was becoming clearer. They were trying to prove that Nyai and I and Darsam were involved in a conspiracy against someone. Against whom, I didn't know. But I concluded definitely that the court was out to get us.

At home I told Mama what I was thinking.

"Yes, they're pressuring us and deliberately wasting time. Your suspicions are right."

"But why are they doing it?"

Mama began to explain. The day before I was brought back from Semarang, there had been a visit by three people: the government accountant, who was a Pure, and two assistants, Mixed-Bloods. They inspected the business's books, as well as the stables, rice lands, and fields, and the dairy too. Mama showed them the audit certificate from Mr. Dalmeyer, but they ignored it.

"Is there something wrong with the examination made by Mr. Dalmeyer?" Mama asked, and the government accountant just replied by giving her a new audit form. "So, Child," Mama went on, "it seems the business will soon be taken over. Perhaps Engineer Mellema will be here shortly or, if not, at least the person he appoints to carry it out."

"But what's that got to do with the trial, Ma?"

"If they can make us look bad in the public's eye, then people will think the business has been run badly as well—run by bad people. So it will seem right that someone like me should be kicked out. Engineer Mellema will be able to take over much more easily. The public will be on his side. They will think it's right that we be gotten rid of."

"Could somebody with education behave as deviously as that?"

"The more educated the person, the more educated the deviousness."

Yes, I had to learn to think like that. Before it had been a kind of hidden knowledge I had. Now it seemed I was going to see the final proof.

"Yes, Minke, you've got to learn to think as daringly as that. They can even do worse things than that, Child." Her words were pronounced slowly, as if nothing had happened at all. "In the ins and outs of this life, Child, what you studied at school was just children's games. You are adult enough now to understand that the law of the jungle rules our lives, amongst them and amongst ourselves also. Soon you will see, Child, that what I am saying now is on target."

I was coming to understand better and better: For the thousandth time and for always we have to keep on fighting back. Just like the Filipinos, who did not know what the future held for them, yet still knew there was something that had to be done. And what was it that had to be done? Yes, they had to fight back.

That night I went off to see Kommer and Maarten Nijman to show them Robert's letter to Mama—the copy made and approved by the prosecutor's office. I even helped Kommer with the task of putting into Malay the bit that concerned Robert's plotting with Ah Tjong. That night, also, the two men wrote commentaries and published them in special editions, separate from their newspapers, which were distributed before dawn.

Kommer's comments were very courageous: The court should not keep pursuing and persecuting the witnesses, especially when it was clear that they were only witnesses and not the accused. The court should return to the crux of the matter, namely the role of Ah Tjong and Robert Mellema in Herman Mellema's death on the one hand, and the Jan Tantang incident on the other.

At the next session of the trial Kommer and Nijman were called as witnesses. They were each asked where they got the quotes from Robert Mellema's letter. Both refused to give an explanation. Kommer was pressed harder: "Was Robert Mellema's letter written in Malay?"

"Dutch."

"If in Dutch, where did you get the right to translate it into Malay and publish it without using a sworn translator from the court, because that letter is presently evidence in this trial."

"As far as I am aware," answered Kommer, "that letter was not written for the court but addressed to Nyai Ontosoroh. It is obvious then that it is not the sole prerogative of the court to possess and control the letter, let alone translate it. As long as I have been a journalist I have never seen a law saying otherwise."

"Do you not understand that the contents of your special edition could influence the course of the trial?"

"It is up to the court whether or not it wishes to be influenced. Everyone is free to reject or accept such influence. And anyway, it is clear now that the letter does in fact exist."

"Where is the original of the letter now?"

"With the prosecutor."

The judge asked the prosecutor whether he did have such a letter. The questions and answers now revolved around the letter.

Mama became involved and explained that she had earlier

gone to the police to ask their help in contacting Robert Mellema in Los Angeles. It turned out that the sender of the letter had since died.

The bench felt the blow of the judge's gavel again and again as Mama had to be reminded to restrict herself to answering the questions.

The proceedings became tense. So many issues came and went so fast. One witness after another was called. I was almost left behind by it all.

"Where is the letter? Why was the trial resumed if there was no new material such as the letter? And why was no more evidence brought forward in Jan Tantang's case?" So shouted Kommer from the pages of his newspaper.

Nijman's comments were almost the same. My dislike for him turned into vigilance. I viewed his involvement in all this as totally commercial. But as long as what he did helped us, there was no reason to hate him.

Both were trying with all their might and with great risk to themselves to ensure that the trial was not diverted from its true purpose. Who, after all, was the accused?

The comments aroused great interest among the more hot-blooded newspaper readers of Surabaya, and among all races. The courtroom became more and more crowded. On the day that the courtroom was at its fullest, the trial was adjourned for several days.

Medical school started without me.

When the trial resumed again there was a new judge, a tall, slim man, Mr. D. Eisendraht. It wasn't clear why Mr. Jansen was replaced. Perhaps he was sick.

The trial now proceeded smoothly, and on a straight course, as though rocketing along a railway line.

The new chief judge asked to see Robert Mellema's letter. Someone was appointed to read it out. Then the policeman who had contacted Los Angeles was summoned. He read out the telegram that was previously received from the Los Angeles police authorities, which confirmed that there had been "a patient called Robert Mellema, a subject of the Netherland Indies, who had died four months and two days ago."

Based upon the letter, new questions were asked about the motive, but again the trial had to be adjourned because Ah Tjong was sick. And when he reappeared again, looking paler, thinner, and broken, he surrendered and confessed to murdering Herman Mellema. He was sentenced to death by hanging. He died before the sentence could be implemented.

The Ah Tjong–Herman Mellema affair had been cleared up, with the aid of Kommer and Nijman.

And the Jan Tantang affair turned out to be a melodrama. This is the story:

Jan Tantang was a police agent, first class, from Bojonegoro. One day he was summoned before the assistant resident of Bojonegoro, Herbert de la Croix. Jan Tantang could give both the date and the time that the meeting took place. As an orderly servant of the state, he had indeed noted everything down.

As soon as he received the summons, he attended.

It was eight o'clock at night. The assistant resident was sitting in his rattan armchair. Tantang stood before him.

"You are the police agent first class that the district chief has sent me?" asked Herbert de la Croix.

"Yes, Tuan Assistant Resident: agent first class Jan Tantang."

"Can you speak Dutch?"

"A little, Tuan."

The assistant resident seemed disappointed that he could speak only a little Dutch.

"Can you read and write?' He looked happy when Tantang said yes. "Who can speak proper Dutch among the police agents?"

"As far as I know, Tuan, no one."

"I need a clever man for a special assignment. Are you willing?"

He admitted to the court he was hoping for a promotion. He had answered: "Ready and willing, Tuan Assistant Resident."

"Good. Tomorrow you leave for Surabaya. You must keep under surveillance the son of the new bupati. His name is Minke. Do you know him, what he looks like?"

"Not yet, Tuan Assistant Resident."

"Wait for him before he leaves for the station. An H.B.S. student. You'll know him."

De la Croix ordered him to report on all Minke's habits: his schooling, his diligence in study, how he mixed with other people, and with whom, outside school as well.

"Why did Assistant Resident Herbert de la Croix give you this task?"

Jan Tantang answered that he didn't know. He had explained what his job was. He sent back reports by letter and telegram.

"Why did you behave so suspiciously? Was that the only way you could carry out your orders from Tuan de la Croix?"

"I was given no guidelines on how to carry out my task."

"Was acting suspiciously the only way you could have done it?"

"No."

He went on to explain that he really wanted to become acquainted with Tuan Minke and so be able to converse and mix with him. But Tuan Minke was a student and Jan Tantang was embarrassed, and felt awkward about approaching him. He felt inferior and so kept his distance.

There was almost a disaster when he asked about my relations with Nyai Ontosoroh. He remained resolute with his answer: "I don't know." Several times the question was put to him in other ways, veiled, but he remained steadfast in his answer.

I reckoned he knew a lot about my relations with Mama. He was deliberately avoiding talking about our private affairs so as not to cause us harm. This moved me. Sometimes I thought he was indeed our friend, as he had told Darsam.

He sat calmly on the accused's chair, always polite, his two hands clasped in his lap. I didn't see his fatness so much anymore, but rather his humanity. His answers were always polite, orderly, and direct. He won my sympathy.

It was he who had been given the task of reporting on me for de la Croix's study of educated Natives. In his race to understand the Native psyche, Herbert de la Croix did not want, it seems, to be left behind by Snouck Hurgronje. He had become a victim of his studies, and had also gotten many people involved in all kinds of problems. He himself had lost his position, and perhaps had to live off uncertain earnings in Europe.

One of the witnesses was Minem. She decided to sit next to me, so I was hemmed in by two women. Among the other witnesses was Darsam.

The questioning went on to Minem. The girl answered in Javanese.

One afternoon a fat man leading a horse passed in front of her house. "That man smiled at me. He stopped and offered me some perfume. Without even asking me, he rubbed a little on my neck. It smelled so nice." Minem spoke fluently, completely unembarrassed and unafraid. "I asked him to come in."

The judge asked Jan Tantang: "Why did you say your name was Babah Kong?"

"The one thing I knew I must not do was to give my own name."

"You were no longer carrying out a task for an assistant resident."

"I was still working for Tuan Herbert de la Croix, even though he was no longer an assistant resident."

"And what were you doing still taking orders from him? You are an employee of the state."

"I only used my own spare time."

"You were paid for your services?"

"No," he said without hesitating.

"Why were you willing then?"

"I slowly came to understand what de la Croix was trying to do, and I wanted to help him."

"And how did you and Tuan de la Croix communicate after he was no longer an assistant resident?"

"Letters."

"And what did he say in them?"

"They were addressed only to me, not to the court or the public."

It looked like Jan Tantang was a man with principles. He deserved to be honored and respected.

Minem continued, "Babah Kong kept asking me about my child, where he was and who he was. I answered that his father had disappeared to parts unknown almost six months before. He asked if we were divorced. And I asked how could we be divorced if we hadn't even been married? Babah Kong took out a little bottle of perfume, poured out a little, and rubbed it on my cheeks, pinching them too."

The courtroom was filled with laughter. Jan Tantang bowed his head. Minem glowed happily at receiving so much attention. That young mother didn't hide anything. Her red, thin lips kept on talking without being stopped by either judge or prosecutor. It seemed they too enjoyed looking at this pretty village girl who spoke so frankly.

Without concealing anything, Minem announced that the child she was now suckling was the son of Robert Mellema, the son of her employer, and so was the grandchild of Nyai Ontosoroh.

Then: "It seemed Babah Kong was jealous of the father of my baby, Rono, Ndoro Judge. He kept on pressing me as to who was the baby's father."

"Did Babah Kong alias Jan Tantang ever propose marriage to you?"

"Babah Kong did once ask me to become his wife."

"And why were you unwilling?"

"My child had to be taken care of first."

"Did not Nyai acknowledge him as her grandson?"

"She has now," she stated with energy.

Nyai was frustrated, annoyed by Minem. Once again her private family affairs were being paraded in public view. The prosecutor didn't allow such an opportunity to go unused, and it became even more obvious that the prosecutor was out to confuse the course of the trial. Question after question was addressed to Nyai.

But the chief judge finally moved to bring a halt to the public's pleasure in these private affairs. The questioning shifted to Darsam: "How may times in twenty-four hours would you meet Minem, Darsam?"

"I never counted," answered Darsam, frowning sullenly.

"And you have never tried to seduce her?"

"A woman like her doesn't need to be seduced," he answered furiously.

"And whom would you have preferred to seduce?" asked the prosecutor, glancing at Mama.

Now it was I who as about to explode in fury.

The chief judge used his gavel again.

"This is important, to fill in the background, Your Honor Chief Judge," objected the prosecutor. "Answer truthfully, Darsam. Why did you never try to seduce her?"

Darsam did not answer.

"You have never touched her?"

"No!" Darsam gnashed his teeth.

"Is he telling the truth, Minem?"

"Yes."

"Did Tuan Minke ever visit you house?"

"No," answered Minem.

"Have you ever spoken to him?"

"A few times, Ndoro Prosecutor."

"And he never tried to seduce you?"

A tear of humiliation, of anger, dropped from my eye.

"A pity, but no, Nodor Prosecutor."

"Why a pity? Did you have hopes in that direction?"

Minem giggled slowly. Mama shifted restlessly in her chair.

Back at home Mama didn't say anything to Minem. I gave Mama my opinion about what the prosecutor was doing. She just smiled, explaining: "He is trying to prove that Rono is not Robert's son, not my grandson."

"But why, Ma?"

"If it is proved that he is Robert's son, then Rono will have rights to a part of his grandfather's property. It is clear now that the prosecutor is definitely in league with Maurits Mellema. But there is nothing we can do. We have no proof."

The next few days at court were spent on the shooting incident between Jan Tantang and Darsam. It could not be proved that there was any enmity between them because of sexual jealousy over Minem. The police presented evidence of a fight.

Both Darsam and Jan Tantang admitted what happened. The motives were admitted by the court: Darsam's suspicions. Darsam was labeled the aggressor; Jan Tantang, said the court, was defending himself.

In the end Darsam was given two years probation on condition he got into no more trouble. Jan Tantang was sentenced to eight months for acting under false pretenses and was fired from the police force.

With the end of the trial this whole convoluted affair was finally over.

16

One morning a man arrived on horseback, dressed in a white shirt, trousers, and a white cap, but no shoes. He was a chocolate-skinned Indo. Very, very politely, he handed me two letters. Mama wasn't in the office but was out in the back doing the work Annelies used to do.

One letter was from the government accountant confirming that the business's finances were in proper order and that nothing was amiss—reaffirming the audit. The other letter was from Engineer Maurits Mellema. I didn't read that one, but left it on the table for Mama.

"Tuan," said the messenger with the letters, "allow me to meet with Minem."

"Minem?"

"She lives here, doesn't she?"

"What do you want with her?"

"Allow me to tell her myself."

I opened the door that led into the front parlor and called the girl over. She came, merry as ever, carrying her baby.

"Young Master called me?" she asked gaily. Her thin lips

were all shiny; who knows what they had just eaten? She stood close and tilted her head.

"In here," and she entered the office. She seemed a bit disappointed that there was another person there.

"This is Minem, if you're sure that's who you're after."

"Minem?" the messenger asked in Malay.

"Yes, Tuan."

"Can you leave today?"

"Leave for where?"

"Tuan Accountant de Visch."

"Who is that? Tuan Accoun—"

"My employer. You said you'd live with him, didn't you?"

Minem thought for a moment, then laughed. "Oh, that tuan? Just a minute, let me take leave from Nyai first. Can you wait?"

She left the office. I was astounded. How freely she behaved, no fear, no embarrassment, not at all like most Native women. Like a European girl from the high school. This child was intelligent, I thought, but hadn't received a proper education. Quite a daring person, game to gamble with her fate. She saw her beautiful body and pretty face as the only capital she had and she could use them to obtain some of the pleasures of life. Perhaps with a proper education, she would have grown up to be an outstanding woman.

Not long after, Mama arrived with Darsam. With no greeting for the messenger, she sat down at her desk, took out some papers, and gave them to Darsam.

"Our regards to them all. Try to meet Jan Tantang. Tell him not to worry because he's lost his job. As soon as he is free, we will employ him."

Darsam saluted, then went again. I went to her and reported that there was a letter from Mr. de Visch, the government accountant, and showed her the letter I had just finished reading.

She read it with shining eyes. A pleasant little smile played on her lips as she nodded.

I observed her face—still so young and fresh, as if she had never borne children. She was always dressed up and adorned, and her skin was always glowing. The events that had just taken place seemed erased from her soul and body. They had left no mark at all on the way her face glowed or on the way she moved.

Now Engineer Maurits Mellema's letter was in her hand. Her

smile disappeared. She took her brass letter opener, but hesitated to tear the envelope.

"The messenger awaits an answer, Ma."

"You brought it?" she asked the messenger in Dutch.

"Yes, Nyai."

"You work for Mr. de Visch or Maurits Mellema?"

"The former, Nyai."

"So this letter was with the other?"

"Yes."

"Is Engineer Mellema at the accountant's office? This letter has no stamp."

"I don't know, Nyai."

Mama knocked the edge of the envelope up and down on the desk. She tried to overcome her hesitation. She put the letter and the brass knife down.

"Read it to me, Child," she said softly.

I opened the letter and read it in a whisper.

"Yes," she then said. "Write the reply, Child."

After it was written she put it in an envelope and called the messenger over: "You can take this back with you." The messenger took the letter and then sat down again. "That's all, you can go now, there's nothing else."

"Yes, Nyai, there's still Minem."

"Minem?"

"I'm taking her with me, Nyai."

"Where did you meet her?"

"Just now, here."

"Here?" Nyai glared, startled.

I quickly explained what had happened. She stood up, took a handkerchief out of a drawer, and started to bite on it. Slowly she walked to the door, took a deep breath, then sat down on the settee with the messenger.

"When did Minem meet Tuan de Visch? No, let me call her."

Before Mama reached the door, Minem entered without knocking, carrying Rono and a bamboo bag. She was dressed up and looked very attractive, slim but full-bodied. She didn't drop her eyes before Mama, as she usually did, but spoke directly: "Nyai, today Minem is taking leave to go to live with Tuan—"

"Sit down here, Minem, so we can talk calmly first. Minke,

come over here, so you're a witness, and you too. What's your name?"

"Raymond de Bree, Nyai."

So the four of us sat in a circle around the table; five of us actually—there was Rono too, asleep in his mother's arms.

"Minem," Nyai began, "you have been living in this house because that was what Robert wanted. You yourself have been living here of your own free will, and because I asked you if you wanted to. Isn't that right, Minem?"

"Yes, Nyai."

"You haven't been here long, that's true, but no one so far has tried to get rid of you?"

"True, Nyai. No one."

"Are you sure?"

"Yes, Nyai."

"You are not pregnant now?"

"No, Nyai. I'm clean."

"Good. Have you been treated well while you've been here?"

"I've been treated well, Nyai."

"Good. So you won't say bad things about the place you're about to leave?"

"No, Nyai."

"You're not going to regret later having gone with Tuan de Visch?"

"No, Nyai."

"Think about it first. Because once you've left here, I will not take you back again. You understand that?"

"I understand, Nyai."

"So you understand. You were taken in because of Robert's request. Now you're leaving of your own accord."

"Yes, Nyai."

"And what about Rono?"

"If Nyai wants to take him, I will leave him with Nyai."

"Are you sure? You've thought it over properly?"

"What's the use of keeping a baby like this without a father, Nyai?"

"Good. Give me the child." Rono changed embraces.

"You won't want the child again, will you? You won't be visiting him? Because that would disturb us and him."

"No, Nyai, but give me some compensation."

"You mean a payment?"

Without embarrassment, Minem nodded.

"I will look after this child well. And I will give you some going-away money, but I will not buy my own grandchild. You yourself are surrendering him freely. You yourself were the one who got so many people to press me to acknowledge him as my grandchild."

The messenger looked restless. He kept shifting his position and moving his bag about. Mama humored his impatience.

"This is about the fate of a human being, Tuan Raymond. We cannot be rash in what we do. Minem, I will give you some going-away money, but I am not a buyer of people. Tuan Raymond de Bree is a witness. You will report all this to Mr. de Visch, yes?"

"Let Minem report it herself, Nyai."

"If you don't want to be a witness, all right. I have a witness: Mr. Minke. But if anything happens in the future, I will still name you as a witness. The day, date, and time you were here and took Minem, I will note down too. You can go."

"But my orders to bring Minem?"

"Take her."

"Come, Minem, let's go," invited de Bree.

"The money, Nyai."

"There must be a letter, Minem," said Nyai, "and you must put your thumbprint to it, if you agree to what it says. If you don't, you can leave without anything. If you want to wait, I'll draw it up now."

The letter was short, explaining that Minem acknowledged that she surrendered her child to Nyai Ontosoroh on the day, date, and time it occurred, with me and Raymond de Bree, the messenger of Accountant de Visch, as witnesses. And that the child was born on a certain date and was her own child with Robert Mellema born out of wedlock.

Nyai read it out and put it from Malay into Javanese. She put her signature to it, as did I. Minem put her thumbprint on it. But Raymond de Bree refused.

"It doesn't matter if you refuse," said Nyai. "Underneath your name it will explain that you heard the whole conversation but refused to sign the letter. Write that down, Minke, and that

Minem was taken by Mr. Raymond de Bree, who did not give clear information where he was taking her."

I wrote all the additional explanation on the bottom of the letter. Nyai gave the messenger the letter for him to read.

Raymond de Bree still refused.

"Good, if you don't sign it, you'll be open one day to the accusation of kidnapping."

The messenger looked frightened. He still hesitated, yet he had no choice but to sign.

They left. Minem left a kiss for her child. For a moment a tear formed, then she left with de Bree. Neither wore shoes and their toes were spread.

"Minem," called Mama, and the girl returned, leaving de Bree waiting under a tree.

"What about your mother? Are you going to leave her just like that?"

"I will come and get her another time, Nyai."

"Who will feed her if you leave her now?"

She didn't answer and excused herself, walking quickly away from the office. Rono still slept in Nyai's arms.

"Wanton girl!" Mama whispered harshly. "You are lucky, Rono, that you will never know who your mother is. Have you ever written about a wild girl, Child? She is a good character for you to write about. You've known her from close up, too."

That was the first time I heard that strange phrase, *wild girl!*

"You can write something as a memorial to this day."

"It's her right, Ma. Perhaps she feels her future here is uncertain."

Mama didn't want to listen.

"In this world there are not many women with that itch—women who seek a profit from their femininity while their breasts haven't dropped and their cheeks haven't drooped. But in all places and amongst all classes there are such women, and they are always disgusting. If I could write like you, Child. . . . Look at this baby; he meant nothing to her. A husband meant nothing to her; a home nothing; her parents nothing. Her youth is being dedicated to her wantonness. Nothing is important to her except if it will help satisfy her lust."

Mama let her anger overflow. I didn't agree with what she said.

"No one knows what fate awaits this child. I hope it's good, yes, Rono, much better than that of your mother and your father. Your nose is certainly like Robert's; your skin is even whiter than his when he was a baby."

Suddenly she remembered something.

"At five o'clock this evening, Child, Engineer Maurits will be here."

I pretended not to hear her reminder. He was undoubtedly coming to order Mama to leave.

"You look pale, Child. Don't worry. Who knows what he wants? Perhaps he wants to kick us all out, except for the wealth we've built."

How ashamed I would be to be thrown out by somebody, kicked out from someone's house, shown no respect. How those people who hate us will cheer and shout. But I must stay with Mama through this final trouble.

She spoke again. "We will arrange a proper ceremony to greet him."

"Greet him!"

"According to the law, he owns all this. He has profited because Robert and Annelies are gone."

"Mama, and what about Mama?"

"You're worried about me? Thank you, Child. Are you afraid that I'll become a burden to you, that I'll want to go with you? No. But let's deal with this man first. You still have an account to settle with him. Indeed we can't fight the law or him, but we still have mouths to speak with. With our mouths we will confront him. And we still have friends."

"What can they do?"

"Friends with you in times of trouble are friends in everything. Never belittle friendship. Its magnificence is greater than the fire of enmity. Do you agree with me that we should call them over to help us make more merry the greeting we give Mr. Maurits Mellema? Jean Marais and Kommer?"

I was silent as I thought over what use that would be. What could they do if the law wasn't behind them? One shy and missing a leg, the other a journalist, speechmaker, and hunter of wild animals.

"You don't agree, Child?"

"Very well, Ma. I'll fetch them."

Rono jerked awake. Nyai rocked the unblanketed baby in her arms.

"Ah, he's wet himself, the baby. Yes, Child, call them over. That's the best thing to do now."

And so I went out, putting behind me the memory of Minem, who was taking her itch away with her, and of Rono and the futility of his birth. My mind was now filled with a new puzzle from my mother-in-law. She was about to confront the man who wanted to throw her out.

17

So that the story runs in sequence, I have put together a selection of writings and opinions that I have heard at one time or another and which are connected with this story of my life. Some of the material I obtained several years after the events, but that is not important.

There had been a rumor that the Netherlands Indies was going to build a navy of its own, which it would call the *Gouvernements Marine*. It would not be a part of the Royal Netherlands Navy. The rumor was not without foundation, and this is what it was all about:

Japan had been given equal status with the white races. Its international position was the same as that of European countries. The Japanese had been taken off the Indies government's alien Orientals list and shifted to the European list. The colonials could shout, roar, and protest, but the decision of the state was more decisive.

The European Indies could hurl all the insults they liked: That the Japanese ships, for a maritime country, were old and decrepit, no better than chicken coops. Certain Japanese admitted that they were like babies just beginning to crawl. In their hearts perhaps they were smiling to themselves—they were one people who had never bowed down and kowtowed to the Europeans, let alone slid along the floor before them—a people whose spirit could not be shaken by international criticism.

I once saw a small poster with a lithograph picture of a fleet of Japanese ships, all in tatters as they were battered by a storm. Their cannons shivered in the cold. A Japanese flag flew on every ship, almost as big as the ships themselves. And the picture's caption read: "In the name of the geisha's kimono, forever forward!"

Whatever insults might have been hurled, the Netherlands Indies military experts felt they needed to organize a meeting, a seminar, to discuss defense matters, specifically in relation to the Indies, and precisely at the time of a visit to Indies waters by a Royal Netherlands Navy force under the leadership of Admiral ——. (I won't give his name.) What was the best defense for the Indies?

Japan was on everybody's lips; its name reverberated around the seminar again and again. They said that the Japanese Navy was many times bigger than the fleet of the V.O.C.—Dutch East Indies Company—when it conquered Java, Sumatra, and the Moluccas. The distance between Japan and the Indies was much shorter than between the Netherlands and the Indies! The rise of Japan should not be met just with colonial insults. A country that has been able to stand up to Western supremacy should not be belittled. Such a people would be able to achieve their ideals. Science and learning had become the property of the world and were there to be used by all who were capable. In this new age, victory in war would not be determined by the color of a people's skin, but by people rising up with weapons in their hands. No race was immune to cannon shot. Modern science and learning were not the sole property of Europeans.

People said that Japan was clever only at imitating. But, said another voice, the imitation of worthwhile things was a sign of advancement, not something base and undignified, as some colonial opinion had it. All people and races began by imitating before they could stand by themselves. People should indeed learn to get used to new realities. Reality doesn't go away because people don't like it, or just because they insult it. Even the European races, before they were as advanced as they are now, could only imitate. And they could imitate the bad things as well, like smoking and sucking on a pipe just as Indians do. Imitating is only a chapter in the life of all children. But then there comes a day when children are fully grown. People should prepare themselves to confront that day. Don't be startled, or shocked and overcome, if on that day reality rears up before you larger than you could ever imagine.

There was no preparation that could be carried out too early.

Yet it sounded like a fairy tale that Japan could force its way onto the soil of the Indies. Japan would first have to face the French in Indochina, then get past the English in that strongest of all Southeast Asian forts called Singapore. Indeed the Indies were guarded by layers of European forts, which could never be penetrated. But don't forget, someone else added, that the distance between Europe and Southeast Asia is very great indeed, and Europe's ships are spread throughout the waterways of its colonies: in the Americas, Africa, Asia, and Australia. The Japanese fleet is together, concentrated in one place, and its ground army even more so.

People should remember that all Japanese who have left their country—whether to become coolies in Hawaii's pineapple plantations, or cooks on the ships of other races, or chefs in San Francisco mansions, or prostitutes in the big cities of the world—nevertheless they remain like the heart and lungs of the Japanese race, inseparable from their country, their ancestors, and their people. And more than that, even though they earn their living from us, they still look upon us as a race of barbarians, and *come that day*, they will try to prove that they are right about us.

We mustn't laugh and think that it is all just the arrogance of an isolated people who have never had contact with the great nations of the world. Japan has opened its doors to Western influence for decades now, and its citizens are busily extracting what is best from the achievements of all peoples the world over. They are a thrifty people who know the purpose of their thrift: the greatness of the Japanese empire. They had practiced the principles of economy and thrift long before they learned it from us.

Some of those attending the seminar, so people said, still refused to acknowledge Japan as significant or to acknowledge the other speakers' opinions as worth consideration.

Views were put forward regarding the appropriate defense strategy for the Indies, given its peculiar geographical situation. In 1811, during Governor-General Jansen's time, the British navy was easily able to take the Indies. That must not happen again. Up until now the Indies army had stood as an autonomous force, a united force, the product of the power of the Netherlands Indies state. But at sea the Indies were still dependent on the Royal Netherlands Navy. Even the transport of supplies to Aceh and the Moluccas for the army, especially before the forming of the K.P.M., depended on private merchant fleets: Arab and Chinese, Madurese and Buginese.

I had never thought about the sea before, but now it began to arouse my interest. My mind conjured up pictures of the centuries during which the wooden ships of the V.O.C. had battled the ocean waves for months, even years on end, seeking out spices. They found them. The profits were huge. And to defend and expand those profits they founded an empire. Mostly, and first of all, upon the earth of my homeland. They created an empire and they kept watch over it across the seas. It was the sea that took them to their greatness. And they knew that every forward-moving nation could use those same seas to build other empires. They were not going to let that happen. They had been cursed with the necessity of always defending what they had founded and what they owned.

The Netherlands Indies needed its own navy for its sea defenses; we could never defend ourselves on the seas while the royal armadas and squadrons were sailing around in the Atlantic. The Indies must have its own navy, and as quickly as possible. The defense of the Indies must adjust itself as quickly as possible to the natural circumstances of the Indies. It must have its own maritime defense strategy. There must be surveys to find suitable spots for naval bases. The bases must be built. The situation cannot remain as it is now, with the visiting Royal Navy ships harboring wherever they like, as if they were on a honeymoon picnic.

The military people at the seminar were quite shaken by it all. And that admiral—people said he represented the concern in the Netherlands—was also shaken.

Reading the news about that seminar left me with the impression that war was going to break out the next day, or perhaps the day after. The Netherlands Indies fighting—I'm not sure whom. How many conflicts there are in this world! Everyone against everyone: people against people, group against group, individuals against their own group and vice versa; groups against their own broader class and the other way around too; women confronting men in Europe and men who didn't confront women; governments fighting their own citizens. And now empires in confrontation. All were just manifestations of one thing: conflicting interests!

And if the Netherlands found itself confronted with a defense problem—which had happened already a number of times—the Indies must be able to defend itself using its own strength. But to try to defend yourself in this modern age without a navy: unimaginable! People reminded each other that there were the Germans in East Papua, the English to the north and to the southeast as well. The American navy was now playing around in the Pacific, playing grave-making with the Filipino rebels and finally throwing out the Spanish.

Changes in "the balance of power," people said, (and how tremendously that idea loomed in my thoughts) had placed the Indies in a new situation.

It was a pity I had never seen that grand epic of conflict, the *Bharatayuddha wayang* story. I had never met a puppet-master who dared to put it on. It was too complicated, and the complexity left an impression of the supernatural. So too it was with this "balance of power." In all these complications and this complexity, with all its supernaturalness, I had a vision of a child's playpen, inside of which was a jumbled pile of question marks. And my mind was tormented like this as a result of thinking about other people's concerns, such as the fate of the Indies without a navy of its own.

In the history of the Netherlands Indies (I did not need to learn this from a book or a teacher) the Dutch were not just proud, but almost arrogant about the strength of their army. But after seeing what happened in the Philippines people began to whisper: A strong land force is meaningless in an island country if there is no navy. The Spanish preferred to retreat from the Philippines rather than confront the American fleet. The Indies had to learn to look after itself, including its sea defenses.

And the seminar itself produced a warning (and I will never be able to forget it): Watch out, gentlemen! In a modern war, if the forts in the countries to the north are penetrated, and we do not have a strong navy, this country will fall in a matter of days.

Not long after the seminar the ship H.M.S. *Sumatra* was sent to the Indies to survey the best places to build a base for the Royal Netherlands Indies Navy of the future. On one of its trips it surveyed the waters around Jepara, on the southern coast of Java.

320

(Later on I found out that three Native girls, one of them with a name famed through all Java, R. A. Kartini, along with their father, had boarded the ship to make an inspection. They were welcomed with full honors. The ship's crew knew them as Native girls who thought like Europeans and they called them the princesses of Jepara.)

As I was writing these notes a question arose in my mind: Did they know what the earlier tasks of H.M.S. *Sumatra* had been?

Why South Africa? Because indeed there is a connection. After the H.M.S. *Sumatra* arrived, another ship followed from that southern corner of the world: The H.M.S. *Borneo*. One of its passengers was a war hero from South Africa: Engineer Maurits Mellema. That warship made its way to where I lived: Surabaya. He was commanding a team of marine engineers.

Now allow me to fantasize a bit about this particular character:

He was still commanding his troops in South Africa when he was summoned by the Royal Netherlands Navy. He had already gone through battle after battle under the command of General Christaan de Wet—victories and defeats. (Indeed there were more defeats than victories and the Dutch were becoming more and more pressed.) But in any case people need heroes to worship. And if there aren't any, they'll scrape up anything. In short, Mellema was made a hero; he was honored and praised by all. He had defended the honor of the House of Orange as well as the veins of gold running through the southern tip of the African continent.

Perhaps I have the right to picture him, sometimes, as an officer whose chest could be covered with medals. I don't know how many Englishmen he had sent to the grave, how many square miles of land he had lost, how many of his men had been killed or taken prisoner or had disappeared or gone mad or deserted. There were no other names along with his. And I don't think I'd be wrong in presenting the picture that from his mouth came a never-ending stream of curses, directed especially at the English general, French.

Probably Holland was proud to have such a great son as Maurits Mellema. Probably he was famous throughout the land . . . and a pile of other probablys as well. My imagination can be squeezed no further.

321

The surveys to find a suitable place for the Royal Netherlands Indies Navy base was finally successful: the Surabaya peninsula. The docks were designed. Remembering Engineer Maurits Mellema's previous experience at Surabaya harbor, when, seven years before, he had helped design new sugar- and oil-loading docks, the Royal Navy summoned him. He was chosen to build the new naval base at the tip of Surabaya harbor.

A telegram was sent to South Africa summoning him. He was seen off by his friends and the soldiers who had served under him. He left Africa with glorious memories. . . .

And if I keep drawing upon my imagination, I can come up with some more ideas.

Every member of the ship's crew taking him home to Holland shared with him the happiness of his return. The journey was a refreshing outing for him, far from death and the spilling of blood, from groans and cries. And if I let my imagination get out of control altogether, this would be the next part of the story:

That morning at the Sumatra docks in Amsterdam harbor, a crowd of people had already gathered. There were many girls there and veterans of the Boer War too. A number of senior officers from the Royal Navy were there, and also a navy band. At exactly ten o'clock the ship from South Africa entered the harbor.

I could see Minister Kuyper, who was so involved with the Boer War, also there to greet the ship.

A woman, dressed all in black, quickly attracted attention. She too was a welcomer, standing in the crowd: the widow Amelia Mellema-Hammers. In one hand she carried a black bag. In the other was an umbrella, also black. And she was ready to shed tears of welcome too.

The ship began to dock. The passengers stood along the deck rail. Slowly the navy band began to play.

The first person to disembark from the ship was none other than Engineer Mellema himself, accompanied by the ship's captain. People shouted and cheered to welcome their hero. The music blared, trying to make itself heard over the cheering. Things became merrier and merrier. Engineer Maurits Mellema smiled calmly. He waved his hand. As soon as he stepped ashore a crowd of people, who knows from where, charged forward and placed a garland of flowers around his neck. The officials and officers from the Royal Navy took turns in shaking his hand. The Royal Navy music corps kept up their playing. Kuyper was forgotten by everybody.

Now, not a single medal decorated Mellema's chest, yet through his veins ran the heroism of his ancestors who had defeated enemies from both land and sea. This great son of the nation was very friendly. He faced the world with a smile that reflected the great experiences now behind him. People said: Whoever returned home from war as victor would see all the difficulties before him become as nothing.

His mother, having longed to see her son for so long now, ran forward to embrace and kiss him. And the hero Mellema loved his mother. There were kisses in return to her cheeks, left and right. This scene of a mother's love continued as she held her son's body. There must not be some irreplaceable part of the hero's body buried back in that unknown land. Amelia Mellema-Hammers suddenly burst into uncontrolled weeping—an expression of gratitude to her God. The body of the child she had given birth to was still whole; the English had not succeeded in breaking it.

The Royal Navy carriage took hero and mother to headquarters to the accompaniment of the crowd's shouts and cheers. In the background the ship and its crew stood along the deck watching this great event.

I don't think I could tell my imagination it was wrong if I said that the papers also reported this event. But there was nothing in the papers about the deaths of Herman Mellema, Annelies Mellema, and Robert Mellema, nor was there any mention that the great hero was about to receive some free booty from Wonokromo, Surabaya.

There was no other news about the hero for a while. Then, later, a small report about a banquet held by Engineer Maurits Mellema and his mother—a banquet with speeches, ringing with cheers. Beneath that report was another about the sacking of an English journalist in South Africa who wasn't doing his job properly but was making up news stories in his bedroom, while in that same room he was composing adventure stories about a white baby who grew up to be the king of the South African jungle. . . .

I'm afraid I must end my fantasy here.

Dulrakim from Kedungrukem, whom I visited to get the address of Khouw Ah Soe's friend, well, he was the kind of person who liked to collect stories—I don't know if just for himself or to broadcast to others. He had a treasury of adventure stories that seemed unlimited. Because he doesn't have an important place at all in my story, I don't think I need say much about him. But he did have something to say about Engineer Maurits Mellema. Only short tales—just some things he had picked up hanging around the harbor.

He reckoned the young marine engineer was quite a friendly person. He said he heard someone say once that heroes were usually like that; great experiences made such people more humble and sensitive to other people. Mellema liked music and was a hero of the dance floor as well.

His favorite topic of conversation was the slowness with which the Netherlands Indies came to realize the need for its own navy. Didn't that great son of the Indies, Daendels, almost a century ago, realize the same thing? Hadn't he even recognized and indeed used Surabaya as a naval base? How quickly the Europeans in the Indies forgot! The lack of an international war for almost a century seemed to have turned them all senile.

According to another story, a Dutch seaman once asked the engineer: When the Surabaya project is finished, where will the engineer go? His answer was simple and strong: to wherever the Netherlands calls me.

Once he had to give a public talk. He talked about how the Dutch first entered South Africa. They had to face the resistance of the inhabitants, the black people who fought with spear and arrow. Do you all know how those black people fought? he asked. They crawled, wriggling along the ground, not standing, but like snakes, moving forward by using their elbows. The Europeans stood straight, rifles ready. The blacks crept forward with spear and arrow—a symbol, and not one of our own making, that the black-skinned people will always crawl beneath our feet. In war and in peace, the white-skinned peoples will always be on top, superior, always standing tall above the crawling coloreds.

Dulrakim never told me if he himself attended that lecture. He couldn't tell me if the people there agreed with the engineer's opinions or not. What he did know was that Engineer Maurits Mellema had been entrusted with the job of building the base for the Royal Netherlands Indies Navy on Perak peninsula, Surabaya, and had been given the rank of Lieutenant-Colonel.

Yes, he is a capable man, Dulrakim commented. He had shown this while leading his men in South Africa, people were saying; and now as a marine engineer he was equally capable at managing the construction of the base. Hundreds of men—perhaps thousands, if you count those not directly involved with the project—obediently carried out his orders. All to bring into being the Netherlands Indies Navy base!

Almost a hundred years ago Daendels knew what had to be done, Mellema was always growling.

Whether these stories are true or not, only Dulrakim knows. I was amazed at the number of stories he had stored away.

It seemed the relationship between Maurits and Herman Mellema would never again weigh on people's minds. Except for mine and Mama's. And it was as though Mellema's way to us, both in my imaginings and in reality, had been swept clean and clear for him. Neither he himself nor his clothes need be dirtied or torn by walking some narrow pathway. He came as a god, the god of the Netherlands Indies Navy base project. It was the pet project of the Netherlands Indies government. It was as though all the power and facilities of the colonial state were being mobilized to ensure the project's success. And Engineer Maurits Mellema was promoted from god of building to god of success.

In Wonokromo a woman would have to confront this double god alone. This woman had been robbed, with the aid of the law, of her child and property, the products of her sweat. She had no legal ground to stand on. She had never traveled anywhere because the Netherlands had needed her. She had at her side only a youth named Minke and a man named Darsam who could no longer swing his machete. What other strength was still stored away in these three people that could help them confront Engineer Maurits Mellema, now so triumphant in all things?

This lone woman wished only for two more friends to be with her. Just two: Jean Marais—painter, one-legged invalid, introvert; and one Kommer—a reporter from a Malay-Dutch newspaper whose writings had never been able to topple the mountainous combined power of the Indies and the Netherlands.

Mama had said Engineer Mellema was coming to kick her out. I thought the word *kick* was too strong. That engineer would never have to raise his foot. He would not have to expend the slightest energy. With just one puff, Mama would be exiled forever from her kingdom and her throne. But Mama still felt she had value and worth. Engineer Mellema would come. He would give a little puff, and all humankind living upon the company's land would be blown off, to flutter away like goose feathers.

Jean Marais bowed his head when he heard Nyai Ontosoroh's request; he went pale, perhaps from fright.

"You don't think you can do it, Jean?" I asked.

He sucked on his cornhusk cigarette, then blew out smoke-rings: "I'm only good with brush and palette, Minke."

"All right, if you won't come, I'm going to Kommer's now, with the same request from Mama. I'll drop in here on the way back." Jean could say nothing, but his eyes watched me closely. "Perhaps you'll have changed your mind by then," I added.

But his face had changed when he heard Kommer was needed by Mama too. He wiped his mouth and said, "Go now. I'll wait for you. Perhaps I'll think differently then, Minke."

I went.

I discovered that Kommer's place was quite large. There were cages everywhere, with their animal occupants: pythons, some mouse deer, a bear, a leopard, forest roosters, orangutans. He himself was fast asleep in his own cage.

The woman of the house—I didn't know if she was a Mixed-Blood or a nyai—who hadn't given him a single child—awakened him. I sat on a rattan settee. He stuck his head out from behind a door, his eyes still bleary: "Have you been waiting long, Tuan Minke?" he asked in a sleepy voice, then disappeared.

He came out wearing batik pajamas. His face was wet and his eyes were still red, but on hearing Nyai's request all sleepiness vanished.

"Good, let's go," he said. "Let me teach this Maurits Mellema a lesson. Give him a good going over, so he knows how it feels, hey?"

This woman followed the conversation from a distance. On hearing I had brought a request from Nyai Ontosoroh, I saw her face change. Her eyes shone with jealousy. She stood up and hurried away, disappearing behind an inner door.

Kommer stood up and went inside too. Not long after there were the sounds of an argument. I heard the noise of plates and cups being thrown about. A woman's scream followed, and crying. But in the end Kommer appeared in fresh and tidy clothes. His hair was parted on the right and shone from too much hair oil. He didn't wear the shoes he wore most days. In their place he had put on a pair of patent leather ones from Europe, the latest fashion. On his coat, as an adornment to his watch pocket, hung a leopard's claw and a silver-bound wild boar's tusk, souvenirs of his proudest hunting successes. He looked handsome and dashing, not down and out, not defeated.

"Can we confront him?" I asked, pretending not to have heard what had gone on inside.

"We'll see what happens."

"You're optimistic," I said as I climbed aboard the carriage.

"All great events should be witnessed first hand, Mr. Minke, and not just so you can write about them properly for the newspapers. Apart from that . . . " He too climbed aboard.

"What, Tuan Kommer?"

" . . . it makes our own lives fuller."

If I hadn't known he had proposed to Mama, perhaps I might have become a devoted admirer of the man. I admired what he had just said, but only a little.

The carriage set off nervously for Jean Marais's house.

"He's coming at five o'clock, hey? Just under two hours," he said as he put his watch back in his pocket.

His eyes examined me. Perhaps he was surprised that I wasn't admiring his wild boar's tusk and his leopard's claw. Perhaps he was surprised that I had no questions about them. Maybe he had forgotten he'd told me the stories of those souvenirs three times before.

Sitting beside me, he emanated an aroma of perfume that sent my head swimming. I sat silently, as if he were the normally attired Kommer. Who can forbid people from falling in or arousing love? Even the gods cannot. The first few pages of the *Babad Tanah Jawi* tells of how a god fell madly in love with a woman of the earth. And even the god of Death, the absolute ruler of Time, could not hold the other back, let alone break the power of their love.

The interesting thing was that the behavior of a middle-aged man who had fallen in love was no different from that of a teenager. Both turned into heroic exhibitionists, out to get everyone's attention. No matter how clever a man is, said my grandmother's maid when I was still very young, if he's been smitten he becomes as stupid as the greatest idiot. Why should Kommer be an exception?

When we arrived at Jean Marais's house, we were met by Maysoroh in a new dress. As soon as I climbed down, she held out her hands, wanting to be spoiled.

"You're grown up now. It wouldn't be right to carry you," I said. She cuddled up to me, so I had to take her by the hand. She looked clean and very pretty. "You're very pretty today, May. Give me a kiss." She kissed me on the hand.

We walked inside hand in hand. Kommer was behind us. He didn't seem interested in his surroundings. Perhaps he was busy readying himself for the big event or preparing himself to look as dashing as possible for Nyai.

And who wouldn't have been surprised to see Jean Marais now? He rose from his chair with great difficulty. His smile was handsome. His mustache and beard had been combed.

"I combed Papa's beard," said Maysoroh proudly. "Isn't he handsome now?"

Jean Marais nodded his impatience to leave straight away. His trousers had been ironed. His vest boasted silver buttons. Fantastic! Had he fallen in love with Nyai Ontosoroh too?

"Afternoon, Mr. Marais," called Kommer.

"Afternoon, Mr. Kommer. A pity you didn't catch that panther. A great pity that trap I designed didn't work."

"That panther escaped, but now we're going after another, Mr. Marais: Engineer Mellema," he said in Malay.

"That's right!" answered Jean merrily.

"You're ready for it by the look of you, Tuan."

"Hmmmm. Let's go."

So it was that we set off in the carriage. I sat next to the driver; Kommer, Marais, and May sat in the back. I couldn't quite catch what they were talking about.

"Is Nyai having a party?" whispered the driver, Marjuki.

"A party, Juki, a big party."

The carriage sped on.

18

That afternoon thick gray clouds hung umbrellalike over the Surabaya. There was no wind, no thunder. The air was heavy with humidity. The trees around the house sleepily awaited the rain, and the clouds would not fulfill their promise.

Kommer and Jean Marais were in the front parlor. They sat close to each other, talking like two old bachelors planning illusory adventures.

In the back parlor, I found Mama talking to Minem's old mother, who had been given the job of looking after Rono Mellema. Darsam was standing near the back door. Rono was nowhere to be seen.

"Ya, Nyai, I don't know what that Minem really wants. She's a crazy girl. A baby still feeding off the breast and she leaves him like he was just a pile of rags."

"Darsam, check the gas tanks now. Quickly bathe and then go and turn on the lamps. Put on your very best clothes. And don't forget to tend to your mustache."

I told Mama that our friends had arrived, all nattily dressed and looking dashing. Mama smiled happily.

"Is the office closed, Ma?"

"No, Panji Darman's there. Wash now, Child; dress in your best. We must be at our very best when we meet Engineer Mellema."

She herself had changed her clothes and put on her makeup. She looked very attractive. For the first time, I noticed, she wore a necklace and a simple bracelet, along with her velvet slippers with silver embroidery and a black velvet kebaya. Dressed all in black like that she looked much younger, very pretty, very charismatic. No one could guess what terrible strength she was going to throw against her enemy later. Those words of hers, which earlier had impressed me so much, now seemed ready to be fulfilled: "Now all I'm left with is a mouth."

After bathing and dressing, I prayed that she would not resort to violence. Her order to Darsam to dress in his best clothes meant that he was to meet the engineer too. Even that instruction to Darsam gave cause enough for worry.

I did not want to see our visitor die, cut down by Darsam's machete. Nyai needed only to move her little finger or give Darsam the slightest nod, and the young engineer would die. No, Allah, no machete must cut apart his body, no blood bubble from his veins. Ya, Allah, protect us all from that horror. Give Nyai some sign, guide her in her confrontation with the enemy. Side now, Allah, with the weak!

Sitting in the back parlor, I observed her quietly thinking. Her face was clear and bright. I thanked God. She was holding Maysoroh's little hand, paying no attention to the girl's prattle.

May then came over and cuddled up to me. For the thousandth time she asked again: When will Annelies come home from Europe? She stopped her prattle when she heard Nyai call Minem's mother. The middle-aged woman entered obediently and bent to the floor.

"Bring Rono here, and his sash too, so that I can carry him," she ordered.

"Rono's still asleep, Nyai."

"Bring him anyway."

May now cuddled up to Mama. Seeing Minem's mother hand over a baby to Nyai, May asked straight away in a loud voice:

"Who's this, Nyai? He's beautiful! Whose child, Nyai? Is it Annelies's brother's child?"

"Yes, he is a beautiful child, isn't he?"

"Very beautiful, Nyai. A boy?"

"Of course, May. Rono, that's his name."

"Rono, Nyai? What a wonderful name."

"You wanted to have a little brother, May. Think of him as your little brother now."

Maysoroh jumped about the room excitedly. Then she took the baby's clean little feet and kissed them.

"Give him here, Nyai, so I can have a turn at holding him," pleaded May. Her eyes shone with great hope.

"He's not a doll, May, he's a little brother."

"Come on, Nyai, let me hold him."

And Nyai gave the baby to May to carry while still holding him herself. Then: "That's enough, yes? Yes, that's enough. Tomorrow you will have another chance." Maysoroh seemed satisfied. She jumped around merrily.

"Ma," I said slowly, "she wants a little brother or sister. She wants one very much."

"You'd like a little brother, May?"

"Yes, Nyai, very much."

"Does Mama remember that holy task, Ma? From her? She asked for a pretty little sister, Ma."

Suddenly Mama's face went gray. She gazed at me silently. She embraced Maysoroh with one arm and kissed her forehead.

"Doesn't my little brother ever cry, Nyai?" asks May.

Only then did Mama and I realize that we had truly never heard Rono cry.

Minem's mother brought in a new batik sash and Mama used it to carry Rono.

"A bottle and a napkin."

As Minem's mother left, Darsam entered, wearing his best clothes, shining black, made from the best cloth. His machete was in his belt. The tips of his destar stood up in challenge like his symmetrical, thick, curling, pitch-black mustache. He saluted with his right hand, now healed.

"I didn't summon you, Darsam."

"But there is something I have to report, Nyai," he said.

"Oh yes. You've met with Jan Tantang."

"That's right, Nyai. He expressed a thousand thanks and will make use of your offer. Such a good man."

"And you were going to kill him. You were crazy!"

"It was his own fault. There are two other matters, Nyai. That Sinyo Robert, the sinyo who came here once and then I took him home . . . "

"Robert Suurhof, Ma," I added.

"He was made chief jail bully, Nyai, and beat up Jan Tantang in the European block. Sinyo Robert was then beaten up in turn by some Madurese. He didn't die, Nyai—just some light injuries."

"And what about your friends, Darsam?" she asked, referring to those who had been jailed for protesting Annelies's being taken. She ignored Robert Suurhof.

"That's the second thing, Nyai. They were sentenced to two months' solitary confinement—no visitors, of course."

"Is that all?"

"That's all, Nyai."

"Good. Wait with the other guests inside."

He saluted once again and left us. Minem's mother brought the bottle and napkin and Nyai tied them to the free end of the sash. Carrying Rono, rocking him that way, Nyai didn't at all look like a grandmother with her grandson, but like a young mother with her first child.

"I forgot to tell you, Child: The court acknowledged the child as Rono Mellema, as Robert's son, just after I received Robert's letter and the police message from Los Angeles."

"That's good, Ma."

I didn't have the chance to check any further whether Rono really had never cried all that time. All my attention was concentrated on Mama. I wanted to be ready to move if she ordered Darsam to kill Mellema. I hadn't heard her give any such order. But who could know for sure? In the meantime I could only hope and pray.

From the front parlor came the chimes of the pendulum clock; it was a quarter to five. Thunder began to growl in the distance, preceded each time by a flash of lightning. The day was becoming even gloomier.

"Come on, May, let's go out front." Maysoroh ran out ahead of us.

"Remember, Child," whispered Nyai as we walked, "you

332

will be facing your enemy, your own enemy. Don't be silent as you usually are."

"Ya, Ma, before him we have only our mouths. Nothing else."

"So you need to understand now"—she observed my face—"he will never read your writings, so he must listen to your voice."

"How do you know, Ma?"

"People greedy for money and property, Child, never read stories; they are barbarians. They have no concern for the fate of other people, let alone people who exist only in a story. His revenge against his father has now turned into revenge against everything that was ever close to his father. It's a pity Dr. Martinet is in Europe at the moment. If he were here . . . "

She nodded to her guests. Jean Marais strove with difficulty to stand as if honoring a great queen.

"Forgive me, gentlemen, that we're a little late," she said in Malay. "We thank you for your willingness to be with us as we meet Engineer Maurits Mellema." She went on, in a somewhat official manner, "We believe that at the very least you have come freely to stand beside us in this matter, even if you should decide not to join us in what we do later." She turned to me and asked, "Where's Darsam?"

Darsam wasn't there. I rushed out back again. I found him changing his destar for the blue-black of a *kain wulung*. And now he was wearing the pocket watch I had given him. Before leaving he took his machete from his belt and inspected it, then walked hurriedly along behind me.

"Do you need to bring the machete, Darsam?" I asked without turning. "It'd be better if you left it at home."

"And what is Darsam without his machete?" he asked.

As I turned I saw him stroking his mustache. His eyes shone; he knew that there was some great work to be done.

"It looks like something important is going to happen today, Young Master."

"Yes. But don't you do anything drastic this time."

"This Darsam here, Young Master, he knows when he has to act. All is under control. Don't worry."

My anxiety was aroused once again on hearing his confident words.

"Watch out. Don't cause any trouble. You have to realize,

Darsam, this time Mama really needs your serious help. Her troubles are very great indeed. Don't you add to them with something new."

"Don't worry, Young Master, I guarantee all will be well."

The wind stilled; the world seemed to have stopped breathing. The layers of thick cloud began to sprinkle droplets of rain, hesitantly. The day became darker. Darsam lit the gas lamps. The front parlor and the back of the house were bathed in light; the house was magnificent in its grandness.

We sat on our chairs, arranged in a row facing the front courtyard: Darsam, Jean Marais, Maysoroh Marais, Mama with Rono Mellema, Kommer, and me. In front of us was a table and on the other side an armchair for the honored guest.

It was all arranged so that the light from the lamps would shine down onto Engineer Maurits Mellema while his welcomers would be sheltered from it. Just like the preparations for a scene in a play, I thought—and that was exactly what it was.

No one spoke. Even Maysoroh, the little prattler, became submerged in the oppressive, mute atmopshere, more oppressive than when we were awaiting the decision of the court.

Three times already Kommer had taken out his watch and told us the time. And again now:"Two minutes past," he said.

Darsam took out his gold watch, but said nothing.

The drizzle stopped. The atmosphere still oppressed us all.

At ten past five a navy carriage at last appeared in the front courtyard.

I rose and went to the edge of the steps. I had been given the task of greeting this man who had murdered my wife. I still hadn't hit upon the right sentence: one evincing never-to-be-reconciled enmity or just the usual greeting to any guest?

The carriage stopped in front of the steps. A sailor jumped down from inside, saluted, and opened the door. A young officer alighted, complete with epaulettes on his shoulders and a sword at his waist. He was dressed all in white from the top of his head down to his shoes and laces. He stood erect on the ground, then straightened his shirt. The sailor, also dressed in white, saluted.

"Good afternoon." I extended my greetings in Dutch. "Welcome, Mr. Mellema."

He merely nodded without looking at me. His attitude was offensive and hurtful. I felt I wanted to punch in his head, though my arm wouldn't have reached him because he was so tall. Yet I escorted my wife's murderer inside. So this, it appeared, was Engineer Maurits Mellema: Tall, with the physique of a sportsman, broad and strong-chested, a long pointed nose like those of Greek statues, handsome, dashing, no mustache, no beard, gray eyes. He strode up the stairs with confident steps.

On entering the parlor, he stopped, raised his hand, and said in Malay, "Greetings!"

The people sitting in the chairs all stood up, as if on command. Jean Marais too, and Nyai carrying Rono Mellema, and Maysoroh too.

"Greetings!" they all answered together.

"Am I now meeting Nyai Ontosoroh alias Sanikem?" He continued in Malay, his gaze focused on Mama, ignoring the others.

"You are not wrong, Tuan Engineer Maurits Mellema. I am Sanikem," answered Nyai. "Please sit down."

"No time to sit," he answered arrogantly. "This will only take a moment."

"It does not feel right that it should be just for a moment. Look, the friends of your business have all come to greet you."

He looked at them one by one, from Darsam at one end to me at the other.

"Let me introduce you to them. Over there, Tuan, is Darsam, our chief of security."

Darsam coughed, and thrust forward his machete. Engineer Maurits Mellema was unsure what to do, and just nodded to the Madurese. The object of the nod showed his teeth.

"Then, there is Tuan Jean Marais, a painter, a French artist."

The guest was even more unsure of himself now. His legs moved for a moment. Forcing himself, he moved forward, closer, and held out his hand. He asked in French, "You are a Frenchman?"

"Yes, Mr. Mellema."

"A painter?" he asked amazed.

"Not wrong, Mr. Mellema. And this is my daughter, Maysoroh Marais. Greet Mr. Mellema, May."

The child held out her little hand, and the guest smiled as he took it. He pinched May's chin, saying in French, "Good afternoon, pretty child."

May quickly started prattling in French, admiring the embroidery and decorations on his shoulders and sleeves and asking if she could feel them. The guest bent down so she could feel his epaulettes, the gold embroidery on his back, the embellishments to his sleeves, even the decorative cords hanging from his sword.

The tension fell away. This arrogant man is a normal human being; he is fond of little children too, I thought.

And at that moment I felt Mama's sharp gaze piercing my back. I turned to her. Yes, her eyes were watching me to ensure that I was not taken in by the pretense.

"Enough, May. Say thank you," said Nyai.

Engineer Mellema straightened again and Nyai Ontosoroh continued: "And this is Tuan Kommer, a journalist, Tuan Mellema."

The guest was startled again, nodding. Seeing that Kommer was an Indo he didn't offer his hand.

"And on the end there is Tuan Minke, my son-in-law, Annelies's husband."

He seemed nervous. Standing erect before Nyai, he turned to look at me. I saw that he didn't know what he must do. With a reluctant heart and obviously forcing himself, he stepped towards me. Nyai went on, "A graduate of H.B.S., a candidate doctor."

He held out his hand to me, saying in Dutch: "Yes, Tuan, I am here above all else to express my sadness to you." He turned to Mama and said the same thing to her in Malay.

"No need for that," said Nyai in Malay when she saw Mellema coming across to her with hand extended. "The loss of my daughter cannot be replaced by the handshake of her murderer." Her voice trembled.

Despite the signs of his grandness—his uniform, his white skin—he shriveled before us. I too shriveled at those words. My breast tightened, knowing I did not have the courage of my mother-in-law.

"That is too harsh, Nyai." Engineer Mellema defended himself. "I understand how sad you and Tuan . . . "—he turned to glance at me—"but to accuse me of murder is going too far. It is not true."

"Tuan has lost nothing except respect in our eyes. Yet you have gained everything from our loss," Nyai went on. Her voice still quavered.

"I can't accept that. Everything has its rules," the guest answered. He still stood, and all his welcomers still stood also.

"That's true," said Nyai in Malay, "there are rules to deprive us and to allow you to profit from everything."

"I didn't make the rules."

"But you have done your best to use those rules for your own profit."

"Nyai can hire an advocate."

"A thousand advocates cannot return my daughter to me." Now it was not only her voice that trembled, but also her lips. "There is not a single advocate who would take on the defense of a Native against a Pure. That is not possible here."

"What can one do, if that is the will of God?"

"Yes, the will of Tuan has become the will of God."

Engineer Maurits Mellema went silent, perhaps because his Malay was limited.

"You don't want to be responsible for any of this, so it is God that you order held responsible. Very beautiful. Why won't you account for yourself to me? To her mother, who gave birth to her, raised her, educated her, and looked after her financially?"

The tremble in her voice and her lips slowly disappeared. She turned to me. Now again I shriveled up, having nothing of my own to fling at him.

"It has already happened," the guest began again. "That's why I have come here, to—"

"—to give up your guardianship over my wife and give it back to me?" I hacked at him, forcing myself, in Dutch.

". . . to-to-to—not to fight."

"You don't need to fight with us. There are many other people you can use to do that, even to kill some of us," parried Nyai. "Tuan Kommer, what do you have to say?"

And with that fluency of his, he spoke in Malay: "Tuan Engineer Maurits Mellema, as a journalist I promise you that everything you say here today will be made public. All of Surabaya will know what kind of man you are. Keep on talking, but maybe you had better sit down."

Still the guest would not sit. He bit his lower lip.

"Tuan Marais," said my mother-in-law, "this is Tuan Engineer Maurits Mellema, about whom you have heard so much. Do you not feel that it is only proper that you accept the honor of using this very valuable opportunity to speak with him?"

"*Monsieur Ingénieur Mellema,*" began Marais in French, "Monsieur was born and educated in Europe, a scholar. So was I, though I did not graduate. But how great is the difference between us, Monsieur; you came here seeking wealth and power, I simply as a wanderer."

"I came here for the Netherlands," answered Mellema.

"You did not come to this house for the Netherlands. There is no Netherlands here, not even a picture of the queen."

The guest coughed; his eyes sought out a picture of the queen but all he found was a painting of Nyai Ontosoroh, in all her grandness, hanging over the door that led into the back parlor.

"We are both pure-blood Europeans, Monsieur," Jean Marais continued, "and I can agree with some of what Nyai has said. You are to blame for Madame Annelies's death. Monsieur owes Nyai and Monsieur Minke a life."

"There is someone who takes care of all that sort of thing, who is responsible," answered Engineer Mellema.

"What you took care of, and what you are responsible for, is that death."

"That's for the courts to say."

"You are a liar! In your heart, in your conscience, do you feel guilt?"

"No."

"An even greater lie!"

"We don't understand French," protested Nyai in Malay. "Now that you have killed my daughter, when do you want to throw us out?"

The guest was still standing, and went pale for a moment; then he went red with impotent anger. Seeing Mellema was still not ready to speak, Mama went on stabbing at him: "Very beautiful."

"So this is what the real Europe is like, the Europe without rival that has been stuffed into my head for so long," I added in Dutch.

This educated man, this marine engineer turned to me. He answered softly: "I understand your sorrow, Tuan, and I join with you in your sorrow. But what can be done? It is all over now."

"Very easy. Do you think your life is more valuable than that of my wife?" I swore. "You thought of my wife as a piece of portable property that you could shift around at will, that could be treated as you wish. You don't recognize Native law, Moslem law; you did not honor our legal marriage."

"I didn't come to discuss all that."

"Yes, you didn't even bother to let us know that my wife had died. You wanted to surprise us with the news of her death. Yes?" I pressed.

Mama exploded in fury when she heard my accusation: "Good. He doesn't want to talk about all this, the sins that weigh so heavily on his heart. Now just tell us: When do you want to throw us out so that your plan may be complete?"

"You are going to do that too?" asked Kommer.

"It's nothing to do with you," answered Mellema.

"Who said so?" Kommer contradicted. "Everything that happens under the sun is the business of thinking people."

Now this person, this officer who was used to having his every word listened to, was stuttering, unable to speak.

"If one's feelings of humanity are offended," Kommer went on, "everyone with feeling will also be offended, except for people who are mad and those with truly criminal mentalities, even though they may be university graduates."

"As a European, and more especially as a Frenchman, I too feel offended. That is why I am here," said Marais in French.

"That's it, Tuan Marais," Kommer encouraged him, even though he didn't understand French.

"Dressed in your navy uniform like that, with your title of engineer, you will surely be the subject of my next painting. And what will I call that painting? This: *L'Ingénieur Mellema, Le Vampire Hollandais.*"

Our guest went pale again. His lips seemed to have been deserted by his blood. He had run out of words.

"For the world, for God, one day I will exhibit that painting in Paris, and in your own country."

"No need to show it in the Indies, however," I added in French. Marais looked at me, shook his head, and smiled.

"There is no need in the Indies, Monsieur Minke," he answered. "No vampire likes to admire another." Marais's voice rumbled in a low tone, like the far-off thunder. "Murdering people's children, robbing the fruits of labor of a woman he should in fact be protecting, and a Native woman too, whom he normally would consider a barbarian!" He laughed loudly, insultingly. "Long live Tuan Engineer Maurits Mellema! Long live murderer and thief."

"There has been no murder, let alone any theft."

"What did Tuan Mellema, your father, bring here from the Netherlands?" asked Mama. "No one knows but me: Two sets of underclothes. Not even a shirt. It was only afterwards that, together with me, he began to keep a few dairy cattle in Tulangan. Listen to me, Tuan Engineer Mellema. Everything he owned in the Netherlands—I don't know whether it was a lot or not—he left for your mother and you. If you know dogs, you would know a dog could tell you that there is none of the salt of your sweat spilled on the floor upon which you now stand. Nor on the land that I now occupy." She coughed and Rono woke up. She rocked him in her arms. "Everything you see around you here would tell you if it could, it is all salty with the sweat from my body."

"The woman you consider a barbarian is speaking to you now, Tuan Engineer Maurits Mellema," said Kommer in Malay. "Now you'll pretend you don't understand Malay?"

"You understand the meaning of *salt* and *sweat*?" asked Jan Marais in Malay.

"I understand," he answered weakly.

"You haven't spoken enough," Mama pressed me.

"Mama, I'm admiring, at the moment, an educated European, civilized and cultured, who has robbed my wife in both life and death. So this is what he is like in reality: a graduate, dashing, handsome, tall and well-built, broad-chested . . . "

Engineer Maurits Mellema turned to me: "Truly, Tuan, I join you in your sorrow," he said.

"He does not know even the name of my wife's husband," I said. "Was this the kind of guardian my wife had?"

"Truly, Tuan"—now he began to defend himself—"I was in South Africa at the time."

"So you're saying South Africa is to blame?"

"Yes, it's indeed South Africa that's to blame," said Jean Marais. "Tuan Mellema doesn't have any business with blame, let alone sin. His only business is profit."

Engineer Mellema, uninvited, dropped to his seat. His white

scabbard got in his way and he shifted it with his left hand. His white cap still sat perched on his head.

Seeing him collapse onto his chair, the others, with relief, sat down as well.

Maysoroh's eyes popped out as she tried to follow the conversation that was going on in French, Dutch, and Malay. She did not understand what was happening, but suspicion shone from her eyes, and it went straight towards the visitor wearing all the gold embroidery.

"Speak, Darsam!" ordered Mama.

In Malay, and with words that he had readied beforehand, Darsam began: "So it is Tuan who took Miss Annelies. Since she was little, I have been the one who guarded over her. Every day I took her to and from school. No one dared worry or touch her. Then you came and took her as if she were some goat's kid. And only now I found out"—he couldn't go on for a moment—"she died at your hands."

The visitor took out a handkerchief. He wiped away his sweat.

"If you like, Tuan, you can unsheath your sword, and we will fight like men."

Engineer Mellema pretended not to hear. He didn't even turn to look at Darsam. Darsam stood up, rubbed his machete, and stepped forward.

"Stay where you are," ordered Mama.

Darsam's face was red with anger. As he edged back to his place, he growled in fury, "It was I. I who gave Miss Annelies away when she married!" He pointed accusingly, still on his feet. "You wouldn't recognize it! Legal and right! Legitimate in the eyes of my religion!"

Hearing Darsam's roars, two sailors came in, gave a salute, and stood on either side of their superior.

"Good. The three of you can fight me at once."

"Go!" the visitor ordered his guards, "and bring that *thing* inside!" he shouted without looking behind him.

They saluted, then went to fetch the *thing*. What kind of weapon was it?

"My job is to guard the security of this family and business. Whoever disturbs it, Darsam's machete is ready to cut up anyone who deserves it."

"That's enough, Darsam. You have to understand that the Tuan before you now is going to take over all this business, everything that the business owns, now that he has murdered Annelies."

"He has killed her, and now he wants to take everything?"

"Yes, that's the man."

"Is it he, Nyai? He did that?"

"Yes, Darsam."

"And I must keep still and do nothing, Nyai?"

"You may only speak. Nothing else."

"Just speak, Nyai? That's all?"

The guest took no notice of the conversation taking place in Malay. He pretended not to hear, but he was struggling to stay calm and in control of himself and the situation.

"But Darsam is willing and ready to fight with him, Nyai"—Darsam's eyes radiated disgust—"now, later, whenever he wants."

One of the sailors came back inside. It wasn't a gun he was carrying, but a large package, not heavy, tied up with silk. He saluted, put the thing down beside his officer's feet, saluted again, then left.

"Sit down, Darsam." Darsam sat down again, still grumbling.

"You shame Europe before Natives," Marais began again, "and in the eyes of Europeans too. If you are the best Europe can produce—a graduate, a scholar—what in heaven's name are its ignorant bandits like?"

"Nyai, Tuan-tuan." Mellema began to regain his confidence and self-control. "If need be, if you feel it's necessary, take me to court. I am willing, I would accept that happily."

"Give me a pencil and paper," said Kommer. He had forgotten to bring his weapons of war. I gave him what he wanted and he began taking notes straight away.

"You of all people know that there is no way for a Native to sue a European."

"You can do it, as a European, Monsieur Marais."

Jean Marais lost his temper. In rapid French he answered: "Good. I will paint you and exhibit the painting both in France and in the Netherlands. And I will not paint the vampire with a tail

342

but just as you are now, in an officer's uniform, representing the barbarian who salutes the law."

"Please, do," answered Mellema.

"Don't worry, Tuan Mellema," Kommer started, "I will publish a special edition in both Dutch and Malay. I will circulate that special edition among the sailors, so that they too may know who you really are."

"Please do. That is your right," he answered, with reviving confidence.

"And to the readers of Surabaya, I will say: Read about Lieutenant-Colonel Engineer Maurits Mellema and find out who he really is. I will tell the newspaper boys to shout out on every street corner: He hated his father, but not his father's property, and now he faces his enemy—a Native woman named Ontosoroh, the person who worked to build the wealth of the father Mellema hated so greatly."

"Superb!" shouted Marais.

"Don't worry, Tuan Kommer," I said. "I will write it all out for you in Dutch: the day I met my wife's murderer, the murderer of his own stepsister."

"No need for a lawyer, no need for a court," added Mama enthusiastically. "Only then will I be happy to leave behind what I have worked for all these years, this building and everything in it, the business and all its wealth."

For the first time, the guest bowed his head deeply and wiped away the sweat again with his handkerchief.

"So, so," Maysoroh shrilled in her pure, clear voice, "Sis Annelies is dead, Nyai?" she asked in Dutch.

"Yes, May, she is dead," answered Nyai.

"This Tuan, he was the one who took her and killed her?"

"Yes, he's the one, May," answered Marais.

Maysoroh now realized what this meeting was about. She went silent as she stared at Engineer Maurits Mellema. Suddenly her two hands seized her cheeks and the cheeks went red. Two tears launched forth across them.

"Sis Annelies is dead! Dead!" she screamed; she pushed out her lower lip as she moaned.

Engineer Maurits Mellema rose, moved to her, tried to caress her hair. Sorrow and rage defeated the little girl's fear. "Murderer!" she screamed, and ran inside. From where I was sitting I could hear Minem's mother ask in Javanese: "What is it?"

Rono, still in Mama's arms, struggled to get free, voiceless as always.

"Sis Annelies, dead, dead, killed by that man in there—the visitor, killed by him."

I couldn't hear whether Minem's mother said anything; all sound was drowned out by May's protests to heaven and earth.

Everyone in the front parlor was silenced as they listened. Mama turned towards the inner rooms and called to Minem's mother: "Quiet her!" Then she soothed Rono, took the bottle of milk wrapped in one end of the sash, and gave some to him.

The guest seemed confused, listening for a moment to May's cries as they faded into the distance, then glancing across to the baby in Nyai's arms.

"Even that little child knows how to grieve for her sister," Kommer went on. "But you want only to profit from her death."

Engineer Mellema didn't reply. His eyes focused on the baby.

"Everyone here loved Miss Annelies," Darsam added. "Only a devil would have the heart to kill her."

"Tuan Mellema," Mama began her accusation, "Tuan needed to have the guardianship of my daughter in order to gain control over her inheritance. Why did no one even visit her before she died? Even when she was buried, there was no one."

"Who said so? That is a lie, she was well looked after and as she should have been."

"Do I need to bring in witnesses? The person, for example, who escorted and looked after my daughter from when she left Surabaya until Huizen and B.?"

"I've a letter from the Huizen Hospital; she was well looked after."

"Who doesn't believe that the hospital looked after her well? But what about yourself and your mother? Tell me it's a lie! Or tell me you were in South Africa. It is no one other than Tuan yourself who knows. Whatever my faults might have been as her mother, I could look after my own daughter better than a thousand women like Amelia Mellema-Hammers."

Sitting in the corner, Darsam was listening attentively to all the conversation, even if he could not understand it all. Every now and then he twirled his mustache or rubbed his machete.

"I don't believe you treated Annelies in the way that even European custom dictates that a sister, even a half-sister, should be treated."

The sound of Minem's mother taking May outside floated in from the back parlor. We could see people trying to peer inside. Perhaps Marjuki had told everyone there was going to be a big party.

Maysoroh was still shouting and crying out, calling for Annelies and cursing her murderer.

Some of the people who were peering in through the windows withdrew from view. Perhaps they wanted to hear what May was crying about. Soon the village people began to gather around the front of the house, men and women, children too, swarming around everywhere. Several women were being shooed out of the back parlor by Minem's mother. Maysoroh's crying wasn't as loud as a minute ago. Coming from not far behind us we could hear her weeping, interspersed with Javanese: "That's him, yes, that's the one, he killed Sis Annelies! That's the one who did it, him!"

The women pushed forward, closer to the door that led from the back to the front parlor. Engineer Mellema lifted his head to look at them. He stood up. But before he could go, Nyai quickly spoke again: "So when do we have to get out of here?"

"I've already appointed someone to manage the business."

"So when do we have to leave?"

"I've decided on a postponement."

"Good. A postponement. And what about this child? Rono Mellema?"

Maurits Mellema looked at the baby. His eyes blinked: "Who is Rono Mellema?"

"You had better take the child with you now. The baby will be easier to kill. If you don't, you'll get a smaller inheritance. You couldn't possibly let him live. The child has never cried. Perhaps he has been mute since birth."

People began to push closer to the door, both at the front and into the back parlor.

Mama held out the baby to him: "Take this baby with you, your own nephew, Robert Mellema's child, also a Mellema heir."

Maurits Mellema looked confused.

"Don't think of him as a rival, Tuan Mellema," said Jean

345

Marais in Malay, in a clear voice so that everyone could understand. "And don't murder him—for the Netherlands."

"You can't even bring yourself to touch your own nephew,"
added Kommer. "He too has property, Tuan; you're not going to
give up his wealth, are you?"

"Why do you hesitate?" pressed Mama, "Take the baby. We
believe you'll be a good guardian."

The guest didn't know what to do.

It was then that Maysoroh ran back into the front parlor. Her
eyes were red and wet. Crying out, weeping uncontrollably, she
lifted her little hand to point at Engineer Mellema: "Yes, here he
is, Engineer Maurits Mellema. He stole Sis Annelies. He killed
her!"

May lost control of herself. She ran up to the big marine
engineer and threw her little punches onto his thighs and stomach.
"Give Annelies back! Give her back!"

Some of the women behind us could now also be heard crying and sobbing. Then somebody asked in Javanese: "Miss Annelies is dead? He killed her?"

"He killed her." Maysoroh pointed accusingly, exhausted
from her punching.

"Why is Darsam doing nothing?" someone whispered.

"I will not throw you out, Tuan Mellema, because this house
is your property," said Nyai. "Go now, before there's a riot. They
know how to feel sorrow, they are all sorrowful and angry."

"Give her back, give her back!" cried Maysoroh, panting.

Engineer Maurits Mellema pointed to the parcel at his feet,
but no voice came from his mouth. The tip of his finger trembled.
He turned his back to us and strode heavily out of the room. His
left hand gripped his scabbard.

We remained seated.

Maysoroh followed him, pulling at his trousers and groaning,
"Give back Sis Annelies! Sis Annelies! Sis Annelies!"

Mellema did not look back. His two arms did not swing. His
body was stooped as he descended the front stops. He looked like
a frog lost among a crowd of humans. He looked small, insignificant.

The crowd parted to make way for him. You could hear them
buzzing beneath the shouts of Maysoroh, who was still tugging at
him: "Murderer! Murderer of your own half-sister!"

Darsam jumped up, pulled out his machete, and began swinging it about: "Animal! Evil, filthy animal!" he roared.

"Miss Annelies, oh Nyai, we didn't realize." The people expressed the sorrow they shared.

Mama didn't answer. She gave Rono to one of the women and opened the parcel the guest had left behind. In it was an old tin suitcase, dented and rusty. She opened it. There were a few sets of Annelies's clothes.

"Good," she sighed, and stood up.

For only the second time ever, I saw Mama shed tears. She could not bear the sight of her daughter's clothes, packed in the suitcase she herself had taken with her when first she was sold to Herman Mellema.

She quickly wiped away the tears.

"Just as we will always remember this day, he too will be haunted by it, all his life and into the grave."

"Yes, Ma, we fought back, Ma, even though only with our mouths."

Buru Island Prison Camp, spoken 1973
written 1975

GLOSSARY

Acehnese	the people of Aceh, the northernmost province of Sumatra, well known at the time for its militant Islamic sentiments
arak	Javanese liquor
assistant resident	for each regency there was a Dutch assistant resident in whose hands power over local affairs ultimately resided
azan	the call to prayer at the mosque
babah	a term referring to Chinese shop-owners, which also has connotations of boss
Babad Tanah Jawi	a classical Javanese literary work, claiming to trace the history of the rulers of Java
bahu	a measure of area equivalent to 7096.5 square meters
bang	older brother, comrade—friendly but respectful
Banowati	a character in wayang, a queen renowned for her beauty
Bapak	literally Father, used to indicate respect
Batara Kala	Hindu god of death
batik	a process for decorating cloth by using wax to prevent some areas from absorbing dye
Betawi	the Malay name for Batavia, the capital of the Dutch East Indies, now Jakarta
Bharatayuddha	a famous Hindu epic, depicting a great war between two families of nobles
biawak	iguana
blangkon	traditional Javenese headdress made from batik and worn mainly by the nobility, or those with pretensions to an elite status

boerderij (Dutch)	firm, company
Boerderij Buitenzorg	the Buitenzorg Agricultural Company, the name of Nyai Ontosoroh's late husband's firm, which Nyai had always managed
bupati	the title of the Native Javanese official appointed by the Dutch to administer a region; most bupatis could lay some claim to noble blood
camat	the title of the native official in charge of several villages
carambol	a kind of billiards
Chinese officer	a member of the Chinese community appointed by the colonial government to supervise tax collection within that community
chiu	Chinese wine
Culture System	This was a system of forced cultivation of certain crops enforced by the colonial authorities; under this system, Javanese peasants had to grow export crops such as coffee and sell them to the Dutch authorities at extremely low prices.
Daendels	Governor-General of the Netherlands East Indies, 1807–1811
dalang	the puppet-master of Javanese shadow puppetry
destar	an East Javanese form of headdress; a kind of headband
dukun	traditional Javanese magician and/or healer
Dutch East Indies Company (VOC); the Company	*Vereenigde Oost Indische Compagnie,* United (Dutch) East Indies Company
Eighty Years' War	a sixteenth- and seventeenth-century war between Holland and Spain, ending in the Peace of the Hague in 1648
Roorda van Eysinga	a writer (1825–1887) expelled from the Indies in 1864 because his writings were regarded as harmful to the colonial government
forum privilegiatum	the right to appear before the court for Europeans
G. Francis	Eurasian author of the early Malay-language novel *Nyai Dasima*
gamelan	traditional Javanese percussion orchestra
gapit	the stick, made usually from buffalo horn, that keeps the leather shadow puppet rigid
garuda	the mythical magical bird upon whom the gods rode
Gatotkaca	a character from wayang stories who had the ability to fly
gus	a term of affection used among the families of the Javanese aristocratic elite by parents towards their male children
haji	the pilgrimage to Mecca or someone who has made the pilgrimage

Hanchou	a city regarded by the Chinese as one of the most beautiful in the world
harvest-time fever	an illness induced by extreme expectations and hyperactivity prior to harvest
H.B.S.	the prestigious Dutch-language senior high school
Dr. Snouck Hurgronje	a Dutch scholar who was an influential adviser on Native Affairs to the colonial government
Indisch	a Dutch term referring to racially mixed persons or cultures
Indische Bond	Founded in 1898, this was an association of Indies Eurasians demanding an end to discrimination against them by the Dutch colonial elite.
Indo	a term used to refer to Dutch-Indonesian Mixed-Bloods (See also Indisch)
Japanese gardens	houses of prostitution
Java Doctor	someone trained in the Dutch-run special medical school set up exclusively for Indies Natives
kabupaten	the formal local term for the administrative area that an assistant resident (through the bupati) administers
kain	traditional dress worn by Javanese women; a kind of sarong wrapped tightly around the waist and legs
kain wulung	a blue-black head-cloth usually worn by Moslem students
Kartini	Most famous woman in modern Indonesian history, regarded as a pioneer of women's emancipation and forerunner of Indonesian nationalism. Best known for the letters that were collected under the title Door Duisternis tot Licht (Through Darkness to Light).
Katasura, Court of	The court of the sultanate of Mataram. In 1740 a rebellion by the Chinese population, backed by a sultan of Madura, attacked Katasura and annihilated the Dutch East Indies Company troops guarding the court.
kebaya	a Javanese woman's traditional blouse, worn always in combination with a sarong
keris	traditional curved-blade Javanese dagger
kliwon	one of the days of the Javanese five-day week
kowe	familiar form of you in low Javanese, considered an insult if used by a lower-class person to a member of the elite
KPM	the Dutch shipping company operating in the Netherlands Indies
kris	see keris
Kyai	Moslem scholar or religious leader
lasting	a kind of plain material
legi	one of the days of the Javanese five-day week
Marechausee	the elite troops of the colonial army in the Netherlands Indies

mas	Javanese term of address literally meaning "older brother." Used by a young woman towards a man, it indicates an especially close, respectful affection. It can also be used between men, indicating respectful friendship; by a sister to her older brother; and also by a wife to her husband.
Max Havelaar	novel by Eduard Douwes Dekker (Multatuli)
mevrouw	Dutch for "Madam" or "Mrs."
Multatuli	pseudonym of Eduard Douwes Dekker, an outspoken humanist critic of Dutch colonialism and author of *Saidja and Adinda* and the anticolonial novel *Max Havelaar*
Mylord	(English) a luxuriously outfitted horse-drawn carriage
ndoro	an honorific used by a lower-class person when speaking to someone in the feudal class or of similar status
noni	miss
nyai	the Native concubine of a Dutch man in the Indies
Nyai Dasima	the heroine of G. Francis's popular Malay-language novel
nyo	abbreviated form of *sinyo*
Oranje Vrijstaat	small Boer (overseas Dutch) states in South Africa
Oriental status	inhabitants of the Netherlands East Indies were divided into three categories: European, Oriental, and Native. European and Oriental status conferred special privileges on those concerned; included in the Oriental category were Chinese, Jews, and, for a time, Japanese.
pak	short for *bapak,* literally father, used to indicate respect
Panji stories	a collection of stories of knightly heroism, based on the legendary activities of an eleventh-century Javanese prince
patih	the chief executive assistant of a bupati
peci	small black velvet cap, originally a sign of Islam
perak	a Malay term for one *rupiah* (100 cents)
plikemboh	a nickname, slang for ugly, disgusting penis
priyayi	members of the Javanese aristocracy who often became the salaried administrators of the Dutch
raden ayu	title for aristocratic Javanese woman, especially the first wife of a bupati
raden mas	raden and mas were titles held by the mass of the middle-ranking members of the Javanese aristocracy; raden mas is the highest
ringgit	2½ rupiah or 2½ perak
rupiah	basic unit of currency (100 cents)
sausing	Chinese wine
SIBA	high school to train Native boys for the civil service
sinkeh	term used to refer to a Chinese immigrant
sinyo	form of address for young Dutch and Eurasian men or Europeanized Native young men, from the Portuguese *senor*
Speceraria	the name of Nyai Ontosoroh's new spice-trading business

talen or *tali*	Dutch East Indies currency, a quarter of a rupiah
thau-cang	the traditional long braid worn by Chinese men
Tong	Chinese secret societies
tricolor	the Dutch flag
Trunajaya	A prince of the island of Madura who led a successful rebellion against the Javanese nobility in the late seventeenth century. The nobles of the Javanese sultanate of Mataram only succeeded in defeating Trunajaya when Dutch military might was thrown against him.
tuan	Malay word meaning master or sir
Tuan Besar Kuasa	Great Powerful Master, a term used for a Dutch administrator or other powerful official
Tuan Raden Mas	the title of nobility of lesser rank
TVK	abbreviation for Tijdeman and Van Kerchem, the company that owned the sugar mills in Tulangan, Tjandi, and Krembong in the Sidoarjo area; called *Te-pe-ka* by the Madurese
VOC	Vereenigde Oost Indische Compagnie: Dutch East Indies Company, the major power in the Indies until 1798, when it was taken over by the Dutch government
Vorstenlanden	the region covered by the kingdom of Surakarta and Jogjakarta in central Java
Vrizinnige Democraat	a liberal democratic party whose members were known as radicals because its first name had been *Radicale Bond* (Radical League)
wayang	shadow puppets